Mr. Darcy's Great Escape

A TALE OF THE DARCYS & THE BINGLEYS

Mr. Darcy's Great Escape

A TALE OF THE DARCYS & THE BINGLEYS

MARSHA ALTMAN

sourcebooks
landmark

Copyright © 2010 by Marsha Altman
Cover and internal design © 2010 by Sourcebooks, Inc.
Cover photo © The Bridgeman Art Library International: The Departure, Green, James
(1771–1834)

Sourcebooks and the colophon are registered trademarks of Sourcebooks, Inc.

Published by Sourcebooks Landmark, an imprint of Sourcebooks, Inc.
P.O. Box 4410, Naperville, Illinois 60567-4410
(630) 961-3900
FAX: (630) 961-2168
www.sourcebooks.com

Library of Congress Cataloging-in-Publication Data

Altman, Marsha.
   Mr. Darcy's great escape : Pride and prejudice continues : a tale of the Darcys & the
Bingleys / Marsha Altman.
      p. cm.
   1. Darcy, Fitzwilliam (Fictitious character)—Fiction. 2. Bennet, Elizabeth (Fictitious
character)—Fiction. 3. England—Social life and customs—19th century—Fiction.
4. Gentry—England—Fiction. 5. Families—England—Fiction. I. Austen, Jane,
1775–1817. Pride and prejudice. II. Title.
   PS3601.L853M7 2010
   813'.6—dc22

                              2009046818

               Printed and bound in the United States of America
                  VP 10 9 8 7 6 5 4 3 2 1

Dedicated to

My mother, who taught me that nothing is impossible,
even things that are *seemingly* impossible.
And
My father, who always has his eye out for another book I might
like, and is therefore partially responsible for the library that
doesn't fit in my apartment.
Plus all their love and support through the years, et cetera.

Chapter 1

DEARLY BELOVED

IN EARLY APRIL OF 1812, four families gathered in Hertfordshire. At this stage, getting them all together was no small task. The guest list of immediate relatives was long and filled with small children, and Longbourn could not host them all. To allow for the proper celebrations of his fourth daughter's marriage, Mr. Bennet had to rent, ironically, Netherfield. Its current occupants were abroad and consented easily, and so for those few weeks surrounding the wedding of Kitty Bennet, it was filled with Bingleys, Darcys, and Maddoxes. Anyone who needed a breather was welcome to return to Town; no one took it, some not having seen the others since Christmas.

The Bingleys arrived first. "I never thought we would be back," Jane said to her husband as they entered, carrying their almost one-year-old, fourth child, Edmund.

"Did you despise it so?" Bingley replied. "Charles! Watch it, that isn't yours to destroy! And if it falls on your sister—" For the Bingley twins were rambunctious six-year-olds and taking full advantage of their new surroundings.

"I did not!" Jane pretended to be affronted as she turned to her eldest. "Georgiana, please make sure your siblings do not immediately destroy Netherfield, or we will have some unpleasant hosts to deal with upon their return." As her seven-year-old daughter ran off to do as she was told, Jane returned her attention to her husband. "In fact, my memories are only happy. But still, it does feel odd."

"Life is full of surprises. Eliza! What did your mother say?" Bingley said to his second daughter, who was now trying to balance a dish on her head.

The Darcys were in before the evening meal. "It is official," an exasperated Darcy said to his brother-in-law. "I never should have taught my son to read."

"Should I ask?"

"He found this book—I don't know where he even found it—on the Roman Empire, and sparing no gory detail too. Would you like to know all about the great battles of Caesar? Because now I know all about them because Geoffrey can't quite read the more difficult words, and so I had to be alert enough to read those segments to him."

Bingley smiled. "The whole way?"

"He did have to take breaks to breathe, occasionally," said Elizabeth, as she saw to the bringing in of her infant daughter Sarah, named after Mrs. Gardiner, who was only three months old. Behind her trailed Anne, now four, and Geoffrey, now seven. "And there was that whole hour where I complained of a headache and he believed me."

"Uncle Bingley!" The two children ran to greet him. Geoffrey bowed, and then looked up and said, "Did you know Caesar married Cleopatra even though he had a wife in Rome when he conquered Egypt?"

"I vaguely recall something of that nature, and I will not doubt your scholarship, Master Geoffrey. But can this perhaps wait until your parents and sisters are settled?"

"How about it waits until forever?" Darcy said. "Or at least until I'm not in the room." He gave his son a playful pat on the head before being escorted to his chambers.

The Maddoxes were the last of the three families to arrive in Netherfield. Their relation was distant, but in her time in Town, Kitty Bennet had fallen under Mrs. Maddox's wing, and though Elizabeth initially had her doubts about the former Miss Bingley training her sister on how to court men, very encouraging letters arrived from both Kitty and Georgiana that put her fears aside. Georgiana Darcy was still unmarried, a situation that was hardly dire, but it was clear she would need some encouragement, as she was still shy and hesitant. If she did see men, she had yet to present her brother with a possibility of a match, no matter how much Elizabeth assured her that he was warming to the idea. In fact, Mrs. Maddox knew the most about Mr. Townsend, Kitty's groom, beyond Georgiana, and she was a wealth of information, because even though marital felicity had obviously softened some of her character, she still did love to gossip. The doctor, of course, hardly said anything, except that he thoroughly approved of the man.

Mr. Townsend had no claim to any titles, but like Bingley, had inherited a fortune from his father in trade, and would provide adequately for Kitty, who now insisted on being called Catherine. He stayed a respectable distance away in Meryton but called on them every night. When the Bennets had a crowded guest list, he was invited to Netherfield. He was an amiable man, young but eager to be settled, lacking brothers or sisters and obviously wanting to buy an estate and build a family, and to do so with Catherine Bennet. Whether they would be a good match in the long run was impossible to determine, of course, but for the moment no one had any objections. He even seemed interested in Netherfield, if the owners would quit it, or a reasonable estate in the county, which suited Mr. Bennet very well.

The distance was long between Hertfordshire and Derbyshire, and until the birth of Joseph Bennet and Mr. Wickham's death, Mr. Bennet had always toyed with the idea, privately, of moving the family up north. Now that Longbourn was filled again, it was out of the question. Though he repeated openly that he loved all of his grandchildren, and no one had any doubt that he did, it was obvious that he cherished little Joseph in a special way, and perhaps the greatest gift Mary had ever given him was having a child out of wedlock. And there were the Wickham children, who he said in letter form, were "doing better under Longbourn's roof, I think," and left it at that.

What he was well aware of, because Lydia made no secret of it, was that Darcy had set up trust funds for both Wickham children after their father's death. George and Isabella would, upon the age of majority, have a decent inheritance. It was meant to be discreet, but since Lydia was denied all access to the funds, she made a habit of regularly mentioning it. To which Elizabeth could only shrug her shoulders and say her husband was a mystery to her sometimes, which he very well was not.

The day before the wedding, as if there was not enough chaos in Hertfordshire, Mr. Bennet requested a special dinner at Longbourn with a very exclusive guest list. Father, mother, and five daughters sat down at the table, sans children, husbands, and relatives.

"When was the last time we were all here?" Jane asked.

"Since our weddings," Elizabeth said, "or perhaps—the day before; I don't recall eating much that morning. I was so nervous." She noticed Kitty's look. "And all for nothing, everything came out perfectly."

"Yes, yes, and I'm still alive, despite predictions of otherwise," Mr. Bennet said. "Who knows—I may outlive Mr. Collins! And then all of that fretting and shouting will have been for naught."

"Naught!" Mrs. Bennet said. "Naught! Who told you to call on Mr. Bingley? Who escorted our girls to balls?"

"Papa, she has caught you," Elizabeth smiled at her father. "Mama did show initiative in seeing us wed."

"Ah, it must be my very old and tired brain that fails to recall something of that nature. But perhaps it was so," he said. "Lizzy, I am sorry to inform you that while you have enjoyed your grand estate in Derbyshire, your poor Papa has been succumbing to senility. And my hearing is going also."

"Your hearing isn't going!" Lydia said. "You just use that excuse to ignore us!"

"What?" Mr. Bennet looked at his youngest daughter. "What was that? I'm afraid you said something and I didn't hear it. Surely it wasn't a comment at my expense."

Elizabeth and Jane stifled their laughter with a harsh look from their mother. "Don't laugh! You don't have to put up with him!"

"One minute you pray I do not expire and let Mr. Collins have the run of the place, and the next you seem to wish me gone," Mr. Bennet said. "Such contradictory notions are positively befuddling to my old mind. No, I promised myself to teach Joseph to speak Italian, and I cannot do that very well from the grave, now can I? So you will just have to wait a few years, my dear." He patted his wife on the hand.

"Mr. Bennet!"

Elizabeth turned to Jane, "So much has changed—and yet, so little."

"On this, Lizzy, I must soundly agree."

The chapel was filled with everyone even remotely connected to the Bennets, which by this time was quite a large crowd. The only person missing from the Darcy family was Grégoire Darcy, who was in a monastery in Austria and was just beginning his long journey to England for a visit and could not be expected until later in May. Similarly missing was Brian Maddox, who had left to marry his Austrian princess and, by very delayed and slow-arriving letters, was apparently doing well and was happy with the arrangements. Or that was all the doctor would say, but he was never known to lie, only to be discreet.

Joseph Bennet was the ring bearer, and the children that were permitted in the chapel were properly shushed for the entirety of the ceremony. Eventually, when the vicar seemed to get around to it, Mr. and Mrs. Townsend were united in marriage, and Mrs. Bennet had yet another daughter married. True, she still had two under her roof; Lydia had thrown off her widow's weeds two years before, but there was no doubt that she would be romancing some officer before long. Mary was another matter, but Mary had (unofficially, for it belonged to her father) a fortune, and proclaimed no intentions to even consider marriage until Joseph was of the age where he could take care of himself. And so, even with two daughters technically unmarried, the

Bennet family was more at peace than it had ever been. In fact, Mrs. Bennet's behavior (besides sobbing at the ceremony) could almost be described as pleasant. The wedding breakfast was long and joyous before they saw the couple off to Town. It was later in the evening, when finally all the children were to bed, that the temporary occupants of Netherfield were alone. Everything was all well and settled in the Bennet family, so talk turned to other things.

"And how is Mr. Maddox?" Elizabeth said, referring to the doctor's brother, as they all sat in the sitting room.

"Currently? I've no idea," Dr. Maddox answered. "But three months ago, he was quite well. It seems to be how long the post takes nowadays from Austria."

"Will they ever visit? Him and…"

"Nadezhda," he said. "I *think* I pronounced that right, but at the moment, no. He is caught up with… baronial business."

"I think my brother-in-law is a concubine," Mrs. Maddox said.

"He is not!" said her horrified husband. "Just because he was won in a bet… with her father… does not mean they are not properly married in the eyes of whatever gods they have in the wilds of the Carpathians!"

"They are Christian," Darcy said, but added, "I think."

"The Russias are Orthodox Christian, are they not? And the Russias are even farther east," Bingley said, "so one could logically conclude they are."

"But the Turks, to their south, are not," Elizabeth said. "You don't think—there isn't any reason why the French would have business in his part of Austria, would they?"

"Have business?" It took the good doctor a second to comprehend her meaning. Women, after all, did not discuss military matters. She must have meant *invade*. "Napoleon would be a fool to go to Russia. It's massive and, from what I've heard, freezing. And Brian is practically on the border."

It was a truth that any discussion of people abroad could only lead to the current politics, which were at the same time both unsettling and fascinating. The self-proclaimed emperor of France was now gallivanting across Europe, having already been to Italy and Africa, and as each country fell, the embargo on Britain tightened, to the point where almost everyone was feeling it. Darcy's fortune was so caught up in local land that it was hardly affected by international politics, but only Elizabeth and the Bingleys knew that he had quietly been settling disputes with his workers, who were concerned by the taxes and their own livelihoods. Bingley had land as well, but not quite so much, and lived largely off his massive inheritance. Time and time again, Darcy urged him to sell his remaining interest in the old shipping company that his father had run, but despite his profession as an idle gentleman with no business in business, Bingley refused. Whether it was nostalgia or actual concern was not something anyone could pry from him, but since the business was the cloth and silk trade, it would likely go under if the embargo did not end soon. All anyone really knew about the specifics was that Bingley was spending an awfully large amount of time running back and forth between Derbyshire and Town.

The Maddoxes, of course, were tied to the Crown, which was in no real danger unless there was an invasion, and England had not been invaded in seven centuries. When asked about the Prince Regent, Dr. Maddox merely replied, "I doubt very much His Highness would put himself in harm's way," which, for the extremely circumspect doctor, was a long answer about his patient.

The only remaining variable—beyond Brian Maddox, who could make himself in danger even in Town—was Grégoire in Austria. True, no one believed that the insane dictator of France would go so far as to start killing his ally's civilians, especially ones who were technically French, but the pesky embargo did mean that the letters between the Darcy brothers were slowed to the point of being almost months apart.

Bingley, as usual, broke the awkward and worried silence, "To relatives far away."

Everyone was willing to toast to that.

"Why can't adults ever say anything interesting?" Geoffrey Darcy said from the other side of the door.

"I know! I want to hear about war!" Georgie Bingley said in disgust. "Give me the glass." As it was passed to her, she put the glass to her ear and against the door. "Still nothing."

"I want to listen! I want to listen!" Charles Bingley the Third said a bit too loudly, causing both of them to scowl at him.

"You're going to make them hear us," Georgie whispered.

"And then we'll get in trouble," Geoffrey said, wrestling with his younger cousin. "So be quiet."

"But I want to hear!"

Geoffrey and Georgie exchanged exasperated glances. They were both a year older than Charles, at an age when it made a significant difference.

"Charles," Georgie said, "if you don't go back to the nursery right now, I'll tell Papa and he'll give you a thrashing because you're a boy, and he won't give me one because I'm a girl."

Charles Bingley, six years old and easily intimidated by his older sister, said only meekly, "*He wouldn't.*"

"He would. Now go."

He ran off, his bare feet making very little sound on the wood, up the stairs and into their nursery. Georgie sighed in relief.

"He wouldn't, would he?" Geoffrey asked.

"Of course not. Maybe your papa, but not *mine*," she said very confidently.

"Why do you want to know about war?"

"You do not?"

Geoffrey shrugged. "I don't know what war is like. But my uncle is on the Continent."

"So is mine."

"But *yours* is batty."

"At least he's not a monk!"

"You don't even know what that is!"

"Do too!"

"Do not!"

"Lying is a sin, you know."

"So is staying up past your bedtimes."

They turned away from the door and looked up at the figure towering above them, wizened and leaning heavily on his walking stick, not like their fathers did when out of doors, but like he really needed it.

"Grandpapa!"

"Grandfather!"

"Now hush or you're likely to give yourselves away to more than one person," Mr. Bennet said. "But I'd think you'd best be off to bed, children. If you've forgotten the way, I will show you. In fact, I insist upon it."

Admittedly, they were much better at scurrying up the stairs of Netherfield than he was and had to wait for him at the top before proceeding down the hallway. Georgie took his available hand. "I thought you were at home."

"And miss time with my grandchildren, who are undoubtedly going to be sneaking out to hear what their parents say behind closed doors? Never!" he laughed. "I take my amusements in this life where I can get them, Miss Bingley. You ought to learn to do the same, though perhaps not by eavesdropping. You might get a story that's not for your young ears." He paused. "Oh, dear, I've just made it all the more enticing. Well, my daughters and sons will just have to suffer."

"Will England go to war?" Geoffrey asked more seriously, looking up at his grandfather.

"I am not a diviner of any sorts, Master Geoffrey, so I cannot begin to tell you the future. In fact, I find it is best to let it rest and expect only that life is going to surprise you, as it—in my lifetime, certainly—has never failed to do."

LADY CATHERINE'S EPISTLE

MAY WAS A MOST enjoyable time at Pemberley, in those intervening years between the master's bachelorhood and his children being out, when he had every reason to be at home for the upcoming Season. It was also special for the Darcys because it was the time that Grégoire made the long journey from Austria to visit them. Georgiana came up from Town, for she had taken to her newfound brother and spent much time walking with him in the gardens.

"He seems to be doing well," Elizabeth said as they watched from their balcony. "I think the Rule of Benedict is much more suited to him."

"I suppose not insisting he drive himself to death is a vast improvement," Darcy said, not looking up from his book. "Maybe we can find him monastery after monastery until we find one that teaches its novices how to be normal men."

"Maybe your brotherly concerns are enough torture for him," she said.

"And when do you intend to tell Darcy?"

"Oh! It is nothing like that, I assure you," Georgiana said. "I've seen him but twice—and only by chance. And of course I can't invite him and he can't invite me, even if he is an earl—"

"If marriage is the intention of courtship, I confess to not understanding why it must be so complicated," Grégoire said. "How are you to see him again?"

"Well... I have asked Dr. Maddox to invite him for dinner, because he is so discreet, and Mrs. Maddox will delight in having a secret from my brother. Oh! Is it wicked of me to say that?"

"I don't believe so," he said with a smile. "But you will have to *eventually* tell him."

"I told you, it is nothing! He is just an old friend who's never been to Town! He doesn't know his way around."

Grégoire just buried his smile in his cowl.

She gave him a little shove. "Promise you will not tell!"

"I will not."

"Promise?"

"Promise."

"Darcy," Elizabeth said as she stepped onto the veranda, where Darcy was enjoying the afternoon breeze with his brother, who was holding Sarah with great delight. Grégoire had no scruples with showing his affection for his nieces and nephew as most men did. "You will never believe this."

Darcy turned to Grégoire and said, "I will not bother to guess. It will take all day. Darling, what is it?"

"Lady Catherine has finally replied to one of my letters," she said, holding it up in evidence. "In fact, she has invited us to Kent."

"Did she give a reason?"

"No. She spent most of the letter berating me, my motherhood, which she is sure is deficient, and so on and so on," she waved her hand as she passed off the letter. "And of course, the only reason we are available is because you are a terrible guardian of Georgiana and will not join her for the Season so that she can be properly married and settled. But since we are so negligent and therefore available, we *must* come."

"We *must*," he said with some amusement and explained to Grégoire, "My mother's sister, Lady Catherine de Bourgh. She was insistent that I marry her daughter, Anne, and when I refused and married Elizabeth, she cut off all contact."

"But—Anne is your cousin, is she not?" Grégoire said.

"Yes. Oh, is there some Catholic injunction against marrying cousins? Is it improper in the eyes of God? Because if so, we must bring that up while we are there, if we should go at all."

"*If* we are to go!" Elizabeth said. "I've only been writing to this woman for eight years for the sake of family harmony, and you consider rejecting her offer?"

"She has thrown us a bone, but that does not mean I am a hungry dog," Darcy said, his tone more serious. "While she is my aunt, her behavior was abominable towards both of us during our courtship, and we are likely to be subjected to yet another tirade if we go."

"Perhaps she has changed."

"But her letter indicates she has not, at least not *enough*. I have only so much tolerance for one who would insult my lovely wife, and if she so much as says one bad word in front of Geoffrey and Anne—"

Elizabeth turned to her brother-in-law for help. "Surely it is some kind of sin to pre-suppose evil?"

"Yes, but there is also the matter of marrying cousins, though the Bible does not forbid it, various papal bulls—" Grégoire shook his head. "It is not my place. I do not know this woman."

"If it is any more enticing," Elizabeth added, "the Fitzwilliams will also be there, and you know how little we see our cousins since they moved to Brighton."

"A regular family gathering," Darcy said. "Now I am even more suspicious. But we cannot go—for the sake of family. My brother has come all the way from the Continent to see me, and I will not leave him to go be lectured by Lady Catherine. Nor would I bring him along and subject him to the highly improper tirade we will all endure for it."

To this, Elizabeth had no immediate reply. She folded her arms in frustration. Darcy rose and embraced her. "Why do you torture yourself over this?"

"Because I am trying to restore normal relations with your side of the family. Relations that were rented by our own marriage, and yet created our own marriage. It was one of her own infamous tirades that gave me hope that you still loved me, after all that happened with Lydia."

"And I, the same," he said. "Hmm, then I must admit, we do owe her a favor. But the problem still stands."

"I am not a problem," Grégoire said quietly.

"We did not mean to imply that you were—"

"No," he said. "I mean, the problem is obviously solved by my accompanying you, if she would have me. I have never been to Kent or met the Fitzwilliams. I have no objection if you would have me as family."

"I would always have you as family," Darcy said, "but when we joke about Aunt Catherine—or mean it seriously—we *do* mean it seriously. She will burn your ears off if she so chooses."

"Do you think my visitation would cause her pain, because she is the sister to your mother?"

He had a point. Remarkably, it was in Lady Catherine's favor. Neither of them had considered her feelings. Likely, she would insult him anyway for any number of reasons, but here was the man who was a result of an injustice on Lady Anne Darcy, who was betrayed by her husband and lady-maid during her confinement with Georgiana.

Darcy debated it and finally said, "If she asks, we will delay your birth date by a few convenient months, after my mother's death."

"Still, I would not want to insult her—"

"Everyone always insults Lady Catherine," Elizabeth said, "just by breathing. We wish to spare *you* being her target."

"I know of my heritage," Grégoire said with remarkable calmness. "I have faced it, and I cannot change it, nor would I wish myself nonexistent. I have done my penance, and while I cannot judge others who would judge me, I am not embarrassed, nor shall I hide in shame."

"You will perhaps think otherwise of your decision if and when you meet her," Darcy said. "Elizabeth, we will discuss this later," meaning, *in private.*

"Of course, Mr. Darcy," she said, and curtseyed like a servant before hurrying out.

"I'm going to regret this."

"Visiting your aunt?"

"Well, of course, but giving Elizabeth an order, even accidentally. In fact, I'd better go apologize to her right now. Excuse me."

"You are quite excused," his brother said and even had a small smile on his face as Sarah giggled in his arms.

He caught up with Elizabeth quickly, as she hadn't made it very far into the hallway, before she spun around and kissed him, breaking his attempt at conversation. When they finally separated, she said, "We are going."

"Do I at least get a say? You know she will spend the entire time berating us."

"Surely not. The woman must take time to breathe. And sip her tea in such a derogatory manner."

"And you would willingly expose Grégoire to this?"

"He is his own man, Darcy. Though, yes, the timing is severely inconvenient, but what can we do? I want to go, and he apparently wants to go, so you must go with us. I've not seen Charlotte in years."

"You've also not seen Mr. Collins in years."

"One does not equal the other. And you would see your cousins, and Lady Catherine would make a fool of herself if she would stoop so low to insult a monk as pious as your brother, whatever his heritage." She put a hand on his shoulder. "I know you are just trying to protect us all, but I would not have written countless letters if I did not want the family restored in some fashion. And now we have perhaps the opening to do it."

"Perhaps," he said. "She has some scheme, Lizzy. Surely you realize this."

"So? She, like the rest of us poor females, can only offer you advice. She can force nothing on you."

"I would say no woman can force things on me," he said, "but there is one. Two, if Georgiana was not so compliant. And four, when the children are out. But otherwise, that is it."

"Then we are perfectly safe in your capable hands," she said and kissed him again, and he found he could do nothing but comply.

The ride to Kent was hot and stuffy, and they rested along the way, though there was hardly any rest as Anne was climbing all over things. "Geoffrey!" Darcy said. "Watch over your sister."

"Do I have to?"

"If it was in question, I would have said it that way. Now, go."

Geoffrey scoffed but did pull Anne down before she got too high in a tree.

They did manage to reach Kent at a decent time of day, good enough to be rested and changed for dinner. Lady Catherine, it was announced as their coats were removed, was taking a rest and not to be disturbed. Not to put up any argument, the Darcys were instead greeted by Colonel Fitzwilliam and his wife, Anne. "Darcy!"

"Richard," Darcy said, "So good to see you. Allow me to introduce my brother, Brother Grégoire of the Order of Saint Benedict."

"Yes," Fitzwilliam, who had been told about but had never crossed paths with him before, offered his hand. "Very nice to meet you, and of course, Mrs. Darcy and Master Geoffrey." He had, at several Christmases, met the Darcys' son.

Geoffrey bowed to his cousins. His sister Anne ran around

him and hugged her cousin's legs. There were greetings all around, and the children were taken to their lodgings.

"I suppose you heard, then," Fitzwilliam said to Darcy, taking him aside.

"No," Darcy said. "Our aunt's letter failed to mention anything special. Somehow I felt she was leaving something out."

"My brother Michael has caught something in India."

"The earl? What is he doing in India?"

"What does anyone do in India? Make a fortune. One has to keep up the lifestyle of an earl, after all," Richard said. "We don't know the specifics. It's very hard to get news, but—the news isn't good."

Darcy nodded. "I'm sorry, Richard. I truly am. Is there any way to bring him home?"

"Only by ship, and he is not well enough to travel, apparently. I would go to see him myself, but I might contract the same thing, and I could not leave Anne with that."

"Understood." Darcy frowned. "Terrible news."

"Yes."

"Do you wish me to meditate on this some more, or may I go straight into speculation that this does not directly involve your brother?"

"It does, but you may do it anyway. If Michael dies... well, you know what will happen then."

"And Aunt Catherine cannot be happy with those arrangements. Or, to be honest, I cannot know what she is thinking. Why can't she come out and say it, as she does everything else?"

"I imagine there will be some discussion. I myself have no inkling. Does your wife know?"

"No. I never saw a reason to tell her. I honestly never thought it would be relevant so quickly. Your brother was a healthy man."

"Yes."

"I am so sorry," Darcy said, meaning it as he put a hand on Fitzwilliam's shoulder. "It is a terrible thing to lose a brother."

Colonel Fitzwilliam decided not to comment on that particular statement.

Retired to their rooms to relax and change for dinner, Darcy was alone with Elizabeth at last and revealed the grave news to her.

"Terrible! I am so glad Bingley has never gone to India," she said, "though I know he's thought of it. But still—this must sound terrible of me to even be thinking, but—"

"Yes," Darcy shooed away the servant and sat down on the bed next to her. "It will improve Richard's standing and inheritance immensely. But that cannot be the reason why Lady Catherine called us here."

"But—how can this relate to this, aside from a probable death in the family? If anything, it improves her situation as well, because Anne will inherit Rosings with the colonel."

"No," he said. "He won't. I will."

Elizabeth stared at him.

"It deals with the specific nature of the entail of Rosings to the Fitzwilliam line," he said. "It dates back hundreds of years, longer than the Darcys or the de Bourghs have been part of the family, and I've seen the document myself only because it was brought to my attention by my father. Now, my maternal grandfather, whose name I bear, had three children—Anne,

Catherine, and Reginald, Richard's father and the one who inherited the earldom."

"Yes." He had died less than a year after Richard and Anne's marriage, but at least had lived to see both his sons married.

"Of those children, the direct line of descent actually goes in order of age of the three original children—of which my mother was the oldest, provided the male did not produce a son."

"Which he did; two."

"I'm getting to that. So, Rosings would of course pass to him upon his father's death, which it did, but Uncle Matlock let it to Sir Lewis de Bourgh for a pittance, because his sister Catherine wanted to live in her old family lodgings instead of the de Bourgh family estate. But until the day Lord Matlock died, he was the technical owner of Rosings. When he died, six years ago, Rosings passed to his son Michael. My uncle made his son promise to allow Aunt Catherine to remain in her home as long as she lived, but he is now dying in India. His wife died in childbirth along with the child, so he has no heir.

"But remember what I said about age of the three children. Now that the firstborn sons of the Fitzwilliam line have all been eliminated, it passes to the next person in line, the firstborn son of the firstborn daughter. I am the firstborn son of the firstborn daughter, as my mother Anne was older than Aunt Catherine. So, it passes to me, and should I die, to Geoffrey, and should he die with no heirs, *then* to poor Richard, the second born and forever passed over."

"Can you not—can you not break the entail and not receive Rosings?"

He shook his head. "An entail can only be broken with a father and son in agreement. And since my father is dead, I must wait until Geoffrey is of age to formally break the entail and forfeit the Darcy claim to Rosings. And, I imagine, numerous other holdings connected to Rosings." Darcy frowned. "But it still makes no sense. Unless Aunt Catherine has lost what little sense she has, she realizes I have no interest in Rosings, as I have told her on numerous occasions, and *clearly* I will happily rent it to the Fitzwilliams for little or no money until I can break the entail in eleven years." He lay back on the bed. "She has some other scheme here. She will make some wild request of me."

"Perhaps we are assuming too much. First, the earl is not actually dead, despite what you all assume. He may well recover. Second, as you said, if she is not unknowing of your own intentions, she may just wish to confirm them. Or she may be unknowing of your current intentions and want to know them. You have not spoken to her for nine years."

"Perhaps," he said. "But I think not. No matter. She would hardly drag us out here without revealing it all as dramatically as she can."

"In that, my dear, I believe you may be right."

In their sitting room, Nurse brought Geoffrey and Anne forward for presentation.

"Do we not have the most wonderful children?" Elizabeth said, tugging on the sleeve of her very tense husband. "Anne, darling, the dress looks very beautiful on you."

"Itches," Anne Darcy said, scratching her chest. Her pink dress did indeed have more lace than she was used to.

"I can't breathe," Geoffrey said, tugging on his cravat.

"Then hold your breath," Darcy suggested, "and be very polite to your aunt."

"*You're* not polite to our aunt!"

"Son," Darcy said, bending down on one knee to face his seven-year-old, "remember what I said about public and private talk?"

"No."

"Hopeless." Darcy sighed, patted his son on the head, and rose to his feet to see Grégoire emerging from his chambers, dressed in the only outfit he owned, his worn wool robes. "Hopeless lots, all of you."

"Lots!" Anne shouted, waving her arms above her head. Anne Darcy seemed to thoroughly enjoy her power of speech, even when she lacked understanding.

"I fear Aunt Catherine will be displeased," Darcy whispered to his wife, though it didn't sound as if he had a lot of fear.

"Lady Catherine has been displeased with me since the moment I met her, is displeased with you and your choice in marriage, and is displeased with Georgiana's delay in choosing a husband. I hardly expect her to act so contrary in her character as to not extend it to the rest of the family."

He smiled and gave her a quick kiss on the cheek. "Well," he said to the rest of them, "shall we go and greet Lady Catherine?"

Chapter 3

THE DEVIL AND THE SAINT

LADY CATHERINE DE BOURGH, now of some two and seventy years, had not lost her composure with age. True, the change in her physical appearance was noticeable. She had lost what remained of the color in her hair. It was obvious (though inappropriate to mention) that she had lost weight, making her appearance all the more skeletal. If anything, it added a certain fright factor to her appearance, to be perfectly plain about it.

Rosings itself had not changed. If anything, it was decayed with time, but still mostly as it had been during Elizabeth's visit to Kent to see her friend Charlotte nine years prior, and Elizabeth realized she was as much a stranger in it now as she had been then. The difference now was Darcy was not standing by her side as an unpleasant acquaintance intruding on her visit but as her loyal husband. This was a welcome relief when she was once again presented to the mistress of Rosings. "Lady Catherine."

Lady Catherine barely acknowledged her as the children were brought forward. If there was anything the Darcy children did understand, it was how to act in front of "proper" people, it being totally different from how they were usually permitted to behave. Geoffrey bowed politely and said, "Lady Catherine," without squirming or making a silly face. His sister did not manage to get the name out, but she did curtsey.

"Come here," said Catherine, holding out a well-bejeweled hand to the little Miss Darcy. "You do not look much like my sister or my daughter. Are those blond streaks in her hair from the sun?"

"They are, Aunt Catherine," Darcy said.

"A young lady has little proper place outdoors, but surely you are aware of that, Fitzwilliam," Catherine said. "I will assume that she will mature when she begins her education. Have you arranged for her tutors?"

"We have, your ladyship," Elizabeth said. "But she is very young yet."

"And Master Geoffrey. Have you learned your letters?"

"I have," he said. "I can even write better than Father!"

Elizabeth had to stifle her laughter as Darcy gave her a cold stare.

"Of that I have no doubt," said Lady Catherine. "You children will take your suppers now. Your parents and I have much to discuss."

Never had Elizabeth seen her children so happy to leave a room. They bowed quickly and scurried out, chasing after the servant who was leading them. Their parents, however, would not have such relief. Her husband, showing no hesitancy, took the lead, "Lady Catherine, allow me to introduce you to my brother, Brother Grégoire of the Order of Saint Benedict."

Grégoire bowed humbly, "Your ladyship."

"How is Austria, Mr. *Grégoire?*" she said. "You will excuse me, but we are in a civilized country now."

"You may call me whatever you wish, your ladyship."

"You are French, are you not? By birth?"

"Yes, your ladyship."

"From Mont Claire, am I correct?"

He bowed slightly again. "You are very knowledgeable, your ladyship."

"Your mother was from Mont Claire," she said. "I remember her very well."

Grégoire's previous composure could not be described as cool, but more of his usual calm, unshakable humility. He did seem rattled by the mention of his late mother, though. "Madam?"

"I was attending my sister during her confinement, so it hardly went unnoticed. Though you do favor your father in appearance."

While it was fairly public knowledge in Derbyshire that Master Darcy had a bastard brother that he had embraced as though a legitimate one, the details were obscured as much as possible. Darcy interrupted the conversation. "Aunt Catherine, are you implying that you knew about the dismissal during my mother's confinement with Georgiana?"

"Of course I did! What, do you think I was blind? I am only surprised that they hid it so successfully from you, Fitzwilliam. Too much time *playing outside*." She glanced at their shocked expressions, but that only raised her apparent indignation. "Why are you all so surprised? Did you not think that Mr. Darcy would do everything in his power to cover up his scandalous affairs? Even if the grief of it killed my sister?"

"You knew?" Darcy said. "All these years, you knew I had a brother?"

"I knew about every servant girl that was dismissed! I knew about both your brothers, Fitzwilliam, but remember that you were to marry Anne, and I would not have tolerated you behaving in such a manner as your father!" She didn't give Darcy time to respond before turning on Grégoire. "You at least had the decency to shut yourself up in a monastery."

"Lady Catherine!"

"For once in your life, be quiet, Miss Bennet!" Catherine said. "I am trying to speak to an actual relation, no matter how disreputable!"

"Elizabeth Darcy is my wife and therefore your niece, Lady Catherine," Darcy said in a chilling voice, "and a very respectable relation, as is my brother. He is a man of the church!" He stepped forward. "If your only intention in this invitation, knowing full well who my brother is, was to insult all of us, then we will take our leave."

And of course, there was no doubt in anyone's mind that Darcy would make good on his threat. Only Grégoire standing in his way prevented his exit. "Please, don't."

"I cannot stand by while—"

"You will admit that her ladyship's motives in disguising the circumstances of my birth were to guard you from sin," he said. "She said it herself."

Darcy looked at Elizabeth in wonder as to why his brother was pleading with him in Lady Catherine's defense, but she could only shrug in reply. "She has also insulted you grievously."

"Fitzwilliam!"

"I am not ashamed of my heritage," Grégoire said and turned to bow again to his host. "Lady Catherine, I am sorry that you lost your sister, and that my mother brought both you and Lady Anne distress in her final days, but I cannot undo my own existence, nor do I wish to. But please accept my apologies on my mother's behalf for your grief, as it obviously still concerns you."

The quiet threatened to overwhelm them all. Darcy and Lady Catherine were connected not only by blood but also by a frustrating obstinacy, which could be volatile when used on each other. So dangerous was the air between them that neither Elizabeth nor Grégoire dared to break the silence.

"Brother Grégoire," Lady Catherine said, setting her hands on her lap, "did you know that Rosings was an abbey before the dissolution of the monasteries?"

"I—I did have my suspicions."

"Suspicions?"

"The façade behind you," he said, pointing to the high part of the wall. "It has been painted over, and false pillars have been added, but I do believe that was once the back wall of a personal chapel, perhaps of an abbot, judging from the size of the room."

"I am a very religious woman myself, and a patron of the church. Even when my own family has abandoned me, I have always found solace in religion, though our religion is quite different from yours."

"Not so different, perhaps," he said.

"I am the patron of our local vicar, who is Mrs. Darcy's cousin and shall be joining us tonight. Perhaps you will find some common ground to converse upon."

He said gratefully, "I would be honored."

The gathering for dinner was short. Elizabeth was overjoyed when the Collinses arrived, as she had not seen Charlotte since early in her marriage, but this was not the moment for renewing a friendship. The atmosphere was too formal, and so they greeted each other warmly, exchanged some information about their children (Charlotte had three as well), and promised to converse the next morn. The Fitzwilliams were also in attendance; only Georgiana, still in Town for the Season, was absent (or to use Darcy's terminology, "excused") from the visitation. It made for a very long table and many sudden rulings from Lady Catherine that seats should be changed to the point where everyone was quite confused and relieved when they finally settled down and she seemed satisfied.

"Mr. Bellamont," Lady Catherine said loudly and sharply to Grégoire, more than was necessary for her voice to reach his end of the table, "it may be different in the wilds of Austria, but in England it is considered rude not to take the food offered you." Very little escaped her notice, and her eagle eyes did notice that Grégoire had partaken of nothing but bread.

Elizabeth wished she could comfort Darcy, who was probably seething at the other end of the table, but husband and wife did not sit together, and she was at a loss.

"My apologies, your ladyship," Grégoire said, not at all bothered by her accusation, "but your food is too refined for my poor monk's stomach."

Elizabeth looked down at her bowl. The soup was rich and quite spicy, and Grégoire had a very simple diet—and, apparently, no shame in admitting it. He had eaten privately before dinner. He rarely had anything of substance after what she understood was Vespers.

Surprisingly, Lady Catherine did not counter, but changed the subject entirely. "Mrs. Darcy, I trust you have secured a governess for your children?"

"No, not yet, Lady Catherine."

"Then you must immediately. I do not see why this has gone to lapse. Perhaps because your mother did not employ one, but my grandnephew cannot be as rowdy as your sisters."

Now it was Elizabeth's turn to seethe. "I would hardly describe my sisters as 'rowdy,' your ladyship. Surely a woman of your superior understanding knows that gossip and reports are often only focused on the most *extreme* examples of behavior and not the daily lives of respectful people. The gossip papers would then be quite boring."

"You read such trash, Mrs. Darcy?"

"I do not," Elizabeth said in all honesty.

"Thank goodness for that at least!" Lady Catherine said. Elizabeth looked over at her husband and observed that his hands were shaking a little on the table as he spooned his own soup. She could only imagine the violent thoughts going through his head and wondered how long his nerves would endure. "Pemberley's library would be tainted with such literature."

"Pemberley's library is quite well," Darcy said. "In fact, my wife has made many useful suggestions for additions to it."

"While it is admirable to take care of your own house, nephew, you must also keep your house*hold*," Lady Catherine said, easily moving to attack apparently every Darcy at the table. "Why have you not employed a governess? Geoffrey is seven years old, is he not?"

"I did not have a governess when I was seven, Aunt Catherine," Darcy said. "My mother and father instructed me personally until I was ten."

Even implying an insult to her sister's behavior was something Lady Catherine would not stand for, let alone do herself. Darcy sneaked a look at Elizabeth, who smiled.

Lady Catherine retreated and did not pester Darcy again for some time, though she did lament at length the poor state of education and how many young men she found to be uneducated (to which Elizabeth sorely resisted inquiring as to why Lady Catherine knew so many young men) and in need of proper instruction. She briefly battered Charlotte Collins with questions about how she was raising her daughters, to which Mrs. Collins had the good sense to smile and look grateful for the wisdom imparted to her so freely. Obviously, she was an expert at it, but she let her husband do the thanking.

The main courses were served, and again, Grégoire did not partake. Elizabeth suspected that even if he were so inclined to break his monastic habits, his stomach truly would be unprepared for the finely flavored meats and poultry from Lady Catherine's kitchen.

"Enough with this Papist nonsense," Lady Catherine finally said. "Mr. Bellamont, I implore you to eat. It is ill-advised for a person not to have a proper diet, even for spiritual reasons."

Mr. Collins added, "As our Lord and Savior said, 'Know ye not that ye are the temple of God, and that the Spirit of God dwelleth in you?'" He had not shown any previous animosity to Grégoire—he was obviously more interested in supporting Lady Catherine.

"Paul," Grégoire said quietly in response.

"What?" Lady Catherine said. "Speak up, Mr. Bellamont!"

"It was Saint Paul who said it. In his letters to the Corinthians," Grégoire said with his head bowed, but Elizabeth detected a small smile sneaking into his expression. "Forgive me. I am not a wise man, but of this, I am fairly sure."

"Mr. Collins is a vicar of the church, Mr. Bellamont. Surely he knows of what he speaks. We read the Bible regularly here, and in plain English so that even *the masses* can understand."

"Your ladyship is right," Mr. Collins said. "I am reminded of Our Lord's saying, 'And this is the word which by the gospel is preached unto you.'"

Catherine nodded her head in triumph to Grégoire, who hesitated a moment before saying, "Peter."

"What?"

"That was Saint Peter, Minister Collins, in his first letters."

Elizabeth had to cover her mouth to hide her laughter.

"Maybe," Darcy said, "we should check the Good Book."

Mr. Collins's face flushed. "That is not necessary."

"No," Grégoire said, almost in support of the flustered vicar across from him, "'For the wisdom of this world is foolishness with God.' I do not presume to be correct." He played with his unused utensils for a moment before adding, "Saint Paul."

Attempting to salvage the argument, Lady Catherine interjected, "I presume that a man who has separated himself from society has time to study the Good Book to an extent that a man with any affairs does not. Tell me, does your order spend the whole day in the chapel?"

"No, your ladyship, Saint Benedict believed that work is a form of prayer."

"And what do you do? Minister to the people? Give sermons? Bless the masses of the poor?"

"No, your ladyship," he said, his head bowed. "I am the newest member of my order. I am in charge of cleaning the chamber pots."

The dropping of cutlery was the only thing audible in an otherwise silent room. Grégoire, unperturbed, picked at the one roll he had been working on all night.

The dinner did not last much longer than that. Grégoire said many apologies and excused himself from after-dinner entertainment, as it was time for Compline and sleep. Lady Catherine did not object to his disappearance and instead began her instructions on what Mrs. Collins should play on the pianoforte.

"Your brother may be a monk, but he is quite the little devil," Elizabeth whispered to Darcy when they finally met up.

"Apparently," Darcy said, sneaking to her a smile. "Though it is not very hard to outwit Mr. Collins. It may have been unintentional." He added, "Though I doubt it was. Pious servant of the Lord indeed!"

The after-dinner entertainment was relatively brief, before the women retired and Darcy took a glass of port with Fitzwilliam in what had once been Sir Lewis' study.

"Your brother is quite a fascinating person," Fitzwilliam said.

"Never underestimate a Darcy," he said with a smirk.

The evening would have gone quite well, all things considered, if not for the servant entering. "Mr. Darcy, Lady Catherine requests your presence in the drawing room." And he left immediately. There was no way for him to excuse himself. It was an order.

"Should I sing a funeral hymn?"

"No, I'd rather not have to bear our aunt and your singing voice in one evening," Darcy said, finishing his port quickly before leaving the room.

Lady Catherine was waiting for him, sitting in a chair very close to the fire, even though it was high summer. Darcy bowed. "Aunt Catherine." There seemed to be no chair for him to sit and still be facing her, but he felt more confident standing. He liked to be on his feet when he was uncomfortable.

"Fitzwilliam," she said, resting in her easy chair. Calling him that was always the first sign of danger. He did not take the seat offered to him, choosing to stand by the fireplace instead. "It has been a long time."

"Yes," he said.

"The situation is obviously very different from when we last spoke; the situation of our families, of course. No doubt your cousin has told you."

"Of his brother's misfortune, yes, he has." She seemed to be coming right to the point instead of berating Elizabeth for a while, which he had expected her to do. "Though it is not a certainty. He may very well return, alive and well."

"Perhaps, or perhaps not. You understand the importance of consideration and planning for the future of our family."

"Of course."

She turned away from him. He could not remember the last time she had done something like that, but she looked into the fire instead. "Would I have employed every gypsy fortune teller in the world, I could not have guessed that Miss Bennet would be a more suitable wife for you than my Anne."

Not knowing what to say to such a dramatic admission, Darcy managed only to stutter, "Neither could I. But I believe my cousins are both very happy in their choice."

"They are. And Anne is much healthier. I should have thought to take her to Brighton." Was this Lady Catherine, admitting to a weakness in thought or idea? He was stupefied as she went on, "The doctors say she might even survive a confinement if she was capable of such."

Darcy said nothing. He could think of nothing appropriate to say.

"But you have a son and so the Darcy line is secure, provided he survives to adulthood. And you may yet have another. Your wife is still young yet. She may have aged you, but she is doing quite well herself."

He looked down. She had noticed, of course, the silver around his ears that had appeared during his recovery from his injuries in the duel with Wickham. "That was not her doing, but my own."

"So I have been informed," she said, looking back at him. "But now we must consider the Fitzwilliam line, which is to die off because of Richard's choice of a bride."

Once again, he could not find the wits for a response that would please either of them.

"Don't look at me so stupidly, Darcy. You know of what I speak."

"If this is a concern over Rosings," he said, "then know that I have no desire to take possession of it and will break the entail as soon as my son is of age."

"That does not solve the crucial problem and is not why I called you here—as you have already guessed."

Of course, he thought. *So why don't you just tell me?*

"The task at hand is not an easy one—for either of us. Long have I considered it, but it is the only possible solution."

"Solution, Aunt Catherine?"

"Yes." She regained her usual demeanor in her determination. "Richard must take a mistress."

Had he been a lesser man, Darcy was sure he would have fainted from the shock. His mouth went dry. Lady Catherine had anticipated this, because she waited for him to gather his response. "*What?*"

"It is, if his brother dies, the only way the Fitzwilliam line will continue. It can be done in secret, of course, so that it appears to be Anne's—"

"But *she* will know! *He* will know!" He was having trouble staying in place. The urge to pace around, to look away—to get away from this insane woman—was ready to overcome him. "Are you intending to propose that they divorce?"

"Of course not! It would bring unimaginable shame to the family—"

"As would your suggestion! Or even more so! A child out of wedlock for no other reason than this stupid idea of family bloodlines? I may have a medieval brother, but I believe the rest of us are living in the same century! If they want children, let them adopt!"

"Like your sister Mary did? So conveniently while in France?" Lady Catherine snarled.

"Yes!" he said without thinking. "No! You are trying to throw me off! You know very well what I meant. If it is all to be covered up anyway, who cares if it belongs to one of them or neither of them? If you are so concerned about outside opinion—"

"I am concerned for this family! The same family whose name you bear, Fitzwilliam; I will not let it die!"

"*Then you should have had sons!*" Even in his enraged state, he could tell—after a moment or so of stunned silence—that he had gone too far. He stepped back, attempting to compose himself as he bowed. "I apologize, Aunt Catherine. But—surely you have not brought this idea to either of them?"

"No," she said. "I need your help to do it."

The blood drained from his face. He felt it, like it was growing cold as death. "You cannot be serious."

"I am very—"

"*No.*"

"Fitzwilliam, I am your aunt—"

"I know who you are, and I will never consent to such a plan," he said calmly, his voice steady in his severity. "It goes beyond all propriety and taste, and I will have nothing to do with it, ever."

"You—"

"We have nothing more to say on the subject. In fact, I find myself in need of refreshment, or I may well be ill. Good night, Aunt Catherine." He bowed again, turned, and left, tuning out her shrieks of his name by slamming the door behind him.

When he returned to his quarters, Elizabeth was already in bed reading. Her head turned up to him in polite inquiry, but he could not bear to speak. He gestured harshly at his manservant to leave, and removed his coat and vest himself. The second was harder, as his hands were shaking in his rage, and it was hard to manage the buttons, but he finally managed to get it off and collapsed on the bed, his boots still on and his hands over his face. To his surprise, Elizabeth said nothing. He heard and felt movement on the bed, and she seemed to disappear, but he had not the strength to go after her before he felt her unlacing his shoes for him. His "thank you" was barely a whisper, and she returned to him after finishing her task.

The rage in him would not so easily dissipate, but he was at least ready to look up at his beautiful wife, the sight of her bringing some relief. She asked nothing of him. Instead she took him into her arms, and so they lay, entwined, as his breathing lined up with hers.

"Your heart is racing," she said with some concern. "I can feel it." Her hand was on his breast. He removed it and kissed her fingers.

"Don't worry for me."

"Darcy," she said calmly, "I worry for you every second of every day. You are my husband. It is not something that can be dismissed."

"Neither can my own feelings, sadly," he said.

"You have lost your good opinion of your aunt forever?"

Her presence and touch must have indeed worked its magic, because he could smile, if a little bit, and most tiredly. "It fell out long ago. Now it has merely been dragged through the mud." He rested his head on her shoulder. "I cannot say it now. You will get upset, and I am still upset, and it will be a vicious cycle. I must settle first."

Elizabeth stroked his hair in complete and obvious understanding.

"I will tell you—in time."

And in time, after a long while of her soothing presence, he did.

QUENCHING THE FIRE

THE DARCYS TOOK BREAKFAST on their own, expressing their regrets through the servants but making no particular excuse. That they did not quit Rosings altogether that very morning had already been decided the night before. They would stay and protect the Fitzwilliams.

"She is mad," Elizabeth said over a very uneasy breakfast in their chambers.

"She is desperate. She has always been stubborn about her opinions, but this is beyond the norm. But she is older than we remember her." He reached over and put his hand over hers, reaffirming that together, they would weather this.

"I did wish to call on the Collinses today," Elizabeth said. "And perhaps it would be most settling for us before facing Lady Catherine again."

"I never thought I would think of Mr. Collins as a settling presence, but I agree," he said. "At least he is predictable."

They shared a laugh at Mr. Collins's expense before rising for the day at last and collecting their children. Grégoire was in his monkish habit of rising at three in the morning to begin his day of prayers, so they found him walking the grounds outside, very much awake and totally unaware of what had transpired. Neither of them could bring themselves to burden him with it—at least, not yet. "Brother. Elizabeth."

"Grégoire," Darcy said with the best smile he could manage. "We're to call on the Collinses. Elizabeth is old friends with Mrs. Collins, and they have not seen each other in years. Would you join us?"

"Of course."

They called for Nurse, who brought down Geoffrey and Anne, who ran up ahead even though they didn't know where they were going. Sarah, Elizabeth preferred to carry herself.

The Collinses were waiting for them, with the two older daughters running out to greet their visitors. Elizabeth embraced her old friend, while Mr. Collins just bowed. He was always intimidated by Darcy and was now equally intimidated by his brother, albeit for different reasons. They exchanged more docile pleasantries as all the children were introduced. The Collins family had three daughters ("The old Bennet curse," Darcy whispered to his brother, but could not further explain in their situation). A single family nurse kept watch over the older children, who played in the yard but were warned not to disturb the garden as the adults went inside.

"You don't have to stay very long," Elizabeth whispered to her husband before disappearing with Charlotte into her private sitting room with Sarah.

"Please, let me see to some refreshment," Mr. Collins said, momentarily disappearing and leaving Darcy and Grégoire in the proper sitting room. A sudden agony washed over Darcy's face, which Grégoire did not miss.

"What is it?"

"This awful room," Darcy said. "I hoped never to visit it again." When an explanation was obviously needed, he said, "I proposed to Elizabeth in this room. Right where you stand now, almost precisely."

Grégoire frowned. "Then should that not bring back pleasant memories?"

"Perhaps I have never told you of our most awkward courtship," he said. "I proposed to her in the most abominable way possible, insulting the whole of her relations and admitting that I thought the match was unsuitable but I was hopelessly in love. She then rejected me in the most abusive way possible without physical violence."

"But you were married."

"Yes. Almost a year later, when I had done everything in my power to convince her that I was not the ogre she thought I was." He saw some movement in the back. "Please do not mention it in front of Mr. Collins."

"Of course not," Grégoire said. "But that is all in the past now."

"Yes. Though I am starting to feel as though visiting Kent brings about awful behavior on the part of myself and my aunt." Unfortunately, Mr. Collins returned, and he could not clarify— for the moment.

The trip had exhausted little Sarah, who was placed in the crib beside Eleanor, only a few months older than she. There, she immediately went to sleep most peacefully. "Perhaps they will be great friends someday."

"I do hope so," Charlotte said. "I have missed you, Lizzy."

"I have, too," she said as they closed the nursery door and went back into the women's sitting room, where tea was ready for them. "So much has changed."

"I must admit most shamefully that there have been times when I thought it a misfortune that you married Mr. Darcy, and we have not seen each other as a result. But that is the fault of Lady Catherine. But—are things beginning to mend between your husband and her ladyship?"

"We thought maybe so, when she finally responded to my pleas for renewing the acquaintance," Elizabeth said, biting her lip. "But now it seems less likely than ever that we will be seeing much of Lady Catherine."

"Why ever so? She was not especially out of sorts at dinner. In fact, I think your new brother silenced her quite well."

Elizabeth looked down nervously at her tea, then back up at her old friend. "Charlotte—will you take the burden of a terrible secret? Though I shan't think it will be secret for much longer, it is the reason we were almost inclined to leave at first light."

"*Lizzy*," Charlotte was almost scolding. "You know you can tell me anything."

She had wanted to tell someone, as it had weighed on her throughout their sleepless night. Grégoire was Darcy's responsibility, and they had decided that they would approach Anne and Colonel Fitzwilliam as soon as possible, but in great privacy and when the mood was right. Plus, they had not the least idea of how to go about it. It was such a relief to unburden herself to Charlotte, who was so sweet and unassuming, so ready to weather Lady Catherine's wild tirades—but even she looked shocked.

"The worst of it is," Elizabeth said, "how she could propose such an idea with no feelings for her own daughter! Is Anne yet again to be the most unfortunate creature of all of us? Surely Lady Catherine is mad?"

"Lady Catherine is older than you remember her, Lizzy," Charlotte said, her own form now tense, "in body and mind. When I heard from my husband that Lord Matlock was sick—and so soon, after the death of his father!—I knew she was particularly concerned about Rosings, as I understand the ownership has something to do with Lord Matlock. Lady Catherine's fortune is of course derived from Rosings, so Mr. Collins has been quite concerned."

Of course. Mr. Collins was dependent on his patroness, or he would be in poverty. Not that he had long before he would inherit Longbourn—but he would not inherit the money to maintain it. Elizabeth chided herself for not realizing the Collinses' precarious situation sooner. How life had surprised them all! "But Rosings will go to Darcy, should Colonel Fitzwilliam's brother pass away, and my husband could not be less interested in the place. He will lease it to the colonel—who I suppose will have to buy out of the army—and the Fitzwilliams are one of the loveliest couples I know! You are in no danger, Charlotte. This will all pass. Darcy has already refused to go along with Lady Catherine's plan, which would never have worked. Colonel Fitzwilliam would never subject his marriage to such a horror."

"He is a kind man. I was sad to see less of him when he moved Anne to Brighton. But—it must be hard on them. Oh, Lizzy, for Anne to not know the joys of motherhood!"

"It is not impossible. I have relatives who took in the child of a woman who died in childbirth, and they raise him as their own son and are very happy!"

"Perhaps. Or perhaps they will have children on their own, and all of this will come to naught."

Darcy was almost relieved when the invitation came, calling him to tea at Rosings. Watching Grégoire run circles around Mr. Collins was interesting enough, but it made the vicar no less odious. For the most part he stared out the window, drinking tea. He suspected there would be very little actual drinking of it at Rosings.

Elizabeth was willing to cut her own visit short, as they had planned to intercept the Fitzwilliams before Lady Catherine did any more damage, and they could not afford to miss this gathering. They said their good-byes and returned to Rosings, first dropping off their children in the nursery.

"Do we have a plan?"

"Yes. You can make polite conversation with my aunt, thereby getting her into a disgusted rage and thoroughly distracting her." He smiled as his wife gave him a look.

They were early by Darcy's pocket watch, which he was inspecting as they made it down the grand stairs, but no further. Rushing down the hallway was the figure of Colonel Fitzwilliam. Darcy turned and said amiably, "Rich—"

Which was about as far as he got before his cousin punched him in the face.

Colonel Fitzwilliam was a military man, while Darcy was merely a strong man who happened to enjoy fencing (and occasionally socking people when he was drunk enough). There was no contest as Darcy hit the floor behind him, fortunately on a very thick and expensive rug. "How could you?"

"How could I *what?*" Darcy said as he was helped up by Elizabeth. Grégoire made a move to also go to his brother's aid, but when Fitzwilliam looked ready to strike him as well, he backed up the stairs a bit.

"Richard!" came a cry from behind them, as Anne ran up from behind, apparently having heard the stir. "What in the world are you doing?"

"Anne," he said more softly, still huffing from the force of it all, "my apologies. This is between Darcy and myself."

"Colonel Fitzwilliam!" Elizabeth said as she forced Darcy to uncover his eye. It was red from the contact but did not look damaged. "My husband deserves an answer."

"*I* deserve an answer!" Fitzwilliam shouted. She had never seen him like this. "How could you?"

"I can't possibly imagine what I could have—" Darcy said as he got to his feet. "—done... Wait—did Aunt Catherine tell you—?"

"So you do know! And you *kept it from me!*"

"Richard, she told me but late last night, and I—"

"You agreed!" Fitzwilliam made another move in Darcy's direction, but was held back this time by his wife.

"Richard!"

"I did not!" Darcy pleaded, his one eye blinking rapidly. "I would have quit this place altogether, but I stayed to warn you!"

"Bloody good job you did!"

"My apologies," Grégoire said, stepping between them in a half-bow. "But what are we referring to?"

"Yes, please!" Anne pleaded at Fitzwilliam's side, but he would not be calmed. At least he was willing to actively stop thrashing his cousin.

"He…" he stumbled in his speech. "Darcy, you are telling me you did not agree to this scheme against us?"

"Of course not! Did our aunt tell you that?" Darcy said. "You know she's delusional! I agreed to no such thing. I told only Elizabeth and we planned to tell you as soon as we saw you, which, I suppose, is now. But I am too late, and I apologize."

Fitzwilliam huffed, but seemed to calm down enough to look less aggressive, but no less agitated by what he had been told. Darcy and Elizabeth couldn't blame him, all things considered. But it was Anne who insistently tugged at her husband's side. "What *is it?*"

"Sadly, I think this is neither the time nor the—ow—place," Darcy said as Elizabeth tried to attend to his wound again. "It is just one of your mother's tirades, sadly."

"Is that what they are to you, nephew?"

All turned, collectively horrified, at the entrance of Lady Catherine de Bourgh. She strutted about as if nothing was amiss, not even Darcy's red and swollen face. "Well? Why do you all stand about in such a silly manner? Darcy, I must speak with you at once!"

"I've no doubt," Darcy said. "But as I have no desire to speak with you, we are in a conundrum. In fact, I cannot think of a person in this room who, knowing your designs, would wish to have any connection with you!"

But Lady Catherine was not unprepared in her always-ready indignation, tapping her cane on the ground. "Do not suppose to speak that way to me, nephew! Who else have you told? I suppose you've told Miss Bennet and that Papist—"

"Lady Catherine," Elizabeth said, trying to be the calming voice, if no one else would. She skipped over the name-calling entirely. "Please, *my husband* has told me nothing I did not deserve to know. The person who deserves to know is your own daughter."

"*What is everyone talking about?*" Anne screamed, and it was the first time either of the Darcys who knew her could ever recall her raising her voice, much less at her mother. "Mama?"

"Quiet! You are the cause of all of this! If only you could bear children—"

Fitzwilliam stood protectively in front of his terrified wife. "Aunt Catherine, you will end this nonsense—"

"You must have children, Richard! Or our family is doomed! My sister's side is polluted by wanton behavior on the part of her husband and son. You must take a mistress—"

At which point, Anne fainted. Elizabeth, not feeling so steady herself, ran to her side and caught her, helping her to the stairs. "It is nothing; she is just in a mood—"

"I am not in a mood!" Lady Catherine shouted, her voice piercing—but unsteady. "I am speaking perfectly sensibly for our family—"

"Aunt, cease this!" Fitzwilliam shouted back. "I think everyone in this room but you is in agreement that you are alone in your conception of what makes a proper family! Your advice has never been sensible, and we have only endured it because we felt an obligation to do so! But if you are to torture your daughter—my wife—with such ideas, then I will cut off our relations, and you will fend for yourself if and when my brother dies!"

"You wouldn't—" Lady Catherine said, grasping her chest.

"I would! You know Darcy will control Rosings, and he will have no cause to tolerate your constant insults towards Mrs. Darcy any longer!"

"No," Darcy said, but in a softer voice, a little put off by Fitzwilliam's frothing rage.

Lady Catherine stepped back unevenly. "You—both of you—my nephews—I treated you like my own sons all these years—and now you will cut me off like so, while you embrace those beneath you so readily—I am the wife of a knight of the realm—I am the mistress of Rosings, and I can cast you out with just a—" But the clutch on her dress began to tighten, and without warning, she dropped to the floor with a resounding thud.

THE CARETAKER

BESIDES ANNE'S SCREAM, THERE was silence in the room as they stood in shock.

This lasted for only a few moments before Grégoire pushed past Darcy and Fitzwilliam and raced to Lady Catherine's side, kneeling beside her and propping her up on his knee. "Lady Catherine?" He felt her chest and looked up at the others. "What are you all standing there for? Fetch some smelling salts!" He had no monastic patience for his gaping brother. "*Now!* Colonel Fitzwilliam! Get the servants to get cold compresses and a blanket!" While they stared for another second, he sighed and picked up the tiny, quivering form of Lady Catherine de Bourgh in his arms and carried her past them, into the sitting room. The servants were accustomed to making themselves absent during a family squabble, so he was lucky to find one in there. "You! Pillows for her ladyship! Make haste!"

Everyone numbly went about their tasks as Elizabeth escorted the shocked and confused Anne to her mother's side. Grégoire was kneeling next to Lady Catherine, holding her withered hand with one of his hands and the smelling salts under her nose with the other. "Lady Catherine," he pleaded. "Please listen to me. Take very careful breaths. I will count with you—"

Fitzwilliam returned with a horde of servants, and Grégoire did not take his eyes off his charge as he gave his next orders. "Get a doctor at once or, at the very least, an apothecary."

Grégoire took a cup of tea, held it to Lady Catherine's mouth, and said, "Please, your ladyship, you must drink." Eventually she was persuaded to open her mouth and swallow the contents of the cup. "There."

"Mama," Anne said, as the servants brought up a chair for her to sit beside the couch where her mother laid, her color gone. Elizabeth stood over, one hand gently on Anne's shoulder, and could not help but note that Charlotte had been correct— Lady Catherine was older in body and perhaps in mind. Her skin was almost colorless as one bony hand clutched Grégoire's.

"What's happened?" Elizabeth ventured to ask.

"I've fainted," Lady Catherine said, her voice weak but still defiant. "What else do you think, you witless girl?"

The doctor arrived as dinner hour was approaching, but no one felt like eating. Everyone was made to wait outside the room, and a dreary silence descended over them. Finally he emerged, looking quite pleased with himself, to give his opinion. "Her ladyship's heart should return to normal with bed rest and some tonic water. They sell bottled water from the pumps at Bath in a shop in the town proper—I recommend it, at least three times a day, and no other liquids. And she must rest, of course, for as long as it takes for her to regain her strength."

"Thank God," Anne whispered, leaning into her husband.

"If her condition changes, please do call me at once," and with that, he excused himself. Grégoire turned to his brother with a look that Darcy understood perfectly.

"Come, Anne," Elizabeth said softly. "I'm sure your mother would appreciate your company. And if she does not tolerate mine, then we will know she has recovered."

With that, they disappeared into the room. Fitzwilliam collapsed on the stairs, speechless. Darcy turned to his brother. "What do you think?"

"I'm not a doctor, Darcy. I am barely an apprentice apothecary. But I think the worst is over."

"Thank God in heaven," Fitzwilliam said. "We almost killed her."

Darcy did not contradict him.

"I will keep a vigil tonight for her ladyship," Grégoire announced. "Perhaps Mr. Collins will wish to join me."

"You've no obligation—"

"I have every obligation," Grégoire said, "to any soul on this earth." With that, he bowed to them and went back into the sitting room.

The next morning, Mrs. Charlotte Collins had just finished feeding her youngest daughter and her husband was getting ready with his gardening tools when there was a knock at the door. She turned to her husband, who scurried to the door. "Hel—Mr. Darcy!" He bowed even lower than he usually did, and Charlotte smiled to herself as Mr. Darcy entered and bowed. "Mr. Collins. Mrs. Collins." As usual, he was quite to the point.

"Lady Catherine collapsed yesterday and is quite ill. Mr. Collins, my brother has been sitting in vigil for almost a day now. I would be grateful if you would take it up in his place so that he can rest." He did not stand on ceremony. "Mrs. Collins, my wife, I believe, could also use some support. Do you have enough staff here to care for your children, or should we send some servants?"

"We have a very competent nurse," Charlotte said, a little shaken, "thanks to Lady Catherine."

Never had they made such quick time to Rosings. Everyone there seemed more than a bit shaken as long as Lady Catherine was still resting and not insisting that she was fine. Darcy dragged Mr. Collins up to Lady Catherine's bedchamber almost physically, where Grégoire was kneeling before the bed. He and Anne on the other side rose at their entrance. "Mr. Collins will take your place. Please." He pulled his brother out of the room. Grégoire could barely stand on his feet. "Now, you are going to break your fast and then go immediately to sleep."

"She—"

"She has a nervous condition and will be fine. Though perhaps not 'fine' in a sense we would all prefer, but physically, yes."

It did not take long after the doctor left for the Fitzwilliams to come to a decision. "We will be staying at Rosings," the colonel said. "The servants say there have been many fainting spells. We wish to monitor her."

The Darcys also decided to lengthen their visit, at least until Lady Catherine seemed to be stabilized. She spoke little unless spoken to but seemed very much to enjoy the presence of her daughter and Mrs. Collins.

"While she may not have been willing to admit it," Elizabeth said to her husband, "I think your aunt has grown fond of Charlotte over the years."

Darcy said nothing, staring out the window, watching his children play on the grass.

The calendar was not their ally. Grégoire looked anxiously at the calendar, and Darcy put a hand on his shoulder. "I know. You must go."

"I don't wish to leave her."

"You've no obligation."

Grégoire played with his rosary in his hands nervously; clearly he felt differently. Together they left the darkness of Rosings interiors for the sunlight of Kent in early summer. "I used to play out here as a child," Darcy said. Rosings Park had a vast expanse of land, including the ruins of what had been a church of some kind with Greek-like columns. "We called this the temple. Sometimes we called it a castle. Richard and I much preferred being out of doors as my mother and father visited Aunt Catherine." He looked up. "We used to climb that—Geoffrey!"

For his son was sitting up in a tree, resting on one of the stronger limbs. "What?"

"What if your mother saw you? Do you know how dangerous that is? Come down from there right now!" Darcy demanded, and then turned to give Grégoire a cold stare as his brother laughed. "You'd understand if you had children. Geoffrey! Now!"

"You were just saying—"

"I know what I was just saying, but you are coming down this instant!"

Geoffrey huffed but did begin his climb down, which included one swing from the branches and landing in his father's arms. "I was just having fun."

"Why don't you play with Amelia?" Darcy suggested. Amelia Collins was a year older than Geoffrey.

"Amelia doesn't want to play with me," Geoffrey said as his father put him down. "She says it's because I'm a *boy*."

"In that, she is quite correct. You are, in fact, a boy," Grégoire said with a smile.

Geoffrey stuck his tongue out at his uncle, mainly because he so easily got away with it. "Georgie plays with me, and she doesn't care. She doesn't sit around with ribbons and dolls and nonsense."

"Georgie has known you since the day you were born," Darcy said diplomatically. "You are the same age and know each other well, unlike Miss Collins. That, and she seems to enjoy frustrating Bingley's laundress by soiling every outfit she has with mud."

"No one will play with me here," Geoffrey said, tugging on his father's legs. "Can I go to Chatton?"

"No, we are staying here for a bit longer, I'm afraid."

"Why?"

"Because," Darcy said and found himself speechless.

"Because? Just because?" His son looked up at him.

Darcy shrugged. "With Lady Catherine, a 'because' is all that is required."

As soon as Lady Catherine was recovered enough to start barking orders again, Grégoire had to say his good-byes.

Darcy pressed a coin into his hand. "Write us when you arrive in Berlin, please. The roads are not safe. And open a box there to write to us from Austria."

"I promise."

"And if there is open war—you will return."

"I am a poor monk and a Frenchman. I cannot see why anyone would have issue with me."

Because Grégoire only sees the good in everyone, Darcy lamented. One of these days it would have regrettable consequences.

Chapter 6

THE MISSIVE FROM AUSTRIA

"Papa! Papa!"

Emily Maddox, nearing five years of age, ran to her father and reached him before his servants did, grasping tightly his leg. She wasn't yet big enough to topple him, but reached just below his waist in height, and she held up her arms in a silent indication of wanting attention.

"Let me at least get my coat off," he said as he shrugged off his greatcoat, handing it to the servant before picking his daughter up. "There. I will assume from your welcome that you may have missed me." He kissed her cheek. His day with the Prince Regent had been long and grueling, going well into the night, and he was just now, in the morning, returning to his home.

"No fair!" his son announced, crashing down the stairs and rushing up to him. "I want to be picked up!"

"Well, I can hardly take you both at once, so you will have to wait your turn," he said, patting Frederick on the head.

"I'll take her," Caroline said, emerging from the sitting room. They exchanged kisses and a child. "She's been waiting by the window all morning. In fact, Nurse has just informed me that it is time for their naps."

"NO!" the children cried in unison.

"I'm not tired! Papa, please!"

"I don't need a nap!"

Dr. Maddox gave an amused sigh. "What did your parents do when you were their age, darling?"

"They threatened to make me watch over my brother," Caroline said. "Nurse!"

The nurse quickly appeared and escorted two reluctant children to their nursery, leaving the parents alone. "How was the ball?"

"Fine."

"You can at least tell me something interesting about your patient," she said. "But I suppose you will not."

"Would you prefer gossip or me to keep my job?" he said, grinning at his wife. "Is the post here?"

"Yes; nothing significant." When the doctor frowned anxiously, Caroline gave him a sympathetic look. "You know how the post is. Especially since Napoleon is near the Rhine."

"That doesn't make me feel any better about it," he said. "If there are no callers, I am going to sleep." He put his hand on the railing. "Oh, and Miss Darcy has been called to Rosings to attend to her aunt until further notice, and so will not be joining us for dinners."

"You didn't tell them, did you?"

He gave her a sly smile. "Of course not."

Dr. Maddox did have a caller the next day, when a messenger arrived whom he was roused for. He hurriedly put on his formal dress and wig, kissed his wife, and was off.

He was not a man to panic. Even the sight of a passed-out would-be king did not start his adrenaline pumping. The servants were dashing all about as he entered, and the squire hovering over his fallen master as Dr. Maddox calmly set his bag down, opened it, and pulled out a small bottle. "What did he have for lunch?"

"Nothing unusual," the squire said, apparently annoyed at Dr. Maddox's nonchalance at seeing his patient on the floor, having rolled off his chaise at some point.

"What did he drink?"

"He had some wine with his bread and some whiskey before, but as I said—"

"Bring me his cup, if you would, sir," he said, kneeling next to the Regent and holding the salts up to his nose. The heavy-breathing prince took one breath before stirring in an angry snort. He was immediately helped up by his attendants into the chair at Dr. Maddox's motion.

"What in bloody hell—" His Royal Highness, Prince George Augustus Frederick, heaved a sigh and rubbed his forehead, bruised from the fall. "Oh, thank God, they've called you."

"Your Highness," Dr. Maddox bowed, but he was more concerned with the goblet he'd just been handed. He took one sniff and held it up indignantly. "What is this?"

"You need a new prescription for your spectacles if you don't know what *that* is, Dr. Maddox."

"I am referring to its contents," Dr. Maddox said. There was still some left swirling at the bottom, and he put his pinky in and touched it to his tongue. "What did I say about this?"

"I am not to be scolded like a schoolchild, Doctor!"

"My apologies," Dr. Maddox said, without the sound of real apology in his voice, "but I am called in to ensure your good health and am therefore, in all good conscience, required to mention when you are ruining it. You know laudanum is addictive. I've told you so."

"Till my ears have come to almost fall off, yes," the Prince Regent said. "So I am perhaps addicted. That means it is part of my daily requirement, or I will die—correct?"

"You will not die if you stop, Your Highness," he said. "You will feel miserable for a few days, and then it will pass. But the longer this continues, the worse the withdrawal will be. Do you want to spend weeks shaking so hard it exhausts you? Do you want to feel freezing no matter how many blankets you pile over your head?"

"Those are just physicians' horror stories."

"So you are content to find out." Dr. Maddox put the goblet on the tray the servant was holding. "You are the guardian of your own fate, Your Highness. I can do no more than to offer suggestions."

"You offer them very insistently."

Dr. Maddox was again unfazed. It was sad, really, to watch a man transform into a drunken, doped bovine, especially when the man was *his* patient and *his* responsibility. "I do, and will continue to do so, because I am apparently the only one loyal enough to you to give you an honest opinion about how you should care for yourself. To my knowledge, you've not raised an issue with it yet." He knew he was treading on thin ice but had realized long ago that the part of the Regent's mind that wasn't addled by opium respected him—or at least liked him—for it. "Do you wish to lodge a complaint about my behavior?"

The Regent sighed. "No, no. Then I'll have to have you dismissed, and some idiot will come in and kill me with their medicine, like they're killing my father. I'm sure of it." For once, he seemed serious. "He was a great man."

"He was. *Is*," Dr. Maddox corrected himself quickly. "God save the king."

"Only God can save the king now." He looked up at the doctor. "Do you think I am destined for the same fate?"

He gave his honest answer. "Seeing as it has struck no one else in your lineage, I do not think it likely if his illness operates like any other disease, Your Highness."

"The only reason I put up with your lack of proper protocol when in service of a royal is because you tell me the truth," the Regent said, "even if I don't listen to it." He picked up yet another glass from the table beside the chaise and raised it. "Cheers, Doctor."

Lacking a glass, Dr. Maddox bowed instead. "Cheers, Your Highness."

The doctor arrived home in the mid-afternoon, when the hot sun was still high in the sky, and the house was relatively quiet, meaning the children were down for their afternoon nap or they were in the fenced garden that he could not help but think of as more of an animal cage. The only person who greeted him was the doorman, who handed him a large, sealed envelope. "From a special courier, sir. Just arrived."

He recognized the paper type and the seal instantaneously and disappeared into his study, where he could sit, remove his ridiculous wig, and properly attend to the letter.

It was in some foreign language, the character set foreign to him, but from the seal, which had been identical to the one from his brother's letters, the doctor knew it to be Romanian. It seemed very official in its wording, or at least how it was presented on the page, and included with it was a slip of a German translation. *That* at least he could read.

It was nearly half an hour before anyone disturbed him. No one generally came into the master's study except Frederick or his wife, and it was the latter. "Daniel?" Whatever business she had, it must have been immediately put aside when she saw him bent over his desk, trying to read the fine print again. "What is it?"

"I admit my German is rusty—that or their German is rusty—but it seems I have been invited to Transylvania to visit my brother, by his father-in-law, Count Vladimir of Sibiu."

"Why would Brian not write it in English?"

"It is in the language of an official decree—as if I am being *summoned*." He removed his glasses. "As if I am not *summoned* by royalty all the time. But I would like to see Brian and his lovely wife, Princess Nade—Nadez—Nadezdah—Her Highness. I would love to meet Her Highness." He squinted. "I'm sure she is a very lovely wife, but could they have not mentioned *my* lovely wife in their invitation?"

"I was thinking the very same thing. But Transylvania—I don't know where that is proper. Hungary, I believe? Or Austria? Near the Black Sea? It is such a small place."

"England is quite a small place, without Ireland and Scotland." He looked up at her with reassuring eyes. "We will of course have to return the favor and invite the count. He will not come, but Brian and Her Highness will."

"And I will not have to get the hem of my dress muddy."

"Do you have a greater fondness for your brother-in-law or the hem of your dress?"

She cupped his cheek. "You will be a very beloved *husband* if you do not make me answer that."

SUMMER AT CHATTON

As the Bingleys celebrated the anniversary of the birth of their second son, they were hosts not only to their relatives but also to the anxieties everyone seemed to bring with them, however unintentionally. The news from the Continent was bad—Napoleon was moving the largest army in history across Europe to conquer Russia. Grégoire had written on his way back to Austria—he was desperately needed in his monastery, but he would try to stay in communication. Dr. Maddox had no intention of bringing up his own travel plans and worry the family, but he was hardly willing (or able) to stop Caroline from alerting every adult. He sighed and braced himself for the inevitable.

For the moment, there was peace. Elizabeth and Jane sat outside, watching the various children who were old enough to chase each other around. "Goodness," Jane said. "Someone in this family must stop, or we'll all be insane."

"I'm beginning to respect Mama more every day for raising her five unruly daughters," Elizabeth replied with a smile.

"Lizzy! You were not unruly!"

"I have a very painful recollection involving a broken tree branch and a sprained ankle that tells me otherwise."

"Oh, I hardly remember that."

"*I* do," Elizabeth said. "I also remember that Papa was forced to replace our tiny tea set."

"Did I toss a cup first or did Kitty?"

"It is hard to incriminate a most beloved sister," was Elizabeth's reply. "But perhaps it was not Kitty." Jane looked at her, and they both burst out laughing.

"Oh, Lizzy," Jane said. "Must you return to Kent so quickly? I must sound very jealous when I say so."

"We are not obligated, especially with the Fitzwilliams there," Elizabeth said, "but we should. Darcy will not forgive himself over the whole event."

"Has he spoken to Lady Catherine about it?"

"No one is willing to bring up the precise circumstances of her fainting spell unless she is willing, and she has made no mention of them." Elizabeth looked out and watched Geoffrey and Georgie toss a ball over young Charles as he desperately tried to intercept it. "She is not her old self yet, for which we all feel grateful, and then we all feel a great guilt for feeling so. It is a vicious cycle. Who knew, by slowly dying, she could turn the tables on all of us?"

Jane put her hand over her sister's in silent understanding.

"I am out of practice."

"You are not."

Bingley and Darcy were a good distance away from the grounds for their shooting. They had discovered shortly after

Bingley purchased Chatton that there was a nice area for spotting birds between their two houses, and would often meet there during the hunting season. Bingley was mistaken; he was not at all less of a huntsman than he had been, but Darcy was himself not doing so well, distracted as he was. He would not admit to the weakness, and Bingley, if he noticed it, would say nothing. It was a long-established tradition; that was why they were good friends.

This time they had implored Dr. Maddox to come, saying that he looked like he desperately needed the fresh air (which he did), but he refused, and they were not surprised. The physician had never been inclined to a sport that involved killing things, or even watching it. He did promise to take a walk. His general countenance was indeed improved by the coming trip to see his brother, whom he sorely missed. Even Napoleon's invasion of Russia could not dissuade him from traveling to the Continent—yet.

"I see something moving, in the woods."

"If it is a stray child, do try not to hit it."

Bingley squinted, "Too large."

"Dr. Maddox? Elizabeth?"

"Too small. Look, there."

Darcy turned his eyes to the edge of the woods, where there was indeed something moving about, but was not recognizably a deer. "A wolf?"

"It wouldn't surprise me. I've seen a lot of them about recently, but they've never ventured to the herds that anyone knows of. I thought you got rid of the lot years ago."

"We did. Or we thought we did. I remember the expedition." During his father's time as master of Pemberley, a local baronet had purchased a pack of what he thought were dogs, while travel-ing in Newfoundland, only to discover they were wolves. He did not have it in him to kill the pups as he ought have, and released them to Derbyshire's forests, assuming they would not survive the winter. They did, and before long the deer population was mysteriously suffering. Darcy was still a young man, barely more than a boy, and thrilled at the prospect to be allowed to go on one of the expeditions to clear out the infestation. "Apparently we did not get them all, and they have recovered some of their numbers. Something to watch over, especially when people come in for the hunt," Darcy said. "I'll alert my huntsman."

"Are you intending to stay long in Pemberley or return immediately to Kent?"

"That is the question," Darcy said quietly, sitting down on a fallen log.

Bingley put his gun down and took a good look at his brother-in-law. "I am sorry for Lady Catherine," he said. "It is all so ill-timed."

"Yes."

"The earl is ill, your aunt is... your aunt, to be polite about it, and Grégoire is in—what is the name of that town?"

"Munich," Darcy said. "He wrote when he returned to the Continent that he was going to Munich, to protect some relics there with his fellow monks."

"Grégoire is in Munich—"

Darcy swallowed and said, "Grégoire is not in Munich." He said it very stoically, but as they always did, his eyes betrayed him.

At last, they had come to the point. "Where is he?"

"I don't know," Darcy said. "All I have is a news report that said the monasteries in that area were all dissolved and the monks were to report to Munich, and from there were sent on their own way."

"You can't trust our papers; you know that."

"I do. So I wrote to Berlin for a confirmation and received it. St. Paul's is no more."

Bingley absorbed this information quickly. "And the monks?"

"Some of them have gone to other monasteries, farther east. Some have gone to Spain. Many have walked out of the convent. But there is no accounting of them." Darcy was still stone-faced, but unconsciously played with his hands. "Before he left, Grégoire agreed to write to Berlin and have the message safely forwarded from there if something was amiss. If something went wrong, he was to return to Berlin and write me from there." He paused. "By all calculations, he should have already been there by now."

"Walking?"

"He promised he would not walk. The roads are not safe."

Bingley frowned. At last he brought himself to say, "He *will* turn up."

Darcy said nothing.

In the afternoon, they celebrated Edmund, who sat on his mother's lap and watched the proceedings with no comprehension whatsoever. The children did manage to be herded in without too much trouble. Only Georgie complained about the ribbons in her hair itching, and Frederick seemed sullen in his jealousy, but everyone else was managed well enough before being dismissed so the birthday boy could have a nap and the adults could prepare for dinner. Dinner itself was not a terribly long affair, and the only missing relatives mentioned were the Bennets. Mr. and Mrs. Bennet were getting a bit old to travel, and did not come up to Derbyshire for every birthday and holiday, or they would be forever in transit, and the Townsends were newlyweds.

Shortly afterwards the men and women separated, as various children had to be put to bed. The port was served in the library; only Darcy didn't partake. It did seem to him a bit odd to be in Bingley's presence after a family meal without having to speak over Mr. Hurst's drunken snoring, but the Hursts were in their summer house in the south.

"I am, if you would, in need of some advice," Bingley said rather calmly. Finally, no grave matter to be discussed. "Financial advice."

"Marry well and get a royal commission," Dr. Maddox said, mainly because he liked port. "I'm sorry, but that is all I can offer."

"Buy land," Darcy said.

"That is not the answer to every investment question!"

"It's not as if there's going to be more of it," Dr. Maddox pointed out.

"Do not get on his side!" Bingley said. "No, this is not related to land."

"Then out with it," Darcy said. "We could use the distraction."

"Thank you." Bingley took another swig of his drink. "Part of my inheritance, completely separate from my personal worth, was a few remaining shares in my father's company in the textile trade. He sold most of it off shortly before his death, when it was worth considerably more than it is now, but he maintained a few shares—I suppose, for sentimental value. Now they are practically worthless with the embargo. In fact, I calculated that I could regain a controlling interest in the company for less than four hundred pounds."

Darcy was skeptical. "And your purpose in doing so would be?"

"Obviously, if the company became profitable again after the war, the shares would then be worth a great deal of money," Dr. Maddox said, and got two looks. "What? I *did* take economics at Cambridge."

"The problem," Darcy said, "is that if the company goes completely bankrupt before the end of the embargo—and we have no idea when that will be—then its assets will be liquidated, and you will be out four hundred pounds. More to the point, if you become the owner of the company, you will have significant responsibilities to keep it afloat, or you will be firing workers and selling warehouses—and workers do not care for losing jobs. It is the same as having tenants, only far more dangerous. You will have to employ a very competent man to run the company, and the expenses will pile up."

"True," Bingley said, "but nothing beyond my ability to handle."

"If you are so sure," Darcy said.

Breaking the silence of Bingley's enthusiasm and Darcy's disapproval, Dr. Maddox said quietly, "Perhaps you should ask Mrs. Bingley."

Both men stared at him.

"I don't presume that she would look over the account ledgers," he said, "but certainly, this venture would send you to Town more often than she is accustomed to. So it would be a concern for her."

"This is true," Darcy said, knowing Jane would be a cool head.

Fortunately Bingley didn't have to answer, because a servant entered and approached him, whispering in his ear. "Excuse me for a moment. My children are being put to bed."

Dr. Maddox raised a glass to him as he bowed to his guests and left. He noted Darcy's scowl. "Come now. We can't all be idle gentlemen. I would go mad if I had nothing to do all day."

"I would hardly qualify owning land and having tenants as having 'nothing to do,'" Darcy said. "But that is neither here nor there, I suppose."

"Yes."

Darcy sighed, paced for a bit, and then seemed to change his composure. "Doctor," he said, taking a seat by the fireplace, looking very uncomfortable. "I understand your brother is doing well, though the invitation seems ill-timed, with all the soldiers moving across the Rhineland."

"It does," Dr. Maddox said, sad but still a bit put off. He'd never spoken much alone with Darcy. They liked each other well enough, but they lived apart, and most of their conversations were related to someone's medical condition. And there was the matter that their wives were not the best of friends.

Darcy hesitated before speaking. "I assume you are going anyway."

"I am to be provided with an escort from Berlin, to make sure I arrive safely."

Darcy said nothing. The doctor didn't push him, nursing his port until Darcy finally spoke, "My brother is... out of contact."

"You've not heard from him? The post is very bad."

"I've not heard from him, but I've heard that his monastery is dissolved and that the town surrounding it had been overrun with French troops."

Dr. Maddox tried to hide his alarm. "When was this?"

"A few weeks ago. I confirmed it as not being total nonsense with a man I know in Normandy, as we're still getting letters from there, but I haven't heard from Grégoire."

"Would he have gone back to his old monastery?"

"It was dissolved in 1809, also by General Bonaparte. Grégoire told me of it last summer. It seems the general is determined to lay waste to organized religion and replace it with the new French rationalism. Which, normally, I would not be so opposed to—if I knew where my brother was right now, and what he was doing," Darcy said. "There was a bit in the paper about a massacre. Elizabeth assures me it's just propagandist nonsense—"

"They *are* trying to recruit for a war."

"—but I can't get it out of my head. Surely you understand?" He looked up at Dr. Maddox, who saw at once the desperation in his eyes. How he kept his anxiety quiet, the doctor had no idea. Daniel Maddox was unable to keep any strong emotion, especially worry, from showing.

"His monastery is on the way to Transylvania."

"I can't ask that of you," Darcy said. "My proposal is to accompany you to Berlin and then split our trails."

"And your wife approves of this proposal?"

"Absolutely not."

Dr. Maddox nodded. "Then at least Caroline will have some company in that, as she is annoyed that she was not invited."

"So you are decided?"

"Yes. You?"

"I have to... further discuss it with my wife," Darcy said. "Perhaps I ought to get to that."

"I have known you these seven years, and you have never

been a man to falter or even hesitate to do your duty," the doctor said. "Mr. Darcy is not to be cowed by anything. Except, perhaps, his wife."

Darcy glared at him before storming off, leaving Dr. Maddox to finish his drink quietly, a smirk on his lips.

"You want to *what?*"

When Darcy said he had to "further" discuss his plans with his wife, he was being a bit liberal in his explanation. He had put off his idea as long as possible, but now that the doctor was so set on going to the Continent… "I will probably find him in Berlin, or a trace of him."

Elizabeth Darcy hugged her bed robe around her, as if the idea gave her chills despite the summer heat. "We saw your brother a few months ago!"

"When he was here, yes. But now we have every reason to believe he is in danger." He had told her of the news from Germany, but nothing of his plan to do something about it. He knelt on the bed, almost pleading with her.

"If someone must go to find Grégoire," she said, "then let it be your steward. Or Dr. Maddox, who will already be in Berlin! Which he does against the insistence of his wife and family!"

"I cannot ask that of him."

"Grégoire *can* take care of himself!"

"We don't know that!"

"We do! You just refuse to believe it!"

"Elizabeth, I have already lost one brother to my own incompetence. I *cannot* lose another!"

It had been louder than he intended, even though Elizabeth had been making no attempt to keep her own voice down. They were in their chambers in Pemberley, and they were not to be disturbed. Still, it was strange, especially with the silence that followed, as his words hung down over them like an ominously dark cloud.

Elizabeth joined him on the bed, instantly embracing him, and he did not shy away, his head slumping on her shoulder. "It was not your fault," she whispered.

"I know."

"But you don't *believe*," she said, separating enough to see the anguish on his face, usually so disguised. "You cannot put yourself in danger for the ghost of George Wickham."

"This is about Grégoire," he said. "I would not put myself in danger for Wickham, ghost or no. But I cannot bear to stand by while Grégoire is missing."

They didn't even discuss her coming with him. With three children, one of whom was an infant, it wasn't an option.

"You understand," he said gently, "why I must do this."

She did not want to admit it. "What if he appears at our doorstep while you are in Prussia?"

"He has a post box in Berlin. I will check it every day. And I will write you if I intend to leave the city at all." He took her hand and kissed it. "I will not put myself in unnecessary danger."

"And your aunt?"

He smiled. "I will not put Aunt Catherine in any unnecessary danger, either." He let her swat him. "In fact, I think I will be putting her *out* of danger by leaving the country."

"You know what I meant."

"I will visit her," he said. "But considering all that Grégoire has done for her, she may well give me her blessing."

"And mine matters not?"

"Yours determines whether I go or stay."

Elizabeth bit her lip. "On one condition."

"Anything."

"You give me a proper good-bye."

Darcy smiled and kissed her. "Most duly granted."

DEPARTURE

When Dr. Maddox opened the trunk readied for him, he nearly screamed as his daughter popped out of her hiding spot, "Papa!"

"Emily!" he said, staggering back. "You scared me half to death." But she continued smiling serenely at him. "I suppose it was very cute. But a trunk is not a good place for a child."

When he tried to lift her out, she grabbed onto the handle. "No! I want to go with you!"

"Darling," he said, turning her around in his arms so she was facing him and not the trunk, "you would not want to come on this trip. It's going to be very long and mostly boring, and you certainly wouldn't want to spend it in a smelly trunk, would you?" He kissed her on the cheek and set her down. In coloring and hair she resembled her mother, and he often wondered if she was similar to what her mother had been when she was a child. Given Bingley's stories, it did not seem out of the realm of possibility. "Where is your nurse, anyway? I'm quite sure we employ one."

Her response was to lift her hands to show that she wanted to be picked up again. He sighed and put her on the bed. "Now what—oh, of course, stay there." He hurried down the steps and into the library. He had already picked out his German dictionary, but it was still on the table. When he returned, Emily was back in the trunk. "What did I say?"

"I was cute!"

He rolled his eyes. "You have until three to climb out of there, or I will call for Nurse. One—"

"No!"

"Two."

"Papa!"

"I'm being serious! Three—"

She reached for the book but was not successful at taking it from his hands. "Read to me!"

"This isn't a storybook. It's a dictionary."

"What's a dictionary?"

"A book of words. Now, what did I say? I said I was going to call for Nurse, and I *will*—"

"Please! Papa!" She tugged on his vest. "Read to me!"

"I'm supposed to be packing—"

"Read to me!"

"Your mother can do it—"

"Mama reads to me all the time! I want you to do it!"

He sighed. "You're as demanding as your mother sometimes, you know that?" Looking around to see that the coast was clear after saying *that*, he sifted through the pile of books on his bed stand and picked one out, sitting down next to her. She wouldn't understand much of the story, but she had never complained about it before. "Your mother gave me this book, before we were married. It's very special." He cleared his throat and began to read, "'When in April the sweet showers fall, that pierce March's drought to the root and all, and bathed every vein in liquor that has power to generate therein and sire the flower...'"

Caroline found him briefly after Emily fell asleep. It was time for her nap anyway, so they quietly called for Nurse, and their daughter was carried off.

"You're supposed to be packing," Caroline said, "since you *insisted* on doing it yourself."

"I know, but she made a very convincing argument for a story," he said, putting the book back on the bed stand.

"And it was—?"

"That I can't say no to a redhead who appreciates good literature."

Darcy assured Elizabeth, "I'll be back before you realize I'm gone." They embraced in front of the carriage that would take Darcy and Collins to Dover, where the boat was waiting to take them to the Continent. He kissed her. "I promise."

"Do not make promises you might not keep," she said nervously, leaning into him and resting her head on his shoulder. She usually did not force Darcy into public displays such as this one, but the situation demanded an exception.

Darcy had wrapped up his business quickly, visiting Kent to wish Lady Catherine well. She seemed, for the moment, to be recovering ("I refuse to die and leave Rosings in the hands of Miss Bennet!") but made no mention of anything else disconcerting. He finished his business with his steward, had Mrs. Reynolds close up Pemberley, and did some paperwork in Town while Dr. Maddox did the same, making sure his will was up to date. The doctor was granted his leave from the royal service, with pay, so Caroline would want for nothing.

"I don't know why His Highness is so nice to me," Dr. Maddox said to his wife with a nervous smile as his trunk was loaded onto the carriage. "All I do is yell at him."

"I'm sure you do it very politely," she said. He had already said good-bye to the children back at their house.

The Darcys' children, who were old enough to understand that their father was going somewhere, were standing with them while Sarah remained in the townhouse. Darcy took Anne in his arms and kissed her before passing her into Elizabeth's care. He looked down at Geoffrey, who did seem pleased with the prospect but was now too old and mature to grab his father's leg anymore.

Looking to comfort his son, Darcy thought for a moment, then pulled off his signet ring and put it in Geoffrey's hand, crossing his tiny fingers over it. "Take this. This was your grand-father's, the first Geoffrey Darcy."

Geoffrey tried it on. "It's too big for me."

His father took the ring and put it on Geoffrey's thumb, which was about large enough for the pinky ring. "There you go. Now you can play with it all you want when you get nervous and think of me. You may have it until I return, because sometimes your father gets nervous too." He patted him on the head and whispered. "Take care of your mother."

"When are you coming back?"

"Very soon. As soon as I locate your uncle."

He stood up, and Caroline approached him. "I will make one final attempt to talk some sense into you."

"Dr. Maddox is going, and he has the most good sense. So if he will not be persuaded, neither shall I."

"He has a point," Dr. Maddox said.

"And he's the most stubborn man in England," Elizabeth added, "unfortunately." She gave him a kiss on the cheek. "Hurry back."

"I will," he said, and stepped into the carriage.

"And if one of you is going to be shot at for some reason," Caroline said, "make sure it's Darcy."

Elizabeth gave her a glare.

Caroline Maddox huffed, pointing at Dr. Maddox. "Because *he's* the doctor, obviously, he cannot operate on *himself*."

"I shall keep it in mind to jump in front of him," Darcy said, "just for that purpose."

Taking the sea route and a boat to Hamburg was a painfully short trip for Darcy. It was so jarring for him, more than he wanted to admit, to be only at sea a few days and then suddenly be in a foreign country with a language he couldn't begin to understand and mountains higher than anything he'd ever seen in France. He'd toured the Continent after Cambridge but had not gone to Prussia. He chided himself for thinking ill of what could be a very short trip. Once he was on Prussian soil, he could write to Munich and inquire after Grégoire fairly easy. But he did not appreciate the trip. He said little to Dr. Maddox, and Dr. Maddox took this as a general incentive to leave him much alone as Dr. Maddox awaited the arrival date of his entourage that would be escorting him to Transylvania.

They arrived in Berlin tired and mangy from their trip, beyond what a good hotel and a night's sleep could fix. Dr. Maddox described Berlin as "more cosmopolitan" than he remembered, because the general chaos brought a mix of people. French soldiers, Prussian soldiers, refugees, gypsies, and émigrés—everyone seemed to be attempting to disappear into the city. That suited both of them just fine—Dr. Maddox's German was relatively good, and there were enough Englishmen about that they did not feel as though they were under any suspicion by the Prussians or the French.

The first morning, Darcy wrote a letter to his wife, assuring her that they had arrived safely and had no plans to leave the area (yet). They were far enough from France that he could hire a courier to make sure it got to England, if at an extravagant price. Dr. Maddox read the German newspapers for him, looking for news of monasteries Grégoire might have fled to.

"It's all about the war," he said, rubbing his eyes with frustration. "Napoleon really is invading the Russias."

"He's a fool to do so."

"How can we know? Neither of us are generals," Dr. Maddox pointed out as they finished their coffee (which was, admittedly, exceptionally good) and went to the post office. Darcy had the spare key to Grégoire's box. "Number 132—number 132—damnit, where is—oh. Finally."

It was hardly empty. Its contents were recognizable as his own letters that he had sent in the last two months, still sealed with wax, and besides that, nothing. He closed the box without taking any of the letters. "He hasn't been here. I will have to write to Munich."

They quickly discovered there was a board near the market square where families were posting, looking for their loved ones in all languages. They decided to read its contents every day, but nothing looked familiar.

Other than that, their days were frustratingly idle, while Darcy waited for the post and Dr. Maddox tried to locate someone who was from southern Austria while still being as discreet as possible. There were many things to do in the city while they waited, but neither of them had an interest in tourism. Sometimes they sat in coffee shops instead of the hotel, just for the change of atmosphere, but every day it was the same: checking the boards, checking the papers, checking the post, then nothing.

"My Romanian is getting better," Dr. Maddox said. "It is very similar to Latin and Italian."

Darcy did not attempt to answer. His black mood would not be lifted.

On the fifth day, Darcy wrote to Elizabeth again. *No progress, but will continue. We are safe.* That was hardly the whole of the letter—he had plenty of time to write it—but those were the key points. He would wait so long to hear news from Munich, and then contemplate going there. It was not so far away.

It was not an hour after he sent the letter that Dr. Maddox returned from lunch very enthusiastically. "My carriage has arrived, with the man who will take me to Austria."

"I am happy for you," Darcy said, sarcasm seeping into his voice.

"But he has agreed to take you to Austria as well! There are still dozens of monasteries there that, if they do not contain Grégoire themselves, they will have some monk who knows him, surely! And you will be safe in the carriage. The count has provided soldiers!"

"I am in your debt." Darcy was relieved. "How quickly do we leave?"

The coach was ready to go the following morning. Their escort, a Prussian named Herr Trommler who worked for the count, was in charge of the guards for the impressive carriage and horse team. None of the guards or the carriage driver spoke a word of English, and they spoke very little German.

"Peasantry, mostly," Trommler said, his own accent rather thick but understandable. "And you vill be joining us, Herr Darcy?"

Darcy bowed just slightly. Trommler seemed like a man of authority, not a low-level servant. "If you would be so kind, for any small distance of the way."

"He is as eager to see his brother as I am to see mine," Dr. Maddox said, and Trommler barked orders in Romanian to the servants, and they departed Berlin, with two horsemen with guns accompanying them.

"For your safety, of course," Trommler assured them. The carriage itself was rather comfortable—not the best, but suitable for long distances. "His Grace the count wishes very much to ensure the safety of your passage to his home."

"And my brother?" Dr. Maddox said.

"I am sure he thinks the same."

"He is well then?"

"I can safely say of His Highness, their marriage is a happy one." His wink betrayed a more suggestive note to his speech.

"His Highness?" Darcy laughed. "Brian is a prince?"

"It is not an official title outside of Transylvania," Dr. Maddox explained, more familiar with the concept ever since

Brian started signing his letters "Prince Brian of Sibiu." "But the family is descended from royalty—or so they claim—so the count has named his daughter a princess and, by marriage, his son-in-law a prince."

"So I am to address Brian Maddox as *His Highness?*"

"If you wish to do what's proper," Dr. Maddox replied. "And I am to understand Mr. Darcy of Pemberley and Derbyshire is considered among the most proper of gentlemen."

Darcy scowled and looked out the window.

The progress was slow, the roads clogged with fleeing villagers and passing soldiers, and they often rode through the night. Trommler and the Romanians never seemed to sleep. Dr. Maddox was hopeful—maybe Brian wouldn't be so pampered by palace life if this was how hardy people were out in the wilderness.

A week down the road, Trommler was less amenable to the idea of veering off the route to stop at monasteries. "They are deep in the wilderness. This is why they have not closed them, Herr Darcy," he said. "It is best if you come to Sibiu, and we can send messengers from there to find your brother."

"I would not want to impose on His Grace—"

"Nonsense. His lands are very large, and we so rarely have guests from so far out of the country."

"Perhaps I should have brought Caroline," Dr. Maddox said.

"I'm sure she would be delighted to be ushered into the presence of *Prince* Brian of Sibiu."

Dr. Maddox grinned. "I am amused at the concept myself. At least I will always have it that I am taller than him." He turned to Trommler. "He doesn't have a crown, does he?"

"He does, Doktor Maddox. It is quite tall—and bejeweled. A very old piece."

"I wonder if his head has grown too big for it by now," Darcy mumbled, and Dr. Maddox had to laugh.

Still they traveled on, to the point where even a well-pillowed carriage ride could not prevent some sores and aches, and they were glad to be informed that they were passing through the lands of Count Vladimir's brother-in-law, Olaf Cisn dioara. Aside from a castle in the distance, almost all of the structures were wooden and mud huts, and the roads could barely be considered that, but the mountains were the highest Darcy had ever seen in his life.

They came at last to a castle that showed its history, built with old fortifications to withstand a siege and high towers to overlook the land. The stone was gray and the roofs, even the spire roofs, covered in red tiles, were worn from what little sun there was.

"He couldn't have married an English country girl," Darcy grumbled. "Or at worst, a Highlander."

"No, Brian never does things halfway," Dr. Maddox said as they were helped out of the carriage—and after two weeks traveling, they really did need help. Despite the summer warmth there was a harsh wind coming down from the mountains, and they were freezing by the end of the walk from the carriage to the front doors, at which point Trommler went in to a side door, and the main ones opened, and a bearded man with a fur-tipped overcoat and a gold chain around his neck stepped out, flanked by Trommler and a guard.

"*Ridica-i!*"

Darcy and Dr. Maddox looked at each other. "Hello, we've—"

"*Cine sunt bărbaţii aceştia?*" he said to Trommler. (Who are these men?)

"*Un anume Dr. Maddox varul lui, Mr. Darcy, Conte Vladimir.*"

The man—obviously a baron or a count or some kind of royalty—grabbed Dr. Maddox in some kind of cross between a warm hug and a grab for assessment, and said, "*Patetic.*" He backed away and said clearly in French, "*Ah bon, vous êtes des relations de Brian?*" (So you are Brian's relatives?)

"*Oui,*" Dr. Maddox said. Darcy understood more French than he spoke and could at least listen with some understanding.

The Count huffed, "*Nous verrons.*" (We shall see.) He barked some orders to his guards, which were probably in Romanian, and stomped off with some ceremony. It was Trommler who snapped for the guards to give them cloaks and lead the Englishmen inside, into the cold entranceway.

"Excuse His Grace," Trommler said. "He's used to a bit more bowing."

"We meant no offense," Dr. Maddox said.

"No matter. As it turns out, we're early; Her Highness Princess Nadezhda and your brother are on a hunting trip. They will be back tomorrow or the next day, depending on the weather. But you are in time for a feast anyway. Some of the count's friends are coming tonight. Come."

Trommler led them straight to their rooms, which were tastefully appointed with beautiful wooden furniture and carv-ings, but still quite drafty. Then he disappeared. There were servants and guards everywhere, but none of them spoke English or French, just Romanian and maybe a smattering of other languages. Dr. Maddox found one who spoke German, but he didn't have much to say, except to point to the things they asked for, like fresh water to use for washing. They were offered indoor coats, as their trunks had not yet been sent up to their rooms and unpacked, and told to rest, as dinners with the count tended to be long. Despite all the questions they had, neither man could put up much argument against this idea.

When they were woken, it was dark outside, and the lamps inside the castle were lit, still making it very dark and gloomy. They barely had time to put their rather elaborate and showy cloaks on over their traveling clothes before being escorted to a long dining table. Count Vladimir sat at the end, with the oddest collection of guests, nearly all male, Darcy had ever seen. The footman with a gigantic and surely ornamental spear announced them in Romanian, then Count Vladimir made some additional comment to his guests, who talked amongst themselves as the Englishmen were seated. There was not a smattering of English among them. At the head, on both sides of the count, were a few men dressed in European fashions who spoke amongst themselves casually. They had no beards, unlike almost everyone else at the table, but only goatees, and were likely the local Hungarian nobility. Darcy and Dr. Maddox were placed next to each other at the end of the table. Beside Darcy was who looked like an Oriental, but he had a graying beard, which Orientals were not known to have, and very, very dark skin. His clothing was not silk but wool, one layer over the right arm, and the other exposed a lower layer, and he had a cloth cap on despite being at the table. Fortunately he had most of his teeth, or the portrait would have been even more disconcerting.

All of the courses were out on the table for them to pick at except the soup, and two silver bowls were unceremoniously dumped in front of the Englishmen, and thick soup poured into them, along with chunks of bone. At least the meat on some of the plates was recognizable as game. Many guests had their own cups or bowls and ate exclusively from those; the server seemed rather put-out having to supply them for the two additional guests.

Darcy looked down at the white soup and the two hoofs floating in it. "I suppose I ought not to inquire what this is."

"I think you can pass on drinking it," Dr. Maddox said. The crowd at the other end was very noisy, so even if they were speaking in a language the others could understand, they would not be heard anyway. "The count will hardly notice." He managed to hide his bowl between goblets and reached with his fork for something green and in a roll. "I believe this is cabbage. Probably with meat in it, I suppose."

Darcy went for the more obvious choice, the duck that was still recognizable as a duck, though it was surrounded by fried things Darcy couldn't name. He was famished, so not eating was out of the question, even if the spices didn't agree with him. Fortunately the meat itself was actually rather plain, if made sour by the cream it was covered in. As Dr. Maddox guessed, the servants were not at all concerned that the soup went untouched. Their main tasks seemed to be constantly refilling the goblets of wine and dispensing a clear liquor. Everyone else was dipping in, and the laughter could at times be deafening. They seemed to be at the quiet end of the table. Darcy looked to his right, and the Oriental was not eating at all. He had a shaker in his hand, with a wooden handle and metal top, and a small metal ball attached by string, and when he swung it, the ball made a humming noise as it circled around. He seemed to be mumbling to himself, his eyes closed.

"He's a fortune teller," said the man across from them in French. When the plate with a pile of stewed cabbage rolls and sweet cakes was moved aside, they could see a very pale, definitely European man with normal clothing under his cloak sitting across from them. He even had a fine pair of glasses. His gray beard was neatly trimmed, but the hair in the back of his head was a little long. "From Xinjiang, northeast of the Manchus' China. You can try to talk to him, but he doesn't speak any language of the white men. He won't lower himself to it."

"He's not... fortune telling now?"

"Oh, no," the Frenchman chuckled, though maybe he wasn't French. He was just speaking French very well. "He's just saying prayers. I hope it doesn't bother you."

Dr. Maddox said with a wary little smile, "Does His Grace normally employ fortune tellers?"

"He's a very superstitious man, though you might have guessed that already." He chuckled. "Yengi always gets all the attention."

"And you?"

"Oh, forgive me." He made a gesture as if he was tipping his hat to them, even though he had no hat. "Artemis Izmaylov. I translate for my friend here. So what are two Englishmen doing in Transylvania?"

"My name is Dr. Daniel Maddox, and this is Mr. Darcy," Dr. Maddox said, a little relieved to be talking to someone at last. "My brother is Brian Maddox, the count's son-in-law. I was invited to see him, and my friend Mr. Darcy is traveling with me."

Yengi the fortune-teller stopped his chant and said something, and Artemis said, "Yes, we met him briefly, the last time we were here, though we did not have a chance to speak. He was busy and so were we. Nice fellow. Refused to have his fortune read, but I can't blame him, to be perfectly honest. Too much English in him." His smile revealed a full set of slightly crooked, almost sharp teeth. "Enjoy the count's hospitality, for what it's worth. He can be a very interesting man."

There was little time for further discussion with the fortune-telling duo, as the various groups dispersed in different directions, and Darcy and Dr. Maddox had to turn down glass after glass, though it was impossible not to take a sip at every toast. When the bell chimed for two in the morning, they were both warm from the wine, and Trommler reappeared from nowhere. "The count demands an audience with you."

"I do not see how we can refuse our host," Dr. Maddox said.

Except for his guards, Count Vladimir was alone in his throne room, a room wholly medieval in nature up to the rusting swords and wooden shields on the wall. His ancestors must have had greater lands and power than he currently enjoyed. "Velcome," he said in German. "You are here to stay." It was hard to make out, and Dr. Maddox did a quick translation for Darcy.

"Yes, I am looking forward to seeing my brother," Dr. Maddox said.

"So are we," Trommler said in English for both of them, translating as the count spoke. "You see, he is missing."

"Missing?" It was the first word out of both their mouths.

"Oh yes, though His Grace is hoping that you will provide an... incentive for your brother's return, Doktor Maddox. He has been quite resistant to the idea since he ran away two years ago."

Dr. Maddox wished he was less drunk, as he sputtered, "But the letters—"

"All of his letters were read. By me, I might add. The final ones were sent late or not at all. We didn't wish to alarm you," Trommler said. "If he'd gone himself, it would be only a matter of honor, and I believe His Grace would have given up by now. But he took the princess, the count's only child, and this of course is unacceptable."

Count Vladamir was still speaking in Hungarian or Romanian, and he slammed his fist on the wood, making quite a sound. Trommler remained coolly calm and said, "He was a very good husband to Princess Nadezhda, you see. I will comment here that he was loyal to her and loved her deeply, and their fleeing was, whatever His Grace may believe, a mutual decision. But there was the small matter that he could not get her with child—for no lack of trying on his part." His grin was downright dangerous. Obviously the count didn't understand what he was saying, and they didn't understand what the count was saying, so Trommler really controlled the conversation. "That Nadezhda couldn't conceive was predicted by the midwife when she became a woman, but His Grace is convinced that a proper husband could overcome that particular difficulty. He gave Brian two years, and when no child was produced, not even a girl, he ordered his execution. A new husband was already chosen."

The horror was beginning to permeate Dr. Maddox's wine-soaked brain. "So he fled, to save his life."

"And being the loyal wife, Princess Nadezhda fled with him. The count assumed he would go west, of course, to England, but that was far too obvious, and Mr. Maddox has a long history of escaping authority. He went to Russia instead, to

Saint Petersburg, and from there the trail went cold. I assume you have no knowledge of this, or you would not have come at our invitation. You should know, Doktor Maddox, that your brother spoke of your kind heart. I knew it would mislead you into believing the best, that your brother was safe and happy in Transylvania, and you would come to see him in his new life without any concerns for your safety." He paused to actually listen to what the count was saying before continuing. "As for the other Englishman, he is just an unfortunate incident but will at least make your indefinite stay a bit more comfortable."

Darcy was aware enough now to dart for the door, but it was shut, and the guards were ready to grab him. They didn't harm him, just held him quite effectively. "You can't keep us locked up here forever!"

"You are mistaken, Herr Darcy, about the extent of His Grace's hospitality. It is quite vast." He made a gesture, and the guards dragged them both away.

"Doctor—" was all Darcy managed to say before he was pulled off in another direction. The terrible thought that he might never see him again went through him like a cold shiver as he was brought to his feet and made to stumble around in the castle. It wasn't like the rebuilt castles of Scotland, largely manor houses. This was an ancient place of stone and torches and winding staircases with no windows. "Look, I don't even speak your language, how can I—" But he was just rewarded with a smack on the back of his head and more Romanian words. They brought him to a room with only two chairs, one off to the side and the other in the center. It was wooden and had metal clamps on it. They freed him from his shackles and locked him into the chair.

They then left him, taking the light with them. They left only the single candle burning down on the wooden table, the only other furniture in the room. As his eyes adjusted to the dark, Darcy took in his surroundings, but there was little to take in. Four empty walls, a wooden door, and a candle. The flickering of it was hypnotic in a way, and his eyes constantly fell to the wick, watching it burn and the wax drip down.

Despite his position, he did not realize he had managed to fall asleep until icy water hit him in the face, thoroughly waking him up. He tried to wipe it from his eyes but found his arms unmovable. His predicament came back to him very quickly.

"*Guten Morgen*, Herr Darcy."

"Once again, I must remind you that I don't speak German," Darcy said, raising his head to the inquisitor. It was Trommler again.

"*Vous parlez Francais?*" (Do you speak French?)

"Not much," he replied, his voice hoarse from thirst. "Please, very little."

Trommler took a very careful seat on the stool that had been brought for him. "We will have to work in English, then, no?" But it sounded more like "*Ve vill haf to vork...*" with his thick accent. "Excuse my accent. We should be acquainted properly now. I am Herr Konrad Trommler."

"Mr. Fitzwilliam Darcy," Darcy replied out of habit. "Look, I don't know why I'm here—perhaps you have your intelligence mixed up or something, because I've not come to look for Brian Maddox; I'm looking for *my* brother, who is totally unrelated and not in Transylvania at all—"

"Have you ever heard of Dracula?"

"What?" Darcy said. "No, I have not."

"His name means son of Dracu—His father was a member of the order of the Dragon. He lived, they say, three centuries ago in Wallachia—right next to us. His real name was Vlad the Impaler. Do you wish to know why he was called that?"

"No."

Trommler smiled. "I think it would actually be worse to leave it to your imagination. Reconsider, Herr Darcy."

"I will not." The circumstances were extreme, but he would not give in to this man's fright tactics. "I suppose you're going to try to intimidate me by telling me the count is his descendent."

"You are familiar with inquisition, Herr Darcy?"

"No. I am a gentleman."

"My opinion on English gentlemen is not very good," said Trommler, "having observed one for over two years."

"Brian Maddox is no gentleman."

"Then you are aware of his habits?"

"I know him. I am related to him by marriage, yes. I have spent time with him, yes. But I've not seen or heard from him in years." He could talk, if that was all they were going to do. "If you think *either* of us knows his whereabouts, or even if he is still alive, then you are mistaken again."

"So *der doktor* said," Trommler told him, "before he passed out."

Darcy swallowed.

"But enough about *Doktor* Maddox. Your brother is German?"

"French," he said, not easily. It was harder and harder to keep up the presentation that he was calm. "Half-brother. He was born in France. Now he lives in Austria."

"Half? How many bastard children did your father have? Or perhaps your mother was a whore?"

Darcy tried, very hard, to break free of his restraints. They were iron, so it was useless, but it was his body's natural response. "*She was not a whore!*"

"Herr Darcy, it was a simple question."

"Calling one's mother a whore is not a simple question!" He was being provoked, and he knew it, but he didn't care.

"Herr Darcy, you had better calm down," said Trommler in an almost concerned voice. "You are only hurting yourself. See?" He stood up and indicated Darcy's wrist, which was bleeding where iron met skin.

He did not want to admit that his inquisitor was right, but Darcy did take a moment to close his eyes and breathe. "It was my father who was unfaithful. For your records," Darcy said. "Are you satisfied?"

"We have a long way to go before we come to that," Trommler said, taking his seat again. "Now, your brother, why did he come to Austria? To take in the sights?"

"He is a monk," Darcy said. "His name is Grégoire. He was living in France, but his monastery was dissolved. So now he is in some town called Munich, or was. We lost contact with him."

"And you came to look for him? You were close?"

"Yes," Darcy said, not particularly liking the idea of *were*.

"Does your mother approve of this?"

"My parents are dead," he added, "Herr Trommler."

"The monasteries have been dissolved by General Bonaparte. You have heard this?"

"Yes." He was tired. He was losing whatever game they were playing. "I heard they were dissolved, and I didn't hear from him, so I came to look for him. I have nothing to do with any of this nonsense with Mr. Maddox. The doctor and I were to part ways in Berlin. We were only traveling together because I don't know German and I've not yet hired a translator. Neither of us has the information you want." He continued, "I am a very rich man in England. My family would pay anything—"

"The treasure he stole was not just from the accounts. It was a treasure beyond rubies to His Grace," Trommler informed him. "He stole his daughter."

"I believe she was Mr. Maddox's wife."

"I was at the wedding, yes. I knew their every movement, their every congress, their every conversation."

"You were a spy," Darcy said. "Did Brian even know you spoke English?"

"Of course not," Trommler paced, temporarily blinding him with darkness and light as he stepped in front of and then away from the lantern of the guard. "I also read his lovely letters to his dear brother *Danny*. They had a somewhat—awkward history, did they not?"

"They did."

"He wrote him excessively and yet left out so many things that one might have wanted a loved one to know. That the princess could not conceive. That his own life was threatened if she was not with child after their second anniversary. That his father-in-law had no problems with putting his new son's head on a spike to remarry his only daughter. That he was planning to make off with her and half the treasury."

"I don't know," Darcy confessed. "I didn't read his letters. All I know is what Dr. Maddox told me, which was that everything was fine. And Dr. Maddox does not lie."

"His brother is very different then."

"They are like night and day." Darcy straightened up, trying to collect his wits. "I don't want to make small talk with you. You must be stupid to not have figured out that I don't know anything about what Brian Maddox has done since he went missing or where he might be! There is no reason to press the point. Brian's ridden to the moon for all I know! And if he were right here, I would strike him for all the trouble he's caused! Now please tell me what I have to say for you to patch me and let me go!"

Trommler luxuriously took his time with his answer. "His Grace, the count, lacks an understanding of subtlety. He will assume that unless you had been put in some peril, you would hold back. But you have nothing for me and nothing that will satisfy him. So we all have to play our little games while we wait for the bigger prize."

Darcy really wasn't very aware of what happened next. He felt like he was floating, between exhaustion, shock, and thirst. This was not supposed to have happened. This was what he had promised Elizabeth would *not happen*. They unlocked him and dragged him down, somewhere farther into the castle, where there was no light but from torches. He put up no opposition as they put him in a cell and put a leg iron over one ankle, as if he had any serious means of escape once the door was locked. The cell next to him was vacant.

Hours seemed to pass, and Dr. Maddox was nowhere to be found. Darcy anxiously stood and paced his cell for as far as he could with the leg iron, which was about half the actual length. When he was hungry enough, he finally tried the black bread and downed the water too quickly. It wasn't water, of course, but some kind of watery alcohol, and it went straight to his head. And this was to be his only drink?

Dizzy, he sat back down on the straw and must have nodded off when he was stirred by the creaking of the bars in the cell beside him swinging open, and a body was tossed in. When the iron was attached, they left the crumpled form of Dr. Maddox alone, saying nothing to Darcy.

"Maddox?" Darcy whispered, and when he was sure they were gone, he said, "Doctor?"

No response, and he had fallen on his side, so all Darcy could see was the rise and fall of his chest, meaning he was at least breathing. "Maddox?" Darcy reached for his jar and used the remains of the local drink by pushing the brim through the bars. Fortunately, the doctor had fallen so that his face was in the proper position to be hit by the flow of watery liquor.

This did wake him. Dr. Maddox groaned and rolled onto his back, revealing his bloodied right hand, which he had been holding against his chest. He cursed in several different languages and curled over in pain.

"Maddox," Darcy said through the bars. "What did they do?"

"My hand," Dr. Maddox replied. "They smashed it. I can feel—it's broken. If I don't—" He could not continue his sentence, distracted by pain. "I-if I don't splint it—"

"You're bleeding."

"I know, I can feel it, oh God, yes."

Darcy felt helpless, watching the doctor suffer while he had been left alone. "Can you see it?"

"Not well enough in this poor light. I—I can see colors—a-and shapes," Dr. Maddox said in a pain-induced stutter. "But it's not distinct."

"May I bandage your wound for you?"

"If you can, please."

Dr. Maddox stuck his hand through the bars, and Darcy removed his cravat and bound Maddox's fingers together. The bleeding stopped, and Dr. Maddox thanked him before passing out.

After what felt like many days—or maybe one, he had no idea of knowing—Darcy woke from his slumber to see Dr. Maddox sitting up, slowly taking bread in small bites. "Doctor?"

"Darcy," Dr. Maddox said; his voice in his long sleep, had mainly recovered. "Thank you."

"How is the hand?"

"I've no idea, aside from it hurting to the pits of hell." Dr. Maddox took a long swig from his jug. They were refilled every day and given fresh bread, so the count had intentions of keeping them alive, at least minimally. "I assume they questioned you. I think I heard it, but... it's all a bit unclear now."

"They did," Darcy added, "not very much. He was convinced I knew nothing of Brian's whereabouts."

"I think I convinced them that you do not speak the language and are only here of my stupidity."

"Thank God for that," Darcy said. "The former, I mean. Though I do hate you for this. Let's be perfectly clear about that."

"Do you have any idea of the time?"

"None. My watch is broken."

"But I must have been out a few days. I can feel it on my face."

Darcy, too, had whiskers. "Probably; I tried marking the days, but I have no window," he said. "If I may inquire—"

"It was a ruse," Dr. Maddox said. "My brother fled the country long before the execution was ordered. They want to draw him out, and they watched his post, so they knew my address and identity."

"So he is alive?"

"He may well be, or not. But to their knowledge, he is."

"Will he come for us?"

Dr. Maddox shrugged. "How would he know we are here? The count overestimates his abilities to be heard. If Brian is hiding somewhere far from here, he's not getting the palace notices."

"And his crime?"

"They did not tell me the story coherently. They assumed I was in league with him and therefore knew every detail. But… what I managed to glean from them was that, despite the very happy marriage he described, the count was upset that his daughter was married two years and was still not with child. So he gave Brian an ultimatum of three months, or his head would be on a spike."

"And he ran." Darcy admitted, "Any sensible man would."

"The very next day. They might have not pursued, but he took Nadezhda with him." Dr. Maddox closed his eyes. "Why did he have to pick this moment in his life to become the white knight?"

"So he loved her?"

"I never doubted that he did. And considering the situation… and my own knowledge, if they were barren, the fault was probably hers. Not intentionally, of course."

"Of course."

"So if he hadn't taken her, she would have been subjected to marriage after marriage, with the same outcome, most likely. I don't know without a midwife's word on her particular condition. But apparently Brian believed in the sanctity of his marriage more than the count and took matters into his own hands." Dr. Maddox almost laughed. It was hard to tell what the sound was. "He sounds almost noble."

"If the story is true, he is. It doesn't excuse his lack of contact with us, or our own stupidity for coming here."

"Knowing Brian," Dr. Maddox said, "he would have only written if he felt it was safe to do so. Or perhaps, the letters simply haven't reached England yet. I should have waited it out." He shook his head. "I shouldn't have dragged you into this, Darcy."

"While I'm inclined to agree with you, I did have my own motivations for the overall trip and would not listen to reason."

"We both should have listened to our wives," the doctor said. "I wrote Caroline a letter."

"When?"

"Unfortunately, after they rather stupidly smashed my writing hand, so I doubt it's legible. I wrote what the count wanted me to write, which was that we are both fine and are helping him look for Brian or some nonsense, and would she be so kind as to send some money to aid us in the search?" He shook his head.

"So we are to be ransomed?"

"No," he said. "Even if the money comes, the count will not let us go until Brian is found, alive or dead. But at least we have the consolation that our wives will know where we are."

"God," Darcy said. "I hope they don't send Bingley. He'd stumble right into this trap."

"He's smarter than you think."

"He's brilliant, but that doesn't mean the man has a lick of common sense."

Dr. Maddox laughed quietly. "And if my brother does appear, do me a favor and promise to sock him for me."

"That," Darcy said, "I will gladly swear on, Doctor."

THE EARL OF MATLOCK

ELIZABETH DARCY HAD NO regrets about one matter, which was her decision to stay at Pemberley instead of Chatton, Town, or Kent. She had now spent a fifth of her life there, and she soundly identified it as her home, in a way that not even Longbourn could replace. It was where she lived, where her husband lived, where she raised her children, and where someday her son would raise his. Every hallway and piece of furniture and portrait distinctly said Darcy to her. Everything reminded her of her beloved husband.

Georgiana returned with them and was a welcomed sister as much as her own sister, who visited as often as she dined at Chatton, which was almost every night. But even Georgiana seemed distracted. Mrs. Reynolds was distracted. Everyone was distracted. The only one who seemed truly content beyond missing the master of all of their lives was Geoffrey, who did not care for Rosings at all with its lack of playmates. He was not a solitary creature. *Well, that he certainly received from me,* Elizabeth thought with a smile as she watched him play with his cousins

Charles and Georgie. Eliza Bingley preferred more feminine distractions than her older sister and was picking flowers.

The letters began two weeks of Darcy's departure by special courier. They were in Berlin safely, and they would begin their search as soon as he put down his pen. His familiar script seemed to reinvigorate Pemberley for a brief moment, as if his presence had returned. For that day, she was happy.

The time afforded her to get to know the Maddox children, who normally stayed in Town year-round and were now almost five. Caroline was invited to Chatton by her brother, and after some hesitation she shut up the Maddox house and came to Derbyshire. Though their history never made it easy, Elizabeth and Caroline were at least united in their underlying fear of disaster. As for the children, Emily was a delight, more like her uncle than either of her parents in her enthusiasm for everything. Frederick was much like Geoffrey had been at his age—exceedingly mischievous and defiant, but even more so. His brown hair was appropriately long and wild for his age. When comparing the children, one could not but speculate on the possibilities and limitations of doing so.

"Has Mrs. Maddox ever said who his parents were?" Elizabeth asked her sister when she thought it was appropriate, as they were sitting on the terrace, enjoying the warm days of summer.

"His mother was a patient of Dr. Maddox," Jane said. "She died of childbed fever. The father I know nothing about, but they do seem to know who he was—or is."

The second letter was another relief, though Darcy did express frustration at not having anything new to report. Dr. Maddox also sent his own letter to his wife, which she said had relatively the same contents. The men would write again next week.

"Next week" came and went. Elizabeth was now sick with worry, distracted and dizzy. Her mood, she admitted to herself, was not the best, and she had to try at times not to be cross with her children or burst into tears spontaneously. Odd, that Caroline seemed calmer. Well, the former Miss Bingley had always been adept at hiding her feelings. She couldn't blame her for that.

With no news after two weeks, she sent another letter to Berlin, this time by a courier, to make absolutely sure it would get there. Her hands were shaking when she wrote it, sealed it, and sent it off without saying anything to anyone.

> *Dearest Husband,*
>
> *When you receive this message, if you have not located Grégoire, I beg you to return home immediately. I am with child.*
>
> *Your Loving Wife,*
>
> *Elizabeth Darcy*

The very next day, she received a letter by courier. It was not the one she wanted.

When Darcy woke, Dr. Maddox was already awake. It really didn't seem to matter when they slept and when they didn't, without any change in the daily schedule of food in, waste out, and nothing else. They didn't even know if that was occurring in the day or evening.

Dr. Maddox was holding his hand up to inspect it. Satisfied, he set it down in its resting place on his lap. "How do I look?"

"From here? Terrible. But if we were to break free, I think we would fit in better with the natives now as hairy as we are." Some time must have passed, because they both had significant beards.

"I hate you," Dr. Maddox said. "I—I don't know why I feel compelled to say that."

"Because we're sitting in prison."

"Perhaps."

"And we're going mad."

"Perhaps."

"Well… I hate you, too. God, that does feel good, even if I actually don't. Though when we get out of here and find your brother, I may very well do something drastic."

"Not if I get to him first," Dr. Maddox replied.

"He could probably take you."

"Why does everyone assume that? I'm tall, you know."

"But he's wily. It is the safe bet."

Dr. Maddox laughed, and Darcy found himself weakly joining him, because it felt immeasurably good.

"So… know any good stories?"

"I can't do the Bard justice with just my memory."

"Neither can I, though if we're here long enough, we may just have to do him the injustice of making the bits up that we don't remember."

"There's always some sordid story from one of our pasts."

"Oh, but I have no doubt that Mrs. Maddox has told you all of those," Darcy said. "Or the ones she knows about."

"Why does everyone think my wife a horrible gossip?"

"Because your wife is a horrible gossip."

To his surprise, Dr. Maddox laughed again. "My God, we're both insane already and it has probably only been a week."

"Utterly hopeless."

"She did tell me some stories, by the way."

"She did?"

"Apparently, Charles is a talkative drunk, and has the convenient problem of not remembering it later. Or so she says that he says. If you know what I mean."

"Ah. So I have no secrets from Caroline Maddox."

"None; even the thing from University."

"What thing from University?"

Dr. Maddox looked at him slyly. Or, more accurately, he looked slyly in Darcy's general direction, "The thing that you threaten Bingley's life over when he threatens to bring it up."

"What?" Darcy paused. "Oh. Yes. Well." He cleared his throat. "University is a strange time in a man's life, experiments with all kinds of things."

"I won't deny it. I did some things that if Brian had any sense in him, he would have pulled me out."

"Really?" Darcy grasped one of the bars between them.

"No one has ever thought to inquire how I obtained that famous, obscure recipe for my opium concoction. The story is the most logical one. I was looking for a good way to consume a vast quantity of opium without having to smoke it. I never cared for smoking. Bad for the lungs, I think, like breathing in a fire. But I could never get the flavor right without ruining it. But I did try very hard and learned a great deal of wonderful things about... say, my hand."

"Your hand?"

"According to my dorm mates, I spent nearly the course of a day staring at it and taking notes. They thought I was making some great discovery, but later it just turned out to be doodles, and something about a rainbow that I've never figured out."

"For someone as fastidious as you are about your health, it is quite hard to imagine."

"Why do you think I am so strict with my own patients?" Dr. Maddox said. "Because, of course, I know the pains of trying to withdrawal from your personal dragon. Specifically, over Christmas, when you're trying to hide from your brother and guardian that you've spent your last semester becoming a dope fiend." He shook his head. "The number of doctors he called! And good ones, too. Money wasted." He raised his jug. "You can never tell him."

"Of course."

"To your dying day, Darcy."

"It may be very soon, Doctor, so you shan't worry about that."

"True enough." Dr. Maddox sighed. "In an Austrian prison, that, I would never have guessed."

"I never imagined I would be married to a country girl from Hertfordshire and have two bastard brothers. Life is just full of surprises."

There was some confusion about whether there should be a funeral for Michael Fitzwilliam, Earl of Matlock. The package that arrived from India contained only his ashes—apparently their barbaric custom in the Indies—and his signet ring. After a brief ceremony in which his ashes were placed in a hole in front of a marker that would eventually have his tombstone, the three of them—Colonel and Anne Fitzwilliam and Elizabeth Darcy—were ushered into the earl state home, where the barrister briefly read over the will. Michael was young, and his will was brief, as he clearly had not expected to die at all, much less abroad.

"I express my deepest condolences for these circumstances," said the attorney, passing Fitzwilliam the ring. "Lord Matlock."

"At least, in address," Fitzwilliam said, nervously putting on the earl's ring as his wife squeezed his arm.

There was a long listing of the holdings of the Fitzwilliam family, which were considerable—Richard Fitzwilliam was now a wealthy man. He would have to retire from the army immediately for propriety's sake. Richard and Anne now could claim a great manor house and a townhouse in London alongside their modest home in Brighton, but neither was thrilled at the prospect. What they could not claim was Rosings, and that made it all much more complicated.

"Mrs. Darcy," the attorney said, "do you wish to have Rosings shut up, or do you wish to reside there until your husband returns from the Continent?"

Fear and uncertainty welled up inside her as she said, "It is my wish that Lady Catherine remain in Rosings. Surely it can stay open for her?"

"She has no claim on it," he said, "so her residence there must be approved by Mr. Darcy."

"He would approve!"

"Yes," the attorney said, "and that is perfectly understandable, but he must be here to approve and sign the papers for it."

"How can we keep my mother in her home?" Anne said.

"Mrs. Darcy must take up residence as mistress of Rosings until legal arrangements can be made by its owner." He was not cruel in his pronouncements; he was stating the law as they knew it to be, but it still seemed harsh.

"Then I will take up residence in Rosings," Elizabeth said without hesitation, "for Lady Catherine's sake. And I will write to Mr. Darcy in Berlin to return home immediately." Not that she hadn't done that several times now—and in the most urgent ways possible. It was leaning on suspicious that there had been no return to any of their letters. He could have gone to Austria to find Grégoire, yes—but wouldn't he have written that he was doing that? Or did he think it would only be a brief trip, only to be delayed while outside Berlin? And that did not explain Dr. Maddox's similar lack of communication.

"Mrs. Darcy," the new Lord Matlock said, "it's probably the post. We'll send his steward to find him immediately. A man can achieve much more than a letter, and his steward will knock some sense into him."

"Surely," Anne said.

For the time, they accepted her comforts as she settled theirs by settling in Rosings to pacify Lady Catherine. Even though she had no great love for the woman, Elizabeth could not bring herself to toss Lady Catherine, who was barely able to move about her house, out of the home that she had lived in almost the entirety of her life.

In the carriage, Geoffrey and Georgiana were waiting for her. The other children were with Nurse in the other carriage. She took Geoffrey into her arms as she explained the situation to Georgiana. "Do you wish to join us at Rosings?"

"Of course," Georgiana said. "And look on the bright side. The post to Kent from Town is much quicker than the post to Derbyshire."

Elizabeth managed a smile.

"Do I have to go to Rosings?" Geoffrey said.

"Yes, darling. You cannot have Pemberley to yourself quite yet. I cannot imagine what destruction you would cause."

He scoffed. "I could stay at Chatton. And I promise to be good!"

"Geoffrey," Georgiana said, "I think your mother wishes you by her side."

Elizabeth blushed as Geoffrey said, "Oh." He looked up at her. "All right, Mother."

She kissed him. "Thank you. It won't be for long—I promise."

And that was how Mrs. Elizabeth Darcy, of Pemberley, Derbyshire, Rosings, and Kent, came to be a most reluctant mistress of Rosings.

Settling in was not as difficult as Elizabeth imagined it would be. She carefully instructed the servants not to defer to her authority in front of Lady Catherine. The woman was well enough to know what was going on around her and to object to it, but also to know that her objections would bear no fruit. Nonetheless, Elizabeth did not want to make her a guest in her own home and tried to keep things as they were, at least in appearance.

Elizabeth had enough on her mind. She was experienced at running a grand estate and could easily tell that the place she now occupied as mistress had fallen into some disrepair during Lady Catherine's deterioration. The place was not falling apart, but it was ill-staffed, and repairs were obviously needed in various places. If it would be a suitable place for Lord and Lady Matlock, it would need some fixing up.

Adding that to her general worry about her husband, Elizabeth was vexed enough when a peculiar letter arrived. Lord William

Kincaid, the younger brother of the deceased James Kincaid, had once vied for the former Miss Bingley's hand while disguising the fact that he was already married. Lord William was traveling through the country on the way back from Town upon the Season's end. He very much wished to call on Miss Darcy, having apparently heard something of Lady Catherine's illness and Elizabeth's position as mistress of Rosings. If he knew the circumstances of her husband's absence, he made no reference to that fact, but she had no idea why he would. They had no formal correspondence since the wedding of Caroline Maddox. From what she recalled of him, he was a pleasant fellow despite his unfortunate relations, but that did not explain his sudden interest at all.

Puzzled, she was still rereading the letter over breakfast when Georgiana joined her and, seeing the letter, immediately inquired as to whether it was from her brother.

"No, it's from Lord William Kincaid. He wishes to call on Mr. Darcy but is aware that he is out of town, though he does not say more than that. So he wishes to call on me, essentially. I have no idea why—" But, upon seeing Georgiana's coloring face, she immediately put down the letter. "Might you have something to say on this development?"

Georgiana put her head down to avoid Elizabeth's eyes. "You can be so like Brother when you wish to be."

"It seems, in his absence, I must, but I am still your sister. Now, Lord Kincaid."

"Yes."

"Should we ramble about the actual subject or will you just tell me what it is you know about him that I apparently do not?" she said, her manner lighter than Darcy's, but still with a degree of semi-parental authority.

"Oh, please forgive me!" Georgiana said, clearly ready to break into tears. "I've deceived you and Brother for so long."

"*Deceived?*"

"Well, not deception—nothing has happened. It was just—we ran into each other, on the street in Town this past spring. He decided to finally pay his dues and attend the session of the House of Lords, and was quite lost. So, I offered to show him the way best I knew it. We chatted, and he asked to call on me, but of course he couldn't, so—" Her flurry of words was enough to confuse Elizabeth as to whether she should be amused or indignant, "—I asked Dr. Maddox to call on him. After all, they do know each other, although they haven't spoken for years. And since I so often dine with the Maddoxes—"

"—he's essentially been courting you? All summer?"

There was little possibility that Georgiana's face could get any redder. "No! No, it was not a formal courtship, I swear! I would have gone to Brother for that! It was so much milder than it sounds. And do not think badly of the Maddoxes! Dr. Maddox kept a stern eye on him the whole time, and Mrs. Maddox was—well, you know, she enjoys watching people come together. I was going to tell Brother—but first he was upset from visiting Aunt Catherine, and at that point I had hardly seen Lord Kincaid more than a few times. Then he got the letter about Grégoire—and you know how he is when he is in an unshakable mood. William—Lord Kincaid—he really did mean, right before Brother was to leave, to go to Pemberley and request permission for a formal courtship. He promised me he would, but I dissuaded him, so as not to upset Brother further. But I confess, since he left and took Dr. Maddox with him, I have not had a chance to see Lord Kincaid, and it does bother me, and I considered even asking the Hursts, but I didn't—"

"Enough," said Elizabeth, now thoroughly amused by Georgiana's exasperated rant. "Georgiana, I understand perfectly."

"—And—wait, you do?"

"Of course," she said without hesitation. "You could have told me though. I would have taken it into confidence if you asked. And your brother is not so against you marrying as you think. If Lord Kincaid wishes to call upon Rosings—I do believe he met Lord Matlock when he was Colonel Fitzwilliam, at the wedding of Caroline, and besides, Lady Catherine had gentlemen visiting her all she liked, despite her thorough knowledge of convention, so why should I not have the same liberties?"

"So—he can come?"

"No matter how the floorboards may creak, I would not deny him the pleasure of seeing Rosings," she said with a smile.

"Oh, Elizabeth—thank you!"

"It hardly requires thanks. The distraction of playing the role of both Mr. and Mrs. Darcy during the presentation of a suitor will be a pleasant distraction for me. And Lord knows I could use one."

THE MISTRESS OF ROSINGS

LORD WILLIAM KINCAID ARRIVED quickly from Kent and was received by the new Lord Richard Matlock in place of Darcy. Elizabeth greeted him as the new mistress of Rosings, and they were spared the awkwardness of it, by Lady Catherine, still confined to the upstairs floors. Elizabeth brought forward her son, whom he had met only briefly and when Geoffrey was not old enough to remember, and her eldest daughter, whom he had not met at all. The last they had seen of him was at the Maddox wedding. It was not long ago, and he still had that pleasant demeanor that Elizabeth remembered. Aside from his accent, he was not recognizably a Scot in dress—this time. In greeting Georgiana, he was polite and abnormally shy—an obvious enough sign of affection. Elizabeth silently swore to write to Caroline Maddox immediately and uncover this minor mystery, though she was sure if their informal courtship had been at all improper, Dr. Maddox would have *instantly* intervened and informed Darcy.

Lord Kincaid was quickly informed of the situation as it was, with Darcy being on the Continent, but most of the specifics were not mentioned. They had a light lunch. No one wanted to discuss the war, so Kincaid was left to explain how he was finding London and the House of Lords. "A privilege you'll be enjoying, I'm sure," he said to Lord Matlock with a sarcastic wink, causing Fitzwilliam to nearly choke on his luncheon meat, which brought a smile to the face of his wife.

After lunch, Kincaid requested to see Lady Catherine's famous gardens, and Elizabeth was generous enough to let Georgiana show him. Their chaperone, she decided, would be Geoffrey, who seemed eager for at least one other male in the house and said, "I like him. He talks funny."

"But you shan't say that to his face. Or perhaps you shall. He might like it," she said, pushing him along. Geoffrey wouldn't be much in the way of a traditional chaperone, but he was sure to get himself into trouble somehow, distracting his aunt by making her watch out for his welfare. In this arrangement, Elizabeth was content.

"He seems like a nice fellow," Lord Matlock said as they watched the couple leave.

"Yes," Elizabeth said. "He is. I always regret that I missed him swinging from a chandelier."

Lord Kincaid and Georgiana returned within a proper amount of time, at which point Georgiana excused herself to see to Lady Catherine, and Elizabeth found herself facing a very apprehensive Scot in what had once been Sir Lewis' study.

"I presume you know why I am here," he said, bowing. "I apologize for the incredibly poor timing—"

"There was nothing you could do to prevent it, Lord Kincaid."

"Yes," he said. He looked nervous. "I understand a date for Mr. Darcy's return is not fixed yet."

"No," Elizabeth replied, feeling uncomfortable herself at the situation, and nauseous from lunch, but that was hardly *his* fault.

"Then, in his absence, I would kindly refer to you for permission to court Miss Darcy."

She was only surprised in that it was not an outright proposal, and that surprise was minor. "I will consent in his place. However, it can go no further without his personal approval. He is most protective of his sister."

"So I have been told," he swallowed. "But—I see no cause not to pursue this courtship. I do care for Miss Darcy."

"I can see that," Elizabeth said. "You have my blessing. You may call on Rosings as you wish, Lord Kincaid."

He smiled, his face flushed. "Thank you so very much, Mrs. Darcy."

"Believe me," she said, "it is my pleasure."

Unfortunately, the already overburdened Elizabeth Darcy, mistress of Pemberley, Derbyshire, Rosings, and Kent, had one more unexpected visitor. The very sight of Mrs. Lydia Wickham tugging along her two children was enough to make her sigh and ring for her servants. "Dress my children and get them ready to see their cousins."

"Yes, marm."

"And have tea sent in immediately. My sister prefers it very sweet."

"Yes, marm."

Georgiana was in Kent, shopping, her spirits brightened by the arrival of Lord Kincaid. That left Mrs. Darcy alone, but perhaps it was better this way, she thought, as she opened her arms to greet her. "Lydia."

"Lizzy! Oh, look at this place!" Lydia was between breaths, shouting for the servants to attend to her trunks and to embrace her sister while keeping hold on her children at the same time. "It's so grand! And to think your aunt lived here all alone!"

"Yes," Elizabeth said. "It was quite dreary for her."

If Lydia caught her meaning she ignored it. "But come, I must see my nieces and nephew, and you must yours, and we must talk. And tea! Some tea would be lovely."

Elizabeth decided not to mention that she had had not a hint of her sister's arrival until someone spotted a carriage coming down the road, and it was not until Lydia emerged that she actually knew the occupants. Or she had not mentioned the odd and distressing situation of having a husband who had just (unknowingly, probably) inherited a grand estate but was lost on the Continent, trying to find his monastic brother. She set those obvious points aside and joined her sister for tea, and there was much comparing of the children. George and Isabella (commonly called Isabel) were older than their counterparts, but not by much.

"This is such a grand house," Lydia said. "You are so fortunate, Lizzy, to have two houses. And one in Town! Papa's finally renovating Longbourn, but it'll never be anything to compare—you're just so *lucky*."

Lydia Wickham, now four and twenty, had to some extent matured in manners. Elizabeth kept her occasional temper with her sister intact by reminding herself that at her age, Elizabeth had been married for three years and (as her husband would readily recall) a bit stubborn, ready with an insult when she felt her husband needed it. Not that much had changed, but she could look back realistically and say that two children, being mistress of a great estate, and a hurried tour of the Continent had had some effect on her general countenance. "I suppose I am, but this is only a matter of entail. My husband has no intention of keeping Rosings. It should go to the Fitzwilliams."

"But to even have an estate to toss off—that's truly rich."

There was some truth in her statement. "Yes," Elizabeth admitted, and sipped her tea.

"Wickham left us with nothing. He didn't die on the battlefield, even if he *was* killed, so the army won't give us anything except some monies meant for his burial. And Mr. Darcy—"

"Lydia," Elizabeth said, "can we not bring my husband into this?"

Lydia gave her a look. It was not particularly harsh, but it was annoyed. "How can we *not?*"

"Because it pains me to think of it, as it does my husband—greatly. But he provided for your children—"

"And he won't let me touch it! Even for a doctor!"

Elizabeth lowered her cup. "Darcy refused a doctor? Who needs a doctor?"

"I didn't ask him. He always refuses me when I want to buy things, so why should he say yes now? He's such an obstinate man! I have no idea how you put up with him—well, aside from the obvious comforts and security—"

"Lydia," Elizabeth interrupted, not sure whether disgust or alarm was going to overwhelm her first, "who needs a doctor?"

"It was nothing—but I wanted one for George. So I had to ask Papa."

"And Papa refused?"

"No, of course he didn't. Papa has all this money now, thanks to *Mary*, but he's so stingy with it, because it's *Mary's*—"

Elizabeth shook her head. Trying to keep Lydia in the same conversational direction was difficult. "So George saw a doctor. What was the matter?"

"Nothing. Or that's what the doctor said. He said it was a fluke thing, and even when it happened again, the doctor said he still couldn't find anything—"

"*What* happened?"

"It was silly, almost," Lydia said, though Elizabeth could hardly imagine anything that required a doctor to be considered "silly." "I took George with me on an errand to Meryton and he wandered off. It was his first time alone in Town, so I suppose it was all distracting, but when I found him in a bookstore, he was sitting on a chair, and the owner was giving him tea and said he had fainted."

"From what?"

"*We don't know*. Didn't I already say that?" Lydia rolled her eyes. "Apparently, there were a lot of people there, and the shopkeeper finally noticed this little boy with nobody by his side, and so he went up to him and asked him who he was, and George just collapsed. He was only out for a few seconds, but he had a little bump on his head for a while from the floor, and so I asked Papa, and we called a doctor, who said he wasn't sick. But if we had a *little money*—"

"What did George say?"

Lydia looked at her as if the question was bizarre. "He's a child, Lizzy."

"I know that, but surely you asked him if something was troubling him? If he had a headache?"

"Oh, of course the doctor asked him all kinds of questions, but he said he didn't feel ill. He just looked up at the shopkeeper, and then the next thing he remembered he was on the floor. But the doctor couldn't find anything wrong with him, and I almost forgot about the whole thing until it happened again."

"When?" Elizabeth said, trying to maintain her composure. She had never been close with the Wickhams for obvious reasons, but George was her nephew on both sides, and Darcy cared enough about him to set up a fund to make sure the boy would not have to worry about money when he came of age.

"I don't know, a few weeks later. We were at church, and you know how Papa always hurries home. I decided to stay and chat for once. Some new people had come to the parsonage, and I wanted to meet them—some of them were very handsome—and I had George with me because he didn't want to leave me. Isabel was with Mama. In the crowd, someone said something to George, and out he went. Fortunately it was on the grass—you know that area in front of the churchyard? It wasn't as bad of a bump this time, hardly anything at all."

"But you saw it this time."

"Yes. But he didn't want to talk about it. He didn't want to see the doctor, but Papa wouldn't hear of it, and so the doctor came and said he couldn't find a reason. It wasn't fits, and George doesn't have headaches, so he's not *sick*."

"And since then?"

"Well, he hasn't been out much. Certainly I'm not going to take him to Meryton if he's going to complain the whole time that he doesn't want to go—"

"Lydia," Elizabeth interrupted again, holding her tongue about Lydia's parenting skills, or the inappropriateness of using church to socialize with the new men in town, "if it happens again, I would like to know. And for the record, if you did not have Papa, we would pay for the doctor."

"But Mr. Darcy has been so stingy in the past—"

"About clothing for you, yes, but not about this. This is your son's health. Our nephew's health." She added, "Thank you for telling me."

The topic extinguished, Lydia began to chat about the goings-on in Meryton, but Elizabeth heard very little.

As Lydia was shown to her rooms and unpacked, Elizabeth had a spare moment to herself and had her tea reheated so she could finally enjoy it. She was beginning to relax when Lord and Lady Matlock entered, taking a break from keeping their mother company. "Are we interrupting?"

"No, please," she said. "My sister Lydia has just arrived. I'm sure she will be making her presence known soon enough. At least Geoffrey has someone to play with—if that is a good idea." She needed to tell someone—unburden herself. She told them of Lydia's minor tirade.

She turned to Fitzwilliam, but he had only a concerned look on his face, like something was bothering him. "Colo— Lord Richard?"

"I was just—remembering something. It is probably unrelated. After all, Master George is only Darcy's *half*-nephew, so—"

Instinctual alarm rising, Elizabeth immediately said, "What is it?"

"It's uhm—well, I can't say I remember it perfectly, but I do remember something about a fainting spell of Darcy's—when he was younger." He frowned. "I must have only been seven or eight at the time, so you will excuse me, but—Yes! Now I remember."

"We are all ears, Richard," Anne said before Elizabeth had to, obviously sensing her trepidation.

"It was—I don't know the year. I must have been about eight, Darcy four or five. I remember I was in Town with my parents and brother. At the time they were more regular theater patrons and had a box or two, and so we were often in Town. But this was something like the first time the young Darcy—well, Master Fitzwilliam—came to Town with his father, who had some business. We knew each other from Rosings, but not that well. Lady Anne was still alive, and so she visited, and we played together in the house in the square. But then a few days into the trip, something happened, and the Darcys went home, and I remember it because I was a little disappointed at losing a playmate, even if he was younger than me, because my brother was in his teens and ignoring me." A sad look passed over his face at the mention of his late brother, but he managed to continue, "What happened was, apparently—Darcy was walking with his mother on the road, I think they were going to see the royal gardens, and Darcy fainted. There was a great fuss over it, of course. They called for all kinds of doctors, but they said it was exhaustion, and he was stuck in bed for a few days. I came to visit, and he complained about not being tired, but his nurse wouldn't let him up. But he seemed fine, so they very cautiously let him out again, this time with his nurse accompanying Lady Anne.

"The second time, I believe it was in a store. Darcy went down, and their first concern was his head, but he wasn't concussed. In fact, once they brought him around, he seemed fine. But as my mother told me later that night, the Darcys had decided that there was something in the air in Town—which, after all, is very bad—that was bothering his little lungs, and they must retire immediately to better climate. I was very upset, but I was too old to be throwing tantrums. I didn't see him again until that Easter for our annual visit to Rosings, and he told me he was fine and didn't want to talk about it. I can't remember the topic ever being broached again. I assume, the next time he was in Town, he was fine."

Elizabeth digested this story with her tea, which had cooled during the conversation. "Darcy has never told me this."

"I don't imagine he would. He was a small child. He may not even remember it. And nothing came of it."

"But it is an… odd coincidence, don't you think?" Anne said.

"If you don't mind my asking, Mrs. Darcy—has Geoffrey ever—"

"No. And he's been to Town for his cousins' birthdays. I can't imagine—" It was a frightful thing to imagine, something strange happening to her son and the doctors not having an answer. But then again, as Fitzwilliam insisted, nothing had come of it. Still, she would ask Dr. Maddox about it when he returned.

When he returned, not *if*, she reminded herself.

Chapter 11

THE PUREST LOVE

"MRS. DARCY? ARE YOU awake?"

She was. Despite the late hour, Elizabeth was sitting on the rug in the corner of her room, trying to find her balance despite her illness. Fortunately it was only her lady-maid, whom she held in the highest confidence out of sheer necessity. "Yes. Come in."

Hannah entered and bowed. "Mrs. Darcy, do you need something?"

"Some of that ginger tea?"

"Of course. Lady Catherine is calling for you. Do you wish me to say you're asleep?"

Elizabeth put her hand on her forehead. "No—I will speak to her. I just need a moment to collect myself." She couldn't possibly have anything left in her stomach. She'd hardly eaten anything today. Hannah was instantly gathering a shawl to cover her and helping her up. Her lady's illness and its origin was a secret kept only between the two of them—at least for the moment. Fortunately, there was no one qualified to notice the signs and not chalk them up to nervousness about her husband's situation. Anne and Georgiana had never been with child, Lord Richard lacked the expertise for obvious reasons, and Lady Catherine rarely left her sitting room. Elizabeth managed to carry her own candlestick, but she needed some assistance staying on her feet until she reached Lady Catherine's quarters, and was ushered in by her ladyship's servants.

Lady Catherine was sitting up in bed, her hair in knots and uncovered.

"Lady Catherine? Are you well?"

"Mrs. Darcy," she replied. Her physical appearance did not match her voice, which was full of vibrancy. "The question is—are *you* well?"

"I am, Lady Catherine."

"May I see your daughter?"

She did not comment on the oddity of the question. "Which one, Your Ladyship?"

"The one I have not met—your youngest."

"Sarah. Yes, if you wish," Elizabeth said, and motioned for a servant to approach, to whom she whispered that her sleeping daughter be brought to her. Sarah Darcy was now eight months old and slept through the night—if uninterrupted.

Her daughter was not kept far from her and was quickly available. Sarah was still asleep when she was passed to her mother's careful arms and then Lady Catherine's. She held her grandniece in her arms until Sarah showed signs of stirring, and she passed her off to the servant. "A strong child. She will most likely survive."

"Thank you, Lady Catherine," Elizabeth said, knowing it was best to take her compliments where she could get them.

"All of your children born have survived—that is quite an accomplishment. Your boisterous nature and my nephew's good breeding seem to have made a good combination." Before Elizabeth could comment, she went on, "My sister was the quieter of the two of us. Isn't it odd how traits seem to skip around in families of their own will? I was the insistent one, and yet it did nothing for my children." Without missing a beat, she met Elizabeth's blank stare. "Close your mouth, you silly girl. I had four of them. Anne was the only one who lived past infancy."

"I apologize, Lady Catherine; I had no idea—"

"There's no reason to go unburying old stories that are better where they lay, Mrs. Darcy," Lady Catherine said, but for a moment her voice was not so arrogant, her tone not so forceful. "Your generation will have your share. As I failed to produce an heir, I tried at least to guide the rest of the family—and look where it left me."

"Your daughter is happily married, as are both your nephews," Elizabeth said, for once not to be mean or clever, but to state the comforting fact. "I would prefer that over many relations in unhappy circumstances, no matter how they benefit the family lineage."

Lady Catherine said nothing for a long moment. Elizabeth even thought she was in danger of nodding off in her chair herself, so exhausted from her illness and from constantly worrying for her husband. Only her aunt's sharp voice woke her from her doze. "You should hope for a boy, of course, if something happens to Geoffrey. Oh, there was a name I never thought I would be saying with any affection again. Fitzwilliam was of course unknowing of his father's nature when he named his son after him."

"Darcy does hold his father in great esteem," Elizabeth said, "even to this day. No man is without faults."

"And would you tolerate the same particular one in your own husband?"

"Oh God, no," Elizabeth said before she could stop herself.

"I was not raised to expect a husband to be faithful," Lady Catherine said. "Lewis was. This was because he dropped dead promptly before he had time to develop any interest in another woman. He literally fell over like that—right on the staircase." Despite the subject, there was no pain or anger in her voice. Elizabeth did not know how to respond, and said nothing until Lady Catherine and she both broke into simultaneous laughter.

"That is your choice, Mrs. Darcy," Lady Catherine said with a smile. "You can have a few children who pop up as adults and scare the daylights out of you, or you can have Darcy take a spill on his great estate."

"If those are my only choices, it is a wonder that anyone is eager to be married at all!"

More laughter. Lady Catherine had some of the cold tea that was sitting in a cup by her bed stand.

"Mrs. Darcy, I do feel for you sometimes," Lady Catherine said, "when my senses don't get the better of me. Shameful familial connections, multiple bastard brother-in-laws—however good one of them may be—a meddling aunt through marriage, and now, a husband who apparently requires a leash to keep him in England."

"It is a shame, then, that your senses do not more regularly fail you."

"Yes. We might even come to some understanding, then," she said, leaning back a bit more. "Good night, Mrs. Darcy."

Elizabeth rose and curtseyed. "Lady Catherine." With her eyes already closed, Lady Catherine failed to notice when Elizabeth bused her teacup, taking it out of the room and shutting the door behind her before taking a sip.

Just as she thought, tea with a healthy helping of brandy.

Charles Bingley arrived to his own bedchamber late. Jane had done her best to stay awake, an admirable effort that ended with her head still on the pillow in a doze, a book still in her hands, and the candle still lit beside her. He smiled and snuffed out her candle before climbing into bed beside her. He had no initial intention of waking her. She did that job herself, rolling over so she was leaning on his shoulder. "What is the time?"

"Late," he said. "I'm sorry—I was caught up in ledgers."

"Are you going to Town this week?"

"Maybe. I've not decided."

"But you do want to do this."

"Ideally, yes," he said, "but the timing is exceptionally poor. I don't want to leave you here with my sister."

"Charles!" Jane said, waking up from the stimulation of conversation. "Your sister is not so terrible!"

"I know you wouldn't think that," he said, kissing her knuckles. "And she is—more like her old self, now that she is settled."

"Her old self?"

"When we were younger, before she was out. Everything was different when my sisters went out. It comes with being the baby in the family."

"My poor Charles," she said, stroking his hair. She did love his hair, which was more of a bright orange. She loved it in her first daughter, even if Georgiana had to be forced to brush it. "Whatever did you do?"

"I remember moping quite a bit. I'm sure Caroline would be happy to expound on the subject without any prompting whatsoever," he said. "Still, that was not precisely what I meant. I do not want to leave you so, constantly with six children, while I go on some business adventure for my own amusement."

"You will hardly be leaving me all alone. Do you forget so easily that I was raised with one maid and no governess?"

"You misunderstand me," Bingley said. "I mean—I will be leaving *you* alone." He kissed her to reinforce the point. It seemed to have the desired effect. It was very hard to respond to that with a contradiction, especially with his hand softly running down her chest.

"Charles," she whispered softly. "Should we?"

"Why not?"

"Because—it seems unfair."

He had to search to find his answer. "My dear, suffering alongside Elizabeth and Caroline will not make this time go by any faster. We love them, we support them, but we don't have to be them." He frowned. "Plus I'd rather not think about this subject in concerns to my sister or yours. It does bring about distasteful imagery."

She giggled. "Now I'm thinking of it! Charles!"

"At least we are of the same mind, the same disquieting mind." He kissed her cheek. "If you think our own abstention will bring Darcy and the doctor back faster, then I will respect your wishes. But we have no evidence of it, or evidence of the contrary being true." He blinked. "I think I just confused myself."

Jane laughed and kissed him. "Your argument was convincing nonetheless."

That, he would not argue with.

Darcy coughed into the hay. More specifically, it was a hack, enough to prick Dr. Maddox's ears. "Darcy."

"What?" he replied, annoyed at the intrusion, taking a sip of his drink. "It's all this damn hay and dust. And the fact that I'm freezing and haven't had a bath in… how long?"

"I've no idea."

Darcy sighed and settled on the more clean and comfortable part of his haystack. Though Dr. Maddox insisted he get up and walk around at least once a day, it was getting harder and harder to do that. Aside from the guard, who didn't speak a word of German, they saw no one.

"Where were we?"

"In which one?"

"*Tristan and Isolde*," Darcy said. "Why do you like that story so much? It ends horribly."

"Most of them do. And yet it is the tale of true, perfect love."

"Wasn't that love induced by a magic potion and not meant to happen in the first place?"

"I believe we covered that part, on the ship. But what love is logical and 'meant to happen'? Does it not sneak up on us? Was the potion not just a device for that idea?"

"I've not thought of this as thoroughly as you, I confess. But I will admit to love sneaking up on me and not going to plan."

"There was a plan?"

"Your wife had a plan, at one time, a thoroughly comprehensive one."

Dr. Maddox did not get up or move in any way, so his expression was not visible. "Oh yes. You were to marry her, and Charles, Georgiana. Bad luck for you."

"What? I am perfectly happy in my choices, Doctor!"

Dr. Maddox didn't turn, but Darcy could practically hear him smiling as he said, "I would put a considerable amount of money on the idea that Caroline does things that your country beauty would *never* do."

"What do you—Oh! God, Maddox, you bastard, for putting horrible thoughts into my head! Intentionally!" His anger only rose as Dr. Maddox chuckled. "If I wanted to know what improper lows Caroline Bingley would stoop to, I would have married her!"

"Why didn't you?"

"Because she was a viperous snake!"

"A viper *is* a snake. It cannot be an adjective."

"You know what I mean! Are you blind, man?"

Without flinching, Dr. Maddox said, "Not yet."

"Besides, it would be like—like jumping Bingley."

"Very funny, coming from you."

"*Shut up!*" Darcy swung his bottle against the bars. "What happened to the shy, modest doctor I met in Town?"

"He came to the defense of his favorite piece of literature and his favorite person in the world through a series of rather low blows. And he's aware that you've still not built up a tolerance for whatever they're giving us, so he can say what he likes without real fear of recrimination, you *lush*."

Darcy growled and turned away. "I'm not talking to you anymore."

"Very well. And I had just remembered where we were in the story."

"Where were we?"

"They had arrived in Wales. Would you like me to continue or not?"

"Maybe. But only to pass the time, not because I'm wanting to talk to you."

"Of course," Dr. Maddox said, and continued.

THE CODE BREAKER

GEOFFREY DARCY'S FAVORITE GAME was "bother Nurse." It used to be "bother Father," but then he would get punished. Sometimes it was "bother Mother," but she looked so tired these days and had to take care of his great-aunt, who was old and sick and shouted a lot, especially to his mother, which seemed mean of her, so he didn't get to play "bother Mother" a lot now. He could play it, but he didn't want to. Nurse it was.

The easy way was to get up before her and run around in his nightclothes. He could never figure out his other clothes, with all the jackets and vests; it all had to be tucked and buttoned, and it was *so boring*. But if he woke up before Nurse and snuck out before Nurse could see him, he was free until she found him again, and then that game was over, and he had to find another one.

First she tried to lock the nursery door; that worked because the door was heavy, old, and creaked a lot, and made a horrible sound when he tried to pull and push it, waking her up. The window was also too heavy for him, even when he had Anne try to help, but she couldn't lift *anything*.

Today he was lucky. Nurse forgot to put the key away, instead just left it on the high shelf. He climbed the shelves, which was much less noisy when he was not wearing shoes, and got the key as Nurse snored and Anne slept on. Sarah slept with his mother still. He turned the key and he was free! Free until she woke!

It was morning, but very early, because only a few people were around, and they were servants. He liked the servants at Pemberley and Chatton, and he had no reason to not like these, but he didn't know them, and they were so much bigger than he was. He thought it would be safer to stay away for now. Every time he asked Mother how long they were staying in this dusty old house, she said, "Not very long, darling," but he didn't know how long "not very" was. It seemed to be *very* long, but Mother didn't lie.

It was getting cooler outside so he stayed indoors, going from room to room. He wondered why everyone in the pictures had curly white hair and a ponytail like servants. Why would servants' pictures be on the walls? Maybe Great-Aunt Catherine *really* liked her servants.

Finally, he wandered into the library, which at first Mother had said not to go in to, because it was so very dusty, but then she had it dusted. He still didn't go in much.

The books were not the only things in the library. George was sitting on the stool by the stacks, with a little pile of books next to him and one in his lap. George was a year older than he was and what was so special was that George could *read anything*. That was almost all that Geoffrey knew about George. At first he was so happy when there was someone here who was almost his age and a *boy*, because all the girls didn't want to play with him, and Mother and Cousin Fitzwilliam were too busy. But George wasn't like Charles or Georgie (who wasn't a boy but got a special honor because she was the oldest and the tallest). George didn't play much, talk much, or run around or surprise people. He read. He was not mean. Geoffrey just did not know the word to describe him, but he was not the same as Charles or Georgie.

"George?" Geoffrey asked. He must have heard him or seen him, but George didn't hear or see people when he should have, not because he was stupid. Maybe he just wasn't paying attention.

"Cousin Geoffrey," George said, looking up, not smiling but not frowning. "What is it?"

Geoffrey smiled. "Do you want to play a game?"

"What kind of game?"

"Well... since I bet Nurse is going to wake, and then she's going to be mad, why don't we hide?"

George looked confused. "Why would we hide?"

"Because if Nurse finds me, she'll make me dress up!"

"So?" George said. Geoffrey noticed that George was fully dressed. "Dress yourself then."

"But it's hard!" He didn't like the way George rolled his eyes at him. Like Father did sometimes. "All right. Do you still want to play?"

"Fine." George put the book down. "Where are we going to go?"

"I'll show you!"

He raced along the corridors, finding more and more ser-vants as he went, as the house began to wake. He could hear George keeping up with him because George had shoes on and they made a sound on the wood. Eventually he came to the entrance to the chapel. "I can't open the door unless someone helps me."

"Why do you want to go in?"

"Because I haven't been."

This seemed a good enough answer for George. Together they put their weight on the door, and it slowly opened with a loud creeeeak! They were inside the stone chapel of Rosings. The stone was cold on Geoffrey's feet, but he didn't want to look like a sissy in front of George, who was older and taller and could tattle on him for this, so he didn't say anything about it as they wandered around the little pews and the altar.

"Did you hear something?" Geoffrey said.

"What?"

"I heard something, like a bird or something. An animal."

Both were silent as they looked around, and the mewing became more distinctive. "I found it!" Geoffrey said, running in the direction of one of the walls where there was a stone missing and a little dirt tunnel to the outside, too small for even his foot to fit through. In that hole was a cat—a tiny kitten, gray with white patches. He instantly picked it up.

"Don't!" George said, running up to him.

"Why not?" Geoffrey liked the cat. It was light enough for him to hold and it was fluffy.

"It's dirty! And it might be diseased!"

"So? I'm not a cat. I can't get cat-diseased."

George said nothing. *Ha!* Geoffrey thought as the cat purred in his arms. "He's hungry."

"She."

"What? No, it's a boy."

"Who says it's a boy? It's a girl."

"No it isn't!"

"Is!"

"Isn't!"

"How do you know?"

George stuck out his tongue. "Because I'm older and that means I'm smarter!"

"But I found it so I get to say whether it's a boy or a girl!"

"You can't just decide! It is or it isn't! It was born that way."

Geoffrey looked at the cat, which looked back up at him and mewed, one paw swatting weakly at his shirt. "What are we going to do with it?"

"It's your cat. You found it."

"I can't have a cat. Father said I could get a dog but not until I'm eight. What if I get a cat now, and then I get a dog, and they fight?"

"You can give it to your sister."

"Anne won't know what to do with a cat. She'll just treat it like a doll, and she throws her dolls around." His eyes went wide as he looked at the cat. "I have an idea."

"Is it going to get us into trouble?"

Geoffrey shrugged. "I suppose. So?"

"We're not supposed to get *in trouble*," George said in a very harsh voice, which he could do because he was bigger and older and Geoffrey needed him for the prank anyway.

Geoffrey huffed. "Georgie would do it. And she's a *girl*."

George frowned and held the cat closely to his chest. "What is it?"

The Darcys' nurse hummed as she entered the nursery. It was no surprise to find Geoffrey missing, as he was no doubt up and making some sort of trouble somewhere, but if she spent every moment searching for that boy, the other children would be in serious neglect. Anne and Sarah Darcy were still sleeping like the angels that they were; girls weren't troublesome until they were older, except for Georgiana Bingley, but she probably just spent too much time with Master Geoffrey because they were so close in age—two weeks apart—and their parents were so close. She needed a more feminine influence, but that wasn't the nurse's responsibility. The Darcy children were.

Anne Darcy was a late sleeper, and a heavy one, which was good for when she roomed with her sister, who had just started sleeping through the night and away from her mother. The nurse checked on her. "My little angel." She then turned to the crib for Sarah, an ancient and uncomfortable monstrosity of medieval workmanship that was made better by lots of blanketing beneath the child, who should be screaming in hunger by now. Her nurse reached for the bundle. "Now, now, my sweet—"

Her shriek did wake Anne, who started crying, but it was the only possible response the nurse could have to pulling the bonnet aside to reveal that young Sarah Darcy had transformed herself into a gray kitten.

"You are in for a punishment, Master Geoffrey!" his nurse said, cradling the real Sarah, who had been in George's arms in the closet the entire time. Their giggling gave them away, of course. Sarah didn't seem to mind any, as far as Geoffrey could tell, so he didn't see what was wrong. All she did was sleep and cry anyway, and she wasn't doing either at the moment. "And Master George—I am telling your mother this instant! You stay right there!"

George looked pale, but Geoffrey just stifled his laughter until the nurse stormed out of the room. The cat was back in George's arms.

He looked at the cat, then up at George. "Does Cousin Isabel want a cat?"

"I don't know. Nobody ever gave her a cat before."

"Well, does she like playing with animals?"

George paused. "Yes. But we don't have any cats at Longbourn. We just have the farm animals, and they smell terrible. Grandmother Bennet gets all mad when Isabel comes back in the house and she smells."

"If we put the cat in a bath, the cat won't smell and then Grandmother Bennet won't mind!"

George smiled. It was so strange to see him smile because he did it so rarely. "You're right! But how are we going to clean the cat?"

"Nurse won't like it," Geoffrey said. "Nurse doesn't let me put *anything* in the bathtub. But the servants wash clothing in bins. We can just put the cat in the bin and take it out before one of them notices, and then we'll have the cat all fixed up for your sister!"

So they embarked on their great plan. It involved a bucket filled with soapy water and a laundress with her back turned, and then it involved a lot of screaming when she turned back around, and then Nurse found him, and *she* screamed—*again*— and it seemed like everyone was screaming until Mother finally showed up. "What in the—Geoffrey Darcy, what have you done now? You're driving us all to Bedlam! Your nurse barely finished telling me about Sarah—who is not supposed to leave her cradle without an adult's permission—and next thing I know, she's shrieking over some new thing!"

Geoffrey ignored her rant. "We cleaned a cat!" he said, holding up the soapy gray kitten for Mother to see.

"Hey! It wasn't my idea!" George said. "Aunt Darcy, it was his, I swear. He wanted to give it to my sister—"

"—but *George* said that it had to be clean—"

"—and then *Geoffrey* said we should clean it in the tub, but Nurse wouldn't allow it—"

"—and then *George* agreed to—"

Mother held her hand up, holding her shawl up with her other hand. "Enough! Where did you find this cat?"

"In the chapel."

"Where is its mother? It is just a kitten."

They looked at each other. They hadn't considered that it might have a mother. "We didn't see any other cats, Mother."

"Well… if it has been abandoned…" She picked up the cat from Geoffrey, despite how wet and soapy it was; she could hold it easily in one hand, it was so small. "George, did you ask your mother if you could give your sister a cat?"

"She is not awake, Aunt Darcy."

"But you did *intend* to ask her."

George stumbled, and Geoffrey quickly said, "Yes, we did, Mother, we *promise*."

His mother smiled. "Very well. I will discuss this with my sister—while you, Geoffrey, will go *get dressed. Now.*"

He had escaped disaster. It was really bad when his mother was angry with him. She didn't seem to be angry with him and she didn't seem to be angry with George. He went inside, and when he was washed and dressed by an angry Nurse (which he saw more often than a happy Nurse), he joined George, and they were told by their mothers that they may present Isabel with a cat, if she wanted it. Oh, and that it was a female cat.

Isabella Wickham, previously oblivious to all of this, practically ran screaming into the room at the sight of the now-clean kitten her aunt was holding, begging to at least hold it, and she was even more excited to learn that it was a gift from her brother and her cousin. She kissed both of them, which Geoffrey thought was quite embarrassing, and was the happiest person there for many days. But Geoffrey was happy too, because George "held him in some regard" as Father would say, which he was sure was adult-speak for "liked him." Why didn't Father ever say anything simply?

The new friendship between Geoffrey Darcy and George Wickham Junior/the Third was one burden removed from Elizabeth's shoulders. Once she had convinced Lydia to let her daughter have the cat by offering up the future expenses of the cat, which was purely conjecture. It made Isabel happy, and it made her son happy. And now her son had someone to play with and distract him from the fact that his father was now officially missing.

It was two months since Darcy's last missive to her, which said he was staying in Berlin. He had not responded to any of hers, all filled with increasing anxiety. She had to consider the possibility that something terrible had happened. Charles proposed via letter to send a man to Berlin to seek them out, and she agreed. His reply told them two things—one, that they were not to be easily found in Berlin; two, more ominously, that the post worked and that was not the problem.

When it seemed as though Elizabeth was ready to burst, Caroline Maddox arrived unannounced. Elizabeth ran to greet her at the door as soon as she heard the news of the approach of a carriage with the Maddox seal, and was both relieved and horrified to see she was bearing a letter as she stepped out.

Caroline handed her the letter, with its rather large and odd script.

"May I—?"

"Of course."

Dear Mrs. Maddox,

Precisely at this moment you must be wondering as to my location. Let me assure you that Fitzwilliam and I are well and arrived in Transylvania. We have met with Count Vladimir and are awaiting Brian's

Return from a hunting trip he has taken with his wife, Her Highness Princess Nadezhda.

In the interest of both our families, now connected by marriage, His Grace has offered to house us indefinitely until Brian returns. Mr. Darcy is staying with me in these lovely apartments and the most amazing purple drapes.

Scenery here is excellent, as is the food.

Over time we are learning much about the interesting customs of the land. We both miss you very much, and hopefully this business can be concluded with Brian's return.

Needing are we of a courier with a return letter from you, to hear that you are well. All our love,

Dr. Daniel Maddox
Mr. Fitzwilliam Darcy

"The letter's not like his writing at all," Caroline said. "He rarely writes single lines when a paragraph would be sufficient, and he never has called Darcy 'Fitzwilliam' before. At least not in my presence."

"Or mine," Elizabeth said.

"He would apologize for sending us such an oddly written letter. He would have no hesitation in that." She stopped only at the entrance of the former Colonel Fitzwilliam. "Lord Matlock."

"Mrs. Darcy. Mrs. Maddox! It has been quite some time," he said as he bowed and they responded with curtseys. While he had come in with his usual broad smile, he immediately sensed the gravity of the situation. "Is there some news?"

"Only a very odd letter," Caroline said.

"More of a puzzle than a letter," Elizabeth said and, with a nod from Caroline, passed it across to Fitzwilliam, who took a seat in the armchair beside them.

"Goodness! I had no idea I was in Transylvania!"

Elizabeth rolled her eyes. "You know very well whom he's speaking of."

"Yes. Hmm." He rubbed his chin. "Are either of you familiar with code? I suppose you are not. It is largely a military thing."

"As much as I enjoy puzzles," Elizabeth said, "I am not enjoying this one."

"Well, I think I have solved it." He turned to the servant. "Pen and ink, please."

Fortunately the servant returned quickly, and Fitzwilliam was quick to fill the pen and put the letter on the sitting room table, where, before their eyes he circled the first letter of the beginning of each paragraph. When assembled, the collection of letters' meaning was clear.

P.R.I.S.O.N.

When the ladies recovered, the mood of the room had changed. Fitzwilliam stood up, pacing very grimly. "I think we'd best call Mr. Bingley. Is he not the executor of Pemberley and Darcy's fortune?"

"Yes," Elizabeth managed to whisper. She summoned the servant and asked for more paper. "Why—why is Darcy there? He'd only intended to go as far as Berlin, not to Austria!"

"Perhaps that was as far as he got," Fitzwilliam said. "If Dr. Maddox was arrested there and Darcy was with him, they could have easily taken him as well."

"Arrested? On what charges?" Caroline said as Elizabeth covered her mouth.

Where other men would sputter and hesitate, the former colonel was calm, collected, and assuring while still concerned. "None, but it makes no sense for Brian Maddox to be continually away on a hunting trip. Perhaps something has happened to him, or he has fled, and they are being held as hostages to bring him back. If it was simply a money issue, there would be a ransom note." He walked back and forth in the sitting room as he spoke. "What we can be sure of is that Dr. Maddox and Darcy are alive, or were when this letter was written. The doctor wrote this letter to provide some clues that something was amiss. What we cannot be sure of is either of their conditions or whether Mr. Maddox is alive or not. That seems to be the open question to everyone."

The servant returned with paper, and Elizabeth quickly scribbled a note for Bingley to come to Rosings at once. It was hardly more than a few lines, but all that he would need. She sealed it with wax and Lady Catherine's signet ring, and off it went. She felt numb. The clarity of Fitzwilliam's explanation, right or wrong, had soothed her temporarily. "What must we do? Should we send money to ransom them?"

"No. He would have said that outright, so there could be no mistake if that was his goal. But it does not mean that if we send a check, we will get them back." He stamped his cane down on the floor. "Time is of the essence. If Mr. Maddox is discovered to be dead or is killed upon returning, then the count's two prisoners—both held illegally—would become worthless to him, and he does not seem the sort of man to let them walk out his front doors. Someone most go and rescue them."

"Rescue whom?" Lady Catherine announced her presence this way, her cane muted by the floor rug. "What is all this fuss about? I would prefer if the mistress of my own house acts like a civilized person!"

"Lady Catherine," Elizabeth rushed to say, "it is a letter from Dr. Maddox and Darcy. They are held up in Transylvania, and we were, perhaps, being a bit dramatic."

"Transylvania? Never heard of such a place. Must be devilishly difficult to spell. Let me see that letter." She said it in a tone that could not be denied, and since it was better than explaining the gravity of the situation after the doctor said not to overexcite her nerves, Elizabeth rose and delivered her the note.

Lady Catherine took a seat and a servant appeared with her reading glasses, which looked more like opera glasses. "Silly man," she pronounced, perhaps the only person ever to call the grave Dr. Maddox "silly." "To waste such a paper with his words all over the place. This count must be very rich. I don't see the problem, and my eyes have always been excellent. They're having a lovely time there, in their 'sumptuous' apartments, while I'm suffering... What's this? Purple drapes? Purple? What is this travesty! A count should know better. I must write to him at once!"

As quickly as she sat down, she now stood back up and took off down the hall, the letter in hand. Elizabeth's move to follow her was halted by Fitzwilliam's raised hand. "It would be less suspicious if there is a return correspondence while we are gone, especially from someone who does not know the situation. And the last time we tried to talk Aunt Catherine out of anything, it was a disaster."

"Yes," Elizabeth said, "I think we have had enough for today."

Chapter 13

PEMBERLEY'S OTHER MASTER

MR. AND MRS. BINGLEY arrived a few days later, bringing the Maddox children with them. They entered a very tense house and a desperate situation. Elizabeth announced it by running up and hugging Jane when she emerged exhausted from the carriage. The mistress of Pemberley and Rosings finally let her emotions flow on her sister's shoulder as Lord Matlock brought a stunned Bingley up to date. Upon hearing the news, Bingley embraced his sister.

"I haven't told the children," Elizabeth said. "I don't know what to say to them. Anne has agreed to distract them. And Lydia knows nothing."

"Lydia?"

"She made a surprise visit."

Jane didn't question it. The children were embraced by their mother and then herded inside as the adults gathered. Bingley immediately offered the obvious.

"Bingley, you cannot go," Fitzwilliam said.

"Both of those men are my brothers!"

"And your legal connections to them are undoubtedly thorough," Fitzwilliam said. "In fact, they are somewhat *relying* on you to stay alive if they do not. Besides, do you speak any languages of the Continent?"

"Not *immediate* Europe," Bingley said, "except Latin. But I do think my Hindi is coming along—"

"*Charles*," Caroline said, in her way that meant, *Shut up, Charles.* Charles looked to his wife for sympathy, and she embraced him but said nothing.

Lord Matlock turned to his wife, taking her hands in his. "It seems that despite leaving the army, I must engage in one last campaign."

"Lord Matlock!"

"Colonel Fitzwilliam!"

"Richard!"

But he was not all perturbed. "Is everyone done shouting my various names now? Clearly it has to be me, if anyone is to go of immediate relation. I have knowledge of French and am accustomed to traveling in hostile circumstances."

"I will go with you," Caroline Maddox said, preparing herself for the courses of exclamations that followed it.

"If I cannot go, then *you* certainly cannot!" Bingley said.

"*Charles*," Caroline said in a way that only the former Caroline Bingley could talk to her brother, "I've been to Berlin, and I speak German and French. Colonel—excuse me, Lord Matlock—do you speak German?"

"No," he said, not looking particularly pleased with how serious she looked about the idea.

"If Mrs. Maddox is going," Elizabeth said, "then *I* am going."

"Yes, terrific. Why don't we all just take a holiday in a battlefield?" Caroline said.

"You said you wanted to go!"

"I have good reason to!"

"So do I! My husband isn't even supposed to be in Austria!"

"If she's going, I'm going," Charles said.

"*Charles!*" Caroline and Jane said in exact concert.

"I sense this would be easier if we all drew straws," Fitzwilliam said with a frown to his wife, who was not so half-flippant about it when she reappeared, having traded duties with Georgiana. "Sorry if we're being nonsensical, darling."

"I am not being nonsensical," Caroline defended. "This is my husband, and I have a valuable contribution to make to the journey!"

"And this is my husband we are discussing as well!" Elizabeth said. "I will not sit back and be a spectator any longer!"

"Lizzy!" Jane said, but was ignored.

"Who will run Rosings?"

"Rosings has been functioning on its own for years," Elizabeth said, "and can remain open even if the mistress—which, sadly, is *me*—takes a small journey while other relatives remain."

"Small journey!"

"If everyone will stop shouting," Fitzwilliam said, "I will say that I will go, and anyone who foolishly wants to come, I don't believe I can stop you. However, I would prefer if we are not carting the *entire* family to Prussia, children and nurses and all!" With that he stormed off, Anne following him with a desperate attempt to talk him out of it.

"I am still going," Caroline said definitively.

"And your children?" Charles countered.

"Louisa and Mr. Hurst are their godparents. They can stay with them in Town."

"They cannot be without their mother!"

"They cannot be without their father, either," she replied coldly. "I will not sit by uselessly any longer!" With that, she rose and stormed off in the opposite direction in a huff. Charles put his face in his hands, and Jane put a hand on his shoulder.

"She'll come to her senses," she said. "Just like Lizzy will. Lizzy?" But Jane did not receive the look from her sister that she wanted. "What is it about this house that makes everyone nonsensical?"

To that, she received no response.

Dr. Maddox was tired of darkness. The choice stood before him—keeping his eyes closed in a perpetual night, or looking out into a blur that contained some light. He could see as far as his arm fully extended, but no farther. If he leaned close enough to the bars between them, he could make out whether he was turned away from him or on the other side of his cell.

He had a system. Every time he found a fresh plate of food, he made a mark on the stone wall behind him with a combination of spit and dirt from the ground.

"How long as it been?"

Darcy's voice startled him. Darcy was on the other side of his own cell and therefore out of range. Dr. Maddox had assumed he was asleep. "I—it depends how often they feed us. And the first few days—week, maybe, I was not recording."

"How many marks, then?"

"Do you really wish to know?"

"Yes, Doctor. I *really* wish to know."

He double-checked his count. "Fifty-two."

There was no sound of surprise or shock from Darcy. Instead, he said nothing. Dr. Maddox pulled the blanket tighter around him. That was one notion of the passage of time—it was considerably colder than it had been at their arrival, where at some point, blankets had appeared with food.

"So, your turn," Dr. Maddox said. "What other dark secrets do you have?"

Darcy laughed softly. Dr. Maddox could tell he was out of sorts. Not that either of them were in peak physical or mental condition, but it was no good to both of them when they sat in silence. The walls around them were too small to start closing in.

"Come on, Darcy," he said, pressing against the bars. "Talk to me."

"I think you know everything I wish to tell." Darcy added, "You know everything about me."

"Not *everything*—"

"You promise you will not say a word?"

"Darcy, we've said that to each other half a dozen times over the last—"

"Say it."

Dr. Maddox sighed and turned back against the wall. "I promise."

Darcy did not speak for a long time. Dr. Maddox suspected him of nodding off, as they both had a habit of doing, until he finally spoke, "My father was not the real heir to Pemberley. He had an older brother." He chuckled. "Grégoire was named after him. I just realized that. It had simply not occurred to me before."

"His name was Gregory?"

"Yes." Again, a long pause before Darcy continued, "I met him twice. Once when I was five or six, and again when I was sixteen."

"Where did he reside?"

Darcy answered, "In a private lodging on the Isle of Man. He was sent there when he was about twenty or so—I'm not quite sure. My father rarely mentioned him." Again, that sick laugh. "When I asked the housekeeper about him, the old one before Mrs. Reynolds, she said he had died—and she really believed it, from falling off a horse or something. That was how elaborate the ruse was."

Dr. Maddox, now beginning to piece together the situation, merely said, "What was the diagnosis?"

"Monomania."

"Was he really ill, or did the family just want him gone?" That was often the case with troublesome relatives, if a scandal could be avoided.

"He was ill," Darcy said. "I don't know what monomania even means."

"It means nothing. How was he ill?"

"I don't know the whole of it. He got along quite well with my father when we visited, actually, and my mother. He could carry on a conversation, and I remember wondering what he was doing, locked in this tiny apartment on an island, when he should have been the master of Pemberley. I thought my parents had conspired against him."

"But they had not."

"No. I asked him if they had—you know, children, they say whatever they please. Geoffrey certainly does. He told me that it was not true—that my father was a good man for sending him away. He liked being away, even if all of his nurses were trying to poison him."

Dr. Maddox said nothing.

"The second time I saw him, I had just returned from a year at Eton. My marks were good, but I had a rough year. I had no friends and I tried to run away—twice. The second time, I got as far as Lambton—five miles from home—before they found me! My father gave me a talking-to, I will tell you that. He wasn't being cruel—he was just being a father. He told me about all of my social responsibilities. Then, some weeks later when I thought it was mainly forgotten, my father took me to the island to see Uncle Gregory. He didn't explain why, but he left me with him for a long time. Much longer than when I was a small boy."

His tale apparently halted, Dr. Maddox pried him, "What did you talk about?"

"Everything and anything. He was adept at conversation one moment, silent the next. And he was older and sicker than I remembered—his hair was white and he told me…" he paused. "He told me never to trust anyone. Ever. He said the bigger and richer and handsomer I got, the worse it would be. Everyone just wanted my money or my body or my connections or me, dead. He grabbed me and shook me as he said this. I was bigger and stronger than he was, but I was terrified, so I let him do it. And then he just started crying and did not recover." Darcy sighed. "He died the following week, on his birthday."

"I'm sorry."

Darcy made a movement, but from the distance, it was unclear whether it was a shrug or not. "The secret died with my mother and father. His name was removed from the records, his portrait burned. There's not a trace of Gregory Darcy to be found in Pemberley. To avoid a scandal that would ruin the family, of course. Even I understood that, naïve as I was at the time. My prospects would be lessened if it were known that I had a mad uncle. I thought—over the years—about telling someone. Georgiana, certainly. Elizabeth would keep the secret. I despise keeping secrets from Lizzy. But—he made it clear to me in our last meeting that he wanted to die in obscurity, so I decided to let him." His head clearly turned in Dr. Maddox's direction. "Does that make me a terrible person?"

"Every family has a skeleton or two in the closet," Dr. Maddox said diplomatically. "I still don't know why my uncle severed contact with my father. All of my memories of my father were happy ones. Brian might know; he might not. I never thought to ask him before he went away. When I was destitute—when Brian left, and his creditors were beating me and taking all of my earnings, and I couldn't make my rent, I went to my uncle in his estate. I had never been there before, even though both my parents are buried there. I tried to talk to him, but I was refused entrance. I only met my cousin—his son, the current Earl of Maddox—a few years ago at a party, and he does not seem to know the reason himself. Another secret too well kept."

"Too many secrets," Darcy said. "I wish my father had told me about Wickham and Grégoire—but especially Wickham. He wreaked so much havoc that could have been prevented—if we knew we were brothers. No matter how despicable he may have been, he would never have tried to seduce his own half-sister." Darcy's voice was wavering, not from weakness but as if he was on the edge of tears. "But some things have to remain hidden. When will you tell your son?"

The question did not require an explanation. "When he's old enough to know. We don't know when that will be, but we both dread it. Hopefully, it won't be until the facts of biology are explained to him, and he realizes he could not have been born two weeks before his twin sister."

"Who are the parents?"

"His mother… his mother was a lady—well, the kind of lady that not many would call a proper lady. You understand? I hate having to say it. She deserves more respect than that."

Darcy nodded. "I understand."

"Her name was Lilly, and I knew her professionally—I used to treat men who fell ill where she worked, usually from drink or heart attacks. That was how I met Frederick's father as well. I treated him for a minor wound on his chest. Never asked him his name. I found out later." He shook his head. "After Frederick was born, Lilly became very ill, and her matron called for me. She had childbed fever, very advanced. She was dead within a few hours. And then, for reasons I'll never understand, Caroline showed up in this horrible flat in the worst part of London, picked up the child, and said 'We're taking him.' And that was that."

"Did you contact the father?"

"He made it abundantly clear that he wanted nothing to do with his bastard son. Though he still sends him a gift on his birthday every year. It scares both of us. The thought that he could come in at any time and take Frederick away from us—*our son*—is…" He put his head in his good hand. "You understand."

"I understand."

Dr. Maddox sighed. "At least he has the good fortune to not inherit my vision. I'm told it happens less often in women, so Emily may escape. We won't know for sure until her teenage years."

"Some things are beyond our control."

"So I would comfort myself after a patient died during an operation that I performed," Dr. Maddox said, "even if he was living when I started and dead when I stopped."

After a while, Darcy said, "Why did you become a doctor?"

"Isn't it obvious? I wanted to save my eyesight. Not so altruistic, is it? But I suppose you can't expect that of someone who is fourteen."

"Considering the doctors who seem to only cheat their patients with expensive tonics, I would consider you a saint by those standards," Darcy said. "They are cheating them, right?"

"For the most part, yes. A giant scam. They make tons of money."

"What's in them?"

"In what?"

"The tonics?"

"Oh, I don't know—they change the recipes every once in a while. Usually water, something with color, and maybe salt."

Darcy laughed. It was not a particularly healthy laugh, but it was nice to hear it.

Nothing was fully resolved that evening, as Lord Matlock began to make his own preparations for the journey. Caroline Maddox held her position quite firmly, to the point where it seemed likely that she would not listen to anyone. Elizabeth held her own counsel, undecided herself. She prepared for bed and was just entering it when there was a knock on the door. "Come."

The door opened. It was Geoffrey, standing in her doorway. "Mother?"

She rose from her bed, unsure of what to say.

Instead, he took the lead. "I know you have to go rescue Father," he said, with some trepidation, but no accusation.

She opened her arms to him and took a seat on the bed, enveloping him in her robe. "I am still debating it."

"You're not. You're going to go," he said. "You should go."

"You think I should?"

He nodded. He was getting so big now, he barely fit in her lap, and she could still remember when he had been a tiny bundle in her arms. "If I was Father, I would want *you* to come rescue me. You're the only one who makes him *happy*."

She smiled, but it exhausted her. All of her worries, fears, and other emotions threatened to overwhelm her, but she could not cry now, when she had to be strong for the boy in her arms and for the man very far away. "You are very considerate of your father's feelings."

"But I don't want to be master of Pemberley," he said, leaning back so their eyes could meet. "Can Uncle Bingley be master of Pemberley for a while instead?"

"Uncle Bingley cannot be master of three places, my dear," she said. "I fear his head would explode."

Geoffrey laughed. He had a hole in his smile, where one of his baby teeth had fallen out and the new one had not grown in yet. It made her heart melt, and she kissed him on his head. "You do not have to be master of Pemberley. Yet."

"Promise?"

"I promise."

"And you promise to come back with Father?"

"Geoffrey," she said more seriously, "I can promise to do all that I am capable of to return him, but you are old enough to know that I cannot do everything."

"But you can *try*."

"Yes, darling," she said. "I can try."

FURTHER DEPARTURES

ARRANGEMENTS HAD TO BE made for those leaving the country, however reluctantly their relatives would let them go. The biggest problem facing Elizabeth was her sister, who was more than a little reluctant to leave her spacious quarters at Rosings ("I don't see why we have to!") and return to Longbourn. Anne stayed with her mother, and Elizabeth made sure not to be present when they told Lady Catherine the news. She heard the shouting from downstairs, even with the thick walls of Rosings.

Geoffrey was right; she was decided. She could not justify leaving her children, but nor could she bear to sit back any longer. She had been alone for too long, except for the child who would go with her. That, at least, she had had the good sense to keep a secret.

Am I putting the child in danger? Yes. But I can't have this child without Darcy.

That, in the end, decided the matter.

The Bingleys, assuming care of her children, stopped in Town on the way back from Kent to see her off and make yet more futile attempts to talk her out of it. The Hursts would stay in the Bingley townhouse, which was regularly kept open for Bingley's own comings and goings, even though he and Jane would officially reside at Chatton, and Georgiana at the Darcy house.

One more awkward conversation was needed. Lord Matlock and Elizabeth Darcy stood before a tense Miss Darcy.

"If—and the chance is so very small—I do not return in time, you know the arrangements?" He was, though not her legal guardian, someone who would grant his consent to her marriage if Darcy were unavailable, for emotional reasons. "When you find someone who makes you happy and Elizabeth's discerning eye approves, you have my blessing."

"Mr. Bingley will be Geoffrey's steward until he comes of age," Elizabeth said, "but it *will* not come to that."

"Please," Georgiana said, oddly calmly, "make sure that it does not."

After heartfelt good-byes from the Bingleys, the three travelers watched England disappear behind them. They were straight to Prussia—not the short trip to France that Elizabeth had once taken across the strait. Slowly their home became a blur in the mist, and then it was gone.

Elizabeth Darcy and Caroline Maddox's unspoken truce of joint worry lasted a full five minutes beyond that. All things considered, Elizabeth would later think that impressive.

Lord Matlock had just gone below deck when Caroline turned to Elizabeth and said, "You are in my debt."

"How so?"

"You and I both know no one would have permitted you along if they knew you were with child," Caroline said coldly. "You are putting yourself in unnecessary danger."

Elizabeth's hand instinctively went to her stomach, though it looked to a more casual observer as though she was just adjusting her shawl against the windy ocean. "If you object so much, why did you not say something?"

"I did not think it prudent."

Elizabeth rolled her eyes. She knew she was lying. "As long as you don't say anything to Lord Matlock—"

"Why? Because he would have you sent home, where you should be now?"

"My husband is in Austria as well. Perhaps you have forgotten."

"At least I offer some service to the cause."

"Lord Matlock could easily hire a guide. He was just unwilling to stand up to you."

Maybe for someone else, it would have been a compliment, but not for Caroline Maddox. She huffed and faced out again. There was no more land to look at, but it was easier than looking at each other.

"Are we going to fight the whole way?" Elizabeth said.

"The possibility has not escaped me."

"Because I warn you, I am not in the best of moods these past three months."

"Neither have I been," Caroline responded quickly. She sighed and then replied more softly, "You should not have come."

"If all you intend to do is raise further objection—"

"No. At least Daniel had the good sense not to leave me in such a state, even if he had not the sense to not go in the first place." She recovered, her voice more steady. "If I do happen upon Brian again, and it is not to everyone's rescue, I will take great pleasure in slapping him."

"On *this* we can agree."

To Elizabeth's surprise, Caroline managed a half-smile.

"Perhaps we can agree also to at least be polite to each other. For Lord Matlock's sake."

"For his sake," she said, and they shook on it.

They arrived on the Continent and traveled to Berlin without incident, but found no trace of Darcy or either Maddox brother. It was not as dangerous to walk openly as an Englishman as they had surmised from home. "An occupied country is never happy about it," Fitzwilliam said as they made it to Berlin. Despite the anti-French sentiments of the general populace, they could find no traces of Darcy or Dr. Maddox's visit there. Nor did anyone seem to know or care about some corner of Austria. After much talking, they decided that instead of a straight shot, they would make their way to Austria and try to recover Grégoire, and purchased a wagon and trained horses for their travels, as uncomfortable as they would be.

"I believe it to be called the Confederacy of the Rhine now," said Caroline, examining a Prussian newspaper.

"What is this nonsense? Boney can't redraw the map every year and expect us to keep up with it," Fitzwilliam said in mock-indignation. "We're going south, and that is that."

Lord Matlock's easy manners at least put some levity in their long drive, made gloomier and bumpier by the well-traveled roads of Napoleon's army on its way to Russia. They drove often through the night, with one or two people sleeping in the wagon on multiple blankets.

"Look there, Elizabeth," Fitzwilliam said, pointing her in the direction of fire lighting up the horizon of the night sky. The moon was in full wane, and there was not much light otherwise. "French soldiers encamped. I heard the general is moving five hundred thousand across Europe to fight the czar."

"Lord Matlock! Do you mean to frighten me?"

"No," he said, "I feel merely compelled to point out that we are literally crossing over what will soon be history. And to think, if not for Anne, I would be now preparing to fight them."

"You think England will go to war?"

"While Bonaparte still lives, it is a certainty," he said. "The question is when. But you must admit that is not a sight you see so often in Derbyshire."

"Or Kent," she lamented. "Were the circumstances different, I might be at ease to appreciate this, but I find I cannot."

"Of course," he said. "He'll be all right, Elizabeth."

She wished she could so easily believe him.

They stopped only when the horses needed to. While Elizabeth got her fill of the German landscape, which had mountains to dwarf everything but what she had seen in Italy, Caroline read from the only book she had taken. At first Elizabeth assumed it was the Bible or a book on the Germanic languages, but one day when they were stopped and Fitzwilliam was caring for the horses, she bothered to ask, "What is it you are reading? For I shame myself by having neglected to bring a book. And to think I consider myself an *accomplished* woman."

To her surprise, Caroline gave her the kind of knowing smirk she usually only reserved for Louisa. "*Troilus and Criseyde*."

"The romance?"

"Hardly a romance. Or a very tragic one," she said. "His favorite."

"I confess to not knowing my husband's favorite book, him having so many he rereads," Elizabeth said, sitting down next to her on the rock. "I suppose it could be *My Account Ledgers* as he spends so much time with them."

"I always thought it was *How to Scowl Indignantly*."

"I've not yet found his copy!"

The sound of their laughter must have been so odd that it distracted Lord Matlock, who gave them a polite but inquisitive smile.

It took them uncountable days—surely, weeks—to reach Munich. For the most part they had bought supplies and stayed out of civilization, so this was a welcome breath of fresh air, despite the fact that the air was not very fresh. The city, clearly, had just been run through by troops, and they were quick to learn that French soldiers were there as late as the day before. The city was dispersed, its residents in shock, many of them not unwelcoming but uninterested in three obviously English travelers. Fitzwilliam hid his pistol in the folds of his greatcoat as Caroline attempted to get directions from a blacksmith. "He says there was a monastery up the street, but it was dissolved a few months ago."

"Benedictine?"

"Yes."

"Where did the monks go?"

Caroline inquired and had a brief conversation with the blacksmith on his porch before returning to them. "Many of them went to Spain or Italy, he says. He doesn't know much more than that."

The idea that Grégoire might not be found settled on them—or, more accurately, unsettled them. Having him lost and learning that there was no massacre of monks was still preferable to a grave for Grégoire Darcy and for them, but it did not give them good feelings.

The abbey was relatively small in comparison to the great cathedrals and monasteries of Europe. It was more of a church that had once had monks, and the town around it on all sides. As Fitzwilliam tied up the wagon, Caroline and Elizabeth entered the church. It was mainly wooden and utterly abandoned. The altar had been looted, and most of the vestments were on the floor. Elizabeth searched everything with her eyes desperately but found nothing.

"They're gone," Caroline said. "We are too late."

Elizabeth looked up at the one stained-glass window that remained mostly intact. The portrait was not of Jesus, but of the Virgin Mary, shown as she always was, with her head cocked to the side for some reason. The only hole was in her hand, and just then, a bird flew through it and entered the vaulted ceiling.

"Elizabeth!"

She turned, and Caroline, not so lost in contemplation, had located a door. It opened not to a side chapel but to a stairwell leading down into the storage rooms. She picked up a candle from the abandoned altar, lit it against the striker, and stepped down into the darkness.

At the bottom was a door. Elizabeth knocked on the door to the storeroom. Inside were some hushed whispers, and then the door burst open on the other side, and a young woman came flying past, weaving between them both to escape up the steps in a hurry.

"Uhm, hello? *Guten tag?*" Elizabeth said, and looked at Caroline, who shrugged, before opening the door further.

Inside, Grégoire was adjusting his cowl over his washed-out robes next to a mattress and a stone box. "*Bitte nicht*—Elizabeth?" He squinted in the poor light of the one window as he tied his rope belt. "Mrs. Maddox?" He hurriedly bowed.

Elizabeth was too shocked, but Caroline apparently felt no need to hold back her laughter, except to at least cover her mouth when she did so. "Did you—"

"It's not—well—I cannot lie, but I can hold my tongue—"

"Did I just see a woman go past? A *half-dressed woman?*"

"Oh Holy Father, what have I done?" he said, crossing himself. "She—I just—she needed refuge—"

"There are different types of refuge!" Elizabeth was having trouble deciding whether to be indignant or just outright shocked. Darcy, no doubt, would shake his hand and slap him on the back. "Excuse *us* for intruding—"

"No! No, no, no, you are not intruding, Sister, I just…" He seemed unable to fully explain it, even to himself. "I will not make excuses. I am a sinner like any man."

"Well, you're certainly more like any man now than you were before, I think," Elizabeth said. "I will be honest—Darcy would be congratulating you right now if he were here."

Grégoire sighed and collapsed on the mattress. All of the important possessions of the abbey seemed hurriedly strewn about, including the massive, gilded box behind him. "What have I done?"

"Finally become a man?" Caroline said, laughing.

Elizabeth could not hold back her laughter either. "Oh, it is not so terrible after all, is it?"

"I have taken a vow—well, I did take a vow—but everyone else took vows, and they just—walked off."

"Then you are the last?" she said, sitting down next to him. "The last monk of Austria?"

"Maybe not the country, but certainly the last Benedictine of St. Sebald."

"Who?"

He gestured towards the box. "His bones. I would not allow them to loot the place. Gold, of course, maybe, but not the holy container of a saint. The relics were brought here last year from the tomb in Nuremberg, in secret." It was, upon somewhat closer inspection, a traditional reliquary.

"So you have been down here guarding this—saint?"

"Yes."

"And the woman?"

"Uhm, her name is Bathilda." He shook his head. He could not speak it. He bunched up his robes to hide from the world. "There was a riot, and it might have ended badly, if not for His Majesty's intervention—"

"His Majesty?"

"Uh, yes," he said. "The Emperor. Napoleon."

"You—*you* saw Napoleon?" Caroline said.

"Yes."

"What was he like?"

"How was he dressed?"

"Was he on a horse?"

"Is he really that short?"

Grégoire seemed overwhelmed by their questions, and his general situation. "I did not—we did not speak very long."

"You spoke to him?"

He shrugged. "Your business was not with Monsieur Bonaparte, was it? Because he is already gone."

"*Monsieur* Bonaparte?"

"I answer to no man but God, Mrs. Maddox," he said. "And my abbot, the pope, and maybe my brother. But that really is it. Temporal forces do not concern me."

"Obviously not," Elizabeth said. "Though you will be concerned by the forces that brought us here."

"Yes," Grégoire said, now realizing the oddity of the situation. "Where is my brother? Why is he not with you?"

"He came to the Continent," Elizabeth said.

"Looking for you," Caroline added.

"I wrote him—I wrote to Berlin with instructions to forward the message to England. I admit the situation here is a bit desperate, but the army is actually polite to men of the cloth, especially Frenchmen—"

"We received none of your posts," Elizabeth said, "so he came looking for you."

"Oh," Grégoire said, looking a little pale. "Why—what has happened to him?"

"For this, I think, you will need to be sitting," Caroline suggested, and he followed her suggestion.

GRÉGOIRE'S STORY

"I took an oath," was Grégoire's reply to the departing brothers and elders of his order. Some were headed to monasteries in Spain, some to safe housing with families, some to Italy. Some were just leaving the cloister for good.

"You took an oath of obedience," said the abbot. "This abbey is dissolved."

"I was ordered to protect the saint," Grégoire replied. "He remains. So I do."

The abbot, a native Austrian who was heading to Rome to seek some spiritual solace there, shook his head. "I had wished you to go to Rome, Brother Grégoire."

"I have already been to Rome, Father."

"And it can teach you nothing now?"

"It is only that I am needed here right now."

Again, the abbot regarded him sadly as the others gathered their things around them. "Your father was English, was he not?"

The question threw Grégoire off. It was not a secret, but

only something he had mentioned in Confession before entering the Order. "Yes."

"Sebaldus was from England, originally." To this, the abbot gave no further comment. "When you applied for Brotherhood, I consulted with the saint. I may have nodded off in my vigil, but he told me something." He leaned over and whispered in Grégoire's ear.

"It cannot be."

"It will be a heavy burden to bear, if it is true. Nonetheless, will you pray for my soul when I am gone?"

Grégoire bowed. "Always, Father."

"Then stay with the saint for as long as he asks you to." He put his hand on Grégoire's shoulders. "Go with God, Brother Grégoire. And remember that humility is the path to holiness."

"Always, Father."

Nonetheless, a disturbed Grégoire did not sleep well in his cell at nights. He rose early to move the reliquary to safer quarters in the basement below the chapel, and when the looters came, he hid there himself.

Grégoire was too distracted from his prayers by the cries. The voice was too feminine to be Sebaldus. His first instinct, to his surprise, was not to chastise himself for being taken from his contemplations by the voice of a woman, but to respond to a cry for help. But what could he do? "Holy Sebald," he whispered into the outer layer of the reliquary. "Help me."

He had no weapon. The church did not spill or touch blood, and for all intents and purposes, he *was* the church, as he seemed to be the only churchman left in this city. He left his sanctuary—and the literal sanctuary—to the streets.

The scene before him was obvious enough. The French soldiers surrounded the woman in question, a woman with her beautiful—*damn it! I shouldn't have thought that!*—dress torn and barely holding up.

"Please, monsieurs," he said quietly in French, which did get their attention, but they looked at him in disgust. They were bloodied and soiled from battle, their whiskers long, and their tone impatient when they answered him.

"Go home, monk," said one of the soldiers. "You wouldn't know what to do with her anyway."

The girl, who apparently did not speak French, just squealed as one of them grabbed her arm.

"No!" Before he knew it, he had run between them and put himself between the girl and the soldier's bayonets, which nearly pierced his robe. "Please. In the name of the Holy Father—"

"Emperor above Pope," said the soldier. "And His Majesty didn't say anything about spoils of war."

He pressed his blade, and Grégoire flinched as the bayonet's blade pierced his chest and drew blood.

"Enough!"

The soldiers instantly turned to the man on the horse, approaching from the south. He rode up carefully, obviously a skilled horseman, with one hand on the reins and the other tucked into his jacket. "Halt! Where are my fine soldiers? Who are these rabble?"

"Sir General—"

"Return to your regiment! Now!" He pulled out his sword, obviously for dramatic effect more than an actual threat.

They did not hesitate. The men departed faster than any of their earlier movements. Grégoire clutched his breast, where some blood had stained his robe, but did not fall over. It was no more than a mild sting compared to what he had suffered in the past, and he felt the woman behind him clasp his shoulders to support him.

"Brother," said the man, approaching on his horse. "Are you French?"

"Yes, Monsieur Bonaparte."

"Do you know this woman?"

He looked back. "No."

"But you would die for her?"

He wasn't sure why he answered so easily, "I would."

The general sheathed his sword. "Your order?"

"The Order of Saint Benedict, Monsieur."

"And your abbey?"

"Down the road. But—dissolved now."

"You'd best take her to it. My men will not violate a church. And Godspeed." He pulled on the reins and rode off.

Grégoire stood there for some time as the woman behind him wept onto his back. Finally the woman—barely more than a girl—turned him around and asked in German, "Are you all right, Brother?"

"I—I will be fine," he said, putting an unsteady hand on her shoulder. Yes, she was definitely a woman. A half-dressed woman. "Come. To the church, please."

"You're hurt."

"It is nothing."

They made their way down the abandoned streets and into what was once the monastery, down the pews and through the back chapel, where he guided her down the steps to the basement. "Here." He had everything that the monastery owned here, what he had managed to bring down, and he gave her a cowl to cover her. "Are you cold?"

"No," she said. "My name is Bathilda."

"Grégoire. B-Brother Grégoire," he stammered.

"And where are your brothers?"

"They are all gone. The abbey is dissolved."

"And you are still here?"

He shrugged. "I will defend Saint Sebald. This is my charge."

"The saint?"

Grégoire gestured to the reliquary. "He is here."

The woman—Bathilda—stared at the box with disbelief, and then at him, and he stepped away. "Please," she pleaded. "You're hurt."

"I have some bandages—and an ointment—it was in the herbarium, but I think I brought it down—"

"No," she grabbed his hand, which had more of an effect on him than if a man had done so, and for all the wrong reasons, he was sure of it. It stopped him in his tracks, even with the light touch of it. "Sit and tell me where it is."

For some reason, he did exactly what he was told, as he instructed her, and she found the items in a crate and set them upon the ground in front of his mattress. He had taken to sleeping on a mattress beside the saint, in the middle of the room. "Now remove your robe."

"I—I cannot."

"Is your clothing that complicated?"

"No," he said. "Please—Madame, I can minister myself. If you would turn around—"

She huffed but did so, and he removed his cowl and his robe, down to his woolen undergarments. The wound was small, or appeared so, and though it did bleed, he did not see any damage that would not heal itself. But when he pressed the bandage to the wound to stop the bleeding, he grunted, and before he was aware of it, she was turned around and by his side again. "Let me, you obstinate monk. What do you think you are hiding?"

"I am trying—" but he found he could not finish the sentence. It had to end with... *I am trying to keep my vows,* and he did not want to say it. "I—" but she had already put her hand against the bandages and began winding them around him. Even though her flesh technically was not touching his, the experience was... difficult to comprehend. If she noticed he was suddenly speechless, she said nothing of it.

"There," she said, tying off the bandage. "Now, was that so terrible?"

Not at all, he thought.

"Stop looking at me like I am the devil incarnate."

Grégoire turned away. This hardly remedied the situation, because she put her hand over his, which had the reverse effect. "Why did you put your life in front of mine, *herr?*"

"Brother," he said quietly.

"*Brother.*"

"Because—because—" and he looked at her, and words failed him. *Because I am a poor sinner and my life is worth nothing. Because it was my Christian duty to protect the innocent. Because martyrdom was the foundation of the Church.* There were so many answers on his brain but not his tongue. But he didn't have to answer, because after enough stammering, she kissed him, and he did not pull away. He did not have the mental capabilities, it seemed, to even contemplate pulling away. It was not true that he had never felt a connection to another human being. He had hugged his siblings, his sister-in-law. He tended to wounds. But this was entirely different, entirely beyond the scope of his imagining that it could ever be.

When she finally released him—and he was very much at her mercy—he pulled away to the extent of standing up. She did not follow him. "What?"

"I took a vow," he said, with what little strength he could muster. He did not have to refer to the nature of it.

"Did you take it knowingly?"

"I cannot honestly say that I did," he said. "I came to the church when I was very young. But that does not change it."

She stood up, and he stepped farther away. "Am I that frightening?"

"No," he said. "No, no. I would never insult—I could never insult—" But when he put out his hand, she grabbed it. "Why—why do you keep doing that?"

"Because you're so adorable when you blush," she said. He hadn't been aware that he'd been blushing. "You saved my life."

"I—there was nothing—" but he was cut off by another kiss. A little voice in his head told him to flee, but that voice was barely heard over the pounding in his ears.

"Tell me," she said between breaths, "am I beautiful?"

"Yes," he said without question. He did not see her disheveled hair, her torn clothing, or the filthy monk's cowl that protected her modesty. He did not see the strain of war and terror on her face. She was an angel. And her touch—he needed more of it. He was tired of doing without, if this was what he was missing.

His senses returned to him sometime when they were on his mattress. He had very little clothing to remove, and hers was not particularly vexing. "The saint," he said.

"What?"

"Saint Sebald," he insisted with what little control he had left, and gestured with his head to the box at the head of the mattress.

"I have news for you, monk," she said, tickling his chest, bare except for the bandages. "He's been dead for a long time."

"He is the patron saint of Bavaria. I cannot—"

She groaned and pulled herself away long enough to pick up a broken piece of what had once been the wall to the confession booth and put it up against the reliquary. "There. Now the bones cannot see us. Satisfied?"

He had to reply that he was. Or he did not care enough to put up further objection.

Everything was new and wonderful, even the strong desire for sleep and the morning light that came when he woke. Grégoire had not seen such a beautiful morning light coming through the tiny window high on the basement wall, at least that he could remember.

"Does it hurt?"

Bathilda was awake next to him, and it took his sleep-addled brain a moment to realize she was referring to the wound on his chest, which had stopped bleeding the night before, sometime that he could not remember, because he was not concerned with it in the least. "No."

"You have had worse."

He sighed. She must have, at some point, seen his back. "Yes."

"Is the Church so terrible to you?"

"No." He flipped over so he could properly face her. "No, I chose this life for myself. Foolishly, at times. But on the whole, I do not regret it."

"But they have abandoned you."

"They fled, yes, but God has not abandoned me, and the saint has not abandoned me. Or I have not abandoned him, and I never shall." He kissed her. "If there is a child—"

"So you are aware of the facts of the human condition!" she said in mock surprise.

"I do have a married brother who made sure to enlighten me," he said. "No matter how little I wanted to hear. The point stands. If there is a child, I have... ways of providing." He had also been advised by the very same brother not to reveal his assets unless absolutely necessary.

"How very noble of you."

"Well, I am a monk."

They giggled. Only the noises of movement upstairs distracted them.

Grégoire finished his story. He hadn't told it quite as it happened, not altering it as much as making a few exemptions for discretion. When he looked up, it was Lord Matlock who seemed to be staring at him the hardest.

"You really mean to tell me that you just—*talked*—to Napoleon?"

He shrugged, staring at the fire. "He is just a man like all of us." He added, almost confused, "Except for the women."

"At least now you know the difference," Elizabeth said, and then buried her face in her hands to hide her guilty grin as she and Caroline burst into giggles.

"And to think," Fitzwilliam whispered as he leaned in to a blushing Grégoire, "these women were once the worst of enemies."

"Why would they be?"

"Ah, that is a long story about a young, handsome, and eligible Darcy who could inspire the jealousy of *many* women. And it seems to run in the family."

When Grégoire finally understood, he blushed.

As quietly as they could, Fitzwilliam and Grégoire loaded the reliquary and a bag of other assorted belongings into the wagon.

"What did he say to you?" Elizabeth said when she caught him alone. "The abbot?"

Grégoire shook his head. "It doesn't matter now."

"Maybe it does."

"No." He had an expression on his face of utter desolation. "It does not. I took an oath and I broke it."

"I thought God was all-forgiving?"

To this, he turned away but had no answer.

Jane Bingley was not one to panic. She had her moments of frantic motherly instincts, but otherwise was well-regarded as a sane, serene person, and Bingley knew that to be true. So her bursting into his office was a little alarming unto itself.

"The children are missing."

"How many of them?" They had seven now, after all. This was not the first time he had heard something of this nature—it was just usually from a servant. "We can't possibly be expected to keep track of them all."

He knew he could smile it away and Jane would relax. "Just two," she said, her body language telling him everything. "But they *are* Georgie and Geoffrey."

Bingley sighed, putting down his ledger. They were the oldest, almost eight, and had wider boundaries than the other children in all respects—boundaries they readily abused. "They're probably planning some horrible prank that I will be the recipient of, and everyone will be laughing for weeks about it. And honestly, if it makes us laugh, we're the better for it."

"I would have agreed with you three hours ago," she said with some concern.

"Then it is a very *elaborate* prank."

Not that he was dismissive of her concerns. He sent out all of the appropriate people to search the house and grounds for them, and by lunch, was becoming quite concerned himself. He entered Georgie's room.

There was no trace of Georgiana Bingley in her room, of course. That had been thoroughly checked. He was just so rarely in here. Maybe he should be more imposing. He was a father to a young daughter—he was *meant* to be distant, and her *mother* meant to be closer, but he had learned long ago that life was not without its surprises. While they both showered their eldest child with love, he had a longer patience for her... well, eccentricities.

Mounted on the wall were various drawings of her family and her adventures, even the noodles incident that he'd rather hoped she'd forgotten and not recorded on paper. Most of them included Geoffrey, or a person who was probably Geoffrey, because she had no siblings with brown hair, only blond and red. They thoroughly encouraged her drawing, because she did it without being forced to, and it was the most ladylike of all of her chosen activities. He sorted through a pile of them on the desk, trying to figure out what she had drawn. Was it of the dogs? No, it was gray and had fangs—*a wolf.*

Hadn't there been wolves in the woods?

"Georgiana!" he shouted on instinct and abandoned her room, darting past the servants and his wife without explanation. There was no time to explain. By the time he reached the edge of the woods, where he and Darcy often shot at emerging deer, his heart was pounding, and yet, no sign.

What *if* something had happened? Yes, he was responsible for Geoffrey Darcy, heir to Pemberley and Derbyshire, but this was his Georgie, the first child of his union with Jane that he had held in his arms—

"Georgiana!" Bingley shouted upon seeing her, her red hair a marked contrast to the green field. He could not yet think of Geoffrey, who was standing beside her, holding up a stick.

"Papa?" she said, confused by his sudden appearance as he ran to her and immediately scooped her up into his arms. He was rendered speechless in his relief for a moment. "I didn't know where you were," Bingley said, wiping away the beginnings of tears to regain composure. "You've been missing. And Geoffrey—come here." Geoffrey approached him, and he took his arm to make sure that he was real.

"We weren't missing," Geoffrey defended. "We were right here."

"But we didn't know you were here! What are doing out in the woods? Something could have—" He swallowed, and kissed his daughter before setting her down. "What were you doing?"

"We were practicing," Georgie said, holding up her own stick. "It was supposed to be a secret."

"What was supposed to be a secret?" But when Georgie would not give, he turned an eye to Geoffrey. "*What was supposed to be a secret?*"

Geoffrey made circles on the ground with his stick. "We were practicing fighting."

"Fighting!"

"Like knights," Georgie said, rushing to her cousin's defense. "In case we have to go rescue Aunt and Uncle Darcy and Aunt and Uncle Maddox."

"You will not have to rescue them," Bingley said, still overwhelmed. "They will take care of themselves, and they will be all right. You understand that, don't you?"

"You're lying!" Georgie said.

"Georgie!" Geoffrey said, trying to hush her, but she was apparently willing to face her father, her expression unwavering.

"I am not lying."

"You are. Uncle Darcy and Uncle Maddox are in prison. I read about prison in a book from the study, and it's horrible. Like gaol but worse."

He knelt down, unwilling to be forceful with her, stupefied by her answers. "You are not supposed to know that. Who told you they are in prison?"

"I heard it," Geoffrey said. "I heard Mother talking about it to Cousin Anne."

"So you *overheard* it," he said. "You are not supposed to be listening to other people's conversations. Who else did you tell? Did you tell Charles? Eliza? Anne?"

"No!" Geoffrey, at least, seemed horrified by the idea. "Just Georgie."

"It's true, isn't it?" His eldest daughter was unrelenting.

He sighed, kneeling so he was eye level with both of them. "Yes, it's true. But they are alive and your aunts and Lord Matlock are going to get them out." He looked at them staring.

"I'm not lying. I believe they will be all right. I *believe it*." And he did, because telling himself that was sometimes the only thing that got him through the day, and he was constantly saying those same words to his wife. "And you should, too. God pays special attention to children's wishes; did you know that? So you don't have to—fight." He took the sticks, obviously meant to be swords from their length and width, out of their hands. "If you want to help, pray for them. And if you *really* want to help, you can stop scaring us out of our wits."

"I thought adults didn't get scared," Geoffrey said.

"I'll tell you a secret, Master Geoffrey," Bingley said, putting a hand on his shoulder. "We do. Especially when our children and nephews are missing. So please, will you promise to try not to scare us like this again?" He was almost pleading with them.

Georgie took the initiative and embraced him, which she could do when he was at her height. "I promise, Papa."

"I promise, too," Geoffrey added.

"Good," he said, still rattled but at least momentarily content. He stood up and took both of their hands. "Now, we must get you home as soon as possible. Mrs. Bingley is very, *very* worried for both of you."

"She'll be upset," Georgie said as they walked across the field, "when she finds out I was fighting."

"Then it will be our secret," Bingley said. "You both promise not to go somewhere without telling us, and I promise not to tell her about your little training meeting."

Her eyes lit up. "Really?"

He finally managed to smile at his daughter. "Really."

After a long period of solitude, Darcy and Dr. Maddox seemed to acquire the new status of an exhibit. Perhaps lacking anything else to do with them, the count had no qualms about showing off his devious nature and helpless prisoners, mostly to people he was trying to intimidate, but this time, Darcy and Maddox recognized two of the guests from the first meal—Yengi the mystic and his translator, the Russian man named Artemis who spoke fluent French. As usual Yengi said nothing, mumbling while swinging his prayer stick, and Artemis listened to the count speak in Romanian. Since Darcy was less conspicuous and healthier than Dr. Maddox, he grabbed his bars as the tour was departing. "Mr. Izmaylov."

With no surprise evident on his face, the gentleman turned in his direction. "Hello, Mr. Darcy." This time he spoke in a very accented English, though the accent itself was impossible to trace. He seemed to be a man from nowhere, even if he was dressed like some kind of French physician and had a Russian name.

"I must make a request. We are being held prisoner here—"

Artemis rolled his eyes. "Yes, I did not imagine with Mr. Maddox absconded, you would stay here of your own free will. But you see, our contract with His Grace is not yet over, and he will not look kindly on us conspiring to free his *guests*."

"I have money in England. I can pay you for your troubles. Both of us can."

"My head is worth more than all the gold and silver in the world."

"At least for the sake of human decency, you can do something."

"I do not traffic in the human, Mr. Darcy. I traffic in the otherworldly." His eyes glinted when he said it, and it made Darcy shiver. "Though perhaps we can be of some aid, as we have little else to amuse us. You could have a very favorable prediction."

Darcy paused, trying to read the foreigner's face. "You're a charlatan."

"I know that in his altered state, Yengi does believe he is seeing something otherwise hidden. But what he sees is entirely open to interpretation."

"Your interpretation."

"Precisely. Though it is not so simple. Count Vladimir will not do anything that is not to his benefit. If I say, for example, that if he frees the Englishmen, his daughter will return, and you are freed and his daughter does not return, we will not be able to escape with our lives. But I could say something in your favor that could be used to your advantage later." He shrugged. "I am afraid it is all I can offer you."

"And your price?"

He stroked his little beard, which unlike Darcy's was well-trimmed. "Yengi would like to read both your fortunes."

"You just admitted it was nonsense!"

"Not precisely. And it may well be, in which case it is a very small price to pay. There are some theatrics involved, but nothing beyond your abilities to handle."

For what it was worth, Artemis worked quickly. That very night they were unshackled for the first time and dragged into a room filled with foreign artifacts and told to wait. There were no chairs, only blankets on the floor, and dozens of tiny candles lit the windowless room, but they were mostly in darkness. It was not long before the door was unbolted on the other side and Yengi entered, wearing a massive headdress of silk and a long cloak over his shoulders with flags attached to the shoulder plates. He moved swiftly between them and sat down on the large pillow against the wall, swinging his Oriental incense bearer, which created a great puff of yellow smoke. Artemis, now wearing woolen red robes, followed him closely and set a cloth down in front of him, and on that cloth a gilded, circular mirror the size of a dinner plate.

"Dr. Maddox, if you would," Artemis gestured for Dr. Maddox to take the seat opposite the chanting Yengi, and Artemis took the doctor's hand and held it out. Only then did Yengi open his eyes and, without ceremony, produced a knife and cut his palm, producing a small trickle of blood. Artemis caught it in a silver dish, and to the disgust of both Englishmen, Yengi drank what little there was to be had. Then he started hissing, his arm flailing back and forth as he tapped the mirror. Artemis knelt beside him, as Yengi's voice was a hoarse whisper, and said, "Darkness. He sees darkness in your future."

"Death?"

"No. A long darkness."

Yengi pointed to his eyes and tapped incessantly on his temple.

"Blindness. A long blindness. Long life for the healer. Happiness. Blessings. Three stars in the sky." Artemis motioned for Darcy. "Come."

"I am not giving my blood to a madman," Darcy said in English, knowing Yengi couldn't understand him.

"Do you want his help or not?"

Darcy looked to Dr. Maddox, who was holding his hand and already retaking his place to the side, and with an encouraging look, assumed the seat across from the mystic. Yengi hissed as he cut him, but it wasn't very deep, only a surface wound to draw blood. Darcy felt his own bile rise in his stomach as Yengi swallowed it, but he kept it down. The mystic's head jerked back and he began muttering again, his finger dragging the plate around and making a clacking sound.

"Indignant. Open your eyes," Artemis translated. "Fear. You have great fear of shadows, but you are surrounded by light. The light will protect you. Look in your dreams. You will never be alone. Look to the true heir."

"What does he mean by that?"

As silly a question as it might be to ask a hallucinating mystic, it was never answered. The door swung open, and Count Vladimir entered, flanked by two servants with Trommler hanging in the back. The servants carried a wooden chair, shorter than his usual ones but still massive, and they pushed Darcy out of the way and set it down before Yengi, who was either swaying intentionally or shaking. It was very hard to see, with the colored incense going and the limited light. The count was accustomed to the sight he was seeing and immediately offered his hand. Yengi drew a great deal more blood, and the count squeezed his hand in a fist so that it would drip into the dish, providing more than a few drops. Yengi drank it, then took the remains and sprinkled them over the mirror before he began his usual incoherent diatribe.

"Four moons… approach," Artemis said. "A man with gold is coming. A great fortune."

"And my daughter?"

Yengi flung his arm out, possibly in distaste but possibly not, as it was rather hard to interpret. Artemis continued, "She goes around you. Circle. All the way."

"That means she must return!"

"Around. *Around*," Artemis said as Yengi drew circles with the blood. "Dangerous games. Prisoners die, your own death is near. They live, you prosper, many years of peace. Many." Yengi cried out and his head dropped, but he was still sitting up. Artemis checked under his eyes and said in French, "I'm sorry. That's all he has for tonight."

"What is four moons? Four months?"

"I don't know. I imagine if it is something else, as always, you will know them when you see them." He bowed to the count, who took his leave. Trommler left last, but not before aiming a skeptical glance their way.

Yengi appeared to be sleeping, or at least in a trance. Artemis removed his cloak and put it over his companion's shoulders. "That was all I can give you for now. Trommler already thinks me a charlatan. If he knew I was doing something for you, it would be the axe for all our necks."

The guards arrived to escort Darcy and Dr. Maddox back to their cells, not offering a moment's reprieve. They cleaned their hands very carefully with the water they had to wash with, but the bleeding had stopped. Where Darcy was merely frustrated, Dr. Maddox was more contemplative. "It was interesting."

"It was superstitious nonsense."

"But *clever* superstitious nonsense. He was deliberately vague or just good at making accurate guesses. Or Mr. Izmaylov was."

"He said you were going to go blind."

"Yes, he did. That was easy to conclude. I have rather thick glasses, but I'm rather young for them, and most men go a bit blind as they grow old. And as for the three stars—that could be anything, but Artemis easily could have asked the count how many children I have, and assumed my wife is young enough based on my own age to conceive at least once more. Even if he didn't, three is a small enough number that I could find something in my life to apply it to." He rubbed his own beard. "Now you are afraid of darkness. Who isn't? And where we don't like darkness, we prefer light, so he said something good about light. And as for the true heir, it could be literal, like Geoffrey, or metaphorical in some sense. You're a wealthy Englishman. You're probably concerned about the heir to your estate. Artemis isn't wrong about that. But the point was, he essentially told the count not to execute us and implied that if we were freed, he would at least hear from his daughter."

Darcy conceded, "There is that." He resumed pacing. "There's no way he could have known about my uncle. I told you that in confidence, and the guards don't speak English."

"The walls may be thinner than we think. Trommler is a very clever man, and so is Artemis, even if they don't work together—or not that we know of. But no, I would not assume that. That would take *actual* prophetic powers."

"I suppose you're right," Darcy said, but somehow wasn't satisfied. He turned on his side and went to sleep. And that night, he slept poorly.

THE ISLE

DARCY DREAMT.

"I think I like it here," Darcy said. "I must be going insane. We must make it official."

"We must," Dr. Maddox said from his cell, not bothering to turn over to face him.

What did it matter to him, anyway? He was blind. Well, not blind, or so Dr. Maddox said. *I have proof. The marks on the wall. He's been telling me how many marks he's made. He couldn't see them if he couldn't see. His eyes only fail him at a distance.* Darcy leaned over as far as he could, looking between the bars. Dr. Maddox still had his back turned away.

There were no marks on the wall.

Liar! Should he shout it? There was nothing Dr. Maddox could really do, even if he wasn't blind or wounded or chained to a wall in a different cell. He could take Dr. Maddox. He could beat him senseless. He could imagine the blood flowing.

I'm not a violent man. I wouldn't do that. "I'm a gentleman," he said.

"What does that mean?" Dr. Maddox said. "Are you a *gentle man*, Master Fitzwilliam?"

"Don't call me that."

"Did you kill your own brother, Master Fitzwilliam?"

"I said not to call me that!"

"Answer the question."

It sounded too much like Trommler. He had to respond, it was instinctual. *I don't want to be hurt anymore. I want to go home.* "Yes."

"Did you enjoy it?"

"No," he said. *I don't know the real answer to that. Does that count as a lie?*

"Did you feel any satisfaction?"

There was only his breathing. He could retreat into his senses no further. He could close his eyes, lie still, even cover his ears, but he could always hear his own breathing. "Yes. Am I a horrible man? Do I have a soul?" *I must have a soul because I'm breathing. I have a heartbeat. I can't turn it on and off.* "I go to church."

"Is that really the same? Does it really matter? We're all heretics anyway; the Pope said so. We're all going to hell."

"Then I can do whatever I want," Darcy said. "I don't have to be a gentleman." He laughed. "My father was wrong."

"You are the son of a long line of gentlemen. You are my heir, my only heir, and the future master of this place. Learn well, my son."

"Liar! You made two others and you didn't tell me! You never told me!"

"Fitzwilliam," Dr. Maddox said, "you were right about going insane. I might have to give you some tonic."

"You're trying to poison me." Darcy kicked away his food tray. "Everyone is trying to poison me. That's why my chest hurts." His chest did hurt, when he tried to take a deep breath of the cold, stale air. There was grime in his lungs, making him cough, hacking up all kinds of things, as if his residence wasn't disgusting enough. *Someone put it there. I didn't put it there.*

"The magic potion, remember?"

"What?"

"The magic potion. It makes you fall in love. Why can't it make you do other things?"

"Can it fix me?" Darcy asked.

"Do you want to be fixed?"

In which direction? Did he want to see clearly or not at all? *"I'm so happy here, Master Fitzwilliam,"* his Uncle Gregory said. *"Your father is not a bad man. Your grandfather was not a bad man. The Darcys are not bad men. I am here of my own free will. Nobody expects anything of me. No one can hurt me unless I let them. Do you know what it is to be safe and warm, nephew? I bet you don't."*

It would have been so much easier to deal with if Darcy could dismiss it. His uncle was a madman. Everything he said was to be immediately dismissed.

"Do you have friends, nephew?"

"I have George."

"Do you trust him?"

Darcy had said yes. He had been wrong. His uncle had been right.

"You didn't answer me," said Dr. Maddox, seamlessly back in. "You have to answer me."

"I don't have to do anything!"

"Yes, you do. You have to be a gentleman, whatever that means. You have to be a father and a friend and go outside and talk to people who don't like you, don't want to know you, only like you for your money and your looks."

He shivered. "Elizabeth loves me, and she doesn't like my money."

"Then you must be the last man in the world, because that's the person she said she could be prevailed upon to marry, no? You're all alone."

"I have you."

"Seriously, Darcy. Who could I be? Who would marry Caroline Bingley? Not even a poor man with bad eyesight."

"True." Darcy flinched. "Wait, then why am I in Austria?"

"*Are you in Austria?*"

He opened his eyes. He liked his bedchamber. It was small and filled with books, so they were right there for him. He didn't have to get up and go past all the servants and go to the library, past cooks and servants who would chat and make fun of their master. He liked that it was small—secure. No one could attack him here. There was no room.

It was a wonderful day but that was outside, and he could see perfectly well from inside, *thank you very much*. He could see the ocean, and he could hear it if he opened the window, but he didn't like opening the window and letting everything in. He didn't even open his door much.

"Mr. Darcy, what are you doing there?"

He was in the hallway. He had gotten up and gone to the hallway. He must have been lost. Silly Darcy, to get lost in such a small, confined place. He was more amused at himself when he smiled at Nurse. "Sorry, sorry."

"Do you want to shave today?"

Why couldn't he be the angry barbarian? Then he would

have to run around and hurt people. He didn't want to hurt people; he wanted to be a *gentle man*. On the *Isle* of *Man*. There, it was especially important. On the other hand, he didn't like the blade in anyone else's hands, and he was not equipped to shave himself. He knew how to balance a ledger or handle a tenant dispute, but not how to shave himself. *What a useless man a landlord is.* "No, I think I'll let it grow."

Besides, it was so cold, and the beard was keeping him warm. Or it was keeping his cheeks warm. He didn't like being cold. He liked being safe and warm. He laughed again; he didn't know why.

"Maddox," he said, "do you think our ancestors grew beards to keep their faces warm?"

No response from Dr. Maddox. He was just a lump on the straw pile, covered by the thin blanket.

He turned back to his room, full of books and lacking space. There was a knock on the door. Funny, he thought it was open, and a young George Wickham looked up at him, not the third but the second. Or was it the first and not the second? Who was George Wickham—son of the steward George Wickham or the master Geoffrey Darcy? Either way, there he was, his playmate, his friend and enemy at the same time, convenient or not. He called him "little" because he was smaller than him, a boy of fifteen, not fully grown into his own skin yet.

"My father sent me."

"Which one?"

"He said I should learn from you."

"That's all well and good," Darcy said, sitting at his desk. "What am I supposed to teach you?"

"I'm supposed to learn how to not be like you."

He could not decide whether to be offended or not. "How so?"

"Because you're a madman. The master of Pemberley has to be a gentleman."

"I'm not sure there's a difference."

George frowned. "Now you're scaring me."

"Am I really? Or are you just amused? Or are you scared because you understand?" Darcy said, pointing to his own chest. "There's a place inside of you that's dark. We all have it, the three of us, our little family heritage. There's a dark place and you can never go there, even though it's safe there because no one else can get there. It's inside you. You have a last resort. You have a trap door. You only have to use it."

"Uncle—"

"You know what I'm saying, don't you?" Darcy stood up, towering over young George. "You understand me exactly. But you have to ignore it. Father will be so upset if you don't. You have to be a gentleman. You have to go to balls and make friends and make female friends and find one to make more little Darcys, all with a little black seed inside them. You just can't water it and let it grow, or it will consume you." He grabbed George and shook him. "That's what I'm supposed to say. That's what Father wants me to say. You have to be one thing. You can't be the other. You have to keep the darkness inside you. You have to put it away where you can't see it. George? George, why are you crying?"

George pointed to Grégoire, in his grey novice robes, even younger than him. "He gets to go away. You get to go away."

"Yes, he's very lucky, isn't he?" Darcy turned to Grégoire. "What do you have to say to that?"

"I have given my life to God."

"Don't be ridiculous; perfectly sensible people can care about God without hiding in a monastery. We're not mindless medieval people."

"I don't see you *not hiding*."

Darcy turned back to his charge, young George Wickham, son of the steward and son of Geoffrey Darcy at the same time. "So go out and make friends. You get people, George. I can't do that. I don't have those skills. I don't want them. Get as many people as you can."

"Try not to get your own sister," Grégoire said, and crossed himself. "You know, by accident. We assume."

Darcy laughed. "We *assume*." It really was very funny. He laughed so hard, and George covered his ears. He laughed so hard, and in came that cold air, and it hurt his chest. When he coughed up, it was black. The darkness had grown inside him, and now it was practically pouring out of him in any way it could. Who knew the seed was in his lungs? It stopped being funny when it started hurting. His chest hurt. His lungs hurt. His throat hurt. His head hurt. He was tired and cold and exhausted from coughing. Exhausted from *coughing*.

"Maddox," he said. "I don't think I'm well. I think you should look at this."

Dr. Maddox did not respond.

"Seriously. Doctor! How many times did I tell you not to nod off while I'm talking?"

Darcy tried to sit up, but he needed to hold on to the bars to do it. His attempt to stand was futile; his legs buckled from the strain of disuse, and he hit not the straw but the dirt ground, with the sound of his leg iron rattling. He groaned.

"…What?" Finally, Daniel Maddox stirred, looking over his shoulder. He was a mass of black hair, so frizzy. If his beard were longer, he would look like a pirate. "Darcy? Are you all right?"

"No, but I don't want any of your poisons, Doctor, thank you very much."

Dr. Maddox sat up. "*What?*" He was squinting. He wiped his eyes and yawned. "What in the hell are you talking about?"

"We were talking—"

"When? Yesterday?" Dr. Maddox positioned himself against the wall. He had not stood for some time as well. "When—what were we talking about?"

"You liar, you didn't mark the wall!"

"Fifty-four days, Darcy." He yawned again, as if he was waking up. "Well, fifty-five now. I really don't know. It is more of a guess."

"I could smash your head in," Darcy said, "but then I wouldn't be a very *gentle man*, would I?"

But Dr. Maddox was frowning. Dr. Maddox did not find his joke very funny. He was trying to see him in the very dim light from the one torch outside their cell. "Look, Darcy, I…" He stopped, a halt in his thinking. Like he had just woken up. But they had been talking! "Listen, if you want, you can see for yourself. You can see from there better than I can see from here."

Dr. Maddox pointed to the wall. The marks were back. They hadn't been there before, and they were there now. Dr. Maddox had been awake before, and now he had only been asleep.

They were there, plain as day.

Darcy couldn't say anything. Nothing came to him.

"Darcy," Dr. Maddox said with a heavy sigh and his "doctor" voice, "last time we spoke, we were trying to remember the end of *The Knight's Tale*. Then I nodded off. Whatever else you said, I'm sorry, but I didn't hear." He was still frowning. "Are you all right?"

Darcy was stupefied; nothing came to him. He was out in the open again. He suddenly remembered he was not comfortable around *people*, and Dr. Maddox was a *person*.

"Darcy?"

Darcy shook his head. His brown hair, never trimmed particularly short, was even longer now, and swayed when he moved his head. His beard hid him, but not enough. He could not hide from that uncomfortable stare, even if the man delivering the stare couldn't see him. It didn't help. "Uncle Gregory said he was *happy*."

"He was a sick man, Darcy. You said so yourself. Or, precisely, it was well-*implied*." He said even more formally, "Mr. Darcy, I don't think you're well."

Darcy couldn't speak. All he could do was nod.

PASSAGE INTO DARKNESS

"Do we have any *real* idea of where we're going?"

Trust it to Caroline Maddox to point out the obvious. "No," Lord Matlock said, sitting beside the two ladies at the front of the wagon. Grégoire sat inside it, next to the reliquary buried under blankets and hay and supplies. "None whatsoever. Brother Grégoire?"

"God will light our path," Grégoire said. "Look to your left."

"That's not God," Fitzwilliam said, readying his gun as a man with a lantern stumbled out of the woods. The man dropped his lantern and raised his rifle.

"Give me your horses," he said in French. Even with his heavy overcoat, torn and bloodied, he was still recognizable as a soldier with his white pants and red colors on his heavy hat. "Just one, please!"

"Stay where you are," Fitzwilliam shouted as he brought the wagon to a halt. He spoke French, and even though he was not dressed as a soldier, his accent made his nationality enough. "Or I'll shoot."

The soldier held his rifle up but had not the strength to aim it properly before he collapsed in the snow, his rifle firing aimlessly. It was Grégoire, of course, who leapt senselessly out of the wagon and landed in the snow, his heavy robes caked in white powder as he lifted up the man and began dragging him back to the wagon. "Lord Matlock..."

"For God's sake, are we meant to carry every man we encounter, living or dead?" Fitzwilliam said with the remains of his good humor. There was no use trying to talk Grégoire out of his Good Samaritan habits, not while it was this cold and dark. They needed to find an inn, but for the moment, settled on dragging the soldier into the wagon.

"He's senseless," Elizabeth said in English.

"Mrs. Maddox, will you please hand me the flask from the front?" Grégoire asked, and she passed it to him wordlessly. "Please, monsieur, drink," he said in French, pressing the open end to the soldier, who eventually opened his eyes and drank. Fitzwilliam started up the horses again, and after some time, the soldier came to his senses, after much drink.

"Where are we going?"

"To Transylvania. East."

"No!" he shouted weakly, attempting to sit up in the moving cart. "Let me off! I can't go back there!"

"Please, monsieur, stay still," Grégoire said, putting his hand on the soldier's shoulder. "You do not have to travel all the way but you cannot be out here, alone, in this weather."

"He's a deserter," Fitzwilliam said in English from up front.

"Where are you taking me?" the soldier asked, his alarm rising.

"We are only traveling through on some personal business," Grégoire said to him in French. "I'm sorry, but we can't give you one of our horses." He implored the soldier to drink more, but was refused. "What is your name?"

"Aubin."

"Like the saint," Grégoire said. "I am Brother Grégoire. These people are my relatives, and sadly, we are on our way east. When it is safe, you can part from us."

"You were fleeing Russia?" Caroline asked in French.

Aubin looked sideways at her, suspiciously, then back at Grégoire in front of him. "Yes. I am a deserter. I was freezing to death. Can you blame me?"

"It is not my place to judge anyone," Grégoire said. "Is there an inn nearby, or some sort of town? We need shelter as badly as you do."

"There is—to the north, about five miles, an inn. I was staying there, but I had nothing to pay them, so I had to leave. And I have to get home—or away from Russia." He did, after a bit, take another nip. "Are you really a monk?"

"Yes." Grégoire removed his hat to reveal his tonsure.

"French?"

"Originally, yes."

"Then what in the hell are you doing with a bunch of Englishmen in Austria?"

"My brother is in Transylvania," Grégoire said. "It is complicated. Is that near here? Are you familiar with the geography?"

Aubin looked hesitant to reveal more of his identity. "I passed through it—briefly, before my horse gave out from the cold. It wasn't my horse. I took it from the stocks. It was the only way to make it through the mountains—the Carpathians." He shook his head. "I am a *voltigeur*."

"A skirmisher," Fitzwilliam said to Elizabeth and Caroline in English.

"We were sent south—through Austria—but it was too cold. I'm from the south of France; so was most of my company. First we started getting colds; then we started dying. We were not prepared. We defeated ourselves."

"The folly of man," Grégoire said sympathetically. "Will you show us the way to this inn?"

Aubin nodded.

It was not far. The night was indeed getting colder, even with all of the layers they had piled on before leaving Munich; their teeth were all chattering when they arrived. Aubin would not enter. He wanted to keep going on his journey.

"Elizabeth," Grégoire begged, "please lend me some coins. I will pay you back."

"For what?"

"I am going to buy this man a horse. It won't cost much. What is a horse worth in this season?"

She dropped a few coins in his gloved hand. "Honestly, I would be surprised if you *didn't* do something ridiculously charitable."

Grégoire quickly purchased the horse from the tavern owner and handed the reins to a confused Aubin, who thanked him profusely before disappearing into the night.

"Will he make it?" Caroline whispered skeptically to Fitzwilliam.

"It's best not to speculate on such things," was all he said as they entered the tavern. Inside they found they were the only patrons, and that the owner and his wife spoke only broken German and no French. Their first language was Romanian, which Grégoire recognized but could not speak. As his hosts prepared a meal, Grégoire had words with the owner, showing him the seal on the letter Caroline had received from the count holding Dr. Maddox and Darcy hostage. There was much talking and nodding in complex, accented German before Grégoire returned to the table. Before him was some kind of soup, filled with floating chunks of beef bones and sour cream. Caroline was looking hesitantly at her own bowl, and Lord Matlock was doing the same, while gnawing on some extremely buttery bread, but Elizabeth had already finished hers. "What did he say?"

"The man we're looking for is Count Vladimir Agnita, who lives in the county of Sibiu," he said, crossing himself before taking up his own spoon. "It is only two days' journey from here, if the weather holds out. If it snows—which it most likely will— then maybe three or four."

"But we don't want to go knocking on his door," Elizabeth said, as the wife of the owner served her another helping, and she began to devour it.

"No," Caroline said, finally resigning herself to her own food, only with a healthy helping of whatever was in her wooden cup.

"The innkeeper says that this count is not well-liked by the local princes. One of them even stands to inherit his lands when he dies, his brother-in-law, a Count Olaf Cisn dioara." He bit off some of the bread, dipping it in the stew. "The owner recommends we see this man, also in Sibiu."

"The enemy of our enemy is our friend," Fitzwilliam said. "Hopefully it will be so."

After eating many small dishes that none of them could identify, but that all seemed to contain a lot of butter and cream, and drinking what seemed to be some kind of orange liquor, they were all ready to retire. Fitzwilliam, ever the vigilant soldier, promised to stay up guarding their doors, but his rosy cheeks said something else.

A few hours later, as Elizabeth crept out to empty her chamber pot, she found him asleep in the hallway, his gun at his side. When she was done with her business, she began to drag him back to his room, only to find helping hands. "Grégoire—"

"Let me. You shouldn't lift," he said.

"You shouldn't have to do—" but he had already done it, heaving the snoring Fitzwilliam onto his bed and tossing the blanket over him, "—do everything."

Grégoire closed the door, leaving them in the tiny wooden hallway in the darkest part of the night. "You shouldn't take so much on yourself. You're carrying enough—aren't you?"

Elizabeth gave him a hard stare, but for once, he did not waver humbly or shyly. His expression was a rather compassionate version of being accusatory. "Did Mrs. Maddox say anything?"

"No, but few people can eat *ciorba ruseasca* with the bones still in it without a second glance."

Her hand, of course, inadvertently fell over her stomach. "Please don't say anything to Lord Matlock."

"I am happy for you," he said, "but I wish the circumstances were different."

"I couldn't stay behind," she said. "I know I'm no use to this mission, but—I just couldn't. He needs me. I know it. *We* know it."

"I know," Grégoire said. "Just be careful, please."

"I will," Elizabeth said, not sure if she could keep that promise, or if she hadn't already broken it.

Miraculously, the snowfall that night was only a minor dusting, and they had skies clear enough to see the mountains beyond them. When they stopped to ask directions, they learned they were indeed the famous Carpathians, now almost entirely covered in snow.

"*Opreşte!*"

It was fairly clear the man in the fur overcoat and the fur hat approaching them through the snow was local, not French. Grégoire came down from the wagon and approached him. "*Sprechen Sie Deutsch?*" (Do you speak German?)

The man was apparently less put-off by the sight of a monk. "*Ja.*" (Yes.)

"We would like to see Prince Olaf," he said in German.

The guard, carrying both a gun and a ceremonial lance, looked cautiously at the odd wagon and its riders. Some questions followed, spoken too softly for them to hear, before they were ushered on.

"We're to be received by the prince," Grégoire said. "For good or ill, I know not."

The castle was massive and foreign. It was not medieval, or how they pictured a medieval castle would be, but it was certainly filled with anciently dressed guards. Grégoire was reluctant to leave behind the reliquary, even though it was hidden in a larger container, but the guards reassured him many times, and Elizabeth finally pried him away from it (almost forcibly) because they needed his language skills.

The stone halls were not much warmer than outside, so they were not relieved of their coats, just the very outer layers, before being ushered into what appeared to be a small dining room. At the head of the table sat the only clean-shaven man they had seen in days, wearing the latest French fashions, with wide sideburns and a mustache. Only an insignia pin on his breast pocket and the fur around his neck noted any significance as he rose to greet them, speaking in plain French. "I am Count Olaf Cisn dioara. I understand you requested an audience?"

They bowed and curtseyed. Fitzwilliam took the lead. "I am Lord Richard Matlock, and this is my cousin Mrs. Elizabeth Darcy, my other cousin Brother Grégoire Darcy, and a Mrs. Caroline Maddox."

Count Olaf bade them to sit with a wave of his hand. "Now, I am going to guess that you are looking for the two Englishmen being held prisoner by Count Vladimir."

"Yes," Elizabeth said, quickly explaining who they were. None of them were interested in eating the food offered as much as they were getting information, but they took some odd drink to be polite. "Please, are they alive?"

"As far as I know, yes," he said, to the audible relief of everyone present. "Though I have not been to his castle much lately. As you may have heard, he and I have somewhat of a—strained relationship."

"We've heard something like that, yes," Fitzwilliam said.

"Everyone has one to some extent or another—Vladimir has alienated all of the princes of Transylvania and Wallachia in some way or another over the years. But for me, it is personal. His wife was my sister. Their marriage was meant to be an alliance between our families." Now it was his turn to look bothered, even sad. "She bore him only one child who lived past infancy, a girl named Nadezhda, before she died. He knows that if his daughter produces no heir, his lands will be mine when he dies, and as soon as my niece came of age, the midwife informed us she doubted Nadezhda would ever conceive. This was several years ago. No one was willing to offer up their son to be his daughter's husband. He brought in many suitors from abroad, but as soon as they learned of the situation, they ran before the ceremony could be performed. He became so desperate; he turned to gambling and tricking the Englishman—Prince Brian—to marry Nadezhda. And then Prince Brian had the bad luck to fall in love with her, or so I am told.

"I met him once, during the ceremony of the opening of the hunt, one of the few that Vladimir attends. Prince Brian was married then, I think, one year, and he seemed like a reasonable man who was very happy despite his position. But after two years, Vladimir became again frustrated that his son-in-law was not producing an heir, but would find no fault with his own daughter. He conceived a plan to get rid of Brian and bring in a new suitor upon his death. Quite obviously, Brian discovered the plan and ran off. He might have been allowed to escape and be assumed dead but he took Nadezhda with him—and her dowry, which was half of the treasury. Both were blows Vladimir has not recovered from. He put a reward on Brian's head that I have no idea of how he would actually pay. He sent spies to Berlin, Russia, and Istanbul. How he came upon your husband, Mrs. Maddox, I know not the particulars of."

"He sent a letter," Caroline said, "inviting my husband to visit his brother, and my husband had no reason to be suspicious. Mr. Darcy happened to be with him for unrelated reasons when he was arrested—or so we think."

Count Olaf nodded. "I cannot tell you if Prince Brian is alive or dead, or if my niece is with him. There are rumors that he was seen in St. Petersburg two years ago, but they may be false. Vladimir has put out notices that he is holding Brian's brother hostage and he must return; the man has either chosen to ignore them, realized that they would just all be killed if he returned, or is somewhere beyond communication. But for the moment, that is neither here nor there. There is the matter of Dr. Maddox and—I am sorry, his name—?"

"Mr. Darcy," Elizabeth said.

"Mr. Darcy," he said, strangling the pronunciation through the French and his own thick local accent.

Fitzwilliam was quick to ask, "Can they be ransomed?"

"Not if Vladimir thinks they are still useful—which, if they are still being kept alive, is true. He will do *anything* to have his daughter back and Brian's head on a spike. No, it will not simply be a matter of money." He stroked his chin. "Tell me—do any of you have any experience in acting?"

"Acting?" Caroline responded.

"Yes," Olaf said. "You see, Vladimir is a terribly traditional and superstitious man, and I can foresee how this would work to our advantage. Yes, it is coming to me now." He frowned. "There is one other concern," Olaf said. "Mr. Trommler."

"Mr. Trommler?" Elizabeth said first. The name was not familiar.

"A Prussian. Count Vladimir's closest advisor and greatest spy. He speaks a dozen languages, has traveled the world, is a master of deceit, and is very well paid by the count. He is also a master of interrogation, or so I have heard. Has quite a reputation." At their ashen faces, he changed course. "The point is he must be bribed. He is an intelligent man and will see through any ruse, but he has no real loyalty to the count. And he will be expensive."

"And why would we not assume he will take the money and then go right to the count anyway?" Caroline asked.

Count Olaf shrugged. "We do not. But it is a risk we will have to take." He continued, "Trommler sits in a certain tavern very close to here in town every Tuesday night. He has a long dinner, but his real purpose is to overhear gossip. He is in disguise while he does so as Theodor Sturdza. Unfortunately I cannot go with you, or it will be obvious, and he will be very annoyed by my intrusion. But we need him—and you must get him, by any means necessary."

There was no reason to wait. Olaf generously gave them clothing to make them appear *slightly* less conspicuous than they already were, and had someone show them the way, promising to guard their things while they went. The reason behind his generosity was obvious—he wanted to hurt Vladimir, and he was willing to use them to do it.

"The enemy of my enemy is my friend," Fitzwilliam repeated softly as they entered the bar, and Grégoire inquired after a Theodor Sturdza. They were pointed to a private room, knocked, and someone from inside told them to enter.

Theodor Sturdza—or Mr. Trommler, whoever he was—was sitting at a lone table picking at his teeth in front of his empty plate. Like Count Olaf, he was fashionably dressed, if in German fashions, and with some allowances for extra cold weather. Shaven, neat, and clean—it was obvious he was a foreigner. He took only the briefest of looks at them before speaking.

"We can skip the formalities," Trommler said in plain, if accented, English. "Four thousand pounds. Notes only. No checks."

They sat there in stunned silence as he put his feet up, looking annoyingly relaxed. "Four *thousand* pounds?"

"Two for each. And the price is not negotiable," he said. "I am assuming you want both."

"How do you even know—?"

"Because, Mrs. Maddox, I am not a particularly stupid person, and having two Englishmen locked away in Vladimir's castle, I would be foolish not to take notice of any Englishmen attempting to quietly enter the country." He pointed casually, "And the monkish brother—your brother was looking for you. Odd how both he and you ended up here."

"It seems you are a very intuitive man," Caroline said, her tone not at all complimentary, even though it was true.

He shrugged. "Information is my business."

Caroline barely managed to maintain her composure as she said, "Tell me he's alive."

"I'll tell you whatever you like," said Trommler. "But he *is* alive. So we shall come to the point. I don't particularly know or care how you go about it, but I will need four thousand pounds worth of some kind of currency tomorrow, at this time, if I am to go along with whatever silly plan you have cooked up to save your husbands. Unless you have any further questions, I must be off." No one interrupted him as he rose, bowed very politely, and left, closing the door behind him.

"Where are we going to get four thousand pounds in one day?" she said after they left the tavern. "In *Transylvania?*"

They had assumed they would have to ransom their husbands, but it was too dangerous to travel with so much cash. Between them and Lord Matlock, they only had a little over two thousand.

"I don't have it," Grégoire said, "but I know someone who might."

They both turned and said in unison, "Who?"

"The saint."

Back at the castle, Grégoire removed the cover over the reliquary to reveal a box with heavy gold plates plastered to it. "There's more," he said, and pulled loose a small drawer hidden in the wooden base revealing a ton of foreign coinage. He crossed himself. "Holy Sebald, please forgive us for our use of the pilgrims' heavenly offerings, but I assure you, it is done only for the highest ends."

"I shall never have cause to insult the worship of saints ever again," Elizabeth said. "May we really have this? St. Sebald will be paid back upon our return to England."

"I cannot imagine how one who walked the path of God would not understand the meaning of charity," he said. "So I imagine St. Sebald will be most understanding."

The next day, four thousand pounds worth of local bank notes were left in an envelope at the bar—at which point Trommler almost magically reappeared. "So tell me this plan you are supposed to have. Or must I invent it for you?"

Dr. Maddox was roused from sleep by the unfamiliar sound. Normally his food tray was slid through a slot in the bars, but this time the cell door was opened with a creak loud enough that he heard Darcy, who had not spoken in several days, start moving around next to him. He opened his eyes to more light than he was used to, and sat up, holding up his arm to protect himself. The arm was quickly grabbed as orders were given in Romanian. He was held up in a sitting position as the man in front of him came close enough to be clearly visible.

"So you are still alive," Trommler said. No matter how ill or insane he got, Dr. Maddox knew he would never forget that voice. "If you want to stay that way, then I suggest you cooperate and not say a word if you're conscious enough to do so—no matter what you hear. Now, drink up."

The noxious concoction, clearly poisonous or medicinal in some fashion, was poured down his throat, and he had to force himself to swallow before he choked. Trommler left, his gray coat disappearing around the corner into Darcy's cell as the guards unlocked his leg shackle and tied his arms behind his back. Trommler had returned, and he hadn't noticed it because his eyes could barely focus at all as the man held one eye open with one hand and held the lantern up with another. Everything was hazy, and he seriously hoped there wouldn't be any questions, because all he wanted to do at that moment was sleep.

"Remember what I said." Trommler's voice was distorted. "Keep your mouth shut, and the two of you may just make it out this night alive."

Muma Pădurii

HERR TROMMLER HAD ONE additional demand: that they, in the process of their theatrics, help him discredit two would-be mystics who had Count Vladimir utterly under their spell and were becoming increasingly influential in his household. As he insisted it would only help the situation, they agreed.

The scariest part was how excited Count Olaf was about this. He hired a costume designer and brought him express from the city. "Does everyone know their parts? And remember to hiss and back away when he produces the cross."

"My face itches," Grégoire said, scratching at the fake fur pasted on his face. "*And* my head."

"I'm sorry, Brother, but *pricolici* simply do not have tonsures," Olaf said. "Try not to accidentally take it off. The glue isn't very strong."

"And if you have to scratch, try doing it with your foot," Elizabeth said. Despite the utter seriousness of rescuing their husbands, there was no use in resisting the temptation to admit the hilarity that was Grégoire dressed up as a hairy wolf man.

"If he manages to pull that off, I want to see it," Fitzwilliam says. "Why do I have to sit outside in the wagon?"

"Because your French accent is atrocious," Caroline said, announcing her entrance into the room. Beside the hairy Grégoire and the wart-covered Elizabeth in rags, Mrs. Maddox was stunning in her black gown and corset. Her red hair was uncovered and tied up with matching ribbons in a sort of beehive. With fake jewelry around her neck, she fit the picture of... whatever she was supposed to fit. "How do I look, and why are we doing this again?"

"Because Vladimir is a superstitious fool," Olaf said. "And you look marvelous. Anyway, I'm a civilized man, not a blood-thirsty barbarian. Leaving him in his misery will have to be enough. Oh, and inheriting his estate when he dies."

"And I'm a what again?" Elizabeth said, still staring at Caroline in wonder. The woman could truly pull off the distinguished look—no matter how desperate the situation.

"A *strigoi*—sort of a vampire witch sort of thing," Olaf said. "You don't speak French well, so just hiss a lot. You're there for atmosphere."

They went over the plan again, and as they turned to leave, the count said more seriously, "Remember—if he does bring the two of them forward, they may not be in the best of condition. It is important that you *don't* react. None of your characters speak English, so you won't have to talk to either of them. Whatever you're feeling," he said, looking carefully at Caroline and Elizabeth, "hold it in. We just need to get them out."

They both nodded, having a feeling that would be harder than it seemed.

Count Olaf had no trouble gaining admittance to the grounds of Count Vladimir after a very tense carriage ride in the evening cold, followed by Fitzwilliam's wagon. In the carriage, Caroline donned the black veil that obscured most of her face but not her hair, lifting the veil only to peek out the window at the castle they were approaching.

This is where Darcy is, Elizabeth thought next to her, and without thinking, gave Caroline an instinctive squeeze on the gloved wrist. *We're coming.*

The castle was indeed very foreboding. Caroline wrapped the shawl around her more tightly as Elizabeth and Grégoire followed behind her, a little better covered but not by much. They all came in behind Count Olaf, who spoke only a moment with the guards in Romanian before they allowed him admittance. He seemed to know his way about the place, and the guards with their lances and halberds nodded to him suspiciously, especially with the party following him. Olaf showed no fear or trepidation as he entered what was the dining hall.

At the head of the long table was a fat, bearded man digging into his dinner of some kind of roast. "*Ce se intampla?*" (What is this?)

"Excuse me, Brother," Count Olaf said, pulling up an empty chair not far from him and speaking in French. "You know I would not intrude on your hospitality without a very good reason, but mine is very grave. I am sure you will understand."

Count Vladimir wiped his hands, shoving his food to the side. He was obviously in no mood for visitors. He was more traditionally dressed than his brother-in-law, in half-robes with a gold chain around his neck and an elaborate hat. He did, however, snap his fingers, and a goblet of something was brought for Olaf, who politely took a sip.

"You will not believe the tale I have to tell you. It is so terrible!" Olaf put his head in his hands for a moment. He did truly look stricken. "You know—we have not been on good terms, I admit, but you know my daughter miscarried last year."

"Yes," Vladimir said, and nothing else as his food was taken away.

"I did not—I did not think anything odd at the time," Olaf said, nervously running his hands through his hair. "We were both so upset, the countess and I. But we assumed it was all part of the natural process. But now... now my son is ill. With what, the doctors know not." He paused, as if terrified with what he was about to say. "You know I do not believe in magic or superstition. I am an *enlightened* man."

"We all are," was all Vladimir offered, very coldly.

"We like to think so, yes. But then we see something so incredible before our eyes—we cannot help but *believe*," Olaf said. Elizabeth had to suppress a smile. He was really getting into his part. "It seems—a *curse* has been put on both our families."

"*Ce vrei sa spui?*"

"I mean—our family has been cursed!"

Count Vladimir took his meaning immediately, various emotions registering on his face before he slammed his hand on the table. "What is the meaning of this?"

"Brother Vladimir, please, be calm," Olaf said, appearing frightened. "Allow me to introduce you to someone I never wished to meet—or believed in, before last night." He rose and bowed, shaking, to Caroline. "Vladimir, this is Muma Pădurii."

Caroline did not curtsey. She approached the table with her "minions" hobbling behind her, pulling their hoods up to reveal one warty, disgusting face and one hairy one.

The effect was as intended. Vladimir stood up, then jerked back, knocking over his chair before recovering enough to bow to her. "It cannot be so."

"It is," Olaf said. "She cursed our children years ago. It seems my sister made a pact with her."

"A pact?"

"It is true," Caroline said in strangely accented French. Olaf had told her to make up whatever accent she wanted, as long as it was odd. "Nicoleta made a deal with me. She knew your desire for a male heir would kill her, and she wanted me to exact revenge. So I cursed your daughter and this pitiful man's as well. And now I will take his son."

"As punishment," Olaf said, "for *your* crimes."

"You made my daughter barren? My Nadezhda?" Vladimir was entranced by the whole spectacle. "Where is she? Where are you keeping her?"

"I am not. She ran away because she knew you would kill her if she could not conceive."

"That's not true!"

"It is," she said. Elizabeth watched in amazement. Caroline Maddox was a fantastic actress when it required her to be composed and tough. "She'll return to you when she can conceive."

Vladimir sat down, trying to compose himself. "I'm not saying I believe you—or Olaf—but why now? What do you want?"

"Your hostages," Olaf said.

"I've never... had Englishmen." The line actually called for her to say "eat" but she couldn't bring herself to do it. "They're worthless to you, anyway."

"We'll see," Vladimir said, and signaled to a servant, who rushed over and took a quiet order. "Please—sit."

Caroline looked skeptically at the chair that was brought for her. She was good at looking at things with disgust. Grégoire yelped for good measure, it came out fairly well, and she finally took a seat.

From the corner door, Trommler appeared wearing a long coat and looking very much the part he was meant to play or had agreed to play the day before. He looked skeptically at Caroline and Olaf before exchanging some words with Count Vladimir in a hushed Romanian.

"Well, she could easily be a vampiress of some kind," Trommler said in French.

"They exist?"

"Of course," he said without blinking. "They eat children, and they drink blood. That is why they have red hair." He made a nod to Caroline.

Even Vladimir didn't seem to believe what his logical, scientific advisor-spy was saying. "I thought you didn't believe this nonsense."

"I believe in what I can see and touch, and I have seen and touched such things," was all Trommler said to that. So he was going to play along.

The count hesitated a moment before whispering again in Romanian to Trommler, who nodded respectfully, and left the way he came. "So," Vladimir said to Caroline, "you will lift the curse."

"Yes, if you provide the payment."

"And why should I do this when my daughter is still missing? Only Olaf would truly benefit."

"Vladimir! You would save your nephew's life!" Olaf said, appearing to be horrified.

"You know one does not mean anything to the other, *Brother*," Vladimir said. He seemed to think he was in control now that he realized he had what they wanted. "I want my daughter back."

"Why? If it's just all about an heir, why not remarry and produce a son, with the curse lifted?" For this, Olaf's voice wavered, but it was barely noticeable.

This, sadly, Vladimir did consider.

"No one will marry me now," the count said.

"That is hardly my fault."

Vladimir sighed as Trommler reappeared, whom he looked to for guidance. Behind Mr. Trommler came two guards, but they were not the items of interest. They dragged along and dropped to the ground at Vladimir's feet two very dirty, very hairy men. Vladimir gestured and the guards pulled them up by their hair so they were kneeling on the floor.

Elizabeth bit her tongue to keep from showing any other expression. She looked only briefly at Caroline, thankful she was wearing a veil over her face. She could at least hide her emotion. Elizabeth had never seen Darcy or Dr. Maddox with a beard; the chief way to tell them apart was the differing color of their hair, as knotted and tangled as it was. But they were Dr. Maddox and Darcy. Darcy still had the tattered remains of what had once been his beautifully tailored green vest. Neither man recognized the scene before them or appeared to even be completely conscious.

"So," Vladimir continued, "I have the Englishmen, but no daughter. You have the curse on your daughter and son, and this person you say is *the* Muma Pădurii. Surely, if that were true, she could further curse me, no?" He looked to Trommler for support.

"This would be true," Trommler said, "if she were so bloodthirsty."

"Then we should ask for an exhibition of her *descântece?*"

Elizabeth did not know what that word meant, but she could logically conclude that it meant something along the lines of "magic" or "curse." Caroline gave her the briefest of glances; they were not prepared for this eventuality. Surely they could talk their way out of it?

"I have a much less dangerous solution," Trommler said, "for all of us." The rest of them tried to hide their sighs of relief.

"Please," Olaf said. "I would like very much to hear it."

"Very simple," Trommler said. "Your Grace, you have for months now extended your hospitality to masters of the profane and otherworldly. Why not put them to good use for a change?"

"Their predictions are valuable!" Vlad said. "Fine, summon them."

Trommler had this prepared, because he only had to wave his hand and the guards retrieved two men, a European and an Asian man, both not dressed for court. They bowed to the count.

"Mr. Izmaylov," Trommler said, with all the false politeness usually in his words when not addressing the count, "do vampires exist?"

"An odd thing to ask in Transylvania," the European said, squirming. "Yes, of course they do. Why do you ask?"

Trommler pointed to the group, specifically Caroline and Elizabeth. "They call her Muma Pădurii, the Forest Mother, and she drinks blood, as do her minions. She has cursed His Grace's family, or so Prince Olaf says. In payment to lift it, she demands two Englishmen."

Izmaylov seemed legitimately confused; he didn't seem to be in on the plot, but he was a quick thinker, "Then I suppose His Grace is lucky he is in possession of two Englishmen."

"Yes, how convenient," was Trommler's answer. Even after four thousand pounds, he was not making this easy. "Surely your mystic Uzbeki has some way of banishing vampires and forest demons." He added in English so the count wouldn't understand, "Unless you are the charlatans we both know you to be."

Izmaylov's expression wavered, then hardened. "Let the Englishmen go," he replied in an accent. His accent was, of all things, American. "They're nothing to you."

"You'd be surprised. Play your cards right, and they're worth a great deal."

"Trommler!" Vlad's patience was wearing thin, especially the language barrier. "What is the meaning of this?"

"Only to say that for what you're paying them, your mystics ought to at least be able to expel some vampires."

"That's not precisely what we do—"

"Yengi is a great holy man of the Kazak steppes!" Trommler boasted, quite loudly and sarcastically. "Surely he can do something against these unholy creatures."

The mystics exchanged looks, and the Oriental stepped forward, shaking in his boots and began to chant, waving his staff with the metal tip and roller on the end of it. When he was close enough, Grégoire, as instructed, leapt at him like a dog and tackled him. The mystic was much smaller than Grégoire was, so it wasn't hard to hold him down.

"Useless!" Trommler proclaimed. "And what of you, Artemis Izmaylov? Her werewolf is making short work of your holy man."

Artemis glared at Trommler and jumped into the fray, pulling Grégoire off Yengi the mystic with surprising speed and strength. Still, he would not approach Caroline or Elizabeth, the latter of whom spat at him.

"I know you're not vampires," he said to them in English. "I don't know what your intentions are—"

"Enough!" Vladimir rose, speaking in German. "Must my house be infested with demons over two Englishmen?"

"A problem I will be taking care of shortly," Trommler said and, with an arrogant smirk, reached behind a tapestry and removed a gigantic wooden cross, so heavy as to be almost unwieldy, with its silver tips and gold inlay. "Be gone, monsters!"

Caroline, Elizabeth, and Grégoire all took the cue to hiss and look away from the cross, but they were drowned out by the two men who stood between them and Trommler, who actually were cowering and growling. Artemis grabbed Grégoire by the neck and said quite clearly in English, but in a very bestial growl, "I know you're not really a werewolf. Tackle him and I'll save the Englishmen!"

This was not according to script, but Grégoire was not really given a choice. Artemis pulled him up with one hand and flung him at Trommler, sending them and the cross right over so they were wrestling over it. Artemis shouted something to Yengi in the language of the Orient, and the two of them leapt up on Vladimir's table, then over, and grabbed Darcy and Maddox, hurling them over their shoulders. Vladimir tried to shout for his guards, but he could barely get the words out as Artemis growled at him—a real growl—and went right back over the table, Yengi following. "Go! Go!"

Their play came to an abrupt end. Elizabeth and Caroline helped Grégoire up and away from Trommler, and they all made a break for the door, Olaf taking up the rear with his own sword and leaving a cursing Vladimir and Trommler weighted down by his own holy weapon.

Fitzwilliam was waiting for them with the getaway carriage, of course, but the crowd that he saw was not entirely what he expected. It was the American Artemis who threw the Englishmen inside and climbed up on the top with him as the women climbed up to be with their husbands. "Go, man! Go!"

"Who are you?"

"Does it matter? Go!"

Inside the carriage, Caroline tore off her veil. Beneath it, she was crying. "It's over, Mrs. Maddox," Count Olaf said across from her as the carriage started up. Now that he had broken character, he looked exhausted and emotional himself. "We have them. We won."

"Thanks to Trommler's enemies, it seems," Grégoire said, pulling off the fur on his face. "I've never tackled a cross before."

"As it was all in good service of saving lives, I think God will be quite understanding," Elizabeth said, patting him on the knee. Beside her, Darcy was soundly asleep, resting his hairy head on her shoulder.

They were deep in the forest when the carriage came to a halt. Fortunately they were not being pursued. "These are my lands. We should be safe," Olaf said and climbed out of the carriage and into the snow. Artemis and Yengi climbed off the top of the carriage and landed beside him.

"All good things come to an end," Artemis said in French, as Olaf didn't understand much English. "Thank you for the ride. I wouldn't want to stay with Count Vladimir so angry at us."

"Impressive thinking with the cross," Olaf said. "It seemed as if you were really harmed by its presence!"

"Yes." Artemis squirmed. "It did."

"But we cannot leave you out in the snow like this. Where will you go?"

He looked at Yengi, who clasped his hands together and bowed. Artemis copied the gesture. "We'll find our way." Without further comment they turned and walked into the darkness, until all that could be heard was Yengi's chanting and the swinging of his metal prayer wheel.

"An odd pair," Fitzwilliam said from his position as the driver. "What's this now about the cross?"

Olaf crossed himself. "I suppose we'll never know. Perhaps it's better that way." He shivered, not against the cold, and climbed back into the carriage for the rest of the trip.

The ride back to Count Olaf's manor was mercifully short. Fitzwilliam checked on Darcy and Dr. Maddox as soon as they came to a stop. "They're drugged," he said. "Just mildly. I don't think it is poison."

"To keep them from speaking," Olaf concluded. "Or trying to escape."

Just inside, a guard was tending to Dr. Maddox's wound but was practically pushed aside by Caroline, who embraced her husband. "Darling," she said. He responded by resting his head on her shoulder, but raised one hand—the one that wasn't bandaged—enough to grasp her hand, if only weakly.

Elizabeth spotted Darcy wrapped in blankets, coughing into a bucket. She kissed him on the small part of his cheek that wasn't covered in hair. "*Darcy*," she whispered. It was not Mr. Darcy of Pemberley and Derbyshire, or Fitzwilliam Darcy. It was just Darcy, her husband, her beloved.

He seemed to be struggling to say something but was unable to. She wrapped her arms around him, around a thin frame under the blankets. They would do everything together—the three of them. "You don't have to speak," she said. "Don't strain yourself." Instead she just placed his hand on her stomach. Though not visible beneath her shawl, there was a small swelling there of what she hoped to God would soon be their next child. His eyes remained unfocused, and he was unable to verbalize whatever it was in his mind, but his hand caressed her belly, slowly and cautiously, in silent acknowledgement. She had told no one—not intentionally—before this moment. This was how she wanted it to be—Darcy, the father of the child, showing the first signs of joy and affection. It was limited to his hand motion, but it was enough.

SOLDIERS OF ALL TYPES

IT WAS UNDERSTOOD THAT they could not stay past the night. Count Olaf was overjoyed at having pulled the wool over his brother-in-law's eyes, but he could not house them for long. He told his men to begin loading up their wagon as the others returned to their chambers.

Elizabeth approached the count, "I know we've been such an intrusion, but might I bother you for a—"

"—change of clothes, yes." He smiled tiredly at her. "It really is no trouble."

"There is no way we can possibly repay you to the extent that you deserve—"

He put his hand up. "I have already secured a favor from the monk. That is enough." He turned and walked off before she could ask him what it was.

That left her with what to do with Darcy, while Fitzwilliam studied the maps. Grégoire was still at his brother's side when she entered her husband's chambers. Darcy had been sleeping since their arrival. It seemed almost cruel to wake him for something as simple as a change of clothes, but— "Darcy?" she said as Grégoire propped him up. He did not respond to stimuli. His eyes fluttered opened, but he made little acknowledgement of either of them.

"Could you hold him up?" Grégoire said, and she held Darcy upright as he cut away the ruined vest and undershirt that had once been white. Grégoire had no visible reaction to seeing most of Darcy's rib cage, but Elizabeth gasped. "I don't think we should try to shave him now. The beard will help in the cold."

"Agreed," she said numbly, staring at her skeleton of a husband. At least there were no apparent injuries on his body or signs of disease. "Darcy," she whispered, wiping the dirt away from his forehead. He groaned something incomprehensible. "It's all right. We're here." In response, he only coughed.

Elizabeth put a clean white shirt over his head and let him lie back down. His socks were disposed of along with his shirt, and he was finally let to rest, which he seemed to be doing regardless of their ministrations.

As Grégoire excused himself, Elizabeth stopped him. "What did you promise the count?"

"The count?"

"Our host. He said you offered a favor."

"Oh." He looked a bit embarrassed. "I—promised to say a Mass so that his daughter will not miscarry. She is with child again." The part about Olaf's son taking ill had been false; the part about the failed confinement of his daughter last year had been true.

"That was it?"

"Yes."

He was hiding something, but she accepted his answer, too tired to do otherwise. It did not seem pressing. Instead she removed her outer layers and crawled into bed beside her husband, listening to his steady breathing and occasional cough no matter how many blankets she put over him. But he was here, beside her, where he belonged. Where they were and how they had gotten there, for the moment, did not matter.

In the morning, Grégoire was already up when she knocked on his door. Of course, he rose earlier than all of them, no matter how tired he was. In the hallway they encountered a tense Fitzwilliam, still not fully dressed. "How is Darcy?"

"Still sleeping. He called out for you during the night, Grégoire," she said to her brother-in-law. "Except he called you Gregory for some reason."

Grégoire shrugged. "Has anyone spoken to Mrs. Maddox?"

"Yes," Fitzwilliam said with a frown. "Dr. Maddox is not well. He has a fever, from the infection in his hand. He needs rest and, at the very least, an apothecary."

Elizabeth felt a pang of guilt; apparently, Darcy had fared well. On the other hand, it wasn't *his* brother who had run off with Count Vladimir's daughter.

"Yes, I discussed it with Count Olaf last night. He says the best thing to do is to make straight for Frankfurt, which is large enough to have a decent surgeon, and from there we can write to Darcy's man in Berlin and have him deliver a message to England. Beyond that, we'll have to find passage somewhere along the coast of Hanover. It's not safe to travel *to* England anymore, just from it." His frown deepened. "I'm not positive that either of them are well enough to travel, but we don't have much of a choice. If we don't leave before the heavy snows set in, we'll have to winter in Transylvania."

At breakfast, Count Olaf joined them, as did his wife and son; they discussed various routes out of the country and various places to stop for shelter. It had not snowed the night before—a good sign, he judged. "The only thing I regret," Olaf said, "is not being able to see the look on Vladimir's face when he discovered our ruse. Perhaps he hasn't, yet."

"And Trommler?"

He shrugged, "That man, as far as I can tell, is the type of person to survive. Unfortunately."

Their few items were packed, and the reliquary was returned to its hiding place in the now well-padded wagon. A hung-over Darcy attempted to get up but eventually needed Fitzwilliam to carry him to the wagon.

Their departure from the castle was an odd one. They were eager to be gone but wanted to say proper good-byes to the man who had so needlessly put himself out and in great danger for them. However, they could not bring themselves to celebrate, and their good-byes were muted.

"Go with God, Brother," Olaf said to Grégoire.

"Go with God," Grégoire said as he made the sign of the cross.

"Uncle Bingley!"

The shouts of two children, probably racing in his direction with the intention to grab hold of him and perhaps topple him, was enough to make a very tired Charles Bingley smile as he entered his London townhouse. "Prepare yourself; I am about to be trampled," he said to his doorman as the Maddox children appeared around the corner. "Hello, chil—" But that was about as far as he got before Frederick and Emily Maddox reached his legs, and he succeeded in standing only by grabbing on to a pillar. "Careful! You're both much too big for this!"

Emily raised her hands a silent question, and he picked her up with a groan. "You're getting too heavy, Miss Maddox. I bet you're going to be at least your mother's height." He looked down and patted Frederick on the head. "And you—you're practically a man now." Actually Frederick was five as of a week ago, but he was unaware of that fact. His birthday was celebrated with his sister's. "Look at you."

Louisa Hurst finally appeared, trying to follow her niece and nephew with a more graceful, womanly entrance. "Hello, Charles."

"Louisa. How are they?"

"Quite eager for next week." She turned a stern eye to the children. "And you are both up past your bedtimes."

With a collective groan, a servant finally herded off the children as Mr. Hurst hobbled in. "Mr. Bingley."

"Mr. Hurst. How are you both? Is there any news?"

"There's a package that was passed on by the Maddox housekeeper, but it's not from the Continent," Louisa said. "It came last week. No return."

"To Dr. Maddox?"

"To Frederick."

He nodded. "Does he know about it?"

"No. We weren't sure what to do."

"I'll handle it," he said. "I'm sorry I'm later than I said I would be—I was held up at the business office."

"I thought you hired a manager for that," said Mr. Hurst. Louisa Hurst had already put in her objections to Bingley reentering the family business, and said nothing at this juncture.

"I did, but—there's only so much he can do with the embargo. The company hasn't had a shipment in six months." He shook his head. He didn't want to talk about this in front of his sister. "Where is this package?"

"In your study, with your other post. None of it from the Continent—we checked as it came in. How is Jane?"

"She is fine. Worried, but fine," Bingley said, which was his regular answer, and he said his good nights to his sister as he went into his study. He left the door open, and Mr. Hurst followed him.

"I hope you don't mind," Hurst said, sitting down on the chair across from him. "You would think having two children would make the house livelier, but it's actually been rather quiet."

"I don't mind," Bingley said as he quickly shuffled through the post, mainly concerning his business venture, and a few from people who had heard he was in and out of Town and were sending their invitations.

"Any hope for the business, Bingley?"

He sighed. "I don't know. I either pay the workers for essentially doing nothing, or throw up my hands and let them all go. The warehouse is empty, and no money's coming in."

"Will you have lost much?"

"Hardly anything. I wouldn't have gone into it otherwise. Still—I feel bad, not paying men who think they have jobs. These are dock workers, not idle gentlemen."

"But they're not actually doing their jobs."

Bingley just shook his head. "Anyway—let's see about this." He pulled the brown package closer to him and retrieved his pocketknife to cut the strings. There was no return address. "I assume it came on Frederick's birthday?"

"Precisely. Or do we really know? Or just the day his mother died?"

"I don't know. I was never clear on that myself. For some reason, I don't want to bring it up, even with Caroline." He severed the strings and tore off the brown packaging to reveal a box. "I feel sort of guilty, opening his present for him."

"My understanding is the doctor does it without a second thought."

This didn't make Bingley feel much better as he opened the box to reveal a set of toy soldiers, half painted British and half painted French, lying against fine silk. "Goodness." He spun the box around so Hurst could get a look.

Mr. Hurst picked one up, examining it. "Very nice. Young Frederick will be ecstatic." He put it back in its place. "Who will this be from?"

"I don't know. Usually the doctor makes that decision, but I don't think he'll be back in time." He crossed his arms. "I bought Emily a doll—I suppose this year it could come from the Bingleys, alongside her present."

"Was the doll made of gold?"

"They can't tell the worth of things. And it's a very nice doll," Bingley said, closing the box and flipping it over.

"Looking for the royal seal?"

"We're not supposed to say that out loud, Mr. Hurst," he said, settling into his chair.

"Someone should say the obvious," Hurst said. "I agree with your plan. Louisa and I already bought him something. He's been trying to find it all week."

"Jane is going to come down for their birthday and bring the children."

"All of them?"

"We thought—well, it might take their minds off the situation. The house might be destroyed in the process, but so be it." He smiled at that, one hand still on the box of soldiers.

The five of them took shifts through the night and the next day, until they had to stop and pay what seemed outrageous for a change in horses. The road was long and brutal, rarely paved except for the old Roman roads. A week at full speed was enough for everyone, and it was obvious that their husbands needed not only proper food (and a shave) but a doctor.

Grégoire held Darcy upright long enough to make sure he swallowed the contents of the container of soup and then helped him back down. Elizabeth climbed up next to Caroline. "How long do you think we should ride?"

"As long as we possibly can. Out of Austria, at least."

The half-ruined wagon rolled into Frankfurt. The best inn they could find was in poor condition from the chaos of war, but it would do. Grégoire was sent off to find a decent doctor, if one was to be found. The reliquary was put in the Maddoxes' room, as it seemed that the doctor needed most any blessings it would bring.

At last, after the innkeeper brought up food and drink, Elizabeth was left alone with Darcy. "Darcy," she said, taking his hand. "You need to drink."

To her surprise, he coughed and responded, "Maddox, I've just had the loveliest dream."

"Oh?"

"Elizabeth was with me," he said.

She kissed him on the forehead, and he opened his eyes. They didn't seem to entirely focus, but enough for him to say, "Oh."

"That's all I get for going to Transylvania to rescue you?"

He smiled weakly. "You are… preferable… to waking up next to Maddox."

"I would hope so," she said, all of the desperation coming out of her. Relieved as she was to find him alive, he was not well. "I'll help you up." "Help" was an operative word, because she did most of the work, as he didn't seem capable of moving much himself or even lifting his own deteriorated weight, but finally she had him resting against the headboard enough for him to drink. It took him a long time to finish the bottle, but he managed, and seemed to stay awake this time as she put it away.

"Where—where am I?"

"Frankfurt. We've just arrived. Grégoire is looking for a doctor as we speak."

"Doctor—" he stumbled. "Grégoire?"

"Yes, you have a brother named Grégoire."

He was too impaired to respond in his traditional way, which bothered her as he answered simply, "He's here?"

"We found him in the monastery. It was dissolved, but he was still there. He posted, of course, but like everything else, it didn't reach us in England."

He made a motion that seemed to be an abbreviated nod. "Dr. Maddox?"

"He's in the next room, with Caroline."

"Bingley?"

"Yes. I don't know another Caroline."

"No... I mean... where's *Bingley?*"

"He didn't come. He's watching the children."

"Oh." After some time, he said, "Clearly... we should have been... more specific in sending for help."

"Would you prefer Bingley holding your hand right now instead of your wife?"

"*No,*" he was aware enough to respond. "But... you know that's not the point."

"I know. But you're safe; everyone is safe." Safety, of course, being somewhat relative. She kissed him and let him drift off again, as he clearly wanted to do. She would have been content to just sit there and watch him breathe, reminding her that he was, despite his state, very much alive and out of harm's way, but there was a knock on the door. "Come."

It was Caroline. "How is he?"

"We spoke. He seemed a bit annoyed we didn't send Mr. Bingley in our place."

"How is that not surprising?" Caroline said. "Daniel woke, but only for a few moments."

"Did he say anything?"

"He asked me to look at his hand and give a description. I'm not sure he really knew where he was, but he was *still* trying to be a doctor." Usually, at this point, Caroline would look annoyed, in her half-jesting, half-indignant sort of way, and roll her eyes. Instead, she just looked tired. Her hair wasn't properly put up. She sat down on the bed next to Elizabeth. "I told him not to go and do something stupid, like get captured by a baron and tortured for information he didn't have. And now—" but her tears prevented her from speaking further.

Elizabeth placed a hand on her back. "But he's alive. And it's only his hand."

"He can't lose his hand! He's a surgeon!" Caroline cried. "Of all the stupid things for him to do—he had to go after that insolent brother of his! Who's smarter than all of us, for staying out of this!"

Elizabeth did not try to talk her out of it. As Darcy slept on behind them, Elizabeth let her sister-in-law cry until she was spent. It took a very long time.

It was getting late when Grégoire returned with Dr. Schauss, who spoke German and some French. The priority was with Dr. Maddox, who was finally roused with smelling salts and a good quantity of juice as his wife explained everything to the doctor.

Dr. Schauss removed the bandages and inspected the hand. "It's infected."

"That I know."

The doctor cut away more infected flesh and cleaned the wound properly, then gave Dr. Maddox some laudanum for the pain, and Dr. Maddox, who could not sit up on his own, leaned entirely on Caroline. "I'm so sorry," he said in his first real words to her.

"You? Sorry? It's that idiot brother of yours who should be sorry," she said, but her usual veneer was cracking. She considered herself fortunate that he could not see her tears. "When I get my hands on him—"

"As noble as he may have been," he mumbled, "I'm inclined to agree with your sentiments."

The first person to arrive in the morning was actually the barber, and Elizabeth Darcy and Caroline Maddox finally could be positively sure that they *had* recovered their husbands and not some random prisoners. Since Dr. Maddox could see no solid shapes with his pain medication, he could not object and got a much closer trim to his bangs than he normally kept, as well as a shave. The barber was thoroughly confused by what Dr. Maddox said to him when he learned of his cut by feeling the top of his head, that he ran out of the room and attended to Darcy. He then proceeded to form the sideburns in the German style, which incensed Darcy to no end, and the poor barber had to deal with two angry customers and two apologetic wives before running off with his payment.

"You look fine," Elizabeth assured him, though she was holding back her laughter as she said it. But in fact, upon closer inspection, he did not look fine. A messy beard and overgrown hair had only disguised how sunken his features were. "My darling," she whispered, and he gave a token kiss on her cheek before collapsing back in bed. "My hairy, mangy darling."

Chapter 20

RISKY BUSINESS

THE BIRTHDAY CELEBRATIONS OF Frederick and Emily Maddox were not muted—there was no way for them to be, with so many children and so few adults to handle them. It was a physical impossibility. Only the age and height factors kept Frederick from lording his presents over Geoffrey but didn't stop him from pestering Charles III into some jealousy, while Georgie turned her nose up at Eliza's fascination with Emily's new doll, and Anne and Edmund ran around with their new-found mobility. With Sarah being passed around, it was almost forgotten how many adults were absent. With the ruckus, only Jane, who had taken Sarah aside to try to calm her crying after having her ears poked by her elder sister, heard the knocking at the door. She quickly passed Sarah Darcy to Mrs. Hurst and disappeared to see to the caller.

Bingley presided over the ceremonies, held in his townhouse, with amusement and delight at the horde of children before him. When Edmund was close to knocking over the writing stand, he picked him up and held his year-and-a-half-old son in his arms.

Trying to put any worries out of his mind, he only looked up when he heard a gasp.

Jane stood in the entrance to the sitting room, holding an opened letter in her arms. Her eyes were already red and her face wet with tears. There was a silence that came over all of the adults to the point where the children even picked up on the changed mood and quieted down. Finally she recovered from her shock and said with a weak smile, "They've been recovered. Elizabeth and Caroline have found them."

Bingley kissed his younger son and set him on the floor, running to embrace his wife. Slowly, after many cheers and assurances to the children—now not halfhearted—the story came out as Jane summarized the letter in Elizabeth's handwriting, but signed by her, Caroline, and Lord Matlock. "After leaving Berlin they found Grégoire in Munich, where he was hiding from the soldiers in the basement of his monastery. From there they traveled by wagon into Austria, and ransomed Mr. Darcy and Dr. Maddox from the count. Mr. Brian Maddox has still not been located—no one knows where he is—but they are all recovered." Her voice broke several times, and she had to pause to recover herself from such raw joy. "Lizzy writes from Frankfurt, where the doctor had to have his hand mended, but he will be all right. She sent this letter to Darcy's man in Berlin, to make sure it would reach us. By now they should be on the coast, trying to acquire passage to England! Charles, they are coming home!"

Congratulations went around so many times that even Mr. and Mrs. Hurst were all misty-eyed, and the children were ecstatic to the point where they quickly exhausted themselves, which was very helpful for getting the younger ones into their cradles for their afternoon naps. ("I've never seen them go to sleep so easily," said Darcy's nurse.) Only Georgie and Geoffrey stayed up longer, playing with Frederick's toys with the real intention of hearing the others talk more frankly. They even attempted to hide behind the settee and be forgotten, but were quickly discovered by the ever-watchful Jane, who immediately sent them upstairs. Celebratory drinks were passed around, and toasts to everyone's health were made, especially those traveling home at last. Jane excused herself to pen a quick note to Anne about her husband, and Georgiana about her brother and sister, while Bingley read the letter for himself. Jane had omitted things in her general reading. There was more to the story of the retrieval of Darcy and Dr. Maddox, but the tale would want to be told properly when they returned, as it was long and complicated, and involved a great deal of trickery and use of superstition on their part. He knew Darcy well enough to know that Darcy would have written the letter himself if he was up to it, but no ailment was described. Grégoire was coming to England for the rest of the war and bringing with him some kind of reliquary for safekeeping, of all things. *At least one person of the two was found*, he thought to himself.

Dinner was a happier affair than they had anticipated. Dr. Maddox had missed his children's birthdays, but he would be there for the next ones, and that was all that mattered now. But even joy brought a certain exhaustion, after many toasts (perhaps a few too many), the four of them retired.

"Perhaps we should send a note to open up their houses," Jane said as she reread the letter in bed while Bingley settled down beside her, feeling a bit lightheaded from so many celebrations with libation. "Or is it too soon? She said they would write again from the coast, if they could." In the letter, it named the town they were traveling to, but their plans were not fixed because of the war. "Should we try to arrange a ship ourselves? It would be much easier from this side of the channel."

"It would be," he said. "I honestly… am overwhelmed." He leaned over and kissed his wife. "It is as if a weight has been lifted from me. I will confess to you now that I do not want to ever have to be the steward of Pemberley."

"And Rosings."

"Oh God, yes. Or would it just pass to the Fitzwilliams?" He frowned and then smiled again. "Well, it hardly matters now. All will be right."

But Bingley did not fall asleep. He was still awake when he heard the bell ring. He did not require his manservant to rouse him, appearing instead in the hallway, throwing a robe over his shoulders, "What is it?"

"A Mr. Kensington sent an express, sir. Nothing to get alarmed about." Meanwhile, a servant dashed up the stairs and bowed, handing his master the letter, which Bingley tore open.

"Charles?" Jane's voice called from the bedchamber, "What is it?"

"It's nothing," he said, reentering the bedchamber. "There's just a fire down at the docks. My manager decided to post me about it." He set the note aside. "It's not near the warehouse. Not that there's anything in it to burn, but still—I'm going to go down and have a look."

"A look!" Jane said. "Charles, you just told me the docks are burning, and you want to go watch?"

"It won't be dangerous. He says it's in a different area. He just wanted me to know." He leaned over and kissed her. "I will be safe, I promise."

"Take someone, will you?"

"Of course." He smiled reassuringly. "I'll be back before you know it." And with that, he stepped into his dressing room to be dressed by his man.

But Jane did know how much time had passed before she heard a knock at the door, because she spent it tossing and turning, listening for sounds, and then staring at the clock as the hours ticked by. When she did hear the bell, she did not wait to be summoned. She threw on her robe, rushed down the stairs, and opened the door herself.

The man who greeted her was *not* her husband.

East London was not very safe—it was rioting. This, however, was hardly an unusual occurrence, especially in these strained economic times. The chief concern of the authorities was to make sure the fires did not spread elsewhere; what the poor did amongst themselves was another matter entirely.

Bingley's carriage pulled up to the warehouse. He had been there often enough in recent weeks; he knew it to be mainly empty, full of wooden storage boxes that would serve as excellent tinder after a particularly dry autumn. If it did catch, he would lose the building and probably the business, even if it were not much to lose.

He sighed, opening the front door. The fires were on the docks proper, some distance away, so he was not immediately concerned. What he *was* concerned about were the workers in the warehouse who faced him as he entered. He knew almost all of them by face and some of them by name—they were the men who had no work and no pay. Most concerning was the fact that one of them, a Mr. Graves (the sort of man who hardly deserved the proper title of "Mister"), was pointing a pistol at the head of Mr. Kensington.

"They made me write it," the old man whispered.

"Let him go," Bingley said in the most authoritative voice he had, which, all things considered, was not very authoritative.

To his great surprise, the man holding him down—a Mr. Goodman, Bingley vaguely remembered—released him and Kensington ran out the back. The gun was then turned on Bingley as the door was shut behind him.

"Look," he said, clutching his walking stick with full knowledge that it would hardly help him when facing an armed gang in poor lantern light, "I know the company is in dire straits right now because of the embargo—"

One of the men at his side grabbed him and pushed him against the wall.

"*We're* in dire straits," Graves said, drawing a knife as he approached him. "Yer sittin' in your posh house, lookin' over books, while we're starvin.' How many courses did ya eat tonight, Mr. Bingley?"

He cleared his throat. "This company is my family's greatest concern. My father—"

"We don't care about your father, Mr. Bingley," said Graves, pointing the knife at his throat. "Or your mother, or your grandfather, or anyone else you care ta mention."

Unfortunately, he was beginning to grasp what they *did* care about. Or at least, the lengths they were going to go through to get it.

"*Yametekure!*" (Hold it right there!)

They all turned away from Bingley without lowering their

weapons to see the figure—figures—emerging from the darkness of the inner warehouse. The man before them was dressed in bizarre silk clothing, but more noticeable was his gigantic hat, which must have been made of some kind of stalk, which was triangular, with holes in the front for his vision, as it covered most of his face. He had one hand tucked into the folds of his robe, the other easily resting on the hilt of two long swords, or one very long sword and another shorter one.

"This is private property," he said in cold but perfectly comprehensible English. "Show your permit or get out!"

"Who're you?" Goodman said, readying his own weapon as the man stepped into the torchlight.

"I will repeat myself once," said the stranger, one finger over the hilt of his blades. "Stop threatening this man and get out!"

"Do what he says," said the woman emerging by his side, wearing a robe and speaking in accented English. Her hair was tied up and covered by a white cloth.

"You and what army, lady?" Graves spat.

"I see you cannot be reasoned with." The stranger turned to a box, onto which emerged a man, hunched over like a bird on stilt shoes. "Mugin. *Iidesuka?*" (Are you ready?)

"*Sehi.*" (Sure.)

Goodman, facing a shadowed and confusing spectacle, decided to take the initiative and raised his bat to the man in the hat. Goodman was larger and fatter, and the man dropped to one knee, drawing his sword enough so that the butt of the hilt slammed right into Goodman's stomach. Goodman stumbled back and dropped like a sack of grain. The young man who had held Bingley up against the wall for Graves now rushed the warrior but was stopped by a clog shoe to the head, tossed with enough force to knock him aside long enough for the second stranger to leap down and kick out his legs before retrieving his lost shoe. He drew his long, curved blade. "*Ikoo! Tatakau!!*" (Come on! Hit me!) he said to Mr. Graves, who now realized he was facing two men armed with long swords, looking quite ready to swing them, the blade in his hand. Beside him, another thug emerged from the shadows with a gun.

"He's got a—" but before Bingley could say "pistol," Graves grabbed him and slammed him against the wall, holding a knife up to his throat. Bingley felt a greater pain when his head hit the wall than from the knife against his throat, and for a moment his world was a burst of colors before his eyes, then returned to a fuzzy version of the man in front of him.

The young thug did not have time to fire his pistol, though; as he gripped his neck in pain, out shot a spray of blood. Neither of the attackers had moved; he dropped to his knees, the flicker of an edged coin highlighted in the torchlight. The woman, previously ignored, stepped forward with a stack of them, tossing one up and down in her palm menacingly at another member of the mob.

"Don't yeh dare," Graves said, his threat on Bingley's person obvious enough. The proximity of the knife to Bingley's throat was dangerous. He was afraid to swallow.

"Threaten my brother-in-law again," said the first man, lifting his hat so they could meet eyes, "and there's no way you'll get out of here alive. In fact, there's little chance of that as it is."

Graves's response was to toss Bingley at the trio that had disabled his gang in seconds. At least, that was the last thing Bingley remembered before he hit the ground.

"Mr. Bingley?" the voice repeated. "Oh, I think he's coming around."

"Me-ester Binguri," said the man with a heavy foreign accent.

"Will he be all right?" said the female voice. Different accent, much better English. European?

"I don't know. I'm not the doctor."

"*Kareshini osake o iidaroo*." (He looks like he needs a drink.)

"He probably needs a doctor, Mugin."

That voice—undeniably recognizable—was right. Bingley was in some pain from being assaulted and then shoved unceremoniously to the ground. At least his throat hadn't been seriously cut. He opened his eyes to the spectators, not quite sure of his perspective, but felt as though he was against an uneven brick wall. Above him, Town's night sky, buildings to his left and right, from what he could see over the ledge, smaller than he remembered. Wait, was he on a roof? Was that where they were hiding? He noticed the man on stilts was sitting, huffing, like he had overdone himself, perhaps by carrying him. He was foreign, strange—but the light was poor.

"Welcome back to the world of the living, Mr. Bingley."

He doubted it no longer. "Brian Maddox." All of his immediate questions did not spring to his lips, maybe because he was exhausted, even though *he* hadn't been the one fighting. Even in the dim light, the sight of Brian Maddox wearing a lampshade for a hat and a silk bathrobe for a shirt was bizarre enough to jolt him a bit. "Where—"

"*Nippon*, Japan," Brian said, "Before that, the *Rus*. I do apologize for my delayed correspondence. I did make every attempt to contact Danny, but it seems he took matters into his own hands while I was occupied elsewhere." He held out his hand, and the woman walked up to him, wearing the most luxurious and beautifully patterned silk bed robe Bingley had ever seen, tied tightly by a thick sash and a cord. "Excuse my manners. Mr. Bingley, this is my wife, Princess Nadezhda Maddox. Mrs. Maddox, this is my brother's wife's brother."

She curtseyed to him. "Mister Bingley."

"Apologies for not—receiving you properly," Bingley said, his voice dragging a bit, "but where in the hell am I?"

"Some rooftop. I hope the family below doesn't mind the racket. We needed a rest. It's still a bit of a ways to the West End. Speaking of which—Mugin?"

"*Nani?*" said the squatting man. Now that Bingley's vision was adjusting to the light, he could see that the man, wearing only a striped shirt, some sort of loose breeches, and an blue coat, was definitely some kind of Indian or Oriental.

"Are you ready to go?"

"*Sa! Igirisuwa konomama tsukareta shiranakatta!*" (Ach, I didn't know England was going to be so back breaking.) Mugin said, standing up and stretching his back. "We take you, Binguri-san."

"Wait, I—" but before he knew it, he was hoisted onto Mugin's back.

"*Dokoni itteirundesuka?*" (Where are we going?)

"Follow me. Though I've never gone this way before," Brian said with a smile and leapt over the edge, onto the roof next door. Mrs. Maddox—*Princess* Maddox—and Mugin followed him with no hesitation. If the idea of jumping about the rooftops of Town in sandals bothered anyone other than Bingley himself, who was carried, they said not a word.

BRIAN'S STORY, PART 1

NO GOOD AT BEING an English gentleman, Brian Maddox decided to be a Hungarian one.

It was late fall of 1807 when he made his way across Austria, far enough south to miss the worst of the early snows and into the hills of Transylvania. His Romanian was passable enough to explain to the border guards of the count's lands who he was. They did seem a bit surprised to see him, but his future father-in-law greeted him warmly enough.

He knew better than to ask to see Nadezhda directly, despite her being the sole reason for his return. The wedding was coming up soon, and his understanding of court culture was lacking, so foreign to him despite his wide travels. Vlad's court seemed to truly be in the dark ages, in stark contrast to even his closest neighbors and relatives, who were quicker to adopt the fashionable European culture of the Enlightenment. Brian could barely make conversation with his chief servant.

"She is very beautiful," said the man. There were an awful lot of reassurances going around. Eventually, mainly from inflection, he was able to discern that he had not been the first suitor to run. He was actually the only one who came back. It bestowed on him an appropriate level of caution. Did she have a tail? Was she a witch? Or was it merely the overbearing count? Brian had to find out and quickly.

The wedding was set for barely more than a month away. The first week he did not see his intended at all and used what little free time he had to perfect his language skills to the local brogue. Hungarian nobility spoke French as was fashionable, with some German and Hungarian, but these were the backwoods of Transylvania, on the very edge of the traditional Hungarian Empire, and the count was a very traditional man. He liked to think of himself as a man of the people despite being quite the opposite, so he spoke Romanian, like the peasants who toiled on his land.

Most of Brian's evenings were spent in long banquets, where he had more time to practice, or would have if the local spirits didn't go right to his head despite what he thought was an impressive tolerance. After the first few nights, before he learned to quietly water down his mug, he emerged with a horrible headache and not much appreciation for the sunlight or anyone who would bother him. There were instructions from what was apparently his manservant, Andrei, on how to dress and how to act, if said in a very polite way. He gave up his cravat but held fast on growing a beard, even if he did allow his sideburns to be a bit wider than permissive in proper society. He wouldn't even give in to the current trend of goatees, preferring a soft, clean face.

Finally, he saw Nadezhda when she was presented to the feast table. She was bejeweled and wearing a complex embroidered gown. Brian could see her beautiful face and her fine form, but he wondered what her hair would look like out from under the silk headdress. She had not changed from their parting in the spring. She smiled nervously to him as she bowed, and he returned it, though he did not know if she saw it. He hoped she did.

That night, after he was permitted to escape the long hours of feasting and storytelling, he sat down with a glass of imported wine in his chambers, and set concerns and fears of his impending marriage aside long enough to ask Andrei when in the hell he was going to see Nadezhda in some kind of privacy. He might have phrased it differently, he might not. All he heard through the pounding in his ears was that it would be arranged.

In fact, it was that very night. He was escorted to a balcony, which was sheltered enough so that it was not terribly cold. On the other side of the open doorway were guards and—he had no doubt—listening people, but she was standing there, and that was enough. "Your Highness," he bowed an Englishman's bow. He would take her hand only if she offered it, which she did not, clamping them together somewhat nervously. She was covered, but less ostentatiously dressed, and it occurred to him that he had never seen her hair. If she was like her father, it was probably black. He found himself imagining what it would be like to run his fingers through it, as she curtseyed to him.

"You asked to speak with me?" she said.

"I wanted to speak with you," Brian said. "I've... not seen you in a while."

"You saw me this evening."

"I mean, privately. Since that night."

"You remember it?"

"Every word."

To this, she was startled enough to have no immediate response. He knew he was not being misinterpreted, but he had no idea of her feelings for him, if there were any. Surely, he would be a fool to think she had fallen for some Englishman with barely a grasp of her native tongue in two meetings, only one of them with any shred of privacy. But he wondered all the same. She was clearly a little afraid, maybe not of him, maybe only of the situation. He took that comfort. He spoke softly, hopefully beyond anyone's abilities to listen, "I returned only for you, Your Highness."

He could not tell from her expression the depths or the nature of her reaction, though there was one. He would give anything for the ability to read her better at that moment, something no tutor could impart. "But I have not been a proper gentleman," he said, to fill the awkward silence, "and asked how you have been, my lady."

"I have been well. I was a bit—surprised at your return."

"Everyone was." He let his hand stray to the balcony rim, which was closer to her hand, without touching it. "Were you happy at the news?" He shook his head. "I apologize. That was too personal a question. My lady, you do not have to answer."

"But you wish to know it?"

With as much muting of his emotion as he could muster, he replied, "Yes."

"I was." And then, when her apparent embarrassment passed, she smiled, but quickly covered her face to hide it.

"Oh, please don't," he whispered. "I so wish to see you smile." This, of course, had that precise effect, and she pulled her hand away. "There." All of his concerns, for the moment, were dashed as he admitted to himself that he was completely and utterly in love.

Their courtship period—which only Brian, in his mind, referred to as such—was slow and complex despite the wedding hovering over him, because he did not want to overstep his bounds. He was advised not to show too much interest in his bride. This he found ironic and somewhat stupid, but he would not stir the pot at this point, even though her father treated him with excitement at their upcoming nuptials as the next great step in the long family history. Although he did see her increasingly at meals, it was never together and they exchanged words only on that balcony and in other places where it was arranged for them. He did not touch her, even to hold her hand or kiss the ring, because he did not know what liberties he was allowed and didn't feel inclined to ask her.

It was the shy Nadezhda who warned him, "Do not trust your servants. Do not trust anyone."

With an obvious smile on his face, Brian said, "Should I trust you?"

"Perhaps," she said. Her shell of shyness was nearly impossible to penetrate, and he found it easier to lead her and let her respond in kind.

Between her hints and his improved language skills, he was beginning to understand the situation a bit better. Her father, the count, lacked a certain social ability to get along well with his neighbors. During his reign, his actions had ensured that they were now all thoroughly aligned against him. They would not risk open warfare, but they would not provide him with a suitable candidate for a husband for his only daughter. So he had to look elsewhere, to the point of winning the hapless Brian Maddox in a bet.

"Brian," Nadezhda said, after many insistences that she call him that, "you should consider your situation."

"I don't understand."

"You—" She stopped and, to his surprise, placed a tense but tender hand on his arm, lightly brushing against his clothing. "There will be expectations of you."

"I know. Your father has made no secret that I must produce an heir."

She shook her head. She seemed to be trembling and turned away from him. Incited by her touch, and out of the concern for her change in temperament, he lightly chanced a grazing of his hand against the outer fabric of her long headscarf. "What? You can tell me."

"I have not told… anyone. Except my father, who will not listen to reason. You will keep it a secret?"

"Of course."

She turned back to him. "You should run, Herr Maddox."

"What?"

"You should run away and never look back. It is the safest thing for you."

"My lady," Brian said, "I have run from many obligations in my life. I decided long ago that this will not be one of them." He moved closer than he ever had dared. "I love you."

"I know." She tried to hide her soft expression in her hands again. "Brian, I don't think I can bear children."

"It frightens you?"

"No. But—do not ask for specifics, but the midwife believes it, and I would not have you bind yourself to me without knowing the truth. If you marry me, your situation will be very desperate."

It took a second for him to comprehend. "But it is not a sure thing."

"I suppose not. But my father is always unreasonable."

It did not take a vivid imagination to conjure up an image of what would happen to him if he ever displeased the count. But maybe his marriage would soften his father-in-law? If he made Nadezhda truly happy? "I am willing to take a gamble. After all, gambling landed me in this situation, and I find it extremely pleasurable. So—you've never told this to another suitor?"

"No," she said. "I never cared for the other ones."

He colored at her implication.

By some stupid baronial custom, Brian did not see his bride for a week up to the marriage. He passed his available hours writing furiously to his brother, expressing none of the concerns surrounding his marriage and all of the joy. He loved Nadezhda. He could not, for a second, consider running away and not taking her as his wife for as long as he should live—however short that would be. Who knew, maybe she could conceive. It had certainly never been put to the test. When they explained (in detail) his wedding night and the presentation of the sheets, he colored and would have run back to his room if he hadn't been standing in front of the count at the time.

He had one other, entirely unexpected, horror to endure. A traditional stag party in England, among friends, might have involved some heavy drinking of whiskey and some tales that were not told often outside of such gatherings, but here it was an entirely different matter. First, he had no friends and dearly missed his brother and sister-in-law. Second, the drinking was much heavier, and he had to work very, very hard to keep himself out of the cups. Third, women were invited. Or, appropriately, women of a certain profession (the oldest) were invited, or paid to come and dance. He sat on a pillow next to the count, who slapped him so heavily on the back that it hurt and made him spill some of his mead or vodka or whatever it was, and was told strongly and in no uncertain terms to pick one of them. Brian excused himself momentarily, and his servant Andrei must have noticed the color leave his face, because the man explained his duties to him politely enough but made it clear that it was a duty expected of him and he could not refuse.

He was not left to contemplate the situation very long before the matter was forced upon him. He helplessly selected a girl in a red costume and was ushered into another room where he proceeded to tell her that for both of their sakes she must act accordingly to satisfy the count, and they spent the next half hour exchanging childhood stories.

If there was one thing Brian Maddox was sure he would never attend, much less be a part of, it was a royal wedding. How luck and fate had brought him here, he had no concept. The weight of the crown on his head was enough to sink him into reality. He was His Highness, Brian of Transylvania. The title wasn't real in the sense that he could use it in any kind of court. The family bought the title at some point in history, and though it was nothing more than a family custom, no one ever called Princess Nadezhda anything but Her Highness (in Romanian), and they would address Brian the same way. Only the velvet beneath the crown made it comfortable on his head, and only seeing a similarly attired Nadezhda beside him helped him through a ceremony he did not even begin to understand. His only pain was with the absence of his brother and sister-in-law, and wishing they could be there at this strange ceremony.

But he put those feelings aside soon enough. Nadezhda was his. His wife... He instantly felt a certain possessiveness towards her. This was not a woman he was courting. This was his wife, his other half, the person he would, hopefully, share the rest of his life with. He wondered if the Catholic priest had said something to that effect.

He was not invited to the wedding dinner. Instead he took a small meal in his chambers and was invited back to the crowd when his duties were performed, as disgusting a notion as that was. That he had to present proof—he shook his head. Well, he would, and that would be the end of it. As his gold chain and crown and outer layer were removed, he took a glass of wine and said a prayer in English to help him to be a good husband, a good person, maybe even a good father... if it was possible.

With utter silence he was ushered into the princess's chambers. To his horror, his wife was stark naked on her bed, as if all he had to do was... No, as appealing as that was, the terrified look on her face was enough to stop him cold. He yelled angrily at the servants to leave them be and shut the door firmly behind them.

"Nadezhda," he said, changing the tone of his voice as he approached her. "You're shivering." He grabbed her discarded robe and put it over her. She must have been freezing. "Here."

"Am I—so terrible to you?"

She was shaking. She did not shy away from his touch, but it was obvious that she did so by fighting her own instincts. Clearly, they had told her something terrible. Not altogether different from what they told maidens in England, probably, which he always thought was outright ridiculous. He finally swallowed and replied, "No. God, no." He sat down next to her, off the end of the bed, holding her hand and nothing else. "Nady, you have no reason to be frightened, whatever they told you." She had, he could now see, long black hair, still tied up, not in the English way, but in many braids. It was silky and beautiful in the lamplight. "I love you."

"But we have to—"

"It's not so terrible," he said. "Trust me. Do you trust me? Of course not, you have no reason to trust me, the silly Englishman. But I am very much in love with you." He held her covering up when she tried to take it down. "No. We have time." He was expected back eventually, but not so quickly. Besides, at this point, he didn't really care what the count thought. "May I see your hair?"

She looked at him blankly.

"I've never seen it before," he said. "Not—down. Or at all. Please?"

She obliged him, of course, un-twirling her long braids of beautiful jet hair that came down past her shoulder blades. He sat there entranced until she was finished, not saying a word as he cupped her chin and kissed her on the side of her head. "I love you."

"I trust you," she said at last. "I do."

"You shouldn't, you know. You shouldn't trust anyone," he said, teasing her, and she laughed. He saw some of the tension leave with the sound of it. "Except maybe me. My Nadezhda." He kissed her again, softly, testing it on her cheek. She did not turn away, but she tightened up. "I suppose they told you some horrible nonsense about marital relations, or relations with

someone other than me. I suppose, I'm not so impressive, but—"
But he couldn't think of a way to end the sentence. I'm experienced. And I love you so very, very much, and I want you to want me as badly as I want you. "Now I'm a little frightened."

"Of what?" she said.

"I—I've never been with a maiden. And certainly, I've never been with a wife," he smiled. "I am, despite all of this Your Highness nonsense, an English gentleman who feels a responsibility to make his wife happy in his conduct."

"You must have a lovely country."

"I am painting a very rosy picture, aren't I?" Brian said. "No, it's a country like any other, but I was raised with morals. I didn't always appreciate them or follow them, but I can try now."

"I heard you are nobility."

"Descended from. But that doesn't mean you're noble. My brother on the other hand is so stupidly noble it's surprising he hasn't gotten himself killed yet."

"You miss him?" she said, taking his hand. She must have been reading his facial expressions.

"Yes. But perhaps one day, we will invite him or visit him. He has a wife and two children, Frederick and Emily. We should have portraits done of us in that royal garb and send it to England. He'll get a good laugh at that."

"Why?"

"Because I'm the scoundrel in the family," he said. "I don't deserve any of this. I don't deserve to be this happy."

She leaned against him, which was indeed making him very happy. "Why do you always talk like that?"

"Because it's true. Your husband was a gambler, a man of vices and a hunted man." Brian situated himself better on the pillows next to her, putting his feet up. "When I was eighteen, my father died. We were on bad terms with my uncle, who is the older brother and therefore inherited the earldom of Maddox, so we had no support. I was left to raise my brother Daniel, who was much younger than I, and to manage our fortune. I wasn't ready for it. I couldn't be a father to my brother. I wanted to go to University and have fun and drink. So I managed for a few years, and then I started indulging myself. While my brother was in school, I gambled away our entire fortune. I took out loans to get him his license so he might be a doctor and have a living, and then I ran from my creditors. I traveled all of Europe, abandoning my brother and my responsibilities. Then when I returned, I betrayed him to someone I held a debt to, and that man might have murdered him if he hadn't been so good at getting away. I didn't know that, but I shouldn't have trusted the man, nonetheless." He pulled back his tunic. "The scar, from where I was stabbed."

"By your brother?"

"Good heavens, no. Danny would never stab me. By the man who meant to stab him. I was in the way. Now I am a cripple because of it, because even Danny couldn't fix me, and he is brilliant at his profession. He serves the Prince Regent, who is essentially our king. Then I ran again, because no one seemed to want me around—and for good reason—and then I met your father. And you." He kissed the hand he was holding. "Then my life changed. Who knows, you may have made me a good man."

"May I see?" Nadezhda said, reaching towards the scar. "I mean, may I touch—?"

"Of course," he said, and removed his shirt entirely. He wasn't covered in scars, but he had a few of them, certainly, and her caressing of him was… making it very hard for him to go this slowly. "I'll tell you the stories, if you like. Behind them."

She giggled and pressed on the line on the left side of his belly. "Tell me."

"Oh God, that's not a good one to start on. A woman did that to me, a girl in Rome, a… woman of a certain profession. It was over money from a certain—service rendered. I thought it was rendered poorly; she didn't. So we had an argument. That's why I'll never go back to Rome, thank you very much. And stop that, it tickles," he said. "Or continue. Whatever you like, Your Highness. I am at your mercy."

"Hardly!"

"A husband is always at his wife's mercy. You should see the leash Mrs. Maddox leads my brother around with," he said, and it took her a moment to realize he wasn't being literal. "May I kiss you?"

"You do not have to ask. Your Highness."

This was not the same type of kiss. It was the first time he had ever truly kissed her fully, and it was incredible. There was very little sense left in him to keep himself together. *Go slow. You have all night.* But he didn't want to take all night, not now, when she seemed comfortable with him, or at least the idea of him.

He let his hand slide down her shoulder and arm, taking the fabric down with it, and she didn't seem to mind. Certainly, it would be hard for her to talk with her mouth otherwise engaged. A woman's body was something to listen to, like an instrument, and there was no outright rejection, just trepidation. No man had touched her like this, he had no doubt. He had no reason to ask. "May I—?" he left it an open question. Would she give him the leniency to explore? She nodded and gave a little gasp when he did. He halted with one hand in a very circumspect place.

"Did I tell you to stop?"

He raised a very surprised eyebrow. "You minx."

His remaining clothes seemed to come off naturally. She was slowly stripping away all of his mental fortitude as well. She was his wife. He had to take her. He had to do that awful thing that would only hurt once, he promised. He kissed her; he lost his head and couldn't speak very much. His senses were gone and didn't return until he was, at least temporarily, satiated, and rolled over in a huffing heap.

"That—was it?"

Brian turned to his wife. "I'm a bit insulted, my lady, by your implication."

"I mean—that was the great pain?" she said. He wasn't mistaken about the whole incident and took great care to wipe up on the stupid ceremonial sheet. "I've had bruises that felt worse than that!"

He laughed and fell onto her. "You're quite a woman," he said.

The doors to the princess's chambers remained locked for the rest of the night and most of the next day.

For the first few months, there was little that could irk Brian out of his marital bliss. He was given very few baronial responsibilities, as his father-in-law seemed to regard him as more of a breeding implement than the future count, but he was required to accompany them for dinners and hunting parties. He had, by regulation, tried to sleep separately from his wife. This regulation was regularly broken, and no one said a word, though he had no doubt that everyone knew that one or another was sneaking off at all hours and not returning after the allotted time. Fine by him. He was the prince now. The only one who could overrule him was the count, who seemed to have no issue with his new son's apparent virility.

One other habit did not waver, which was to write to his brother. He was besotted, and he knew his letters were probably dreadful because of it, but he cared very little. The point was, he was writing to Danny, and it made him feel less lonely, when he did feel lonely, at least for his brother and his extended family.

He did leave out any anxieties he had, and there were few, until the third month. He was barred from Nadezhda's chambers by her maid, who would not take any reasoning for quite a while before she gave in to his demanding stare and allowed him entrance. He found her not in her bed but hunched over on a bench, weeping and clutching her stomach, surrounded by servants who looked very upset by his intrusion.

He ignored them all. "Nadezhda—" He ran to her side but was bodily stopped by an older woman.

"Please, Your Highness," she said. "This is a woman's business."

"This is my wife's business! Will you not allow me to comfort her?" he shouted, and Nadezhda tried to wave him off as he took a seat beside her and kissed her on the forehead. "Nady. Tell me what is wrong."

"Nothing is wrong," said the woman. "This is quite normal for her. It is her affliction, and you have no business in it."

"And who are you to say that?" he said, putting an arm around his shivering wife.

"The midwife, Your Highness. Please. She has dealt with this for years."

It took a moment, but slowly it came together for him. It occurred to Brian that for not a single night had he been separated from her, when he should have been by basic necessity for a few days a month at the very least. He knew that much—and much more—about feminine biology. Though many women were told they were ill during this period and had some pain, it was nothing like this, something manifesting like a physical ailment. There was something irregular about her system, and he was damned that he did not know what it was. This was what she had spoken of before their marriage. But she did bleed, so maybe she could conceive.

"Nady," he whispered in her ear. "Do you want me to go or stay with you? I will do as you wish, but I wish very much to stay and help you."

"You cannot help me," she whimpered. "No one can help me."

"I will search the ends of the earth and speak to every doctor, but until then I will not be satisfied that no one can help you," he said, and kissed her on the cheek. "Do you wish me gone now?"

Her face was hard to see with her hair so loose and so bent over, but she did manage to whisper back, "No."

He kept vigil with her through three horrible days of pain. When she was too tired to speak, his mind wandered to all the possibilities. She was not undeveloped, so perhaps she could conceive, perhaps it would be the best thing for her. This was what she had dealt with since the end of her girlhood? And yet, he could not bring himself to write to his brother. First, Daniel Maddox was too proper and modest to be any sort of expert on woman's matters, something he was forced on many occasions to repeat. He could do something if there was a problem during childbirth, but that was the extent of his knowledge. Second, Brian could not bring himself to break the illusion that all was well. He was, when she recovered, very happy with her, and did not for a moment regret his choice to marry her. What he could do—and what her father did not seem to have the sense to do—was demand, quite adamantly, that a decent doctor be sent to examine her.

A man did arrive from Russia. Brian had said France, but at the moment, he settled and endured the harsh looks from his father-in-law when he allowed Dr. Petronov into the princess's chambers. In fact, he held her hand for the inspection, which was apparently unpleasant. The doctor, who spoke no Romanian, had to speak through a translator to Brian, whose Russian was equally bad, but essentially the conclusion was reached that while she was probably not totally and utterly incapable of conceiving, it was a highly unlikely prospect, and there was no way to be sure.

Brian called for another doctor. This one came from Prussia, looked utterly confused at the whole matter, and made the graver conclusion that she could not conceive, and in fact, would not live a normal lifetime. Brian, out of sheer mental necessity, had to dismiss the latter idea as too radical of a pronouncement.

The count took the news dismissively. He wanted to hear nothing of his daughter's failings, nor would he hear of calling a French doctor. He was not endeared to the young upstart Napoleon. Brian, feeling helpless, resolved that if his wife had a very narrow and unknown time for conception, he would do his best to happen upon it by sheer persistence. Nadezhda, no longer the terrified girl he had found on their wedding night, seemed happy with at least that prospect. She was, in front of her father, still the same little girl, but her mood changed behind closed doors, and she opened up to Brian. Her life was beyond sheltered, her only activities beyond the castle walls being the hunt, and she wanted to hear all of his wild tales. Inside her chamber or his, behind closed doors, there was total bliss.

Two years came and went, and he helped her through seven more devastating "afflictions." He was now established in the palace, and though his position carried weight with everyone but the count, his father-in-law did not waver in his blind insistence on his daughter's health and his son's failures—though certainly, there was enough palace talk to know his son was particularly prestigious in the area of being with his wife.

On the anniversary of their marriage, when he much preferred to dine privately with Nadezhda, Brian was called to a hunting expedition. The cold and snow did not bother the locals at all, and he had adjusted to it as well, though he still stubbornly insisted on being clean-shaven, and had to cover his face. It was there, when they were mainly alone, that the count clamped a hand on Brian's well-covered shoulder and said, "Three months."

"Excuse me, my lord?"

"You have three months." He gave him a shove that could be interpreted as friendly or not. Brian did not have to question what the answer to "Or?" was.

Returning, he did not join them for dinner. He took a glass of wine in his room before joining his wife in her chambers, dismissing the servants but this time taking extra care, for he was sure they had their looking-holes and places where they could hear. As he climbed into bed with her, he pulled the covers over their heads and whispered what her father had said.

"You have to go," she said.

"I know," Brian said. "Immediately, preferably. But I cannot leave you."

"I will be fine."

"Nady," he said, "you are my wife, and will be until the day I die. So either I stay and have my head on a spike, or you go with me, because you cannot be with another man. Surely, your father has one in mind or will find one." He ran his hand along her hip. "You are my wife. But the question remains— would you put your life in danger for me by leaving? It would be very dangerous."

"It would be dangerous for me to stay," she said. "I'd end up like my mother, after all."

His blank look must have asked for more.

"Brian," she whispered. "My mother did not die in child-birth. He had my mother killed because she could not produce a son."

She said it so matter-of-factly, as if it was nothing. The silence pervaded them for some time before he stammered out, "He—he killed your mother?"

"Yes."

"A-and you don't despise him?"

"I don't remember it. I was too young, and he's taken down all of her portraits. Besides, he is my father. He can do what he likes."

Brian grasped her hand very tightly. "No, he cannot. Nady, you must go with me."

"What will he think?"

"I don't care what he thinks. I hope he goes mad with rage and falls on his own sword," he said. "It is not in question. You are going with me."

"If you go alone, he might decide not to chase—"

"No," he said, exasperated. "I will hear no more of it. I will not abandon you to him, and I cannot stay, for it is basically the same thing. So I am going, and you are going with me." He lowered his tone again. "Tomorrow."

"Tomorrow!"

"I am experienced at escaping. It must be tomorrow. Hopefully, I can take your dowry with me, as is my right anyway, and we will have some money for the road. We cannot go west, because he will expect it, because England is west. We must go to the Russias. You speak Russian and I will learn. It will be very dangerous, but it is weighing one danger against the other." He kissed her. "Say nothing of this to anyone."

"Then how will you get my dowry? Do you trust your servants?"

He frowned. "No."

"Well, I trust Anya, my maid. If I give her your keys, she can get access to the vault without suspicion, perhaps, and take what she can." She cupped his cheek. "I have known her almost all of my life, Brian. If there is anyone here I would trust beyond you, it is her." She pulled away. "But… she will be questioned, when it is obvious we are gone."

"Then don't tell her in which direction we are going. Don't tell her anything unnecessary, and she will have nothing to tell. Give her money to run, if you want her to live," he said. "We will go to St. Petersburg or something. It depends on the weather. But we will manage." *Somehow.* "Are you scared?"

"Why do you ask?"

"Because," he said, "I am, but not enough to prevent me from doing this. My life is nothing without you, so you are my only concern."

"Then, we will be a little scared together, but we will spread it out," she said, and hugged him close. They fell asleep that way, after a long night where talk was not needed, but touch was.

The next evening, they took two horses, an assortment of as many weapons as Brian could carry, and a bag containing half of the barony's treasury, and they left.

Chapter 22

A Man Walks into a Bar...

JANE BINGLEY HAD BEEN raised to expect hardship in her life. Her life, for the most part, had been a pleasant surprise. She was quite happily married to a man of no small means who loved her, and she had four adorable children. Her sisters seemed to have had some, if not as much, luck as she in finding mates or a life that made them content. It was sad enough for Lydia to lose her husband while she had two children to raise. In rare moments of perfect honesty with herself, Jane would admit that perhaps Wickham was the easiest death she could have been asked to deal with. But Mr. Darcy was another story entirely. Lizzy loved him, her husband treasured him as a great friend, he was uncle to her children, and she admired him despite all that he put Lizzy through. His death would be unfathomable, with Geoffrey so young—or at all, really. He had lived through so much, why not continue? Dr. Maddox was loved by everyone, never said an unkind word about anyone. He was, somehow, the perfect husband for the former Caroline Bingley, who was now a reasonable companion, even a friend. Their lives were all so locked together in an intricate web of relatives by blood and marriage that it could not stand another hole. To lose two of them at once because of some miscommunication overseas—that was unfathomable.

Despite the weight removed from her shoulders with Lizzy's letter earlier that day, the evening brought an ominous tone she could not shake. Then a flustered Brian Maddox appearing at her door, bearing his mysterious princess bride and some kind of Oriental guard, was no consolation. They had apparently, quite innocently, arrived from the Japans that evening, gone straight to the Maddox townhouse (with no knowledge of the events occurring because of them—they had been at sea for months!), only to find it closed down in the absence of both mistress and master. The Mr. Maddox who arrived at the Bingley house was distraught and would not entertain questions about his appearance until he heard *her* story about his brother and Mr. Darcy, which distressed him greatly as he repeated it back to his wife and servant in Oriental. He then inquired after Mr. Bingley, was alarmed, and said he would see that he was safe.

Jane did not go back to sleep when the three guests left, despite the hour. There was no chance of that now. She did not wake the Hursts, who normally slept like the dead, and she prayed Edmund and Sarah would sleep through the night and not wake their siblings and cousins.

She did go upstairs, where her lady-maid was waiting, and was quickly dressed so she could properly go downstairs and sit before the roaring fire. She tried pacing but eventually settled in the armchair, occasionally glancing at the clock. She could not reasonably expect them back so soon if they were walking there, which they appeared to be doing. It was the docks, after all.

"Mama?"

Stirred from her half-slumber, she opened her eyes to little Georgiana standing before her, dressed in her nightclothes.

"Georgie!" she said. "Did something wake you?"

Her daughter shook her head.

"You shouldn't be walking around without slippers. The floors are very cold, and you could get sick," Jane said. Georgie's response was to climb up into the armchair with her, wrapping herself with the edge of Jane's shawl. Now that she was so much older, it was becoming harder and harder to do this, and Georgie had always been so differing in mood anyway that Jane could not recall many incidents where her eldest daughter wanted to be held by her mother. Eliza was different, more physically demanding of affection. Georgiana said nothing, just nestled into her mother's side. Jane was tempted to ask her what was wrong, but she had no desire to get her daughter worked up when she didn't seem distressed, while Jane herself had her own fears to deal with.

There was no noise from Georgie. Jane was about to check if she was asleep, when the door burst open before the servant could open it. Brian Maddox entered, carrying Bingley in his arms, blood staining his clothing. "He'll be all right," he said in response to her gasp. He laid Charles down on the sofa. "Someone should look at his head, though. Not because he's dizzy. Just because he's Charles."

"Papa!"

"Georgie!" Jane said, covering her daughter's eyes. "He will be all right."

Sadly, Nurse was probably asleep. Brian turned to the woman who was his wife and said, "Can you take her into the next room?" He added in Romanian, "She is your niece. Her name is Georgiana."

"Yes," she said in accented English. She curtseyed to Jane. "I take Georgiana."

"Thank you," Jane said. "Georgie, this is Princess Nadezhda. Go with her for a while."

"Will Papa be okay?"

"Karega naoshitekureru dekiru to omoimasu," (I think I could patch him up) said the Oriental, who turned to the terrified, little redheaded girl before him. "He okay. Promise."

Nadezhda finally herded Georgiana into the next room, and Brian continued his conversation, *"Tashika ni?"* (Are you sure?)

"Nani, saki ni kowareta hone ga nakatta to omoimasuka? Kimi, ude o kowattemiru, sukideshouka?" (What, like I've never had a broken limb before? Try breaking your own arm; would you like it?)

"Please!" Jane said, noticing her husband was returning to consciousness. "Will someone tell me what is going on?"

"Mugin says he's familiar with broken limbs." Bingley was still in a daze. Brian said, "He's just been roughed up is all."

An exhausted Charles simply put his head back on the pillow Jane put under his head. He needed to stay still, while his manservant went to seeing to his comfort. Charles opened his hazy eyes once more at the crowd of people standing over him. "Mr. Maddox?"

Brian knelt beside him, putting a hand on his shoulder. "You just rest, Mr. Bingley. When you've regained your health, I've a business proposition for you."

Georgiana was brought into the room. "Papa!"

"Georgie," he said, his speech slurred. "My little Georgie."

"Your father will be all right," Jane said, more sure of it now than she had been before. Georgiana kissed her father on the cheek; he was asleep before she left his side to go back upstairs.

Jane would not leave her husband, but they did move out of earshot as Brian briefly described what had happened. She sensed he was leaving out details, such as how blood got on his strange silk clothing, but the point was her husband was safe. Now there was the less immediate, but no less important, problem of the rest of the family stuck on the Continent.

"For that," Brian said, "we have a plan."

"Colonel Fitzwilliam," Darcy said, not attempting to rise from his armchair as Fitzwilliam entered Darcy's room at their current inn. Elizabeth had said that having him up and out of bed was an accomplishment unto itself. He had weathered the trip to the coast but still wasn't eating enough to regain his strength. His stomach was not used to the foods they were giving him.

"Darcy," Fitzwilliam said, "I suppose I should tell you, it's Lord Matlock now, but I tend to go with Lord Richard. You may call me whatever you like."

This seemed to be new information to Darcy, even if his reaction was muted. That or he hadn't absorbed it the first time he'd heard it. "I've missed much, it seems. I'm sorry for your loss."

"Thank you." He knew Darcy had lost something also, but it was internal. Darcy had gray hair coming in around his ears and in some of his hair. His cheeks were sunken, his expression scattered and distracted. "Anne is staying with her mother at Rosings. We intend to continue to care for her—with your permission."

It took Darcy a moment to process this. Fitzwilliam frowned; maybe he was bringing up too much at once. Darcy just looked away, "Of course." His mind seemed to wander towards less complex topics. "Where are we?"

"The Prussian coast. I'm trying to arrange passage, but it is very difficult, with all of the retreating soldiers."

Again, if Darcy knew anything about it, he gave no indication. "Dr. Maddox?"

"Another complication; he can't be moved easily. He has a bad fever. They're keeping him under with laudanum." He did not know if Darcy wanted to know more; he was very hard to read. "How are you feeling?"

"I want to go home."

It was simple enough. The frightening part was how desperately he said it. This man was not Darcy. He was a shell of Darcy. Austria had hollowed him out. "As soon as we can get a ship and move the doctor."

Darcy looked down, playing with his hands. He looked up at Fitzwilliam. "You can understand, maybe. You are a soldier. You have seen things."

"Yes." He'd actually only seen live combat once, in a pitched battle, but it was enough. "I've bought myself out now because of the earldom and Anne. I said, 'This is my last campaign.'"

Darcy smiled weakly at that but said nothing.

Fitzwilliam rose. "I'm off to look for a ship. Is there anything you require?"

"I'm well, thank you." It was a lie, but that was all right for the moment.

Fitzwilliam bowed and took his leave with a heavy heart. He knew Pemberley would restore Darcy, and his family, all of whom were now safe. He just knew it would take time and, until then, would be painful to watch. "Good day, Darcy."

"Good day, Richard."

Fitzwilliam left and shut the door. The inn housing them was small but clean and rather pleasant, except for the strain of war all around them and the harsh winter winds beginning to blow in. They were all tired; home was so close, and yet so far. Even Grégoire, first hesitant to leave, agreed to come and take the patron saint of Bavaria with him. "Well, he *is* from England," he finally rationalized, "originally."

"Stay with your saint and Darcy," Fitzwilliam said. "I'm off to the docks."

Grégoire bowed, fully understanding the gravity of his charge.

Lord Matlock was gone for quite a while, to the point where Elizabeth was worried that it would be another fruitless day of searching for a ship that was willing to take them home. Napoleon's blockage was quite strong on this side of it, and while they could go north into more favorable territory, it was obvious that Dr. Maddox could not, for the moment, be moved again. He tossed and turned in his sleep as Caroline put another cold cloth on his forehead.

"It will break," Darcy assured her. He had insisted on seeing Dr. Maddox. "The fever will break, and he will be fine."

Caroline tried to look assured but failed. Elizabeth passed Darcy off to Grégoire and had conference with Caroline in the other room. "We must do something."

"Agreed." Caroline looked especially tired from tending to her husband, who was getting worse, not better. "Perhaps the docks are the wrong place to look. We could at least ask around."

Since they knew Darcy would not accept the idea of them venturing out on their own, they did not tell him. They merely went down into the tavern beneath the inn, a seedy place that they had only walked through, having had their meals sent up. It was awful, but it was the best place in town. They had been here two weeks and not found anything better.

"Yer lookin' fer passage?" said the barkeep. Surprisingly, many people were also English, in the same proverbial boat or just current residents for one reason or another. "There's a cap'n over there." He pointed, a rather rude thing for him to do, but Elizabeth held her tongue as they looked around. The place was mostly empty. There was a French soldier splayed out on a couch in the corner by the door, smoking a long pipe. There were a few people playing cards, natives speaking German. And at one table, two men, who very much looked like sailors, were devouring a plate of unrecognizable food.

The ladies curtseyed. "Are you the captain?"

"Name's Jack," he said. "This here is Handy. Which 'e is," he said.

"My name is Mrs. Darcy, this is Mrs. Maddox," Elizabeth said as they semi-reluctantly seated themselves across from these unsavory-looking men. "We're looking for passage to England."

"I heard. You got that lord, been askin' around," Jack said.

"Yeh can't go to England," Handy said. "Boney's got ships attackin' the Grand Old Navy. They're holdin' up, but yeh gotta get across them. 'S dangerous."

"Please," Caroline said. "We must get to England. Name your price."

"And my reception when I return? Fer that I wouldn't take the royal treasury," Jack said. "But—we're all English. Let's not be unreasonable; 'haps there could be some 'greement—" And he slid his hand across the filthy table and over Elizabeth's.

"Sir!" She instantly tried to withdraw, but he held her hand fast. "Unhand me at once! You know very well my husband—"

"Isn't your husband laid up?" Handy said. He turned to Caroline. "And isn't yours Irish?"

"I am *not* Irish!" Caroline furtively looked around, but the few patrons of the bar didn't seem interested in what was going on in the corner. She wondered how far it would have to go before they did. When he reached for her, she slapped him, but it had little effect on such a burly man.

"Hey," said a voice from the other side of the room. It was the smoking soldier. "*Yameroo.*" (Hold it.)

"What? Hey, feller, stay outta this."

The man lazily got off the couch; his posture was all slack and unconcerned. As he emerged into the light of their table's candle, it became obvious from his expression that he meant business. He also had something strapped over his shoulder that could only be a weapon, probably a sword. He was wearing the long, blue overcoat of a soldier, but a brown tunic beneath. He seemed to be wearing wooden shoes with stilts, different from the Danish clog shoes. He was also wearing a French officer's hat, turned backwards, and it did not obscure his face, which was decidedly not European. He stared down Handy, the man who had tried to scare him off. "England. They go."

"What did I just say? Or do you even understand me?" Handy said. "This is just a business matter, and yeh're in hostile territory, so you might as well take a walk. That is, if you don't speak in clicks and whistles."

"*Kore de sugita.*" (I've had enough of this) he said, knowing that they would not have understood a word. "Leave them alone."

"Or what, Chinaman?"

It was faster than any possible reaction as the man pulled the long sword from his scabbard and swung it at Handy, who was only able to scream and tear himself back, clutching his severed limb as his hand and forearm dropped lifelessly to the ground. The Chinaman seemed unaffected by this but did not replace his sword, grabbing Jack and slamming his hand on the table with his own slender, tattooed arm. "Now." He held it so Jack could not escape as his partner thrashed about behind them and the few other patrons hid behind the bar. "I take finger. Count to three. *Ichi*—"

"Please, sir, I beg of you—"

"*Ni.*"

"All right! All right! Just—leave me in peace! I'll go!"

"Is shame," said the Oriental, and with only a hold on Jack's hand, hurled him across the room to join his severed partner. "Go."

They did. Following them were the rest of the patrons. The Chinaman turned to the two women, horrified at the bloodshed that they had just seen, and very aware that if Jack and Handy had been at his mercy, so would they. He put his sword on the table. "Madokusu-san?"

"I am Mrs. Maddox," Caroline's voice was trembling as she unconsciously linked arms with Elizabeth.

He bowed, and pointed to Elizabeth, "Darushi-san?"

"I am Mrs. Elizabeth Darcy." She rose and curtseyed to him. "Are you looking for us?"

"Madokusu-san and Nadi-sama send me. You go to England?"

"Yes. We were trying to arrange it—"

"He arrives. Ship." He looked out the window. "Soon."

"We'd best leave, anyway," Caroline said. "After all the carnage you've caused, Chinaman."

"Mugin," he said. "No Chinaman. *Nippon*."

"I'm afraid we do not fully comprehend you," said Elizabeth, "but our husbands are upstairs, if you would follow."

"*Hai*." He put his blade back in the scabbard and bowed to them.

As they climbed the stairs, they could hear the clonking of his wooden shoes following behind as Caroline whispered, "Why are we listening to him?"

"Because I'd rather listen to him than lose my arm!" Elizabeth replied and opened the door to their room.

Darcy was in the armchair. He rose with his cane at the entrance of his wife. "Elizabeth. Mrs. Maddox—" and then he caught sight of the very angry and dangerous-looking person following them. "Sir?"

"This is—I have no idea," Elizabeth shrugged, "but he just saved our lives, if in a very gruesome way."

Darcy did not seem to have the energy to ask for the details. "Sir," he said, with a very small and stiff bow, "I am indebted to you."

"Please, don't strain yourself," his brother pleaded beside him. "Sir, we are grateful."

The man shrugged it off. "Go to England." He pointed to the doctor, still unconscious on his cot. "Madokusu-san?"

"Dr. Maddox," Elizabeth said. "He's very sick. We'll have to arrange—"

But the man slid past her, without any hesitation, picked up Dr. Maddox and slung him over his shoulders. "We go. *Junbi dekiteru?*" (Are you ready?)

"If I might inquire—"

"Darcy," Elizabeth said, grabbing his arm. "I think this man was sent by—Brian Maddox. I don't think we have the option of not listening to him."

For it seems they didn't, unless Caroline wanted to raise her pistol at the man carrying her husband over his shoulders with surprising ease for someone on clog stilts. Elizabeth gathered what little belongings they had and put her husband's arm over her shoulder, helping him follow the Oriental down the steps and out the door as Grégoire carried the box containing the reliquary.

It was a small town, and he seemed to know his way to the docks. Aside from their feet against the cobbled stone, they made very little noise. The water was in sight when they heard it.

"*Halte!*" It was an occupational guardsman, coming up with a lantern and a pistol.

"*Nani?*" said the Oriental.

Several others joined the guard, with bayonets.

"French," Darcy said. "We have to go, Chinaman."

"No China! *Nippon, gaijin!*" He slid the doctor's body off his shoulders and onto the ground. "I take care." He drew his very long sword.

"Darcy, don't let him," Elizabeth whispered. "He'll kill them!"

"*Nanika atta?*" (What's up?) came a voice from behind them. A lone figure standing in front of the entrance to the docks, wearing a lampshade for a helmet, from what it seemed in the light. "Mugin? *Daijoubu?*" (Are you okay?)

"*Saikou da!*" (Couldn't be better!)

"Remember what I said," the lampshaded figure said in the King's English. "No killing, Mugin."

"*Hai, hai, Madokusu-sama,*" said Mugin as he approached the three very confused soldiers. Actually, what he did was not so much approach as it was to duck off to the side, catch the tip of the raised bayonet between the grooves of his wooden shoes, and stamp his foot down, punching the man in the jaw as he went down. The leader fired a shot with his pistol, but Mugin was already gone from that spot, leaping over him and clocking him from behind with the butt of his sword. The third man might have reached him had the lampshade-hatted man not used that time to join him, drawing his sword and swiping it across the bayonet, slitting it in half. Between that and a hit in the head from a flying shoe, all three men had been sufficiently incapacitated in a few brief seconds.

"We should go," said the man, turning to his English spectators, "immediately. Nady has the ship waiting. But first, tell me—is my brother alive?"

"Barely," Darcy said. "And if it were not for your wild Oriental there and my own infirmity, I would sock you for it, Mr. Maddox."

"That I can't help," said Brian Maddox, lifting his hat, which seemed to be made of some kind of straw, so they could see his face. "What I can do is get you all to England—now. Mugin?"

"*Hai?*"

"We're leaving." He re-sheathed his sword—he had two of them—and attempted to pick up his fallen brother, but the doctor was much taller than him and therefore much heavier, and it was Mugin who took him fully.

There were screams and alarms in the distance. After all, they had caused a ruckus in this little town. They barely made it onto the ship where Fitzwilliam was waiting. "What—" but he got no response as they ran past, with Brian using his small blade to cut the ropes as they went. Shots were fired as the mainland disappeared behind them. The doctor was wrapped in a blanket by a woman in a silk robe and eased onto the deck floor. Mugin, completely relaxed by the whole series of events, merely kicked off his sandals and laid down against the side of the bow.

"Some—introductions are in order," said Brian Maddox, removing the hat and revealing an oddly shaved head, long in the back and tied up over the front. "Mr. Darcy, Mrs. Darcy, Mrs. Maddox, Colonel Fitzwilliam—this is my wife, Princess Nadezhda Maddox."

Upon closer inspection, in the light afforded to them by the full moon and the various lamps on the bow, they could see that despite her clothing, the woman beside him was dark, but certainly not Oriental. She was undeniably European, and curtseyed to them. "Pleased to meet you all." Her accent was heavy but certainly excusable. She whispered something in another language, presumably Romanian, to her husband, and he laughed.

"No, I assure you, she's not," he said and, without explanation, turned to Darcy. "You must sit down. You look horrible."

"Yes," he said. "Amazing what months in captivity by an Austrian count does to you."

Brian didn't flinch as he ordered the hired crew to settle Mr. Darcy down on something soft and attend to the ladies as well. It was only then that he fully turned his attentions to his brother, whom he could not wake. "Danny?"

"Laudanum," Caroline said, kneeling on the other side of her husband, "for his hand. And the fever."

"His hand?" With all of the bandages, it was obvious.

"If only we'd known, we wouldn't have—"

"I know," Brian said. "I know. I wrote every day I was still on the Continent, I swear. I sent couriers and couriers to say we were safe, but none of them reached you because of this... bloody embargo!" He fumbled in anger and tore at his hair, pulling down the carefully tied topknot. "Danny, I'm so sorry."

"How did you find us?" Darcy asked.

"Mrs. Bingley filled me in on the particulars upon our arrival from Japan."

"Japan?"

"Yes. We took the rather long way home to avoid my father-in-law. I think I'll be happy never to be on a ship again in my life."

"And your—I don't know his name, the servant."

"Mugin. He isn't a servant. He's just sort of... traveling with us," Brian said, sitting down beside his brother and resting his arms in the sleeves of his silk robe. He added, "And he can understand you, even if he pretends otherwise."

From his position, Mugin huffed, but said nothing.

BRIAN'S STORY, PART 2

1810

EMBARRASSINGLY FOR BRIAN'S SELF-ESTEEM, it was Nadezhda who was the chief reason they survived the first few weeks. She was a far better huntsman than he was, having been raised with it as a means of sport in her native homeland. She was also a better cook, so she was largely responsible for the food, and he only the fire, which she often chastised him for being too high or too low to bring the meat to a proper temperature. He had spent more years on the run, and in this he bested her, knowing how to hide (which they did from every passing authority figure, no matter from what country), how to make shelter, and how to treat burns from the frost on a particularly chilly evening. He was surprised that they made it to St. Petersburg without having to eat their horses, and still managing to stay off the well-traveled roads. There, he was mainly lost. He had been there once on an errand, and his Russian was poor, while hers was fluent.

"I don't know which one of us is being rescued," he said to her with a smile as they enjoyed what they considered the luxury of one-room lodging with a pipe stove. The bed wasn't very large, but neither of them minded. In fact, it helped pass the time.

Paper was expensive, but they had her dowry, and he slowly began to quietly convert small amounts over to Russian coinage, with multiple trips to multiple banks. He spent his spare time, while she shopped for food, writing to his brother, carefully not revealing their location but relaying the events of the past few months. He sent every letter with a prayer as it dropped into the iron box.

"If we stay here much longer, we'll have to winter here," he said.

Nadezhda curled up against him. "The sea is frozen by now. We can't sail to England."

"Maybe we could skate."

Nadezhda giggled.

He'd been frightened—she had never been more than a few miles from home, and here she was, fending largely for herself in a foreign country with a foreign husband. She never complained. "I am alone with you for the first time. No spies."

"That we know of."

She laughed again and kissed him.

Any degree of tranquility they enjoyed was shattered, but with enough time for them to make it out of St. Petersburg before it became too cold to do so. For this, Brian was grateful, but in the days to come, he would look back on their weeks in that tiny apartment with great affection, as if it had been their true honeymoon, drab as the surroundings were.

She came home that afternoon and said, "Someone called me by my name."

Brian sighed. They had to go, no matter how innocent it might have been. They could not go east, and they could not wait for the thaw of the sea to take them to safe harbor. They had to go west, into the terrible steppes of the Rus. They went south as well, where it was slightly warmer, but not enough. They went from village to village. Nadezhda's horse died, so they sold the meat and rode together on his. They both had a bad cough, and many times were tempted to stop and seek shelter in some village for the winter.

"We cannot go farther," he announced. They stopped at the next set of wooden buildings ahead on the road, now disappearing into the snow. With half of Count Vladimir's treasury in Russian rubles, strapped to a sack beneath his clothing, he took his wife's hand, and they walked into town. He tried his Russian, but their accents were too heavy. The men were wearing beaver fur hats and long black coats, and as far as he could tell, they were speaking some unknown dialect when they talked amongst each other. They all had beards; that was hardly unusual, but the way they talked—they did not speak directly to Nadezhda; however, they understood what she said and talked amongst themselves for some time.

"Here," he said in Russian, holding up some coins. They would probably not take paper money here. "Please. Help."

"We can't stay," Nadezhda whispered to him in Romanian.

"Surely if we give them enough—"

"We can't stay. It's dangerous."

"You are sure?"

"Brian, they're Jews."

He blinked. "So? I've met Jews before."

"You have?"

"People are people, Nady," he said, "people with warm houses. They could have horns for all I care." He smiled as one of them looked at him. "Hello."

The men were still talking when another one came out of one of the houses with a long beard, carrying his hat as he was clearly unprepared to be walking about outside, and began yelling at them. It was vaguely Russian, vaguely not. "Yiddish," Brian said at last.

"What?"

"A Yid. A Jew. They speak it in Germany."

Whatever they were saying, every man hushed when the old man approached them and started sermonizing. Eventually, they all scattered, and a woman emerged from behind him and waved Brian and Nadezhda in. "Thank you," Nadezhda said in Russian.

The old couple spoke fluent Russian, they soon discovered, and Brian understood more than he spoke, so he was able to follow the conversation fairly well. He offered money, but the man waved it away.

"We need shelter," Nadezhda said nervously. Aside from his black skullcap, the man did not have horns. "Please."

"You come from where?"

"St. Petersburg," Brian said.

Their host said no more about the obvious lie as his wife disappeared, reappearing with a steel tub of soup, which she portioned off for the four of them.

"I am Rabbi Shneur Zalman," the man said. "My wife, Sterna Zalman."

"Brian Maddox," he replied. "My wife, Nadezhda Maddox."

"You are English?" the rabbi said in perfect German.

Brian and Nadezhda exchanged nervous glances. "I am," Brian said in German. "My wife is not."

"She is Polish?"

"No," he knew he couldn't say she was German—her accent was too Baltic. "To the south."

The rabbi didn't inquire further, said something in Yiddish to himself, and began his soup. That was their signal. So they dug into their food, drinking down every last hot, salty drop, and washed it down with vodka. Feeling warm again was delightful; Brian only gave a dreamy glance as his wife was removed with the rabbi's wife, leaving him alone with Zalman. "So, you are from here? Where is here?" He fell into a natural Romanian without thinking, only realizing it after it came out of his mouth.

The rabbi answered in Romanian, "I was born in Liozna. It is Lithuania now, I believe, then Vilna, and then St. Petersburg. But we are in Liadi, Baruch Hashem."

"You are—I don't know—noble here?"

"No," the rabbi said very modestly. His home did not look like a noble's. It looked temporary. The walls were bare, the furniture comfortable but plain. "The voivod was who invited me to come here, Prince Stanislaw Lubomirski. Now his son rules. He stays away, thank God. The czar, he always makes trouble." But he waved it off. Brian noticed that beneath his black coat, he had scars on his wrists. "You will stay for the winter, Herr Maddox?"

"Please. We will pay anything."

"Did you do something bad?"

He was put off by the question, perhaps because of the strength of the vodka and his general exhaustion. "I—yes, we are in trouble. But we didn't do anything wrong. Please, you understand?"

"I was in prison in St. Petersburg, for three months," said the rabbi, "for giving charity."

Brian smiled despite himself. "What kind of charity?"

"I gave money to my homeland. The Turks were very upset." He must have read Brian's look of confusion. "My homeland is the land around Jerusalem, in their empire. It is now Palestine. The goyim, they change all the names."

"Jerusalem? As in, the Bible Jerusalem?"

"*Ja*, the Bible Jerusalem," said the rabbi in German. "Every year I ask God to go. Every year He says no. Someday, I find out why."

Brian laughed.

Brian and Nadezhda quickly learned much about their hosts. Rabbi Zalman—"*der Alter Rebbe*"—was the leader of the community and had been a big man in Vilna before his arrest. He married into wealth, so he could devote all of his time to study. Their house was plain, but it had a considerable library. This was no Englishman's collection of gothic novels. The texts were gigantic and smelled ancient. Some were still scrolls or hand-bound—all were in languages neither of them could read. "I feel like I'm at home," Brian said to the rabbi when he first entered.

"You read?"

"Not like my brother. He is a doctor. He reads—all the time. I was going to send him something before I left Austria, but I didn't get the chance." He sighed. "He probably already has a copy. It's an old German poem or something."

The rabbi spoke maybe a dozen languages. "A doctor is a great profession."

"I know. I'm very proud of him."

Brian had some trouble finding use for himself. Nadezhda could at least cook and did not mind doing such a mundane chore. There were no servants to be had, only dozens of students following the rabbi, who seemed to walk to and from the synagogue. Brian offered to find them food when he noticed they ate little game.

"No hunting," said the Rebbetzin, the rabbi's wife. "It is cruel to the animals."

"Then how are we eating meat?"

He got a demonstration from the rabbi himself the very next day, when they slaughtered a calf for dinner. The rabbi calmly herded the calf away from the other animals, took a large butcher's knife, and slit its throat. It died almost instantaneously as the blood poured into the snow. "You slit the throat just so," said the rabbi. "It is very hard not to hurt it."

"What if you hurt it?"

"Then we chop it up for the wild dogs to eat. We don't eat it."

"Why would you feed wild dogs? You don't eat them."

"When the Jews were sneaking out of Egypt in the middle of the night, not a single dog barked to alert the authorities. So we feed the dogs, if we can."

Brian did not question it. He had never taken Bible passages so literally.

Eventually they found industry for him—and were grateful for it, so "others can learn." He cut wood, essential for the freezing Russian nights, and he carted around goods. Fortunately these obviously religious people did not have a rule about sleeping in a different room from one's wife, and he could collapse guilt-free beside Nadezhda; he found his own way of keeping warm in the long nights. There was far more darkness than light. He was happy to an extent, because he had his wife and he had shelter. As the winter passed, he began to dream of England—its rolling hills, the small hills he had once considered mighty mountains, even the awful smell of the Town square on a hot day. Surely their trail had gone cold? (Everything else had.) Once they were in his homeland, they would be untouchable, even if the count wanted to pursue. Nadezhda seemed to silently accept never going home again, why couldn't he?

Brian watched the snow melt with an unspoken anticipation. He wanted to go—somewhere—that would bring him home. East? Maybe he could go south, to Mongolia, and then to the Turks?

"You can bribe your way through the Turkish Empire," said the rabbi, "if you can get there."

"We can't go back to St. Petersburg," he said. "What should I do, Rabbi?"

"If you must go east, go east," said the rabbi. "We wandered forty years in the desert, and we came out all right."

"The Bible didn't happen yesterday, you know."

"Every Jew who would ever live stood at Mount Sinai. We are all old souls." He always said things with complete confidence, at least on spiritual matters. That was why, Brian supposed, the people listened to him like he was the next prophet, even though he made no prophecies. He sat and read, and occasionally wrote on some religious thing he was working on—something about the soul and how to elevate it. It was beyond a vicar's sermon that was for sure. He even wrote in ancient script. Brian watched him write a letter to his friend in Poland in what he explained was Hebrew. "It is to congratulate him on the birth of his son, Nacham Franzblau."

They could not stay in this place forever, however removed from their reality it seemed to be. At night, Nadezhda and Brian sat in conference.

"We go east?"

"We go east."

They consummated the deal the best way a husband and wife could.

It seemed silly to be going off in the wrong direction. Brian's horse didn't survive the winter, so they purchased a wagon and two mules, which was the best they could do. The Rebbetzin gave them more preserves than they thought they could ever eat, which was a pleasing prospect. The rabbi gave them the only book he owned in a European language—a copy of some French travelogue, so old it had writing in different hands in the margins and inside the cover. Brian took it gratefully.

"So they didn't have horns after all," he said to his wife as they watched the little town of Liadi disappear behind them. "Or drink our blood."

"So I was ignorant! Like you're so wise," she said.

It was not very warm, but it was warm enough to see the roads again, and that was enough. They had come full circle, living outside and traveling until they would both collapse. Brian didn't try to keep track of the date, or ask it of the villagers they passed. All he knew was that it was warmer, so it was spring. There was a port to the east, the villagers said. By the time they got there, it would be thawed and ships would come again. They could go to America; it was so close. America? At least they spoke English there. One could get to England from

America—that much, he knew. He wondered how far across it was.

It was late spring, almost summer when Brian and Nadezhda Maddox arrived in Magadan. They shuddered to think about how long they had been on the road. Brian had written letters again; he posted them from the first place he saw suitable enough to possibly guarantee a delivery. In this tiny town, there was at least a kind of civilization, where he could get a shave from a barber and speak to someone in German or French. He saw the ships coming in and began to inquire. There was one bound for this place called Alaska, near America. They booked passage.

A day before they were to leave, he decided to write to his brother again to give yet another assurance that he was safe, his wife was safe, and that they would someday come home when it was safe for them and for the rest of the family. He slipped his message in the box and turned around to see the face of his Transylvanian manservant, Andrei.

"You are a hard man to find," Andrei said, holding up a pistol from within his heavy coat.

Brian followed his signal and left the public place, to a more secluded area, but he had already decided on his actions. "What do you want?" he said, facing him.

"Do you know how much His Grace would pay to have his daughter returned to him, much less with your head beside her?"

"Even if you care nothing for me," Brian pleaded, "you're leading her into death. You know she can't conceive. Everyone seems to know it but the count. Have some loyalty to your princess."

"My princess?" Andrei said. "You assume a lot about my loyalties, Prince Brian."

"Then you can be bought," Brian said. "How much?"

"I know you have half the treasury."

"I spent it in St. Petersburg. If you are so good at following me, Andrei, then you would know that." It was a lie, but he needed time.

"I'm not your servant," he said. "How little you know of me. Do you even know my last name? It is Trommler."

"Name your price, Trommler."

"I've already said it. You have most of it, I know. You lived like a pauper in St. Petersburg."

"St. Petersburg was a long time ago."

"So you say. I also know you carry the money on your person, beneath your clothing."

"You have bested me," he said. "Please—let me—" But he reached with one hand for the satchel and the other for the gun. Yes, he would risk his life for Nady—without question. He hadn't spent a winter chopping up wood for nothing. The gun went off, and he didn't care; he grabbed it and beat Trommler on the head with the wooden handle. Trommler dropped like a sack. He was still breathing. If he would stay that way, Brian knew not. He took the gun, still hot, and ran to the flat where they were staying. "Nadezhda!"

She was standing over a pot and the last of their preserves. "Brian! You're bleeding!"

He hadn't even noticed. He was honestly too concerned for her. "We have to go. We can't wait. Andrei is here."

"Your servant?" she said, grabbing a towel and placing it against his skull. Now that he thought about it, he did feel like something had hit him, though he knew Trommler had not. "You were grazed. You need to sit down."

"We need to go. Board the next ship. I don't care where it goes."

"What happened?"

He could barely breathe. He did have to sit, as much as he didn't want to, as she pressed the cloth against his head. "He had a gun—he wanted all of our money. I hit him and he fell. T-that's all I stayed for. Oh, and I took the gun." He pulled it out. "We have to go before he wakes up."

"Brian, you're going into shock."

"I'd rather do it on a ship."

She listened to him, quickly gathering their things. They abandoned the cart, which had little in it anyway, and took only what they could fit on their backs. Brian could barely walk, Nadezhda had to hold him up, and he shoved a mildly insane amount of money into the hands of the captain of a ship bound for a port in the south. The crew was male with no passengers. "Just keep it quiet," Brian mumbled. They showed him to a spare room and brought him a mattress, which he hit rather soundly.

When he woke, they were already at sea. He felt the rocking of the boat and found it comforting. *We're moving.*

The days passed quietly. He recovered quickly and checked the ship—no Andrei. They were safe. Nadezhda didn't venture far outside the cabin, not with a male crew. They mainly stayed to themselves until their food ran out; they then shared meals with the crew, again, at extra cost.

It doesn't matter, he told himself. *It's like farthings.*

It wasn't worth that, when they all started getting sick. At first, he thought he was seasick, even though he normally had a strong stomach. He could hardly blame Nadezhda, who had never seen the sea, much less been on it before in her life. But then there were sores, fevers, and the boat began to veer off course because so many crew members were ill…

"Typhus," he said as he rejoined Nadezhda in their cabin. "Bloody fucking typhus!"

Nadezhda managed a weak smile.

"I may sound as if I've gone truly insane," he said, "and this would not be the first time I would have said something that made people think that, but there's land ahead. We could take the boat and row."

"But—the captain—"

"If we stole it—went at night—" He slumped down against the wall. "I know it's wrong, crazy, and stupid. But if we stay here, we're going to die."

She nodded weakly. She always agreed with him. She was never afraid. She was so perfect, so wonderful—she didn't deserve to die. He would do anything to make sure that didn't happen—not on his watch.

That night, in a feverish haze so bad he could hardly tell left from right, the two of them took the boat off the side and lowered themselves into the water. Everything proceeded smoothly—most of the crew was below deck, dying. Two had already been thrown overboard.

The waves were heavier than he expected. He tried to row alone. Several times, his strength failed him, and Nadezhda took his place. He lay down on the floor of the small wooden boat, listening to the waves, falling into the comforting silence beyond Nadezhda's desperate breathing. That was, until the boat crashed into a rocky coast; he heard the wood splintering and noises from afar—his cue.

Nadezhda was unconscious. He rose somehow, his pack still on his back, and lifted her into his arms, stepping out of the ruined boat and into the water that went up to his knees. Slowly he waded to shore, his night vision failing him against the torchlight. It was all a haze, and then there was shouting. He set Nadezhda down when she murmured something.

His only thought was of Nadezhda, half-collapsed at his side. He was inclined to join her, not feeling well on his feet. He was very aware, not only of the lapping water against his boots but the presence of others around him, swords drawn. He drew his pistol, though he doubted he had the strength to do more than hold it up and fire once or twice. "Stay away," he said in Russian, even though in the poor light, these people did not look Russian. They were positively Oriental, with their strange hair in buns, their odd swords, and their eyes. They had left the mainland, he was sure—so they could not be in Cathay—"If you touch her, so help me God," he said in Romanian.

Someone shouted at him. It was an order, but it was incomprehensible. He did not know if they recognized what he held in his hands when they came after him. He'd been in similar straits before, certainly, but not with a wife by his side, and not when he was so utterly sick and exhausted.

How the gun went off, he could not properly recall. It fired harmlessly into the air, gunpowder drifting down as he was knocked in his side by the butt of a weapon, and he collapsed. "Nadezhda…" he whispered. She was gone, and so was everything else.

Chapter 24

DAWN BREAKS

1812

THE SKY WAS GETTING light when England came into view, first in the form of the waning light of the lighthouses, then the lamps of Dover. Darcy eventually gave in to his wife's *subtle* suggestions, as well as his own body's, and fell asleep on a pile of blankets. In fact, almost none of them were able to make it through the night except the crew.

Elizabeth woke first, from her uncomfortable position leaning against the beam. In the early morning light she was surprised to see Brian Maddox seated on the bow, the longer of his two swords against his shoulder for convenience, staring out at the approaching skyline. His wife was curled up beside him, very much asleep. He managed to rise without waking her to bow to Elizabeth. "Mrs. Darcy."

"Mr. Maddox. Have you been awake all night?"

"Yes." He put his sword back in his belt, or sash, or whatever it was, and stepped further out to the edge with her, away from the sleeping crowd. "It seems I am the cause of all of your troubles again, Mrs. Darcy."

"Not all of them," she corrected. "But—most."

He blinked in the light. "I would not take it back. I certainly didn't ask Danny to come rescue me. I wrote many letters telling him to do precisely otherwise, which he didn't get or didn't listen to."

"The former."

"And Darcy chose to accompany him?"

"Darcy was also looking for his brother. He just had the misfortune of falling into the count's trap first."

Brian nodded. He had been changed, undoubtedly, by whatever he had experienced himself. How, it was difficult to tell. "I am sorry for the difficulties, Mrs. Darcy, but my responsibility was to my wife, and I had to see it through. That I do not regret."

"We've heard different tales, and I'm sure you have your own, but as I understand it, your father-in-law gave you little option but to run."

"Yes. We ran so far east to escape his agents that we wound up at the end of the world."

"'Here there be dragons.'"

He chuckled. "Indeed. Coincidentally, they're positively obsessed with dragon imagery. In the Orient, I mean. If I must now return to the backward Englishman stance and call it that."

"You must have quite a story."

Brian smiled. "You must be somewhat forgiving of me now, to be so casual about it. Yes, in fact, I do."

"How long were you in England?"

"Only as long as it took for me to arrange this ship. The night we arrived and found the house shut up, we went to the Bingleys', and then there was that," he shook his head. "A long story. Excuse Mr. Bingley's absence; he is nursing a concussion."

"You didn't!"

"Certainly not! But my brother-in-law has to learn a thing or two about warehouses in Town and facing unpaid workers by himself. Fortunately, we were there in time. Between that and here, I believe, it was three days. Mugin offered to go ahead."

"By boat?"

"I believe he swam, at least some of the way."

Behind them someone said something incomprehensible, which Elizabeth took to be Japanese, indeed, it was Mugin standing there.

"He says he swam about halfway, but it was freezing," Brian explained. "And then a ship happened by and picked him up."

"Is that true?"

"Probably," Brian said, giving a knowing look to Mugin, who shrugged dismissively and walked off without a bow to either of them. "He's temperamental, but he's saved my life more times than I can count. So no argument here."

"Is he some type of hired warrior?"

"I guess that's one way to describe him. He wanted to get out of Japan for a while, so he rode with us, all the way to England." He turned away. "I suppose we should start waking everyone. I can see land there."

Land. For a brief moment, Elizabeth thought she had never heard a more beautiful word in her life.

Brian knelt beside his brother, putting a hand on his forehead. "Danny?"

Dr. Daniel Maddox opened his eyes, looked up at his brother and whispered, "My God... Y-you've... gone bald."

Brian laughed. "It's just shaved, I assure you." He glanced up at Elizabeth. "His fever broke."

"So... I'm not hallucinating," the doctor said.

"No," his brother assured him.

"And I grew up? Got married? That... all happened?" he said, gasping. "Not just... recovering from some cataract surgery i-infection?"

"No, Danny. I really did marry a princess, and you have two children and a royal commission. Oh, and everyone thinks I've gone insane. They may be right."

Dr. Maddox smiled but was too exhausted to say anything else. He laid his head back down on the pillow, with Caroline still asleep beside him.

Their arrival was greeted with little fanfare. There was no precise time on the boat arrival, but Jane abandoned her husband's side (with his encouragement) to be there to meet the carriage from Dover. The sun was barely up when they all arrived, truly a dirtied, bloodied, over-exhausted mass of people who somewhat resembled the people she loved. Darcy of course insisted on stepping out of the carriage himself, if with the aid of a cane and Elizabeth. "Hello, Mrs. Bingley."

"Mr. Darcy," Jane said, curtseying. "It is so good to see you." There was so much joy in her heart, but this was not the time to express it. He needed to get into his house, where Georgiana and his children awaited him. "Brother Grégoire." He seemed to be carrying a large box on his back.

It was Dr. Maddox who was not conscious and needed to be carried by his brother and Lord Fitzwilliam. All of the men had a few days' worth of beard on them, except Mugin, who seemed to be wearing a French officer's coat. "Mr. Mugin—"

"*Hai?*"

"Your coat. It's uhm…"

"Was cold."

Nadezhda whispered in Japanese in his ear, and he bowed to her. "*Gomen nasai.*" He removed the coat, bowed to Jane, and kept walking.

"How is Mr. Bingley?" Elizabeth managed to whisper to her.

"Cranky, but he will be fine, I'm told. He sends his regrets—he does wish to see both of them, but he cannot be moved."

Elizabeth hugged her. Only briefly, because her coat was soiled and there was just so much to do, but enough to acknowledge: *It is over. We are home.*

The children were not up when the Maddoxes arrived at their house, and Caroline checked on them both but did not wake either in their nursery. She didn't want them to see their father until he was at least cleaned up.

Fortunately or unfortunately, Dr. Maddox seemed to slowly be returning to consciousness when he was carried up to the master bedchamber. Brian immediately turned to the shocked servant and gave instructions to contact the physician who had treated his brother since he was a child. "Where does he keep his opium?" he asked Caroline.

"In his study, but no one knows the recipe."

"He didn't write it down?"

Caroline shook her head and turned to her husband. "What is the recipe for your opium medicine?"

Dr. Maddox, his voice stilted by pain, merely said, "No."

"Well, I don't care what he says; I'm getting him laudanum." With that, Brian disappeared. As servants came and went, forced into a rush to open the house for the master and his wife, the door remained open, and there was a knock on the doorframe. Nadezhda Maddox stood there pensively. She was still wearing her silk robes, which Caroline had to admit had the most beautiful prints of flowers on the corners that she had ever seen, but the princess now also had her hair covered in a complex set of veils.

"*Entschuldigen Sie*," she said in German. (Excuse me.) "So sorry, know small English."

"I speak German," Caroline replied, continuing in that language, "And so does my husband."

Princess Maddox—if she was still a princess at all—curtseyed. "I am so sorry, Dr. Maddox."

"It wasn't your fault," Caroline said for her husband, holding his good hand.

Nadezhda cautiously stepped into the room, as if she was violating some sacred temple, even if servants were running to and fro. "My failure as a woman caused all of this. If I could only conceive—"

"Your Highness," Caroline said, not really sure how she was supposed to address an ex-Austrian princess, "everyone has a little trouble. My sister is barren, and her husband supports her nonetheless." Actually, her brother supported Mrs. Hurst, but that was neither here nor there.

"I drove my father mad—"

"Your father was not mad," Dr. Maddox gasped. "Just… cruel. Not your fault." He shifted in bed. "I think I have a spare—pair of glasses. Mine are rather filthy. In the lab, darling?"

"Of course," Caroline said. In the hubbub of returning home, she had almost forgotten. She kissed him on his forehead, picked up the keys from the dresser, and excused herself.

Dr. Maddox immediately opened his eyes and turned them in the general direction of Nadezhda. "Has my brother been a good husband?"

"Yes," she said. "Brian is the very best of men."

He chuckled. "I never thought I would... hear someone say that." He swallowed. "Thank you. I feel—much better."

Dr. Hulbert arrived within the hour. Dr. Maddox was sitting up, with the help of many pillows. Hulbert checked his hand, listened to his chest, looked in his mouth, and looked carefully into his eyes before giving him an exam with Dr. Maddox's glasses on. Dr. Maddox passed, but he said very little over the course of it. Normally, Daniel Maddox was most prodigious about his health and would probably be babbling on about it. Hulbert frowned. "Well, the news is mainly good. The infection does not seem to be spreading, though the fever may continue for a few days. In fact, the most distressing thing aside from your weight loss is... lice."

"Lice?" the Maddoxes said in unison.

"Your hair is infested. I'm surprised the doctor in Prussia didn't notice it." He closed up his bag. "And you should tell the other fellow you were with to have himself checked. Now get some rest, Daniel. Mrs. Maddox?"

She gave Dr. Maddox's hand a squeeze and followed the doctor outside, where he shut the door behind them.

"I've never seen him like this," she admitted, finally able to release her worry, if only a little.

"Is he more aware than he was when he was first rescued?"

"He wasn't even *conscious* when he was first rescued."

Hulbert was a much older man, his hair mainly white, but still very spry. "I understand he's been through a lot in the past few months. He's malnourished and in pain. He needs rest, but he will recover. I don't think there is any permanent damage."

She sighed with relief. "And the lice?"

"He needs to be shaved and his head dunked in whiskey. It can be bad whiskey, as long as it's strong."

She paused. "The children are here. I don't want them to see him like this."

"How old are they?"

"Five."

"They'll hardly notice, though I would buy him a wig of some sort."

"Mother?"

They turned toward Frederick Maddox, standing in the hallway, almost pulling on her dress to get her attention.

"Frederick!" she said, unable to hold back her affection as she knelt down and hugged him. "My darling. I'm home and your father is home. He's just very tired." She kissed him on both cheeks and then on the head. "Where is your sister?"

"Sleeping." He looked up. "Who are you?"

"Dr. Hulbert," the old man said, bowing.

"Frederick Maddox," the boy said in a proper little bow. "Who are you?"

"I'm your father's eye doctor. I've known him since he was—well, almost as small as you, but not quite. But he was very young."

"Am I going to go blind like him?"

Caroline looked at her son in shock, but Dr. Hulbert didn't miss a beat. "I don't think so, Master Frederick. His condition is very rare."

"Frederick," Caroline said more sternly, "why don't you have Nurse dress you so you can properly see your father?"

This idea the boy took very well, and he disappeared down the hallway the way he came.

"I never told him about it," Caroline said. "I've never said it in his presence—"

"Children are smarter than we think," said the doctor. "Or, at least, more intuitive. I remember a young Master Daniel whose older brother and I conspired to keep his fate from him. So he read every medical book he could find in English until he figured it out. He was twelve."

"How long do you think he has?"

Dr. Hulbert spoke very kindly. "The specialist in Scotland gave him four years. Obviously, I gave up guessing a long time ago. He told me he's determined at least to see his daughter come out." He turned his head at the sound of someone ascending the steps. "And if it isn't—good God, man, what happened to you?"

"Dr. Hulbert," Brian said, bowing. "In short: marriage, Russia, Japan. That will have to do for the moment. I have some medicine to shove down my brother's throat." And with that, he bowed again quickly and disappeared into Daniel's room.

"That was short," Dr. Hulbert said. "I cannot fault him for that."

At the Darcy townhouse, Elizabeth had a real fear that Darcy would crush his sister. Georgiana was so small and so readily embraced him, unaware of how much support he needed to keep standing, and it was a lot of weight to take on. The servants fortunately rushed to help their ailing master and take the box containing the reliquary off of Grégoire's back.

Darcy's manservant, Mr. Reed, appeared almost in tears as he attended to his master, removing the torn coat they had picked up in Austria, and helped him to the stairs. Darcy responded to queries, but mainly in a "yes" or "no." The only thing that finally made him stop was his son, standing at the top of the stairs. "Geoffrey."

Mr. Reed and Elizabeth were there to brace him as Geoffrey raced down the stairs and crashed into his father. "Father! I was so scared, I didn't know—"

Darcy smiled sadly but said nothing, only patting his son on the head. There was something removed about his reactions.

Anne Darcy was quick to follow her brother and was raised by Elizabeth to kiss her father so that he could retreat up the stairs and into his bed. He left in his wake a nervous silence for Elizabeth, still holding her eldest daughter, as Grégoire and Georgiana had their own embrace.

"Father—he's going to be all right?" Geoffrey said, tugging at Elizabeth's dress.

"Yes, of course," she said, hoping her voice carried more assurance than she felt in her heart.

Chapter 25

UNEXPECTED GUESTS

A BRUTAL THREE DAYS passed before Jane received word that Darcy was willing to receive visitors. It was some time before Mr. Darcy made his appearance, slowly shambling down the stairs with his walking stick and awaiting them in the sitting room. As Jane entered, he retained his English manners, however a struggle it was.

"Mr. Darcy," Jane said. "Oh, please don't—"

But Darcy was still Darcy, and he paid no heed as he struggled to rise to his feet to properly bow to her. He did sit back down rather quickly though, instead of waiting for her to be seated as she passed him a letter. "Charles sends his regards," she said.

"Of course." Sadly, both of them were stuck in their own homes for the moment. Darcy would probably recover enough in a few days, but Bingley was still resting from his head injury.

There was something oddly formal about the situation in the sitting room, despite the three of them, because of so much that could not be said. Elizabeth had prepared her for seeing Darcy, but it hadn't been quite the same as seeing him with his clothes hanging off him, his face sunken, with no proper sideburns, wearing a brown wig that Elizabeth said was his father's. He was distracted—by what, she dared not to imagine. His eyes were unfocused and rarely concentrated on her or any particular thing in the room. His usual veneer of intensity was gone, even if his words were formal.

"How is Bingley?" Darcy said. "I'm not—entirely clear on the circumstances of his injuries, though they have been explained to me." His eyes darted around like he was lost. "It seems much has occurred in my absence."

It occurred to Jane that she had no idea exactly how much he'd been told, or even if he knew of his inheritance of Rosings. Elizabeth said nothing but squeezed his hand as Jane spoke. "He is very frustrated at being incapacitated, especially right now. It seems he unintentionally picked a fight with his warehouse manager, who was upset about not being paid."

"The business is under, then?"

"No, actually. It seems Mr. Maddox returned home not only with his wife but with a significant stock from the Orient. If not for my husband's injuries, he would be spending much of his time assessing its worth."

"I must say that Mr. Maddox has an amazing capacity for appearing only when he is most needed or least wanted," Elizabeth said. Darcy seemed to half-smile at that. "Or both. Have you spoken to him much since our arrival?"

"A little. He is very busy taking care of his brother. He's barely left his side," Jane said.

"And his wife? Her Highness?" Darcy asked.

"I spoke with her through Brian. She speaks five languages fluently, but her English is limited. She and Mr. Maddox—forgive me for saying this—they *have* been through a lot." She watched Darcy's reaction very carefully, but he didn't seem bothered by it—or all that aware of it—and Elizabeth nodded for her to go on. "The story is that they went east instead of west, deep into Russia, where they were pursued by her father's men all the way to the coast. They boarded a ship, but had to abandon it when everyone contracted typhus. Their tiny boat washed up on an island in the very north of the Japans, and the locals took them in. From there they had to walk to—I can't pronounce it, but it's a port in the south where the East India Company docks. It took them a year just to travel through Japan, and then three months at sea to return to England."

"On foot?"

"On foot. Mugin—the man who rescued you—went with them most of the way as a bodyguard. So did another man, but he died in the city. His name is very hard to pronounce or remember." She added, "They have promised the story in full—when everyone is ready." She rose. "I won't take any more of your time, Mr. Darcy. But you do look much better than you did when you arrived."

"Thank you," he nodded, and did not attempt to rise without the aid of his servants. It was obvious he was beginning to fade, and she didn't want to tax him. He exchanged a brief word with his wife and was then helped back up the stairs.

As soon as he was gone, Jane embraced her sister. "He will be all right."

"I know. It's not how he looks. He was so upset when they cut his hair, but I didn't mind—I just can't bear to see him so—*troubled*. I told him about Rosings, but he didn't have a response. The papers are being drawn up, and he'll sign, but I don't know if he really cared."

"He needs time, Lizzy. Caroline said Dr. Maddox is the same way."

"I only wish he would tell me what happened to him, what he's thinking—"

"Lizzy—was Mr. Darcy *ever* one to tell *anyone* what he is thinking?"

That brought a smile to her sister's face. "I suppose not. He is safe, and all are delivered from danger, even Grégoire—oh, Jane, I never told you about Grégoire!"

"What about Grégoire?"

Her sister was now fully smiling. That in and of itself was a burden off Jane's shoulders. "God, I shouldn't say it, but I suppose if I don't, Caroline will. When we found him, he was—well—not exactly tending to his vow of celibacy. Our timing was most unfortunate for everyone."

"Grégoire? No! It cannot be true!" Maybe the others were right. Maybe she could only see the good in everyone. But still—this was their family monk.

"He was so embarrassed—it was the only time, or so he says, and I think he may be believed. But I admit, we had a few chuckles on his behalf, especially because after Darcy has spent so much time chiding him about his monastic impulses, we find him with a woman!" They broke into laughter. "He saved her from some soldiers, and she was *very* appreciative."

"Lizzy!"

"I know! I shouldn't be saying such things about a brother! But still—" She covered her mouth. "It is so good to laugh."

Jane could not contradict her about that. Unfortunately, she was silenced by the casual entrance of Grégoire. "Is everything all right?"

Neither of them could think of what to say to *that*. They only managed to stifle their giggles for a few seconds before breaking into full laughter as Grégoire looked on, dumbfounded. They eventually recovered but excused themselves from enlightening the poor monk.

There were many legal matters immediately pressing, and Darcy, without reading them, signed the contracts regarding the Fitzwilliams living in Rosings despite his ownership of the property. He just nodded when it was explained to him, ignored their concerned looks, and retreated to his chambers. He was "not at home" to any further visitors unless it could not be avoided.

One person did appear unexpectedly and was received by Elizabeth very gratefully. Mr. Bennet did not however ask for Mr. Darcy's presence nor have any wish to bother him. "Being assured that he is back in the country will be sufficient," he said to his daughter, "for the time being."

"At least wait until his sideburns grow back," Elizabeth said. "He is most self-conscious about it."

"Mr. Darcy? Self-conscious? I've never heard of such a thing!" he said. "Now, where are my grandchildren? Your mother will not relent about my superior age, but I am still quite sure my mind is sharp enough to remember having them."

Elizabeth laughed and asked for the children, who were in the middle of being bathed and was told there would be some delay, as young Master Geoffrey was most resistant to the idea. "How is everyone at Longbourn?"

"I confess I had become so used to your mother not having attacks of nerves that it quite surprised me when you were gone.

She did worry for you, though she will not be quick to admit it," he said. "And Mary prayed most extensively. Unfortunately, it was often out loud and over grace, so I was subjected to many dishes that had gone cold by the time she was done."

She embraced her father. "How is Lydia? Is she remarried yet?"

"Sadly, she is finding that a widow with two children and little inheritance is not the most pleasing of prospects. But I imagine she will find someone when all the soldiers come back from war and are too muddled by their experiences to notice," he said. "It is good to have you back, Lizzy."

"It is good to be back, Papa."

"Master George has been enquiring about his uncle most prodigiously," he said. "He seems eager to renew his acquaintance with his cousin."

"How is George?" she asked. "The most I've seen of him was at Rosings."

"He is well. Entirely a different person from his mother and father—more like his uncle, I would dare to say. He reads without instruction, and he says very little. Quite confounding in some ways, but I am not one to complain about a well-mannered boy. And his sister—well, it does help pass the hours to have Mrs. Bennet up in arms about that cat."

"She is not too upset, I hope? It was I who agreed to it and convinced Lydia."

"She would be more agreeable to the animal in general," he said, "if it was not so intent on playing with the strings of her needlepoint." He sighed with a smile. "But in comparison to her many speeches about marriage and poverty, I can manage with a few complaints about a kitten."

Dr. Maddox was in his sitting room, trying desperately to concentrate on the words on the page in front of him. That in of itself was enough of a distraction for a while, but not for long. He was still too weak from his long imprisonment and subsequent fever to go out, or attend a lecture at London University, and he did not have it in him to ask others to provide distractions for him. He had learned many years ago to be independent, and that lesson was not so easily forgotten.

The task before him he was finding too difficult. Many times he closed his eyes or dropped the book as exhaustion lulled him into sleep, only to be startled again by a fresh wave of pain in his hand from his healing wound.

"Dr. Maddox," said the servant, bringing his presence to Dr. Maddox's attention. "Your wife insists." The man was bearing a tray with only a glass of juice on it.

He grumbled and had to put down his book, which he wasn't doing much of a job of holding up anyway, to take the glass. The sight he'd seen in the mirror wasn't pretty, but that didn't mean he had much of an appetite.

"Darling," his wife said, entering the room. "Oh, don't stop on my account. You haven't eaten anything today, have you?"

"No," he said after he finished the glass. "Ugh. I think the oranges are off or something. Anyway, my appetite *will* come back, just not today." He added, "And please don't give me that look. I don't want to argue about the opium again. I'm tired of being cross with everyone."

"We know you don't mean it," she said. She had not come in to have the same fight they'd had every day since he'd regained consciousness. She sat down next to him, and he put his arm around her. Yes, having one's wife leaning on one's shoulder could be suitably distracting. "Well, you have permission to mean it if it's to thrash your brother."

"I'm not capable of thrashing my brother."

"He doesn't seem to think that. He is still walking around *armed*."

"That is because my brother has gone completely and utterly betwattled. The *armed guard* is for whenever we all decide to exact our revenge."

"At least, there, we can call it cultural differences. Though Nadezhda has given me the impression that Mr. Mugin was an oddity even in Japan."

"How is she? What is she like? We've not—had much occasion to talk."

"She is a… strong woman," she said, not unkindly. The wives had a shared language of German, so they could converse. "She has been through quite a lot. Her father was very kind to her, but he had expectations she could not meet."

"Maddoxes like strong women," he said with a smile. "We're notorious for it." He looked at her. "Dear, your hair is… well, it's more of an orange. I don't know why they say it's red. It isn't." He kissed her on the forehead. "It's orange."

"Thank you so much for noticing it," she said. "Are you feeling better?"

"I don't know why I—didn't, before. So much." He took off his glasses and then put them back on again. "There's so *much* of it."

"Yes, dear."

"What color is Nadezhda's hair? I don't—I haven't seen it. She wears the—the thing—" He waved his arms around his head to indicate the veils.

"I think it's black. 'The thing'?"

"'The thing.'" He laughed. "I'm a very articulate man."

"It is the reason I married you."

They descended into laughter, and it felt so unimaginably good that it was only in the silence following that he tried, very hard, to focus on the glass, on the table, in front of them. And couldn't. "You—you drugged me." He detangled himself from his wife and reached for the glass, but his coordination was so poor that he only succeeded in knocking it over, where it rolled harmlessly on the ground. "The juice."

Caroline stroked his hair, even though it was still considerably shorter than his usual cut. "Darling—"

"I promised—I promised myself—"

"Daniel," she said more seriously, "it was years ago, and you weren't trying to recover from an injury, however small." She helped him straighten up and to lie back with his head against the wall, because he found his body too heavy to do it himself. "I know for a fact that you haven't slept well in two days. Look at you. What kind of doctor doesn't take his own medicine?"

"I took an oath," he said, expending most of his concentration to say it clearly. Caroline, despite being beside him, was becoming a blur. "Caroline, I took an oath."

"Well, I didn't, and I'm tired of dealing with an obstinate husband who won't let his body rest, is making himself sick, and is cross with us because of it." She kissed him on the cheek. "I did it because I can't stand to see you suffer for one minute longer. And I don't regret it. I love you, Daniel, but you sometimes have no idea of what's best for you and must cede that authority to your wife. Now, lie down and rest."

"I—here? Now?" Because, honestly, he was feeling quite wonderful and had no desire to just sleep it off. Well, maybe exhaustion was finally getting to him, but this was the first time he wasn't in pain… in as long as he could remember. It was all a little fuzzy.

"Yes." She helped him lie down on his couch. "I'll see that you're not to be disturbed. Now be still and rest, Daniel."

"Yes, marm," he said, trying to raise one hand to touch her before she left, but it just flapped up and fell down. She seemed to blow him a kiss as she had the double doors to the room shut behind her. She'd taken off his glasses too, so that didn't help. Yes, there was no reason to fight it. It felt different this time. He'd been drugged for the surgery, of course, but that was unavoidable and necessary to protect his heart from the pain. And then there was darkness after that, and he was back in England, falling asleep in his sitting room like any lazy rich man with a house in West London, while his wife did some pretty embroidery and his children ran circles around Nurse. Nothing had happened or changed, and all was right in the world. He could, at last, rest.

That was the last thing he remembered until he was listening to the same servant repeat something over and over again. He had the feeling he'd heard it many times now, without any recognition, as he was cruelly pulled out of sleep. He had a crick in his neck from his position. He managed to grab his glasses and put them on to face the very nervous but insistent servant. "Yes?" But it came out more of a *yesh*.

"The—his Royal Highness to see you, sir."

He was hallucinating. How delightful. "Terrific. Send him in."

SICK VISIT

"MY GOD, MAN," SAID the Regent. "I've never seen you so content. You must be taking some of your own medicine, if you know what I mean."

"I do," he slurred, gesturing for His Highness to take a seat. He was still lying on the couch, his head propped up by the pillows. "Wife—drugged me."

"Is this a regular habit of hers?"

"I *wish*," he said as they shared a laugh. "Seriously—I swore off it all years ago. Years and years. You know." He closed his eyes. "I'm *serious*."

"You are a terribly serious man. It is good for a doctor, but a bit frustrating at times. I imagine you will be in some fits when you come off this stuff and realize whom you were talking to."

"Oh, I'd be in a *lot* of trouble," Dr. Maddox said. "First, I can't even—even get up to bow. You have to do that a lot with royalty."

"Of course," said the Regent. "And your patient is probably an incomparable arse."

"No, but I'm sick of treating his venereal diseases," he said. "God. I told him not to sleep with people who must be so *obviously* diseased—"

"Come now, Doctor. Not all of us have your expertise."

"Must I write an essay or something? Honestly." He tried to pick his head up as he heard the sound of metal clinking and saw his son running through the exasperated legs of two guards with gigantic ceremonial lances, barring entrance to the now-open doors. Frederick Maddox was only five and so had no real trouble maneuvering around them and racing to his father's side.

"Aunt Nady wants to know if you want to eat with us later."

"Where's—where is your mother?"

"Out. She said she had to get Uncle Brian new clothing because he dresses all crazy."

"Your Uncle Brian does dress like a crazy person," he said, petting his son's mop of brown hair. "Now turn around and say hello to our guest."

"Yes," said the Regent. "I would be delighted to make the acquaintance. I assume this is the young master."

Frederick turned around and bowed politely to him. "Frederick Maddox, sir."

"You have a sister, don't you?"

"Emily. But she's taking a nap." He said, "Don't you know any manners, sir?"

"I know quite a bit about manners, Frederick!" said the Regent, and Daniel laughed. "Why do you ask?"

"Because you're supposed to stand up, bow, and say your name. It's polite."

"Did your father teach you that?"

"He did! He taught me everything I know."

"Well, then," said the Regent, "he should have taught you that I am a prince and, therefore, not required to bow to anyone but my own father, who can't tell me from a tree anyway."

"Really? My father can't see too well, but I think he could tell me from a tree," Frederick said.

"You are much smaller than a tree," Dr. Maddox said. "That is the giveaway."

"See? Your father is very clever," the Regent said, putting one of his hands on Frederick's tiny shoulders. "He is one of the smartest men I know. You'd do well to listen to him, even when he's out of his senses, which I suspect he is at the moment." He patted him. "Now, run along and play or whatever normal children do at your age."

That was all Frederick needed to scamper off at top speed, leaving confused guards in his wake. The Regent was silent, and Dr. Maddox was sure he was close to nodding off when the Regent finally said, "I am not in the custom of visiting my doctors in their homes. Perhaps I should inquire beforehand as to whether they are sitting in a drugged stupor before making my appearance."

Dr. Maddox giggled.

The Regent stood up, walked over to stand over Maddox, who put his glasses back on so he could see him more clearly. "You should know you were missed. Your temporary substitute is terrible."

Dr. Maddox's mind couldn't quite process much of this. "Thank you?"

"And I commend you on your parenting skills. Good day, Dr. Maddox."

"Good day. Night. Either one."

He was already asleep again when the supposed apparition disappeared the way he came.

Dr. Maddox awoke some time later—how much, he could not tell—to a red blur that eventually became the form of his daughter, scrunched next to him on the couch. "Hello, darling," he said. He had a foul taste in his mouth, but otherwise felt fine, almost calm, the pain in his hand reduced to a mild throb. He pulled her in and kissed her on the cheek. "I missed you."

"Mama is very upset," Emily said.

"Oh? What did your uncle do now?"

"It isn't Uncle Brian."

"Oh?" he said, straightening his glasses. "What did *I* do now?"

"You got a letter."

Mildly intrigued, he eventually sat up, set his daughter down, and meandered out of his sitting room. He made it only a few steps into the hallway when his wife held up a letter to his face. "What is *this?*"

"Hmm." He took it from her—carefully, for it looked to be on very expensive paper—and held it up to his eyes, pushing his glasses up, where they promptly got stuck in his ridiculous wig. "It seems to be a letter from the Crown."

"Well, read it, why don't you!"

It was indeed a very expensive document, not folded, and with the royal seal hanging from it. The handwriting he did not recognize, but all of the documents he received from Charlton were always written by the steward or some lesser person.

To Dr. Daniel Maddox,

I will excuse the lack of proper reception on the grounds that you were positively senseless, and a physician's home staff is not usually accustomed to a Royal Presence. Nonetheless I am relieved with your return, as the substitute surgeon is terrible in numerous ways that I will no doubt enumerate at my next appointment.

Your permission for leave with payment is still in effect for the remainder of your convalescence. When you feel well enough to return to the Service, do not tarry. Say hello to your wife, whom, I am assured, is nothing like my own Caroline.

His Royal Highness, The Prince of Wales,
Regent of the United Kingdom of Great Britain
and Ireland,
George Augustus Frederick

"Oh God," Dr. Maddox said, "I thought that was a dream."

"How could you possibly think a visit from the Regent was a dream?" Caroline shouted. Actually, it was more of a shriek.

"Well, I was... quite *senseless*," he said. "I don't quite remember what was said, something about a tree." He thought to himself that it was probably better that he didn't remember what he might have said, as it would just lead to a lot of panic that neither of them could actually do anything about. "Was anyone else here?"

"Nadezhda and the children, but they were not requested, apparently. He came and went, according to the servants."

"So Brian was not here? He is a prince, you know. They could have chatted about... princely things, I don't know."

"You are not taking this seriously!"

"I suppose not," he said rather calmly. "I think I am honestly too exhausted to care. Besides, he clearly wrote that there was no harm done." He handed the letter back to her. "Where is Her Highness?"

"In the garden."

"In the garden? In November?"

"She did grow up in Transylvania," Caroline said, clearly trying to accustom herself to his unnaturally mellow mood. Caroline Maddox would keep her composure, thank you very much.

The still-befuddled doctor excused himself and put on a coat before opening the door to the small garden in the courtyard, where Nadezhda Maddox was working in the soil.

"Your Highness," he said in German, standing in the doorway. Instantly his son came around the shrubbery, considerably better insulated than the foreign princess.

"Father! I met the king!"

"Really," he said, frowning. "You mean the Regent? Come inside; you'll catch cold." He turned his attention back to Nadezhda, who rose and turned to him and he bowed. "Was the Prince Regent here, by any chance?"

"Yes," she said in German, unaffected by the searing winter winds. "Very briefly."

"Did he speak to my son?"

"He did."

"So Frederick was asked to join us?"

"No, I believe he ran in to ask you something, and ran out."

"Oh." He was not quite sure what to make of it. He wondered if she knew the connection. Come to think of it, probably. "Well... this will probably never happen again, but if it does, keep Frederick somewhere else."

"*Ja*," she said, curtseyed, and then returned to her gardening.

Freezing himself, Dr. Maddox closed the door and turned immediately to Frederick, still bundled in scarves. "What did you say to the Regent?"

"Things."

"Things?"

"Mother *already* asked me about it," Frederick said, annoyed. "He's very fat."

"He is, but I hope to God in heaven you did not say such a thing," he said, trying to maintain some semblance of calm.

"Aren't you his doctor? Can you make him less fat?"

"I have tried, believe me, but every man is in charge of his own destiny," he said, kneeling beside his son so they were eye level. "What did he say to you? Do you remember?" He put his arms on his son's shoulders. "Please, it is important."

"Nothing! He just said you were smarter than him and his dad can't see very well, or something. He told me to listen to you."

"Really?" he said.

"Yes! Why does everyone care so much? He is just a man."

"Yes," he said, laughing softly. "I suppose he is." He pulled his son in and, despite some resistance on Frederick's end, held him as tightly as he could. "I love you, son. Always remember that."

"Yes!" his son said. "Everyone's so queer today."

He laughed, feeling his eyes tear up. "I wish that was the least of it."

Darcy had no wish to visit Rosings. He did not make it known by words, but by expression that he had even less desire to be sociable than normal. He had irrationally resisted having his head shaved before giving in at the doctor's insistence and would not even be seen until his sides were beginning to grow back. He made his desire to return to Pemberley, as soon as possible, readily known. In fact, it was often all he said in a day that was not a monosyllabic answer.

There was one remaining issue that needed settling in Town. Sensing his reaction would not be an easy one to handle, Elizabeth had instructed Georgiana to keep the business with Lord Kincaid to herself, and instead fill him in on whatever else he was willing to listen to with a rather blank expression on his face.

Lord Matlock came by once before leaving with the papers for Rosings and reassured Elizabeth, "He needs time."

"I've never seen him—"

"He's in a state of shock. It will wear off." He added, "It cannot be made to happen any faster."

When she decided it could be avoided no longer, Elizabeth sat down with Darcy in the study and carefully explained the long courtship between Georgiana and the earl, William Kincaid. She modified some of the dates, so it would not seem that Georgiana had already been in the earl's acquaintance while Darcy was still in England, to soften the blow.

There was a brief silence before Darcy, devoid of any passion or emotion, simply said, "No."

She was not quite sure what to say to this. "Husband, you must further explain your answer."

"I am not obligated to do so."

"You are assuming too much of my abilities to read you. Do you mean you do not wish to consider this now, or you reject my consent for the courtship, or you simply do not believe me?"

An expression passed over his face. "You know what I mean."

"Lord Matlock also agreed—"

"He was her guardian when she was a child," he said coldly. "He is not her brother. This matter does not concern him."

Elizabeth tried to be patient with him. She was told, quite clearly, by the doctor that being made continuously upset was bad for her condition, as if that had not happened enough times already in the last few months. "I am merely saying that I counseled with the next available authority in your absence, and we both agreed upon speaking to Lord Kincaid that the arrangement was entirely acceptable—"

"There is no agreement!" he shouted. It was a fearsome thing even without him moving much to do it. "Georgiana is not marrying—or courting—that Scot!"

"Do you have a complaint to lodge against Lord Kincaid's person?"

"I am not lodging a complaint!" he said. "This is not a court where I petition for a movement. He is not courting her, and she is not marrying him, and if she wants to hear that herself, she can come in here, and I will tell her!"

Elizabeth did allow herself a bit of loss of temper. "May I remind you, Mr. Darcy, that she is no longer of an age where she requires your consent?"

"Georgiana would not do something I did not consent to," he said. "I know her, and I know she would never do such a thing." She wanted to respond (even though he was technically correct in this regard), but he continued, "If she is so intent on marrying this man, why doesn't she make the request herself? Why must it come from you? Do you think you need to protect her from me?" His voice was now officially above the norm.

"This is *my* sister, whom I have given my life to protecting! Do you think I do not have her best interests at heart? Or that you, of no blood relation, would have better ideas?"

"Mr. Darcy!"

"Mr. Darcy *what*? Yes, yes, I am Mr. Darcy!" he said. "You think yourself more intelligent than me? *You think I'm mad?*"

He did not break his stare, so it just hung in the air like a stale thing; the silence that followed it was unbearable as Elizabeth covered her mouth to hide her sob. Darcy's expression softened when he heard it, and he rose, came around the desk, and held her hands, which was as close as he'd come to voluntarily touching her in days, despite their sharing a bed. "Lizzy." But his eyes were still unreadable. They were not soft or hard. "Just—no more talk of this. Please."

The way he said it, she could not deny him. Very uncomfortably, she said, "All right."

She dealt with Georgiana's tears later, in privacy, while her husband slept. In the morning, they departed for Pemberley.

The Bingleys were set to depart for Chatton but were delayed slightly by Bingley's delicate head injury, as a carriage ride was not immediately recommended. As Dr. Maddox recovered, Brian Maddox spent much of his time at the Bingley townhouse. "We're going into business together," he said to his brother in Dr. Maddox's study. Brian still refused, except when invited to dine at the Bingleys', to dress like a civilized man and was walking around in his silk pleated pants and robe. He was totally unconcerned about the opinion of the Town passing in the streets. His wife did not go out much, but when she did, it was with Mugin, who was even more of a spectacle.

"There's really no need for the armed procession," Dr. Maddox said. "We *are* in England."

His brother, with two swords in his belt, merely said, "I promised to carry these swords, and I will. As for Mugin, I don't recommend asking him to leave his sword behind unless you want a sandal to your head." He added with a smile, "He will do it. I've seen him do it." He reached into the folds of his robe and removed an envelope, which he passed over the desk. "I know this is little consolation for my absence when you needed me, but I did write when I was in Japan. There was no post at all, but I wrote to you, in hopes of someday delivering it. Some of it may sound like nonsense, but it is all true. Except, of course, the things I left out."

Dr. Maddox nodded. "Thank you." Brian bowed and left.

Dr. Maddox was not heard from for several hours, until it was nearly time for dinner, and Caroline knocked on the door. "Come."

"Your presence is required for dinner, Dr. Maddox," she said, her eyes passing over the pile of rice paper letters in tiny handwriting. "What in the world is that?"

"Brian's journal, in the form of letters to me," he said. "It's really quite fascinating."

"Oh God," she said. "First my brother with India, and now *your* brother with the Orient. Am I to have any *normal* dinner table discussions ever again?"

He passed her one of the piles. "Here. So you can at least contribute to the conversation."

Caroline gave him an indignant look. She did, however, take the letters—not returning them until late the next day, when she requested to see the rest.

Chapter 27

BRIAN'S STORY, PART 3

1810

THE PEACE WAS POSITIVELY beautiful. The chirping of unfamiliar birds, the sound of cooking and rustling outside, the sounds of the ocean not far away... Was he in Brighton? No, it was too bright for that. And his surroundings too wooden, too square; the woman facing him was not a proper English nurse. She forced broth down his throat, salty and fishy, then bowed and disappeared, leaving him on the white mattress on the floor.

He was vaguely aware that he was alone, and from the windows, that it was daylight. He was stripped of everything but his undergarments and shirt, but he was not chained down. They must have made a guess that he was incapable of movement, much less escape.

There he lay for he knew not how long. Slowly it came to him. *Nadezhda!* If they'd done anything to her, they would pay. Surely they realized she was his wife? What had he done, to throw her alone among such savages? He had to get up, he had to recover his strength, and he had to save her.

He sat up only with great dizziness and sat there until it passed. When he finally managed to get to his feet, Brian could only stay upright with the help of the wall, which seemed to be made of bound stalks. His limp was more pronounced than usual as every part of his body screamed out. He slowly shambled over to the doorway, where he found a richly colored silk robe more ornate than anything he had ever worn in his life and a pair of sandals made from the same grass-like stalk.

There was no guard outside. He wandered onto the porch, grasping the railing for support. Several times the world went into a haze, but then refocused, and he continued down the porch looking for another room, maybe containing his beloved.

There was a man around the corner, dressed differently, and obviously Oriental. He was wearing a black robe, pants that were wide enough to resemble a skirt, and sandals, and his head was curiously shaved like a balding person, with long hair in the back tied up in a knot above it. He seemed to pay little attention to the limping figure of Brian Maddox, looking out at the ocean instead, resting his hands within the folds of his robe. Then, from nowhere, he said something in quite a forceful voice to Brian and walked away.

Brian could not go on. He knew that much. He rested, if only for a moment, on the wooden steps, warming himself in the sunlight. The world went out again, or almost. He must have nodded off, because the man in front of him had appeared out of nowhere and was poking him awake with a stick tied up with gourds. This man was different—paler, with a long white beard and truncated pants like breeches but no proper shoes, just wooden sandals on stilts.

"Speak—speak Russian?" Brian finally murmured.

"Yes. A little," he answered.

"Where is Nadezhda?" It was then that Brian noted that the man had not one but three curved swords in his rope belt, one hanging on one side and two on the other. He said a bit less forcefully, "My wife. Please."

"Not Russian, *gaijin?*"

"I ask again," he said in his own semi-broken Russian. "Where is Nadezhda?"

The man hit him on the shoulder. Right on that injured nerve that went all the way down to his leg. He must have known—but he could not have known. The man only smiled and walked away with his stick rattling from the various implements tied to it, leaving Brian to writhe in pain.

"You should have known better," said the man next to him, a man dressed similarly to the old man, but younger, his Russian perfectly fluent. "You cannot make empty threats."

"It was not empty," Brian growled.

"You have no force. You are injured and sick. And you have no respect for Kayano, who declared that your life be spared."

"I—apologize," Brian said, trying to remember his Russian in an agitated state. "Sorry."

"*Gomen nasai.*"

"What?"

"Sorry. *Gomen nasai,*" he said more clearly.

Brian understood. He knew enough smatterings of languages to understand when he was being taught one even if he didn't know which one it was. "*Gomen nasai.*"

"Good." The man offered his own hand and helped Brian to his very shaky feet. "She is your wife?"

"Yes."

"Not your lover? Running away?"

"No. But we are—run away," Brian said. He should have learned more Russian. Nadezhda was so much better. "Where is she?"

"*Doko*. Where."

"*Doko*," Brian said, it coming out more impatiently than he would have liked.

"Follow," said the man. "I am Tahkonanna."

"Brian Maddox." He reached out to shake hands, but apparently, the man didn't know what that meant so he retracted it. "Where am I?"

"Otasuh."

"Cathay?"

"Nippon."

Did he mean the Japans? How did they ever get here? It must have been closer than Brian imagined. Or they had been truly lost at sea for longer than they thought. He forgot all that when he was helped into the next room and found his wife on a similar bed being attended to by the woman in the tightly wrapped silk robe. She scampered out, bowing stiffly, like a man, to Brian and Tahkonanna. Brian would have run in, if he could walk without the Oriental's help. But Tahkonanna stopped him. "Shoes."

"What?"

"Your shoes. Please." For the man had already slipped his off.

Brian did so, treading barefoot to his wife's side. "Nadezhda." Whether the Oriental took his leave or not, Brian paid no attention as he cupped her cheek. "Nady?"

This seemed to jostle her awake. "Brian," she said, her voice weak but less clouded than his, possibly because she had the sensibility to be resting when they were both obviously still weakened. "Are you all right?"

"Fine," Brian said in Romanian, kissing her hand. "Now."

"Your color—you should lie down. Now."

He was happy to oblige. He was feeling drained and if in this strange country it was terrible for a husband and wife to lie together, then they would have to suffer the embarrassment. "I love you," he whispered, nestling his head into the crook of her neck, and then his strength was truly and wholly gone again.

Now that the immediate problem of locating his wife and seeing that she was being cared for was solved, Brian did not attempt the same feat of moving about again for some time. Nor did they interrogate their hosts, whom they saw little of except for the old woman with the food who spoke no Russian. They barely moved at all beyond the basic necessities of life.

"Do you know where we are?"

"Japan, I think. We must have been driven south by the currents."

"Japan is not so far south from Russia."

"No?" To be honest, his non-Western geography was not particularly well-researched. "I suppose not."

They eventually learned Kayano was the head of the village, and Tahkonanna his son, who was fluent from some trade with the Russians. They had every intention of forcing their guests to learn their language. Instruction began immediately, but it was so foreign (and Brian's Russian not so perfectly fluent to begin with) in nature that they could barely pronounce it.

The days fell into a familiar routine. In their weakness they spent much time sitting on steps of the porch of their hut, watching the villagers go to and fro, and listening to their conversations.

There was one ritual that was never altered, not even for Sundays, whenever Sundays were here and if they even existed. Every morning, the man in the blue pants and black shirt would fight Kayano in the sort of town center in front of them. They had determined that he was from a different tribe because he dressed and acted differently, and seemed most aloof and unhappy to be there. Every day he took up a wooden sword and charged at Kayano with fury. Every day Kayano fought him off with only his staff, without drawing any one of his three swords. Despite his advanced age, Kayano was wiry and seemed impossibly accomplished at not only walking on those wooden stilt shoes but also fighting in them. Once, they even saw him block the wooden blade with his own shoe, balancing on the other leg, to which the man in black threw down his sword in frustration, bowed, and walked away.

"His name is Miyoshi," said Tahkonanna.

"He is not from here?" Nadezhda said in Russian.

"No. He is *ronin*." When they looked at him, he shook his head. "Warrior is the best similar word, but not the same. He is not Ainu."

"Ainu?"

"Us. Not Japanese."

Brian decided to hold back his remark that they seemed similar enough. "What is he doing here?"

For this, Tahkonanna had to switch to Russian. "Father took away his swords, and he cannot leave until he gets them back."

"Why?"

"He insulted his honor. By law, Father had every right to take his head. He chose this way instead. Now the stupid samurai will win his swords back and take his own head over the shame." He shook his head.

Brian looked at his wife; they decided to interpret that as a mistranslation because it made no sense and they did not want to offend their hosts. Instead, Brian changed the subject as Miyoshi was knocked off his feet yet again. "Miyoshi keeps saying something to me. I don't understand it." He attempted to repeat the Nipponese phrase to the best of his ability.

"'In the land of the Rising Sun, even if dogs, cats, and bugs can live, there is no law that Westerners can live,'" Tahkonanna said.

"Is that true?"

"By law we should have killed you on sight, Madokusu-san."

Brian wondered if they were saving it up.

When he procured a pen—more of a brush—some ink and paper, Brian "Madokusu" began to write. Specifically, he was writing to his brother, but the utter lack of mail service prevented him from sending anything. That did not discourage him from pouring out every fascinating detail onto the page. It was also nice to write in English again, a language he'd used only to mutter to himself in the last year. He also ticked off the days as soon as he became aware enough of their passing. They had been in Otasuh nearly a month now. As unlikely as it was that any of his posts from Russia had made it to England, he had literally dropped off the map, and he doubted if he could find where he was on a map.

It was also a comfort. They were gone beyond the known world and certainly beyond the count's now terribly extensive reach. They had found shelter at last. Maybe they could, somehow, return to England. Brian knew that the Dutch East India Company stopped in Japan for the silk trade. When he inquired where, Kayano said, "To the south."

"How far?" he asked.

"Very far."

In the evenings, most of the men smoked long, wooden pipes in front of the fire, where their language skills increased tremendously. Brian brought up again the most important subject to Tahkonanna, switching back and forth between Japanese and Russian when needed.

"You have discovered you cannot stay here," his host said, and Brian nodded. "If the authorities find you, they will execute you."

"And you, for taking us in?"

Tahkonanna nodded.

"Where should we go? Back to Russia?"

"Can you travel to your home from there?"

"No. We cannot go the way we came. We must go to Cathay."

"The Middle Kingdom does not tolerate *gaijin* much more than we do."

Brian sighed.

"Miyoshi-san says there is a port for foreigners. Nagasaki. From there, you could ride a ship to the west."

"How far is Nagasaki? Did he say?"

"It is the length of Japan. Very far."

"How would we get there?"

Tahkonanna seemed surprised by the question. "How else? You walk."

"But—we cannot travel in Japan. As *gaijin*."

"No." The Ainu blew a ring of smoke. "I will ask Kayano-sama."

Later that night, Brian retired with his wife. No one had any opposition to their sleeping arrangements, or if they did, they expressed none. Tonight, they did not do much sleeping. Brian propped himself up, and they spoke in hushed tones, even though they doubted anyone spoke a word of Romanian. "We cannot stay."

"I know," Nadezhda said. "But Lord Kayano is thinking of a plan."

He rolled onto his back. "I don't know why he's being so kind to us."

"I don't think the Ainu like the Japanese, or the other way around, or both," she said. "Miyoshi looks down on all of them. Haven't you noticed?"

"I have. But he looks down on us too, so it's hard to tell if that's not just his general disposition."

"But he has not betrayed us."

"That we know of."

There was a call at the door. It was not possible to knock with the paper sliding doors. Brian had accidentally destroyed his twice already.

"Coming," he said in Russian, as he closed his sash and went to the door. It was Kayano. "*Nani?*" (What?)

"*Kinasai,*" (Come!) Kayano said, with a little urgency in his voice. Brian nodded to his wife, slipped on his sandals, followed the old man out the door and out into the woods surrounding the forest. Kayano stopped in front of an old lantern and a statue of some sort. It seemed to be a sort of shrine. "Now," he said. "Take this." He passed him a wooden sword. Brian held it in his hands in confusion. "Now. Defend!"

As slow of an attack as it was, he was not ready for it. He barely got the sword up in time to block the staff from hitting him, and the force of it threw the sword right out of his hands.

"Get it!" Kayano demanded, and Brian scrambled to the wooden sword. This time, he took a proper stance against him, holding it up in his right hand. "Stupid *gaijin*! Reverse!"

"Reverse what?"

"Side! Reverse your side!" Kayano insisted. "You are weak on your right. Don't reveal it!"

He meant, of course, to fight left-handed. "But—" He did not know the proper translation for "un-gentlemanly." Not that he had considered himself a gentleman in a long time, but that did not mean he forgot how to fence. "Not—proper."

"Left side! Now!" Kayano beat his staff against the ground impatiently. Brian hesitantly took up his left side. Still, the old man was not happy. "Both hands on blade!"

Brian did not attempt to argue this. He put his hands on the blade as he had seen Miyoshi do time and time again, even though at least Miyoshi fought properly, on his right side.

"Now. Block!"

He was stronger on his left but untrained. He barely managed to block again, but this time he did not lose the sword.

"Again!"

So it continued. Block, block, block. By the end he was sweating and exhausted, while Kayano's response was to strike his feet. "Move them!"

"I can't—"

"Motion!"

Brian stepped back in a sort of shuffle, maintaining his stance.

"The Buddha says change drives the world. Change is inevitable. You must change!" Kayano said, but then more calmly continued, "But you know this."

Weakly, Brian nodded.

"You have changed many times. Many, many times. Like a wheel moving too fast."

Again, he nodded.

"Miyoshi cannot change. Japanese, they cannot adapt. Every day, the same strike! Every day, the same block! Useless samurai. He would be better use to you," he said. "Change or die."

With that, he let Brian hobble back to his room, where he collapsed next to his wife and fell promptly asleep.

At the next meeting, it was decided. "Pilgrims," Kayano said, and the others nodded.

"Pilgrims cover their faces and speak little," Tahkonanna said. "You will go to visit a shrine in the south."

"Apologies," Nadezhda said, "but how will we find our way?"

"Miyoshi-san," Kayano announced, to Miyoshi's surprise. The samurai, whatever that meant, stood off to the side of village meetings, his hands in the folds of his robe. Kayano rose, pulled out the two swords on his right side, and presented them to Miyoshi. "You will escort them to Nagasaki. Do you know the way?"

"*Hai*," Miyoshi said, obviously shocked at the gesture.

"Then take them there, samurai," Kayano said, then handed him his swords, which Miyoshi quickly slipped into his belt. "And then do what you will."

Miyoshi bowed to him before Kayano turned his attentions back to the couple. "We have obtained a traveler's permit, some money, and provisions for the road. When you are well enough, you will go."

"We have no way to repay you," Brian said, bowing low to the ground from his kneeling position as he'd seen others do before Kayano-sama, Lord Kayano.

But Kayano just laughed and slapped him on the shoulder before walking off.

Their instructions on how to dress and act like pilgrims began in the morning; first thing to do was to learn how to wear gigantic hats that were little more than overturned rush buckets with slits to see through. These illogical contraptions were not at all heavy and would thoroughly hide their features, but they had to be tied because, to the best of his knowledge, Brian hadn't seen a buckle or button since they left Russia.

Tahkonanna aided them. Miyoshi went off somewhere, and they did not see him but were assured that he would keep to his assignment all the way to Nagasaki. "He is an honorable man."

"He is a bit..." Nadezhda searched for the word in Japanese. "Rude."

"He is proud. Samurai. The warrior class. Nobility."

"What is he do—here?" Brian asked as the village head's son showed them how to tie up their white pilgrim's outfits with all the proper knots.

"Doing here," he corrected. "I don't know what he did, but he had to leave his lord, a very dishonorable thing. He came here to die. *Seppuku.* So sorry, I don't know the word in Russian."

"Kill himself?" Brian said.

"Suicide?" Nadezhda said in Russian.

"Yes." He gestured with his hand as if he was holding a sword and thrusting it into his stomach. "*Seppuku.* A very honorable way to die, the proper action, for one who has brought shame to themselves."

Then I would be dead many times over, Brian mused. "Are you serious?"

Tahkonanna gave them both a look of mild surprise, which indicated that he was, and they decided not to push the matter any further. "Here." He handed him what appeared to be a walking stick but upon closer inspection it had an obvious handle and a longer portion.

Brian pulled it apart to reveal a thin sword. "I don't know how to use this."

"You've never held a sword?"

"Oh, I have, but—never in serious combat. We use guns."

"Your gun was destroyed, Madokusu-san. Miyoshi-san is your samurai. It is only for emergencies," he assured him. "Nadi-san," and he passed her a much smaller one, which could be concealed easily in her robes.

There was another town nearby that had regular trade with the Russians, however illegal. Through them, Brian and Nadezhda were able to convert their fortune to Japanese coinage. Brian offered some to Kayano, who refused. "You will take this instead." He pointed to his head.

Brian wasn't quite sure how literal he was being. "What?"

"Memories," Kayano said. "We have lost. The Japanese came from the south and defeated us. In time, we will be gone. But you will remember."

Brian understood and bowed.

That night, they shaved his head or most of it. His usually wild mane of hair was particularly hard to trim, as it was naturally frizzy and overly knotted. They shaved off his long,

Russian-esque beard, including the sideburns. The only thing they left long was the back, to be tied up in a knot of some kind, and he left the room feeling more naked than he had ever been in his life despite being otherwise covered in clothing.

When he entered his chambers, Nadezhda made no attempt to hide her laughter at his bizarrely tonsured head.

"It's not funny," he said in Romanian with mock indignity.

"Oh, darling, I've not seen you this way for a long time. Or ever," she said, holding out her arms as an invitation. He sat down on the mattress beside her as she caressed his face. "Though your cheeks do feel good again."

"I had no idea you took such pleasure in them."

"Now that I have told you, you must be as fastidious in your shaving habits as you can."

He kissed her. "Of course."

She continued to massage his face and then his neck. Over their long flight and then even longer recovery from typhus, they had had understandably little time for any intimacy.

"We will have to be very quiet," he whispered into her neck. "I don't think these walls are particularly good at disguising sound."

"Then they must be accustomed to it," she said simply, because she always seemed to take things with greater ease than he did. She had learned the language better than he had. She had no provocation against approaching elders and speaking for herself, and they seemed unruffled by it, here in this tiny barbarian village at the end of the world. She was his Nadezhda, and she was constantly surprising him. He had already decided, long ago, that he liked that part of their marriage very much.

"We don't know how to thank you," Brian said to Kayano, meaning it somewhat literally. The leader had already refused what little Russian coinage they had, saying they would need it in Nagasaki.

"Taking Miyoshi-san off our hands is enough," said Tahkonanna. "Good luck."

"I would say we would never be this way again," Brian said, "but luck keeps surprising me." He tightened his grip on his wife's hand, and though with the bucket of straw over his head he could not see her smile, he could feel it.

Miyoshi was waiting for them, up the road, as they said their good-byes to the village. Other than wearing a hat that resembled a lampshade, which covered the upper half of his face, his traveling clothes were no different from his regular ones. "It will be good if you remain silent," Miyoshi said. "Your accents give you away."

"How far is Nagasaki?"

"Very far. Months."

They were going to be walking for months? Brian looked at Nadezhda through the holes of his *tengai* nervously. Could she take it? Could he take it? Miyoshi seemed to have no hesitation at such a long journey on foot, even in sandals.

"Have you ever been there?" Nadezhda asked.

"No," Miyoshi said.

"But you've been close."

"Edo."

That was, or so Brian recalled, the capital. "Are you from there, Miyoshi-san?"

"No." That seemed to be the end of his answer for a long time, before he added, "I worked there."

Both of them had enough sense to know this was not something to probe further. The rest of the day was passed mainly in silence.

THE HARVEST FESTIVAL

1812

THE DARCYS RETURNED TO Pemberley as quietly as was possible, which was not very quietly, and Elizabeth discreetly tugged on her husband's hand as he observed the crowd greeting him as if he was a distant, uncomfortable observer. He did nod and acknowledge them in every necessary way required of him, and then retired to his chambers until dinner. Though he did not express it, he was obviously most displeased that they had delayed the harvest festival until his return, which meant he had to preside over it. Decorations were thrown up as quickly as possible, and he made only a minimal appearance. Georgiana was also in a state of despair but managed to put on a smile as Elizabeth reassured her that Darcy would come around. Still, Elizabeth imagined that to have one's future put on hold by an overprotective elder brother was clearly its own strain.

Settled at Pemberley, Darcy's physical recovery continued, but he remained retreated from everything except the basic civilities required for social life. He saw his children but didn't play with them; Georgiana and Grégoire were officially charged with distracting Geoffrey and Anne from their father's infirmary. Sarah Darcy was not old enough to notice.

There was also the other matter, that of Elizabeth's own increasing girth. Since Austria, Darcy had made no attempts to involve her in conversation about her condition. She knew that her own emotions were not as they normally were, after the strain of both what was happening with her own body and what was happening to their family, but that could not help her dismiss her fears.

There was one resident also hurt by Darcy's infirmary, whatever it was, and it was Georgiana. Georgiana Darcy, a child no longer, was sitting on her heels impatiently but *so patiently*. She loved her brother, yes, but he was not her responsibility. Elizabeth doubted that in the throes of love she would have so much patience for her own father if he had not consented to her own marriage, but Georgiana sat in silence.

In their time as sisters, Elizabeth and Georgiana had treated each other as such, and the younger of the pair had blossomed, but perhaps now was the time to stop unconsciously looking down at her as a young girl.

Her mind guiltily set, Elizabeth found Georgiana in her sitting room, reading. The book was in French. "Georgiana."

"Elizabeth." She set it aside as if she was ashamed of it.

"What are you reading, if I may inquire?"

"Oh, it's—I borrowed it from Mrs. Maddox. It's a history of Scotland. They were allies for many years, the Scots and the French, against the English." She picked it back up and caressed it. "It makes me feel nearer... somehow."

"Your brother will give in."

"He shouldn't have to give in," Georgiana said with a surprising amount of anger. "He's my brother, and I'm in love with a man who will care for me and isn't terribly far away from Derbyshire. Why should he resist? I am sick of his protectiveness." She put her hand over her mouth. "Forgive me. I don't understand him sometimes."

"*Sometimes?*" Elizabeth said. "But—in regards to yourself, to all of us, may I ask you something?"

Georgiana looked up at her. "Of course."

"Do you think Darcy is well?"

Her sister-in-law did seem to grasp the severity of her meaning, because she looked down at the book again, and then away, before answering, "I don't know. I'm perhaps not the best person to ask."

"You've known him all of your life."

"But he's always been distant—or he was, before he was married. You know he's been more a father to me than a brother." She shook her head. "I cannot judge."

It did not settle Elizabeth. It had the opposite effect, but she made every attempt to hide it in order to continue the conversation. "Has Darcy said anything—odd—to you?"

"What do you mean?"

"Off. Strange."

Georgiana frowned. "I think he meant it in privacy."

"You don't have to say it, then."

"But," her sister-in-law considered, "he didn't *say* it was private. I just don't think he meant to be heard. That's... fair, isn't it?" She looked to Elizabeth for approval and was nodded on. "He said he never left Austria. He said he never will." She paused before going on. "Forgive me, but I could not think of what to say to that."

"I cannot imagine he was asking for a response."

Georgiana's voice was wavering. "You don't think he's well, do you? Something rattled him in Transylvania?" Before Elizabeth could respond, she said, "Should he see a doctor? Not Dr. Maddox, I suppose."

"No," she said. "I've... thought of it. But I cannot bring myself to subject him to that. Besides, even Dr. Maddox's opinion of mind doctors is poor." *I'm not sending him to Bedlam,* she thought. *I'm not giving up what little of him I have left.* "He needs to talk to someone."

"Then of course it should be you!" Georgiana said. "Lizzy, you are the only person I know who can alter anything in him. Believe me when I say, if anyone is to reach him, it can only be you."

Determined to do so, Elizabeth returned to the house, went into her study, and sat down to write the hardest letter of her life.

If Darcy knew anything, he said nothing. He said little at all. He did have a lot of business to conduct, having been gone for half a year between his trips to Rosings and his stay on the Continent, and often spent hours with his ledgers in his study. At the end of very late nights, as Elizabeth stayed up waiting for him, he slipped into bed clothed and with barely more than a good night. Her enforced celibacy continued. He was often up and about when she awoke.

So it continued, for two unbearable weeks, until the Maddoxes came up to visit Chatton. Darcy pleaded business to excuse himself from the call. He had not been outside Pemberley's doors in nearly a month. Elizabeth did not fight him this time and went to call on the Bingleys—and Dr. Maddox.

The months had obviously been better to the doctor, who had returned to his old pallor for the most part. He didn't look the best she had ever seen him, with gray hairs coming in at the roots where there had once been black, but he was a man who had returned to health and society. "Mrs. Darcy."

"Dr. Maddox."

He waved off the servant and closed the door before settling into a seat next to the table between them. In his hands was her letter, now a bit rumpled from use. He glanced through its several pages before putting it on the table and turning his attention to her. "Have there been any changes I should know about?"

"No."

"Well, then," he said. "I spoke to Sir Richard Gregory, former doctor of the mind research at Oxford and the current head of the staff in charge of His Majesty."

"I am impressed," she said, "and grateful."

"We do cross paths on occasion," he said. "He agreed to review the case with me and studied my set of notes without the patient's identity. He is one of the few mentalists I respect as a doctor. That said, I cannot honestly say I recommend his advice."

"So he reached a diagnosis?"

"He said he could not without examining the patient. Then again, he's had half a dozen different diagnoses over the years for His Majesty. It isn't quite like looking at a wound or listening to a cough, as you can no doubt imagine. Eventually he said monomania, but that is really a diagnosis for someone whom the physician—and the family—wishes to be committed."

She knew the blow was coming and had been attempting, for these weeks, to brace herself for it.

"This is why I do not care much for mind doctors," he said grimly. "If Darcy is, to be plain, not fit to reenter society, then taking him away from it will not amend the situation; it will make it worse."

"Do you think he is unfit?"

"I think he's unwell." Dr. Maddox had no hesitation saying it. He never seemed to have a problem speaking with the formality of a doctor. "He is more withdrawn than some men, but that is not a great flaw in his character by any means. In fact, I have always regarded Mr. Darcy as one of the most upstanding gentlemen I have ever met. He is not cruel, he is not malicious, and he is not abusive. He does not turn his anxieties into anger. For the most part, he has managed them. Then, of course, we had Austria." Now he did lose some of his composure, if subtly so. "We tried to keep each other sane by talking about anything. We recited poetry. We told stories. We recited as much literature as we could remember, but there were long hours, and there was a darkness there—metaphorical and literal—that could not be escaped. Eventually you just... gave in."

Elizabeth put her hand over her mouth. She wanted to cry. It seemed odd that she was more upset than Dr. Maddox, who was speaking of his own experiences. "But you are well."

"I am a different case entirely. I have withstood loneliness before. Not on that scale, but I lived alone. Many years in poverty in the East End, surrounded by disease, and hunted by Brian's less scrupulous creditors. In a way, I was more acclimated to the circumstances." He sighed. "The chief difference between me and Darcy is the desire to return to normal life."

"What did the king's doctor recommend—beyond Bedlam?"

"Some pills that he gives the king, which I see no sense in, as they obviously don't work and the king has a completely different condition, more of a disease than something the result of trauma. The one suggestion I would actually follow is a certain tea, which mixed with certain ingredients can be very calming. When mixed with others, it can help a person sleep. I will venture a guess that he is not sleeping well. That, at least, I think we can convince him of." He continued, "Beyond that, my own recommendation—though I am no expert of the mental realm—is to talk to him. After all, he should not be excluded from his own treatment." Before she could respond, he said, "If you would permit me, I wish to speak with him."

"He might not take well to it."

"Maybe not. But we have at least some common ground on which to chat," he said grimly.

OUT OF AUSTRIA

THE NEXT DAY, a terrible downpour descended on Derbyshire. It was not the gentle May showers that the children enjoyed playing in before Nurse discovered them, but the cold, harsh rain of early winter, not quite snow yet, but cold enough to be almost sleet.

Elizabeth seemed surprised when Dr. Maddox made his scheduled appearance, even though the walk from the carriage to the front door had him thoroughly soaked. "Mrs. Darcy."

"Dr. Maddox," she curtseyed. "I did not expect you, to be honest. I would not want you to put your health at risk."

"I was more concerned for the carriage driver than myself. Please alert me if he takes ill, but I never miss my appointments."

He was rushed at by the servants, who attended to his coat and hat and provided him with all the towels he needed. Beyond that, he was not interested in wasting time. "Where is he?"

"He's not yet left the bedchamber. He is not seeing visitors. I told him Bingley was coming, and he said to say he was busy with his ledgers."

It was half past noon. Dr. Maddox refrained from comment. "Do I have your permission to intrude on the master's quarters?"

To his surprise, Elizabeth blushed as they climbed the grand staircase. "Mr. Darcy has always preferred the mistress's quarters."

Again, no comment. "So I have your permission."

"Yes," she said, as they headed into the private wing of the master and mistress of Pemberley's rooms. "I dismissed all the servants except for his manservant, who is aware of the situation." She added, "I think Darcy has his suspicions."

"They are not unreasonable suspicions at this point," he said as he was brought to the doors that led to her chambers. "Thank you, Mrs. Darcy."

She was emotional as she had to leave him to his business. As a physician he was normally accustomed to this, but not so much with a relative, especially when he had little idea of what he was doing. "All will be well, Mrs. Darcy. Time heals all wounds." The quotation was not actually true, as he had certainly never seen anyone's leg grow back, but it seemed to comfort her enough for him to enter the room and close the door behind him.

The sounds of rain and thunder filled the room, as everything else was perfectly quiet. Darcy, sitting in an armchair that was turned to face the window, could have easily heard the shuffling on the carpet and said without turning around, "I do not recall summoning you to my private chambers."

"As you seem to be unwilling to greet guests, I had to resort to more drastic measures," Dr. Maddox said, slowly approaching Darcy's end of the room. It was terribly dark, the only light from the dreary sky and a candle by the bed stand.

"Maddox," Darcy said, his voice less harsh, but not lightened. "Doctor. Please don't come any closer."

"We lived together in a space half this size for months; I can hardly believe that you are so bothered by my presence." Without Darcy's permission, he strode up to the window, his hands behind his back. He did not eye Darcy like a specimen, but looked only briefly enough to tell that he was dressed, even if none of his clothing matched, and he hadn't shaved in a day or two. Beside him was a tea tray on a stand.

"So, I am not to expect a straitjacket? Or are you the distraction while burlier men sneak behind me?"

"No," Dr. Maddox said quietly. "Nothing of the sort, I assure you."

"You have no bag, I see."

"I have no instruments that can help you, Mr. Darcy. I am only here to write a prescription, and I can do that in any room of the house." Again without permission, he pulled the other armchair formerly by the fireplace and placed it on the other side of the stand.

"People die from those magic pills," Darcy said. "I am not a fool."

"That is why I so rarely prescribe them," Dr. Maddox said, sitting down and pouring himself a cup of tea. Darcy was apparently stupefied by his presence, lacking all of his usual healthy demeanor and assertiveness. "It's actually just a recipe for a tonic that aids in a night's sleep."

"You wish to drug me?"

"I wish to recommend it. I assume you've not been sleeping well."

"So I am to have no secrets from anyone?"

"It is not a secret. It is plainly written under your eyes." He sat back, dish in hand. "I did not know of it until it was prescribed to me by my own physician. I take it every night and it works wonders for me." He sipped the tea, and then put down the dish. "The tea is cold. Should I ring for more?"

"No!" Darcy said, alarmed. He recovered quickly, saying more passively, "No. You shall not. These are my chambers, in my house, and I will decide who rings for what. Am I not the master of Pemberley?"

Dr. Maddox said softly, "It seems more that you have made yourself a prisoner of Pemberley."

Darcy did not respond in anger. He didn't fret or fidget. He merely retreated into himself, gazing out the window. That, at least, was unchanged from the old Darcy. "I can leave if I want to."

"I don't think you can."

Darcy considered this for a moment, gathering his answer. "I know you think I'm mad. I know you've been watching me since our return."

"Then apparently you knew about it before I did, for I was only informed of your suffering a few weeks ago."

To this, Darcy had no answer. He did look eager to give one, but words seemed to fail him.

Dr. Maddox turned and looked into his eyes. Darcy's eyes were the only part of his body not slackened. They betrayed the turmoil inside him. "Darcy, I am not here to have you sent away or to encourage your family to do so. I came here primarily to give your housekeeper instructions for a drink that will help you sleep. My secondary motive was more in line with your suspicions, but not quite so wild. Your family *is* concerned for you, and *did* contact me, and *did* answer my questions about your behavior."

"So there is a conspiracy."

"I would not use that term."

"I would call any number of people planning behind my back to do something against me a conspiracy. You can call it what you like, Doctor. I really don't care."

"I'm going to ring for more tea."

He rose, but as he did, Darcy grasped his arm very tightly. "Please don't. Have pity on me!"

There was a sudden surge in Daniel Maddox, and he left his formal doctor mode entirely. "Have pity on you!" The shocked Darcy slumped at this wild deviation from the mood, as he faced a towering man with a loud, raw voice. "You! You, who sat in a cell while I entertained you, while I wanted to die from the pain in my hand, as my flesh rotted away from infection! You, who were not so easily discarded by the count, who was looking for someone to mindlessly take his frustrations out on!" None of this was calculated. In fact, it was the very definition of sudden. His mood had varied unexpectedly since he had returned, but he had restrained himself in company. But now he grabbed Darcy by his vest and nearly pulled him out of his chair. "Do you know what they did to me? First Trommler and then the count? Did you sit in a chair for three days without food or water while being interrogated? And yet I have to go on, like nothing happened, because I don't own a great estate that I can hide in and turn into my own private cell! All because I'm not rich enough to ignore everyone beneath me, even my own wife!" He found himself, once he had shaken the life out of Darcy and shouted more than he had in his entire life in one breath, quite woozy. He released the petrified Darcy and stepped back, first leaning against the window and then, when his legs failed him, sliding down to the ground, with his hands over his face.

A meek Darcy said, "Neither of us left Austria."

"You're wrong," Dr. Maddox said, still not recovered. "We brought it back here with us."

Outside, the rain continued unabated.

"What do we do now?"

Dr. Maddox lacked a prepared answer. He had only throttled one other patient, also a relative, and there he felt he was justified. He had reason to lose his head while intoxicated. He had no reason to do so with a disturbed patient. "I don't know."

"So there are no doctors to heal the mind?"

"It is not possible. In this we are quite inept." Dr. Maddox was exhausted. Facing Darcy had reopened wounds he thought healed.

"Then why are you still here?" Darcy's tone was not insulting. It was more a desperate inquiry. "Why do you not leave me alone?"

"Because if I do," Dr. Maddox said, "we know there is only one option before us, and though it might seem a relief to you to remain confined, I will not stand to see your family—*my* family—suffer it."

Darcy stood up and walked to the window for a moment before offering his hand to the doctor, who got to his feet. Darcy couldn't meet his eyes, distinctly looking away but in no particular direction.

"I'm sorry," Dr. Maddox said. "I should have been more professional."

"It depends if you consider me a patient or a friend."

Dr. Maddox half-smiled. "I suppose you're right."

Darcy removed his wig. "I hate this sodding thing." He tossed it on the bed. His hair was beginning to come in again, enough to cover his head adequately, but he still looked quite different than he normally did. "I can go outside if I want to."

"Prove it."

Darcy visibly steeled himself before running out of the room. Dr. Maddox followed curiously, but not particularly quickly, as Darcy bypassed his wife, servants, and by-then curious doorman, and ran out the front doors of Pemberley, into the rain.

"Darcy!" Elizabeth said, chasing after him.

Dr. Maddox sighed to himself and walked up to the window, watching her disappear into the forest after her husband.

"Are you in the habit of just letting your patients run away from you, Doctor?" Mrs. Reynolds asked next to him.

"No," he said, "but I suppose I can't be expected to hold on to every one."

Elizabeth lost Darcy, but she never felt like she truly lost him. She knew where he would go, almost instinctually—like a child, he would go somewhere he felt safe. She knew all of his spots. He had, after all, spent the first happy months of their marriage showing her every inch of Pemberley's vast grounds and explained every spot where he might have fallen, or played, or caught a fish. With the downpour, there were very few options. The trees did little to lessen it. But there was a shelter—near the waterfall—that was so beautiful in the summer. There had even been a bench there, but it was brought in for the winter now. She was lucky it was such a warm December. "Darcy!"

"Go away," he said, and she turned to her left. Her soaked husband was indeed sitting under the little wooden canopy, or had been sitting, but he rose in alarm when she approached. "Just—please. Leave me."

"Darcy—"

"I don't mean you any disrespect—"

"I'm sure you don't!" she shouted, which had its intentional devastating effect.

"How can you know what I feel?"

"Yes, sir! How, indeed, can I know if you do not tell me?"

Darcy turned away; she was not sure in anger or in befuddlement. Even with nowhere to escape to, he was doing his best to try, but she grabbed his arm and tugged on his coat. "Darcy," she said, softening her tone. "I am your wife of nine years, and I take it with insult that you do not share with me your concerns. Please, *tell me*."

He said nothing. He did not move, either away or closer to her. His face was partially hidden in shadow. She waited, and she lowered her hand so that it grasped his, cold and wet, and for a while, there was only the rain to make sound.

"I cannot," he said at last.

"Why?"

"I cannot explain it."

"Are you afraid of me?"

He turned his head to her at last, his eyes full of desperation and surprise.

That was enough of an answer for her. "You don't have to be."

"I know."

"You're ill, Darcy."

He whispered, "I know."

She reached out to embrace him, but again he shied away, going as far to the end of their shelter as he could without being soaked. More than he already was, anyway. "I told you," she reminded him.

"I know." He was, it seemed, fighting his own instincts. "Lizzy, I can't."

"You can't? You can't even touch me?" She did not let his hand go, as much as he twisted and tried to escape it. It was her last hold on him, a tether into the abyss. "Have I become too disgusting to you?"

"No," he stumbled. "No, of course not."

"Then you know your thoughts are irrational."

"So you presume to know them?" he spat back.

"You are making them obvious enough, sir."

To this, he had no response. Actually, he did stare at her, rather blankly.

"Do you still love me?" She wanted it to be with force; instead, it came out as a scared whimper. Damn it! She was madder at herself than him.

"Of course," he said, stepping closer to her.

"As much as the day we were married?"

"Yes," he answered without hesitation.

Without provocation, she crossed the length of distance between them—still considerable—and kissed him, wrapping her arms around his neck. He was not entirely unresponsive, if a little spooked. With enough time that passed, she felt the uneasiness release from him. When she pulled away to breathe, he was still trembling. "I need you," she whispered. "I need my husband. And don't tell me he's still in Transylvania, because he's right here with me; I can feel him." She caressed his cheeks, probably the only thing that kept him from fleeing.

"Lizzy," he said, "are you admitting to a weakness?"

"Not a weakness," she said. "A need. A want. I want you, Fitzwilliam Darcy. If you've been so paranoid to that end about your wife's concerns... *there*, you were quite correct. I won't stand for it any longer." She kissed him again, more insistently, less wary of his own reaction, which this time was strong enough to illicit a response of shock. He was quite willing to be the recipient of several more, to be backed up against the rock wall, to let her hands wander and find his.

"Lizzy," he said. "This isn't a good place."

"Would it shock you to hear that I have little care of that?"

"Very little you could say... could shock me."

They removed their overcoats and spread them on the ground, which would serve its purpose. This was not their first amorous adventure beyond the bed, but this was the first time she made it abundantly clear, in words, that she wanted him—*needed* him—and she would not wait a moment longer.

It didn't matter that it was cold, raining, and quite a bit damp, even on the high terrain, under the shelter. Nothing mattered beyond husband and wife, finally together after a long separation, first physical and then mental, but ultimately dissolved.

It was growing dark as the Darcys ran across the great lawn of Pemberley, Darcy holding his overcoat over his wife in a futile attempt to shield her from the rain. The door opened to a horrified Mrs. Reynolds. "Mr. Darcy! Mrs. Darcy! We've been looking for you all afternoon!" There was a slight and unintentional scolding tone to her voice, as if they were two children who had run off and gotten themselves all soaked and muddy. They certainly must have appeared that way. "I will call the maids."

"Please do," Darcy said. "We are quite exhausted, Mrs. Reynolds, and I believe my wife would like to retire for the evening. Will you have our meal sent up and have Georgiana informed of the arrangements?"

"Of course, Mr. Darcy. We shan't have you catching a cold. Either of you!"

"We were caught by the weather," Elizabeth said, a bit amused at the way Mrs. Reynolds fretted about, as it seemed to bring out a smile from Darcy.

Her husband, smiling.

"Is Dr. Maddox still here?"

"He's in the library. Since he does not know the grounds, we discouraged him from following you."

"Give him our thanks," Darcy said.

"And serve the poor man some food," Elizabeth said.

They did have an acute interest in returning to their chambers. As if being wetter was a good idea, both master and mistress submitted to a hot bath and then finally a dry change of clothes before the tray appeared, whereupon they dismissed everyone and shut the doors.

They were exhausted, as could only be expected from a physically and emotionally draining day, however well it had ended. Elizabeth found that, even after hastily finishing off the meal and retiring to bed with her husband, all of her fears and worries of the past months were not so easily discharged. Darcy stroked her hair, but said nothing, lost in his own thoughts as well.

"Did you consider sending me to Bedlam?" He sounded a bit worried, but not overly so.

"No," she said, resting on his shoulder. "It was thought of but not seriously considered."

"I do not mean to be the way I am," Darcy said. "My father was not like this."

"I did not fall in love with your father," she replied. "All things considered, I might not have wanted to. You are willing to admit your faults. Though sometimes it takes a bit of badgering."

She felt him laugh. Just a little, but it was enough to create a rumble in his chest.

"Perhaps I have not been... completely rational with Georgiana," his voice was pained, "or—anyone. But allow me to at least concede to one person at a time."

"Do you have any real objections to Lord Kincaid?"

"I have objections. They keep running through my head, and I cannot dismiss them. It is very hard for me to do."

"Somehow you've already managed it. Darcy, you are stronger than you believe yourself to be. You have survived so many things—gunshot wounds, death duels, prison, and a headstrong wife—that you can survive Austria. Maybe you can survive the idea of Georgiana in love and happily married to a Scot."

"He has your good opinion, apparently, and your good opinion is not so easily won—"

"It is to *polite* people with *social abilities*—"

"—that perhaps I will concede that your judgment is better than mine in the matter of Lord Kincaid."

So. There it was.

"Let me sleep on it," he said, as she hugged him tighter. "A momentous decision should be made after a good night's rest, preferably beside one's wife."

To this, she put up no argument.

Chapter 30

CHRISTMAS RETURNS TO PEMBERLEY

CAUGHT BETWEEN HIS DESIRE not to leave Pemberley and his desire not to endure being the host of many guests, Darcy eventually mumbled to Elizabeth that she should decide with the Bingleys on the Christmas celebrations.

"What do you want?" she asked, knowing it was not a simple question.

"I don't know," he admitted after a moment. "What do *you* want?"

"Well," she said, repositioning herself on the pillows, "I think either would be good for you, and I love Christmas at Pemberley." She leaned in. "It will be small. Just close family."

"So, Pemberley will be overridden by a horde of small children."

She kissed him on the cheek. "Precisely."

Before the decorations were up or any guests arrived, Darcy invited and entertained a visitor at Pemberley. The winter winds had set in, but it bothered neither man as they strolled around the dying gardens. Lord Kincaid was accustomed to the northern winters, and Darcy to a cold cell. For them this was a mild fall day. Darcy took off his gloves and wrung them out as he walked. "My behavior, however indirectly to you, was of course inexcusable."

"The timing was poor," Kincaid said politely, to soften it.

Darcy stopped in his tracks and turned to Kincaid. He stumbled over his words, his usual ability at words failing him. "Georgiana is everything to me. I mean—not everything, but she is my sister."

"Miss Darcy has only the highest respect and admiration for you, Mr. Darcy."

He liked that Lord Kincaid was formal and proper about it. It made him secure in what, he had been assured many times, had been a courtship within every boundary of propriety. "I was told the circumstances of your meeting, but I'm afraid I was told a lot of things upon my return—I'm really not normally so deficient in the retention of information." He trailed off. He had come fairly close to destroying his gloves by now. "If you would indulge me, Lord Kincaid."

"Happily," he replied. "This spring I decided I could put it off no longer and came down to my session of the House. One day, I found myself quite lost in the West End, where I came upon the only familiar face I had seen since my arrival, that of Miss Darcy. It was a beautiful day, only her lady-maid escorted her, and she offered to show me on my way. I inquired as to your family and the Maddoxes, and that was our conversation. That might have been the end of it, but we ran into each other again, at the theater, where she was attending with Dr. and Mrs. Maddox, whom I got to talking to during intermission."

William Kincaid had, after all, been at their wedding. "It was on the way home that I realized that within the strictures of polite society I had no proper way of seeing her again without applying to you, but you were not in London, and so I fell into a state of despair. I asked my sister-in-law Fiona to come down, but she refuses to leave the Highlands, saying the one time she left it was to marry my brother, and what a disaster that came to be."

"Yes, of course," Darcy said.

"A few days later Dr. Maddox was good enough to invite me to dinner at his house. I did want to know how his brother was getting on—but of course, he had little idea. When Miss Darcy did come up in conversation, I said how nice it was to see her again and left it at that, even though I was eager to say more."

Darcy just nodded.

"When I was invited a second time, as my home was no place to host anyone at the time, Miss Darcy was there, and we chatted. We came to a mutual understanding that we might see more of each other through the Maddoxes. We did wish to apply to you about this, but you were busy with your aunt, I believe, and she didn't wish to—"

"Yes, yes," Darcy said, waving it off.

Kincaid continued, his walking stick making a soft sound on the stone pathway. "So, unfortunately, it was all kept very quiet until you abruptly left for the Continent and Miss Darcy went with Mrs. Darcy to Kent. Not being able to write her or even run into her, I was in despair." He tried to meet Darcy's eyes, which was a challenge in that Darcy kept avoiding contact. "Your sister is the kindest, sweetest, most beautiful woman I have ever met. She is all goodness, and she is a great companion. It took me only a month to realize I could not do without her, and wrote to Mrs. Darcy that I happened to be in Kent. I hoped Miss Darcy would be informed, but if not, I was resigned to wait longer. I was invited to meet the new Lord Matlock and his wife, and that was when I applied to court your sister."

"I never thought a Darcy would fall for a Scot," Darcy said. He wasn't sure it was polite or why he said it, but he did.

"I never thought I would fall in love with an Englishwoman."

The way Kincaid called Georgiana a woman again and again—it made Darcy stir. She was five and twenty, and out—she deserved to be considered a woman, not a child. She would always be his little sister (and she would always be shorter than he was), but she was not a child. Elizabeth was right—she deserved to be treated as an adult who could make her own choices. "Are you applying for a courtship or her hand?"

"I wish to ask her myself, first," he said, "but I have not yet done so. This conversation should have happened in the summer and so had to happen first, did it not?"

"Do you believe she will accept?"

"I surely hope so. I will be heartbroken if she does not."

Marrying an earl was not a bad prospect for Georgiana. She would bring wealth, and he would bring land and a title, provided his estate was not in complete disrepair—which, Elizabeth assured him, it was not—further fortune in investment. Derbyshire was not so terribly far from the Lowlands—he had many Scots servants and tenants. She could easily marry farther south, far away from him. But so young? Elizabeth had been twenty when she married *him*.

How long could he deny his sister something she truly wanted? She was not a little girl; this was not a flight of fancy, or did not appear so. Their courtship had apparently been long—nearly eight months—and arduous, with her moving about and his being unable to follow. All who knew him were willing to stand up and testify that he was genuinely interested in Georgiana, if not in love with her. He was young, but not too young—in his late twenties, as Darcy had been when he married. He had been an earl unofficially for almost a decade and officially under English law for several years, since the death of his brother. He was responsible, polite, and proper. He was probably within shooting distance if he ever hurt her. Despite everything that had happened in the last few months, the image of hunting down a wild Scots in a full kilt brought a smile to his face. "If she responds favorably to your query... I will consent to the marriage."

The smile on William Kincaid's face could only be genuine. "Thank you, Mr. Darcy."

Because he didn't want to be touched, Darcy bowed. When they returned to the warm house awaiting them, he discarded his torn gloves.

Elizabeth, as always, found him first as he headed up the stairs, her look a question.

"I will retire for a bit before dinner, for as long as there is peace in this house," he said. "If you wish to join me, I think now would be a good time for Georgiana and Lord Kincaid to accidentally be alone."

Only Elizabeth could embrace him so quickly and without warning, kissing him on the cheek. "I love you."

He did not reply. He was tired, mentally. He did not want to sleep so much as rest. He dismissed his man, shed his waistcoat and scarf, sitting down on the settee with his head in his hands.

"He's a good man," his wife said, sitting beside him. "You did the right thing." She took one of his shaking hands in hers. It dwarfed hers; it was his scarred and numbed hand, but it didn't matter. "If you want to, you can practically shoot him from here."

"At least we are thinking the same thoughts," he mumbled.

"*Yes*," Georgiana said, her height and weight being the only things that prevented her from tackling William Kincaid with her enthusiastic hug.

Overwhelmed himself, Kincaid blinked the tears out of his eyes and kissed her on her forehead. It was the first time they had really touched. He decided that he despised English propriety more than anything else about the country, if only for the frustration it had forced on him. He was sorely tempted to cart her off like a wild man and be married on a glen somewhere, just them and the vicar, like olden times. But if he had to wait for her brother to reappear, so be it. She was worth it.

Marriage hadn't been particularly on his mind when he went to London, though he was getting to be of age where the others around him were giving him that knowing look. He was so exhausted from the fight with his brother over Fiona's marriage—where he felt it was just to take her side—and then James's death that he put it aside. He was the younger brother and was busy running the estate in James's absence and then officially afterwards. He went to London, only most reluctantly, to find it as full of smog and soot as he had been told, but still very sophisticated, far more than Edinburgh, and he was so blindsided by city life until he met Georgiana. She was no longer the girl she had been when they had briefly met seven years earlier. She was a woman, she was out, and she was beautiful. Her brother was an extremely honorable man. William knew he was in love, but he also knew that it would be an uphill battle, and this time with no surprise entrances and quick resolution.

"I feel awful for leaving my brother," she said, "especially now."

"Your brother will want a formal engagement period, and there can be no proper wedding until the spring," Kincaid assured her, however un-assuring that news was for other reasons. "By then, he will be much recovered, I am sure."

"He did grant his consent?"

"Yes," he said. "Though, technically, could I not have gone to your *other* brother?"

"Oh!" Georgiana laughed. "Oh, I have a terrible idea."

"If it brings a smile to your face, it cannot be so terrible," he said.

The first person to hear of the engagement of Lord Kincaid and Georgiana Darcy was not her beloved elder brother, resting upstairs, or her dear sister-in-law, also absconded. They found Grégoire in the chapel, where he spent most of the day. Beneath the altar was the reliquary of Saint Sebald, though they were hardly making it public knowledge.

"Grégoire!" Georgiana said as she rushed into the room, and he stood to greet her. William kept pace but stayed behind for a moment as she curtseyed formally to her confused younger brother. "May I have your consent to marry Lord Kincaid?"

The look of puzzlement on Grégoire's face was truly priceless. William bit his lip to hold his laughter and bowed. "...D-do you need my consent?"

"Well, you *are* my brother."

"Oh. Yes. Uhm," he scratched his head. "Yes, yes, of course." He bowed again to Lord Kincaid. "You... have my consent to marry my sister."

"Oh, thank you!" she said, hugging her overwhelmed brother. That was approximately when William and Georgiana lost their composure, and their laughter only seemed to relieve Grégoire.

"Do you need me to perform the ceremony or something?" he said, still quite befuddled.

"No, thank you. I'm a heretical Presbyterian," William Kincaid said.

"Oh. Well, I'm a Papist monk, but I shall enjoy attending the ceremony anyway."

The guest list quickly became paramount to the preparations for the holiday. Lord Kincaid had other prior obligations; he would spend the holidays as he normally did with his family, in the north, to return as soon as it was possible.

Darcy entertained another guest the following day. Though they had been in correspondence, he had not actually seen Bingley since his arrival from the Continent, as neither was able to visit the other for different reasons. "My God, man."

"Yes, yes, I know, I'm an idiot," Bingley said. "Needlessly putting myself into danger. At least I managed to do it without leaving the country."

Darcy managed a thin smile as Bingley was helped into an armchair. "It is good to see you."

"The same. You scared the daylights out of me. I do not want to be steward of Pemberley *and* Rosings for the next ten years." He gladly accepted the drink that was offered to him.

"Thank you for caring for my children. I hear they actually behaved themselves."

"I was thinking Geoffrey was a bad influence on Georgie, but it may actually be the other way around. It's rather hard to tell," he said. "I am willing to have Christmas at Chatton, if you wish it."

Darcy refused. Bingley was perhaps the one person whom he had no concern about looking nervous around. "I'm very eager to be at home. We would just prefer to have a smaller list this year."

"Understandably, but there is one matter—Brian and Princess Nadezhda."

Darcy said nothing. He could think of nothing to say.

"I know—it is awkward. I believe Mr. Maddox is truly penitent about his disappearance and the havoc it caused. But he did save my life."

"He has a strange habit of causing mischief and then making up for it in the most dramatic way possible."

"He certainly does. Nonetheless, my sister and Dr. Maddox won't come without them. This is Nadezhda's first Christmas in England. They don't even have a house yet."

Darcy knew the right decision. Why was he having so much trouble making it? "All right, but no swords. That is my only condition. Besides, it *is* Christmas."

"I'll see to it myself," Bingley said. "Oh, and Mugin would come with them."

"Who?"

"The man who rescued you? In the tavern?"

Darcy shook his head. "I'm sorry, I—" He leaned on his hand. "Yes, him."

Bingley did understand. "He's their friend from Japan. He barely understands English. He'll be no trouble; they promise."

Darcy nodded numbly.

Bingley got to his feet. "It is good to have you back, Darcy."

It was only because of Bingley's smile and his tone that only spoke of his words being genuine that Darcy was able to stand and shake his hand before his friend left.

"There," he said to Elizabeth as she rejoined him, "is a man I did not realize how much I truly missed."

Despite all the things to prevent it from happening, Christmas was held at Pemberley that year. The guests were hosted at Chatton but festivities were at Pemberley. Three miles away, the Maddox clan had their challenges. In fact, just about everyone upstairs could hear the shouting.

"*Ore no katana wa hanasenai. Kenrin ga nai,*" (I'm not leaving my sword behind. I have a right not to do so!) Brian's voice was defiant.

"*Tadashikamo. Kare wa samurai da to omoimasu kara.*" (He's right you know, if he thinks he's a samurai.)

"*Mugin, kare o ganbaranaidekudasai. Anata mou katana to ikemasen,*" (Mugin, stop supporting him. And you're not going armed, either,) Nadezhda said. "*Oshujin ni daremo okorasenai. Koko wa Igirisu desu. Daremo anatatachi ni tatakawanarimasen!*" (No one is upsetting our hosts! This is England. You won't be attacked!)

"*Shoshiki,* Pemberley *de mou semerareta...*" (Actually, I have been attacked at Pemberley before...)

"Brian, *Atashi o shitagatte!*" (Brian, you will do what I say!)

"*Shitaganakereba, nani?*" (Or what?) Brian decided to challenge his wife.

"*Sou dattara, Mugin no mae de hanasenai!*" (Or—something I can't say in front of Mugin!)

"*Oi. Hazukashinaide...*" (Hey, don't be embarrassed...)

"*Mugin, uruse!*" (Mugin, shut up!) the Maddox couple said together.

Outside, Daniel Maddox just scratched his hair—what little there was of it, barely enough to start curling. "Should I interrupt?"

"I did inform you of the incident with the man in the bar losing his arm, did I not?" Caroline said.

"Oh. Yes. Well, I'm sure this will sort itself out in time. Why don't we wait as far away as possible?"

They eventually emerged, proving that Brian remembered how to dress like an Englishman after all. Princess Nadezhda had procured a more modest style of dress than the English gown and still walked about with her medieval headdress. Mugin finally emerged *sans* sword, wearing Brian's black robes, blue pants, and sandals, which must have been some kind of Japanese formal wear. "Personal attack, I hit his head with fist," he said warningly to Bingley.

"I will make sure our host is informed," was all he said in response.

An enthusiastic Elizabeth and Georgiana, and a polite, somewhat mellow, Darcy greeted them. Dr. Maddox took one quick glance at Darcy's pupils and kept moving. Dinner could not help but be a celebratory affair. Elizabeth was preparing to enter her confinement, and Georgiana was engaged, a notion to which Darcy had no comment. If he had any nerves at all that evening, none of them showed. He looked remarkably calm, almost sleepy.

They retired to the sitting room after the children were sent to bed, overeager for Christmas, while the adults waited for midnight mass.

"Will Mr. Mugin be joining us?" Elizabeth asked Nadezhda.

"Do they have Christianity in Japan?" Bingley asked.

"They did, at one time," Brian answered, turning to Mugin. "Mugin, are you religious?"

"Three," he said.

"The trinity?" Grégoire offered.

"No. Have three religions, *gaijin*. Not need more."

"Well, is *one* of them Christianity?" Dr. Maddox asked.

Brian translated for Mugin. When Mugin replied, Brian and Nadezhda both colored. "I'm not translating *that*."

"Now you're not being fair," Caroline said. "Tell us what the Oriental said."

"I really don't think—"

"Now you're just teasing us, Mr. Maddox," Elizabeth said, "unless it was crude."

Brian sighed. "I explained what we meant by Christians, and he said, 'Oh, those are the guys we crucify.'"

Mugin had a sort of gloating smile as he guzzled whatever the servant had filled his glass with.

"So… no, then, he won't be attending," Bingley said.

"No, I don't think so."

"This may be mildly inappropriate for the night Our Lord was born," the doctor said, "but it *is* very ironic."

Caroline stifled her laughter, or tried to, as she nudged her husband.

When the hour did come, the carriages were prepared for church, and as they stepped outside, they saw white. It was beginning to snow very lightly, in that sort of beautiful way when it comes down, in soft, slow clumps.

"Happy Christmas," Dr. Maddox said to Darcy as the others stood admiring the sky. "When I said, 'Take at night'—"

"Shut up; it was only two cups," Darcy whispered back. His speech, now that he was actually talking, was a little slurred. "Three. That was it."

"Generally you should not venture from the written prescription. It could be dangerous," Dr. Maddox said, slapping him on the back. "But for tonight, I'll excuse it. Happy Christmas, Darcy."

"Happy Christmas, Maddox."

Chapter 31

THE HUNT

DARCY'S FIRST WORDS ON Christmas morning were, "We did bolt the doors?"

Elizabeth rolled over. "Yes. Why?"

"Because if I have to endure another Christmas of our children rushing in here—"

She kissed him. "One day, you will miss it."

He smiled and rubbed her swollen stomach. "But not *very* soon." His voice was steadier than it had been. She could still sense the anxiety he had not yet let go of, even as it dissipated. "We *did* get the children something, didn't we?"

"Yes. We did."

"As long as there's no inquiry—"

"Geoffrey has wanted toy soldiers so he can play with Frederick. Anne is to have a play tea set, and Sarah is getting a new doll."

"Thank you." Banging on the door interrupted any further conversation, a very low banging on the door. "And it begins again." But Elizabeth's laughter made it all worth it.

The Darcys and the Bingleys had one tradition that was inevitable—the regular jealousy of the other children, because the Bingley twins also received their birthday presents. They tried once to break it up during a different time in the day, but it hardly mattered, and so the adults just shrugged.

The most interesting presents in terms of surprise came from Brian and Nadezhda, of course, having newly returned from the very exotic Orient. The moment Charles the Third was distracted, his father immediately picked up the wooden top of a fat man that would remove and put back on the mask in his hands when the cord was pulled. "Yes, Charles, I know. It's lovely," Jane said to her husband in the exact same voice she used with her children when he demonstrated it. He turned to Caroline, who just rolled her eyes.

Georgie had already opened her new set of colored pencils and disappeared into a corner for a bit before approaching Mugin, who remained off to the side for most of the morning.

"Mr. Mugin," Georgie said, startling the Oriental as she approached him. So far, she was the only child who seemed to be able to do that without some apprehension. "Happy Christmas." With that, she handed him a piece of paper with a drawing on it.

"What is-a this?" he said in obvious confusion.

Nadezhda Maddox decided to come to his aid, peering over his shoulder. "It seems to be a picture of you, Mugin-san." For it was. Georgiana Bingley was an accomplished artist for someone her age, even though she'd drawn him squatting with pencil-thin limbs and shoes nearly triple their normal height. "A present."

"Oh," he said, and turned to the little red-haired girl in front of him, and bowed. "*Gomen nasai. Demo, kanoyoni nanimo o mottekuremasendeshita.*" (Thank you. But I don't have anything for her.)

"*Sore o suru no o nozomanai to omoimasu,*" Princess Maddox assured him. (I don't think she expects you to.)

"Idea!" he announced and whispered in Nadezhda's ear. Brian, now showing some interest, approached them and, upon hearing their discussion called for paper, ink, and a brush. When they were retrieved (it took some time for the servants to find a brush to Maddox's specifications), Mugin knelt beside the sitting room table, bunched up his sleeves, and tipped the brush, meant for restorative painting work, in the ink. "Name?"

"Bingley Georgiana," Brian said.

"Binguri Jorujiana," Mugin said, and began to draw on the paper with smooth strokes. The other children, and some of the adults, turned their heads as he formed complex and unfamiliar characters, one after another, going down to the bottom of the paper, before handing it back to her. "Here you go."

"He's written your name," Nadezhda explained. "In Japanese."

Georgie took her present and squealed. "Thank you! Happy Christmas!"

Mugin bowed as Georgiana ran to show off her present. "Papa! Papa!"

Unaccustomed to such behavior from his normally reclusive daughter, Bingley handed Edmund off to Nurse before examining the paper himself. "How interesting!"

One could count the seconds before every child, cognizant of what had happened, wanted one. Mugin obliged, though the warrior did not seem quite sure what to do when surrounded by a pack of overexcited children yelling at him in a foreign language. "So sorry, name again?"

"Geoffrey Darcy."

"Darushi Jefuri," Mugin said, taking a second to figure out the letters for that.

"It seems your companion has brought his own set of gifts," Darcy said to Brian. "In fact, I doubt ours are comparable. He *is* writing their names, yes?"

"My lettering is not particularly good, but I believe he is attempting to," Brian assured him.

After the Christmas feast, some overexcited children were put to bed, and the roads were deemed too dangerous from the snow for a return to Chatton. That wasn't entirely true, but Darcy was feeling charitable, though he excused himself for most of the afternoon. Elizabeth eventually found him in the chapel with Grégoire, but did not disturb them. She waited instead until Darcy emerged. "Did you know he knew all along? Georgiana told him in May. May!" He shook his head. "Little bugger."

"*Darcy!*"

"What? He is smaller than I am." His hapless smirk was too endearing for her to say anything against him, and he knew it.

The next morning, the snow finally ceased, and Derbyshire was encased in white powder. The guests had had necessary items brought from Chatton, which was truly not that far away, and stayed the night, staying up much later than was good for them and resulting in some very late risings.

Geoffrey Darcy, who was sharing his room with Charles, was up first. He was always up first, to the annoyance of many people, but the servants were quite used to it, and most paid little attention to him except for a polite smile. He was still not entirely awake when he was surprised to find someone else up. Georgie Bingley was staring out one of the windows of the great hall, wrapped in a blanket. *It was hard to heat large spaces in winter, Father said.*

"D'you know how early it is?" Geoffrey said, rubbing his eyes.

"Shut up!" Georgie commanded, not taking her eye off the window. "Do you want to see it or not?"

Geoffrey yawned and nodded. He had to wipe away the condensation on the glass to see out. White snow blanketed Pemberley, including the long stone porch. At the end of it, facing the forest, Mr. Mugin stood on one leg, the other braced against his knee like a bird, his left sandal abandoned. There he stood, arms braced together, quite still and silent for some time. Geoffrey doubted he could get into that position, much less stay in it for so long. Mugin was wearing only a scarf and his bizarre hat over his regular clothes; he must have been freezing.

"C'mon!"

"Georgie! You can't be—" But apparently she was serious, because she tossed him a blanket, wrapping her own around herself as she opened the door and stepped outside cautiously.

"Mr. Mugin-san!" she called.

"*Hai?*" he said, without moving an inch.

"Aren't you cold?"

"Ar-en you? Englishmen very weak."

"We're not!" Geoffrey said, and decided to race out in front of her, knowing his blanket and his shoes would be soaked in moments. Georgie followed quickly, shutting the door behind them, and they ran around Mugin's side. "See?"

"Are you praying, Mr. Mugin-san?"

"*Nani?* Ah, no," he said, lowering his hands from the prayer position. "Don know word. Thinking."

"What were you thinking about?" Geoffrey asked.

"Nothing. Is point, Darcy-chan."

Georgiana attempted to climb onto his unused sandal, which would put her above the snow. She quickly lost her balance but Mugin caught her before she could topple over, holding her above the snow, as he slid back into his other shoe. "Good?"

"Good," she said, though she sounded a little rattled. Mugin did not set her down, but instead took her into his arms, even though she was seven and not many adults could do that.

"I put you down?"

"Yes, sir."

He set her down without any trouble, beside Geoffrey, picked up his sword, which was lying in the snow, and put it back over his shoulders.

"May I ask you a question, Mr. Mugin-san?"

"Not Meester," he said. "Mugin-san; means same."

"Mugin-san, have you killed a lot of people with your sword?"

Geoffrey was put off with the question; Mugin was not and only shrugged. "I very bad at counting."

"Is that why you went to prison?" Geoffrey asked. "My dad said you went to prison. That's why you have tattoos."

"Not why. I—stole from ship, get arrested. Very stupid of me."

"So it's okay to kill people in Japan?"

Mugin shrugged. "People fight me, I kill them or they kill me. Is fine."

"Anyone? Not, like, women and children?"

"No!" Mugin said. "Some women, fine."

"Do women have swords in your country?" Georgie said, tugging at his pants.

"Some. Women can be very dangerous."

Geoffrey huffed. "We don't kill people in England, Mr. Mugin, unless they've done something really bad."

"But you kill people in France," Mugin countered. "Big war. No war in Japan."

"That... is true."

"Ha ha!" Georgie said. "Mugin outsmarted you."

"He did not!"

"Did too!"

"Good children," Mugin said, patting them both on their heads. "Cold. We go in."

"Mugin-san! Look!"

Georgie pointed in the direction of the field. The forest was not far away, and because it was so white they had not noticed the quiet approach of a white wolf, sniffing curiously, some distance away from them. They were not far from the door. Geoffrey was going to run when Mugin grabbed him by the shoulder very strongly. "You stay. She go for small thing first. Wait."

"Mr. Mugin—"

"Not move," he commanded. "I take care, you go for door. Understand?" He looked down at them. "*Understand!*"

They both nodded.

"Good children. I distract her. Then you go." He released Geoffrey, herding them behind him as he drew his sword.

Neither of them dared to say a word.

"You not look. Understand? Just run for door."

They nodded again.

He cautiously stepped out farther on the terrace, approaching the wolf. "Go!" he whispered, and they ran.

The wolf did not attack Mugin, who continued to approach it, his stilt sandals keeping his feet out of the snow. Geoffrey and

Georgie ran inside and closed the door behind them, but not all the way. Geoffrey wanted to run and tell someone, but Georgie grabbed him.

"But he said not to look!"

"Do you want to see it or not?"

He did. They stood by the window as Mugin shouted at the wolf and pointed to the forest. It growled in response. He jumped up and down, trying to scare it off. It circled him. There was a silent gesture back and forth, and Mugin looked over his shoulder and winked at them, only a moment before the white wolf launched herself at him. He leaned back and let the wolf bite down—on his sandal. Her teeth caught, and he rolled back into the snow and flipped her over with him. The ensuing action was obscured by the spray of powder, but Mugin stood, covered in snow, and wiped his sword across his maroon shirt to clean it before putting it back in its case. He kicked some snow over the wolf, which lay motionless, and turned back to the house, entering as if nothing had happened and there was no reason why he was covered in snow and breathing heavily.

"Mugin-san, you're bleeding!" Georgie cried out.

He looked down at his foot, the one the wolf had tried to bite off. There was a small mark there that was bleeding. "Huh. Caught me. Good opponent." By now, some servant had passed through and was standing in horror at the spectacle of an armed Oriental facing him. "You have cloth for foot?"

When the Darcys were woken (which was quickly) and the panicking finished (which was not as quickly done), the children were sent off with a minor scolding for going outside in the cold, and to be watched more carefully by their nurses. Meanwhile, the adults held conference as Dr. Maddox bound Mugin's foot.

"Bath," he said to the servant who was the least terrified about approaching him. "Now! Very hot."

"Yes, sir; right away, sir."

Mugin bowed to Darcy and followed the servant.

Stunned by Mugin's appearance and the news of a wolf threatening his children, Darcy struggled to maintain his composure as the master of the grounds; he turned to a curious Brian Maddox, who was the first one to speak to the Japanese man in his native tongue. "Is there some way to—pay Mr. Mugin?"

"He wants the white wolf's hide. He says she's still on the lawn."

Darcy nodded. Glad that the job was done, he pushed it away in his mind. Aside from entertaining the children with some stories, the whole matter was set aside, and the holiday festivities continued as the Christmas decorations came down and the Twelfth Night ones were put up. In the ensuing chaos, the whole event was largely forgotten, and Darcy never bothered to inquire about the hide, or even think of it again.

Chapter 32

BRIAN'S STORY CONTINUES

1810

"SEEN ENOUGH COUNTRYSIDE TO last a lifetime?" Brian said to his wife. "Even if it's in Nippon?"

"It is very lovely," she said. For it was incredibly beautiful, unspoiled and natural, nothing paved, rarely a sign. They occasionally passed travelers, who either ignored them or moved away at the sight of Miyoshi with his hands (casually) on his blades, but besides that there was no one.

Eventually they took a road that looked barely wide enough to be passable. Nadezhda privately admitted to being a bit exhausted from sleeping in the open, however good Miyoshi was at setting up a shelter with his cloak, and Brian felt that old tiredness seeping into him. "Can we stop here? At an inn or something?"

To their surprise, Miyoshi nodded. That was, until he saw a sign, which he spent some time studying before announcing, "We cannot enter here. We must go around."

"Will we lose time?"

"It doesn't matter," Miyoshi turned away from the posted note. "We have to go around."

"What's wrong?" Brian said instinctually.

"There's a wanted criminal about, and that means they will be searching all travelers." He added, "We will find another town soon."

That did not mean they were free of company, as there were people going to and fro. They had to journey some distance off the road to find any sanctuary. This Japan place was filled with forests and rivers, and they were low on food.

"Can we fish?" Brian said, wondering if there was a law or something.

Miyoshi's response was to remove his *ronin gasa* and tie up his long sleeves. "Yes. Do you know how?"

"What man doesn't know how to fish?" Brian replied, and tied a string to the end of his walking stick as Nadezhda worked on the other end, pinning a piece of their remaining bread to it. "There we go. There are fish here, right?"

Miyoshi grunted, which meant that he was unwilling to admit to not knowing. Brian had barely got his make-shift fishing rod into the water when Miyoshi held out a hand. "Quiet."

"I was being—"

Their bodyguard looked at them seriously, silencing them, and Brian slipped his hat over his face. Miyoshi's left hand was on his sword hilt and not lightly. He took a few steps straight into the water, which was not especially deep, barely inches above his ankles, and his blade came out fast enough to drop the man who leapt in front of him. In a spray of blood the man fell down into the water, but Miyoshi did not hesitate, drawing back to protect the Maddoxes as the other bandits emerged from the woods, armed with spears and swords.

"You are outnumbered, *ronin*," said one of them.

"It does not concern me," Miyoshi said, his voice as steady as a rock. "Come closer, and you shall suffer the same fate."

"If they want money," Brian whispered, "give it to them and be done with it."

Miyoshi grunted. Clearly it was not up for consideration. He was true to his word, because when the first man came forward, he cut his spear in half before letting his swing slice through the man beside him. Brian instinctively put himself in front of his wife, his hand on his walking stick. "Don't look," he whispered to her in Romanian, because the water was looking a bit red for his taste. Yet Miyoshi was unconcerned. His attention was apparently on cutting them all down without thought, and he was very good at doing it.

"Don't move," said a man behind them, putting a sword to Brian's shoulder, the tip piercing enough to make him bleed. "Tell your samurai to stop."

"What do you want?"

"Money. And your woman. Surely worth your life?"

It was Nadezhda who screamed as, without hesitation, Brian drew the sword hidden in his cane and spun around. He meant to at least put some distance between him and the bandit, but it didn't have a hope of working, as the man laughed and knocked it out of his hands. He was out of his league.

"*Haaaaaaaaaaaaaaaai!*"

The cry came from above, the man landing before it was finished. He was different from the others, moving in a blue blur from his *haori* coat, his bizarre sword drawn and ready as he sliced the man's head off before his stilt shoes hit the ground between them. He then turned to Brian and Nadezhda. His hair was wild and not shaved or even tied up, his clothing mismatched and worn, obviously a collection of other people's outfits. He had tattoos around his wrists. He laughed and ran past them with no explanation, sword still drawn, and with a flying leap, landed on the man whom Miyoshi was attempting to fight off. While he stood on him, he swung his sword around, missing Miyoshi by inches on one side, decapitating the last bandit on the other while one drowned beneath his *geta* shoes.

"So," Miyoshi said, not sheathing his sword, "you're the villain they've put up warnings about."

"Me? Signs?" the man said. "I'm honored."

"What did you do *this* time?"

"Who knows?" he said, and swung at his opponent—Miyoshi. Their blades met, and the man leapt off the now-dead bandit and back into the water, catching Miyoshi's swing in his shoe, and stepped down, bringing the sword with it. "See? At my mercy again?"

That was when Miyoshi dropped his sword and drew his shorter blade, hitting the man in the hand with the butt of it, disarming him again. "Not so easy, Mugin." He recovered as Mugin lifted his foot, allowing Miyoshi to recover his blade. "I can't do this now."

"You won't fight me?"

"Not now," Miyoshi said, putting away his blades.

"So, you're protecting foreigners? The very opposite of the law."

"You must be very familiar with it, as you've never done a lawful thing in your life," Miyoshi said, stepping out of the now-red stream and returning to land and his charges. Mugin gave an exaggerated gesture as if he was offended. "We'd best be on our way," Miyoshi said to his charges.

"He knows," Brian felt compelled to point out.

"Yes, of course. I'm not an idiot, no matter what Shiro-chan says," the fugitive said.

"How long have you been following us?"

"Does it matter?" Mugin said, walking across the water and onto their side of the lake, ignoring the pile of bodies behind him as he put his sword back in its scabbard, which was over his shoulder. "So, Nagasaki it is, then? It's very far."

"You're not invited," Miyoshi said.

"Ah, but then I could report you, of course."

"That would mean showing your face to the authorities."

"Heh! I'm not a wanted man in every village, though I am proud that you think I'm such an esteemed criminal," the man said. "Besides, it looks like you could use the help, no? All I want is a few good meals. A good deal for you."

Miyoshi, for some reason, seemed to be considering it. Despite the fact he had just fought this man with ready blades, there was some faltering in his usual stoic expression, and his hesitation forced Brian to push the matter. "Miyoshi, can we trust him?"

"No," he said. "But it seems he's coming anyway."

"Besides, I can fish better than Shiro any day," the man said and, without hesitation and fully clothed, ran to a deeper area of the river and dove in, resurfacing a minute later with a fish speared on a knife. "There." He removed the fish and tossed it to their shore. "Back in a minute." And he dove under again.

"Who is he?" Nadezhda asked as Miyoshi watched on in stunned silence.

"Mugin," Miyoshi said at last.

"A friend of yours?" Brian dared to ask as yet another fish was thrown at their feet.

"No," Miyoshi insisted, and said no more.

When Mugin had provided them with a pile of fish, they walked some ways down the river, far away from the bodies, and started a fire to cook the fish. A soaked Mugin shook his hair out like a dog and sat down by it, putting up his feet in a mode of complete relaxation, as Miyoshi tended to the fish.

Brian was the first to remove his hat. When Mugin didn't bat an eye, he encouraged Nadezhda to do the same. "Mugin-san," he said, bowing to him. "I am Maddox Brian, and this is Maddox Nadezhda, my wife."

Mugin did open his eyes at this but showed no surprise. "*Hai*. Greetings."

"May I ask how you know Miyoshi?"

"I don't know—he might get annoyed. But he gets annoyed at everything, so who cares?" Mugin said, sitting up. "I'd rather Shiro-chan tell it."

"Why do you call him that?"

"Because I know him," he said, thinking he had to explain the significance of *chan* to the foreigner. From Brian's expression, he did not. "He was so formal with you; he didn't tell you his name? Miyoshi Shiro? How rude. And yet, how like him."

"You traveled together?"

"For some time."

Brian quickly realized that Mugin would be a wealth of information about their bodyguard, who grumbled at basically everything that came out of Mugin's mouth but still did not order him away. That, however, could be handled in time.

As night descended on him, there were other things on his mind, thoughts that he had been distracted from by the sudden appearance of Mugin, who they gathered was at least partially mixed-race, as he laughed at the suggestion and dismissed it. They had been witness to nothing less than a mass slaughter, even if those men had been bandits. Nadezhda was tense in his arms under their shelter and Brian knew why but could find no words to comfort her. In the nearly three months of being on Japanese soil they had come to feel a peace. That had been shattered by the reality of violence that was taken for granted by the men who protected them. They were not safe.

After he nudged her into sleep, Brian slipped out of his shelter and approached Miyoshi, who had taken up watch on a rock, his longer sword resting against his shoulder. Mugin was asleep next to the fire, snoring loudly.

"Miyoshi-san," Brian said, bowing to him.

"Yes?"

"What happened today—"

"Mugin will not be a problem," Miyoshi said. "As obnoxious as he is, he is actually quite useful."

"So I saw," Brian said with a swallow. "I also saw you kill five men."

Miyoshi merely replied, "I am your soldier."

"Would you have done it anyway? If they attacked you alone for some reason would you have run?"

"I am not trained to run, Madokusu-san. I am samurai. I have every right to kill as I please." He looked up and took note of Brian's horrified expression. "Are you *gaijin* all so squeamish?"

"We're not... adjusted to the idea of such a... violent society." He was tripping over his own thoughts as much as his vocabulary. He could not upset Miyoshi. For the first time, he was truly afraid of him, aware of what he was capable of, apparently without regret.

"Then what do you do to bandits then?"

"Try to fend them off, or have them arrested. And then they—" He realized he did not know the word, so he said it in Russian. "Stand trial."

Miyoshi looked at him blankly.

"Go to prison," he said in Japanese.

"Ah," Miyoshi said. So they did have those here. "So you never kill? Even in defense of yourself? Or your wife?"

"Maybe in defense," he said. "Maybe... a few times; twice." He shuddered, shivering in his robe. "But I feel horrible about it. I pray for those men's souls."

"They attacked you?"

"Yes."

"Then they knew death was the only possible result."

"Perhaps they did not."

"Then they were fools. You cannot suffer for fools, Madokusu-san." At Brian's silence, he continued, "I will make this clear now. I am to take you to Nagasaki because Kayano-sama asked it of me and I consented. Along the way, I will kill anyone who stands in our path, and people will stand in our path. If you find this arrangement disagreeable, you can turn yourself into the authorities and be crucified. Then I will have failed and must end my life. So we will all die. That is your choice. If you find my behavior disgusting, it is because you are ignorant in the ways of necessity."

Brian didn't know what to say. For once, his clever tongue failed him. Miyoshi was so perfectly serious. The ideal world around them—so beautiful and peaceful—was marred by a severity of law, or lack thereof. Which it was, Brian couldn't tell. By Miyoshi's count, his actions were lawful, and it was clear he would not hesitate to repeat them. He cared little for either of them, and yet he would leave a trail of bodies in their wake to get them to shelter in the foreigners' port. "I cannot understand it. It is so different from—well, the rest of the world."

"It is Japan. It is not the rest of the world."

He could not bring himself to dispute that unshakable logic, at least, not at the moment. "So sorry, I did not understand." He still didn't, but he returned to bed less uneasy. At least Miyoshi was on his side. And having Nadezhda literally at his side was enough to lull him into sleep.

Their trip around the village was not terribly costly. Mugin knew his way around much better and directed them to a quiet inn and bathhouse of some sort.

"Seems we'll be like the Romans," Brian said to his wife in Romanian. "Will you be all right by yourself?"

"For a bath, I'd do almost anything," she said, and they parted. The bath was an open hot spring, separated by gender with a wooden wall. Brian waited until his wife had gone, but hesitated in his robe and sandals at the carved stone steps leading down in the water.

"Shy *gaijin*," Mugin said, leaning against the rock wall, completely nude. Fortunately the night and the water disguised his lower half. Next to him was a meditative Miyoshi, eyes closed. "Come on. We want to see if you barbarians have tails."

Brian colored. "We don't." *Us? The barbarians?* Although he did feel particularly barbaric in his filthy state.

"We won't try anything, Madokusu-san."

"I won't," Miyoshi said, not opening his eyes.

Brian sighed, untied his obi, and slid into the water as quickly as possible. "Ow! Hot!" he said in English purely on instinct.

"Baby," Mugin said.

The water did, when he was adjusted to it, feel immeasurably good. Tension that he had unknowingly been holding in began to be released, and he took his own position across from them, against the rock wall. For a while there was silence and steam, and when he finally opened his eyes, he saw the hundreds of fireflies that lit up the sky above them. *I hope Nadezhda sees this.* It occurred to him that over the past months—no, for maybe two years now—he had rarely had a waking thought that did not involve her in some way. *I am a very lucky man, despite everything.*

"Madokusu-chan?"

"Brian," he said, stirred out of his stupor. "My name is Brian."

"Bri-ayn," Mugin sounded it out. "Is Madokusu-san really your wife?"

The audacity of the comment received only a raised eyebrow from Miyoshi. When Brian calmed a bit, he realized it was a reasonable question. Why would a husband and wife be on the run together? They would more logically be lovers. "Yes. We were married in the sight of..." He pointed upwards, not knowing Japanese for God.

"So what is the problem? Ah, right, family didn't approve."

"Actually, family did approve," Brian said, mimicking Mugin. "Nady's father is a... so sorry, large landowner with title?"

"*Daimyo,*" Miyoshi offered.

"*Daimyo.* The marriage was arranged, and we were very happy. But... it is personal."

"Aha!" Mugin splashed in the water. "You couldn't get it up!"

Brian's ears were burning when he answered, "No! That wasn't it!"

"So insistent. Shiro-chan, think he's telling the truth?"

"He is," Miyoshi said. "Stop bothering him. He is not your plaything."

"And who is my plaything?"

Miyoshi gave an odd grumble and turned his head in disgust. It struck Brian as very odd, but he didn't mention it. "May I ask you a question, Mugin-san?"

"I'll answer yours if you answer mine."

"The tattoos—are they religious?"

Mugin lifted his arms out of the water. "What? No. I was in prison."

"It's a mark," Miyoshi said, "of a convict."

"What did you do?" Brian said, having no compulsion against asking him, if Mugin was going to do the same.

Mugin, however, had no problems with the question. "I got caught stealing supplies from a ship. Now, you answer mine."

Brian huffed, and then said, "The—*daimyo*—was upset that we cannot have children."

This was news even to Miyoshi, as it had not been asked of them when they were in the village. There was only a hint on his face that he was interested in this new information, but as usual, he said nothing.

"Excuse me," Brian said, and after dunking his head under for good measure, he did excuse himself, put his robe and hat back on, and returned to his assigned room. Nadezhda was waiting for him on the first real mattress they had slept on in months, even if it was on the floor. "Hello," he whispered in Romanian as he joined her.

"Brian?" She willingly took him into her arms as he took his place next to her. "Are you all right?"

"I'm fine," he mumbled. "Just… I get overwhelmed, sometimes."

"By what?"

"You," he answered, because it was the truth. "Last time I had to care for anyone, someone I truly, truly loved, I utterly failed him."

"Wasn't he a child?"

"Yes."

"Do you think I'm a child?" she said in her subtle way of teasing him.

He smiled. "No. I assure you, I do not."

Mugin was far more talkative than his companion, if Miyoshi could be called that. He was also, at the same time, spry and lazy. He would oversleep and then be called in a second's notice. He made crude jokes, or just chewed on a grass stalk, or complained that he was hungry. For a slim man, he ate a lot.

"Why are we protecting two people who can protect themselves?"

Miyoshi only responded, "I was hired to protect them. You have no obligation."

"*Sa!* You know what I'm saying!" Mugin huffed. "They have weapons; you can teach them to fight. What, you think only samurai should know *bushido*? Who knows, maybe it would be good for *gaijin*; better than to have them stand there while we fight."

"Mugin-san has a point," Nadezhda interrupted. "With respect, Miyoshi-san, we would like to contribute."

"Yes," Brian said. "Otherwise I am just carrying around a very heavy walking stick."

"You are supposed to look injured."

"I can limp without the stick. I do it anyway."

To this, Miyoshi's response was to turn and walk away. Mugin ran in front of them, preventing them from pursuing. "Let him go. He's always like this. He'll give in eventually. It's his pride that holds it up."

"Why don't you teach us?"

He looked surprised. "Me? I don't know *bushido*."

"If you didn't learn in Japan, where did you learn to fight?"

"Guangdong," he said, "in China."

"What were you doing there?" Nadezhda asked as they continued walking, following Miyoshi who had begun ahead of them.

"After I escaped from prison, I went to the Middle Kingdom," he said. "It didn't seem like I was wanted here; wasn't really wanted there, either."

"How old were you?"

"Uh, don't know. Must have been about..." he rubbed his chin, which had the beginnings of a goatee. "Kansei Seven Year so—I was ten, eleven maybe?"

"That was when you got out?"

"I went in when I was a kid," he said. "I was an orphan. I wasn't killed, because I was a kid. They sent me to prison instead. It was hard, but it was better than being dead."

"Kansei Seven... and this year is?"

"Bunka Eight. Why are you obsessed with numbers?"

"We've been trying to guess how old you are," Nadezhda said with a smile. "That you keep renaming your years doesn't help."

"Barbarians," Brian said jokingly in Romanian, and then continued in Japanese, "So you must be eight and twenty, or so?"

"Maybe."

"How old is Miyoshi-san?"

"He is—hey! Shiro-chan!" Mugin ran ahead of them, circling around Miyoshi, who stopped. "What year were you born?"

"Kansei Two, pest."

"He's lucky I like him," Mugin said, running back to them. "Or I would kill him."

"You can try," Miyoshi said, without looking back at him. It was obvious from his voice he was serious, but he was always serious.

"The way you joke always makes me so uncomfortable," Brian said, using his free hand to count off the years. "So Miyoshi must be—two and twenty." He hadn't realized his bodyguard was so young, barely more than a boy, really. "I'm twice his age."

"Is someone jealous?" Nadezhda said in Romanian.

"As long as you're not looking at him," Brian replied with all the severity he could manage through a screen of stalks. Then he broke out laughing.

When they ventured far enough south, the weather began to change for the worse, merely with the passage of time. "We'll have to find an inn," Miyoshi said "to wait out the weather."

Brian was too exhausted from walking so long to put up any complaint. His back, which usually was fine when walking, was starting to bother him from the strain of his unnatural limp, and there was only so much that Nadezhda's backrubs could do, no matter how much he enjoyed them.

They put it off until it became impossible to travel farther in the snow. They found a quiet inn that was empty but for the owner and his wife, who were willing to shelter two foreigners and their samurai guardian (and that thug following them around) for the right price. Considering their lives were on the line, Brian could hardly fault them for the "right price." They didn't seem to have names, but none of the peasants did.

"Peasants don't have names," Miyoshi said one night as they sat around the hearth. "Only nobility or people in a clan."

"Like Mugin?"

"Mugin is a peasant," he said. "He got a name when he was in China. Moo Shin. His ego wouldn't allow him to relinquish it." As he spoke, he was running an oiled cloth along the length of his katana with great devotion.

"Talking about me?" Mugin said, entering with a plate of food. Even in the cold winter months he was barefoot.

"What clan are you from, Miyoshi?" Nadezhda asked.

He huffed and didn't answer.

"Fuma," Mugin said. "Shiro, you can't hide it anyway. You're wearing their insignia. They just can't recognize it." He turned to Nadezhda. "Fuma is a very powerful clan; used to be even more powerful centuries ago." He stuffed rice into his mouth. "Still very powerful. Close to the government. Ever meet the *shōgun*, Miyoshi-san?"

Miyoshi closed his eyes, put away his blade, and with great care, rose, and walked out onto the patio, sliding the door closed behind him.

"Why do you do that?" Brian said. "Why do you make him upset? You know our lives depend on him."

"Because I can't respect people who carry around their shame like it's a badge of courage," Mugin said. "What he did was so terrible he can't even speak of it."

"What did he do?"

"Ask him. Besides, I don't know the whole story. I only know what he used to do in Edo."

"Which was?"

Between mouthfuls, Mugin said, "He was an assassin."

Brian gently took Nadezhda's hands off his back, rose, and excused himself. He took his walking stick with him. "I'll be back." He opened the door to the patio, limped through it, and closed it behind him.

Outside, the snow was lightly falling over the small garden. Miyoshi was standing on the rock path to the well, almost oblivious to it falling on him, but it was probably hitting the heavy layer of wax that kept his topknot straight and his hairline from growing back. He at first did not react at all to Brian's approach, the shuffle in the snow. In fact, Brian had removed the wooden staff and held up the sword to swing it before Miyoshi even made a movement, spinning around and simultaneously drawing his blade, meeting Brian's and forcing it down. Brian fell forward, only to be caught by Miyoshi's strong hand, which pushed him back so the Englishman stumbled backwards and collapsed in the snow, his blade falling to his side. Miyoshi said nothing, his frame blocking the moonlight, as he replaced his sword.

"You're not the only person who's ever done anything bad," Brian said. "If I was not a barbaric foreigner, I would have committed *seppuku* in shame at least ten times now." He attempted to get to his feet and was surprised when Miyoshi offered a hand.

He was taller than the samurai, but being a cripple didn't make it seem that way. "Do you want me to list all my offenses? Because it's cold, and we'll be here all night." He bent over to collect his sword. "I ruined my family's standing, made my brother destitute, ran from my creditors and all responsibilities, drank, gambled, consorted with prostitutes, lied, cheated, stole—" As he straightened up, Miyoshi was holding the wooden sheath to his sword cane. "Thank you."

"I was a personal assassin for the *shōgun*," Miyoshi said. "My family is very powerful, but I was more interested in *bushido* than I was in politics. I didn't want to be an administrator. I wanted to be a real samurai, so they found another outlet for me." He watched as Brian closed his blade in its case and set it down to support him. "I was very good at it. If I had been as ruthless in politics as I was at doing my job, I could have gone far.

"I was not his only assassin, of course. I have an idea of the numbers, only those that are employed within my clan. We have short lives, but not necessarily for the reason you think. One night, I was given a mission to punish a couple that had married against the wishes of their parents. One of the fathers was an imperial notary—very close to the *shōgun*—one of his spies, I believe, on the emperor. I didn't question it until I met the couple as they tried to make it to the port. They intended to escape to China but had not found passage, and that night they pleaded for their lives. The husband was my age—his wife, maybe the same, I'll never know." He turned away. Brian was glad his hair had grown back because it was protecting him from the snow before it soaked in, though this was still nothing compared to Russia. "As you may suspect, I did not complete my mission. They escaped to the mainland; I will never know how they survived there, or if they did. I returned to the palace, reported to the *shōgun*, and requested permission to commit *seppuku*.

"He refused. I was to be executed like the worst type of criminal—I was to be crucified. This I could not accept. My pride was greater than my ability to follow orders. How I made it out of the palace, I will never fully understand. I pledged to Amitabha that I would succeed on my mission to commit *seppuku*, if only He would grant me exit and help me fell all in my path. He did, and I ran north. Mugin, I already knew from some past assignments. He popped up and helped me get fairly far, and when he refused to be my second, I realized I had to continue. I made it as far as Otasuh, where I reached the standstill with Kayano that you witnessed. From there, you know the story."

They had calculated that Miyoshi Shiro was two and twenty. What had Brian been doing at two and twenty? He had been raising his brother, trying to manage their funds, and see to the education of a boy who was losing his vision. He took him north to Scotland for a dangerous cataract removal surgery. Danny, who had yet to hit his growth spurt, cowered at the sight of the table they had to tie him to so he wouldn't move his head. Brian was forced to talk him into it. The surgery was successful but an infection followed, throwing Danny's life into danger instead of just his eye. When his fever finally broke, and his young body defeated the infection, Brian brought him home to London, exhausted in a way he could not describe. While still unacceptable, the stupor into which he fell as soon as his brother left for Cambridge was, on some level, understandable. "You don't believe in redemption, Miyoshi-san?"

"I do believe in redemption. A samurai's redemption is in his death."

"Are you so sure?"

"Yes," Miyoshi said without hesitation. "Whatever it may seem to you, I made my pledge to the Amitabha Buddha and I will keep it." He spat. "What do your gods expect of you?"

"Repentance."

"And how do you go about doing so?"

"Prayer, admitting that you were wrong. Not as dramatic, but still…" He shrugged. "It is our way. If I had taken my life, I never would have met my wife. For me, I think this was the best way."

Miyoshi turned back to him. "Put your sword in your obi, like I do."

Brian did so, sliding it into place. His blade was straight, and Miyoshi's was curved, but the effect was largely the same.

"Kneel."

Swallowing, Brian did so.

Miyoshi knelt across from him, some distance away. "The first lesson I was taught is to expect attack at any moment. You must first learn to draw your sword from a sitting position. The release of the blade is the deciding moment of the battle. Now, do like so…"

The Labors of Brother Grégoire

1813

AFTER THE MADDOXES (AND company) returned to Town and the other guests had gone, Elizabeth retreated into Pemberley to begin her confinement. "I admit it snuck up on me," she said to Jane. "Did seven months really pass?"

"Thank God they did," was Jane's reply, and Elizabeth could not help but agree.

Life began to return to normal at Pemberley. Urged by his wife, brother, and sister, Darcy immersed himself in the ledgers and the maintenance of his estate, which had been almost entirely left in the hands of his steward even since his return. Fortunately for everyone, it did not seem to be a particularly harsh winter, and some travel was possible, not just between Pemberley and Chatton, but also as far as Lambton. Lord Kincaid, who thought their weather was a gentle breeze, came down to Lambton to call on Georgiana. Over time, Darcy's manners were less distant toward his future brother-in-law; it helped that his children adored the man who would be their uncle. William Kincaid was a man of perpetual good humor; he did have an amusing accent to the sheltered Darcy children, and anything that made Geoffrey and Anne happy was good enough for Darcy. Sarah was now trying to walk, which was a rather tiring delight, because Elizabeth was exhausted from chasing her, and it was yet another thing for Darcy to focus on.

News continued from the Continent, and while Darcy paid little attention to it, the winter was not a good one for Napoleon or his troops, with a botched invasion of Russia. When some news did pass by his ears, Darcy could only feel relieved that his brother was home in Pemberley, safe from all of it.

Grégoire did not always join them for meals and spent most of his time in the library when the chapel was too cold; the stone was not a good protector against the winter climate. One day, Darcy inquired as to his brother's whereabouts, and Mrs. Reynolds said that Master Grégoire was taking his meals in the chapel for the time being.

"Is there some holiday I am unaware of?" Darcy said as he entered the chapel, a room no larger than his master bedchamber, with three rows of wooden pews and an altar. Grégoire sat on the stone steps to the altar, drinking from a teacup.

"No," Grégoire said quietly as he drained the last of the tea and set it aside. "I am sitting in vigil with the saint."

"Oh," Darcy said, glancing at the reliquary beneath the altar. "What is a vigil?"

"It is a period of prayer and contemplation in honor of the saint."

"Is it his day?"

"No. His feast day is in August," Grégoire said, standing up. "I promised Count Olaf I would do this."

"Who?"

"The count who helped us rescue you," his brother replied, "in Austria." He made no comment at Darcy's blank look. "His daughter, Nicoleta, was with child when we left. She is due to deliver about this time. He asked that I pray for her and the health of the child. I could not help but accept after all he'd done for us."

"Of course," Darcy said, not recalling a Count Olaf but not doubting for a moment that there had, at some point, been one. "That *is* it—prayer and... contemplation? No fasting?"

"No, no fasting." Grégoire added, "I will stay awake until it is over."

"And how long is that?"

"Until it is over, Darcy," Grégoire said, "not very long."

"Because—"

"I will not harm myself, if that is what you are thinking."

Darcy looked away in embarrassment, because he *had* been thinking it. "Of course. Well, I will not interrupt." He put a hand on his brother's shoulder, and Grégoire did not sway or look ill. In fact, he looked the healthiest Darcy had perhaps ever seen him. "Good luck."

"Thank you."

"And if you wouldn't mind—terribly—putting in a prayer for Elizabeth?"

Grégoire smiled. "Of course."

While he did not consider himself duplicitous, Grégoire Darcy had become a master of knowing when to leave out important details. He had made a promise to Count Olaf that he would sit in vigil for his daughter's health; because of the length of the vigil, he would not fast. Instead, he would stay awake.

It was harmless, but difficult and increasingly so. He ate little because food brought on sleep. He drank tea excessively and began chewing on the leaves more often than drinking the actual drink. When he felt himself tire, he took off his sandals and walked across the cold floor barefoot, or took a walk outside, where the frigid air was enough, for the time being, to restore his senses. Eventually he conspired with the servant assigned to him—Thomas—to occasionally ring a bell when he seemed to be nodding off. "Thank you, Thomas," he said politely, which never failed to surprise Thomas, who was unused to this level of informality from his master.

On the third day, he quizzed Geoffrey on his vocabulary, reading him passages from the Bible, the ones children would like. Geoffrey, now too large to sit in his lap, would constantly ask him questions that his mildly impaired mind could not always process.

"Why did the Izrealishes get lost in the desert?"

"Israelites, Geoffrey."

"That's not what you said."

"Did I say Israelishes?"

"Now you said it a *different* way!"

He smiled, pushing up his reading spectacles so he could rub his eyes again. "I meant Israelites. Your uncle is very tired." He tried to focus on the page. "They didn't get lost. They were made to wander in the desert for forty years."

"Why?"

"Because they built a golden calf."

"Why?"

"Because a golden calf is an idol. The Egyptians worshiped them. This made God very angry. He did not want them to worship false idols."

"How do you know if an idol is real or fake?"

"Because—I don't know, Geoffrey," he said, and his nephew looked up at him. "I do not know everything."

"Are there still people in Egypt?"

"Yes. Napoleon invaded Egypt a few years ago."

"Do they still worship calves?"

"No. I believe they worship—I forget his name. Mohammat. S-something like that." He took another swig from his jug of tea. It was cold, but he didn't care. "That is enough for today; perhaps tomorrow, if I am not asleep."

That night, Thomas presented him with a caged bird. "The damned thing won't stop squawking," he said. "It was meant to be a present to my younger sister for Christmas, but no one can stand the poor thing."

"It does certainly provide a lot of noise," Grégoire said, covering his ears and staring at the bird fluttering around in its wooden cage. "Thank you, Thomas. You are a lifesaver."

On the fourth day, he attempted to have a rational theological conversation with Lord Kincaid, which was an utter failure because his mind could no longer maintain one path of thought, much less an argument, and before long they had ventured into why things were shaped the way they were.

"No, Brother Grégoire, I have no idea why the sun isn't square," Kincaid said, laughing. "Are you sure you don't need a quick rest?"

"I am sure I need one; however, I will not have one until my promise is fulfilled! And so, I have defeated you! There!"

"You're right; the Pope is the true Vicar of Christ. What was John Knox thinking? If only he'd talked to an overtired monk, Scotland would surely never have fallen into heresy!"

"Overtired and *hungry*," Grégoire corrected.

"Are you fasting as well?"

"No, but food makes me sleepy. It is better not to fill my stomach." He chewed absently on a scone. "This is horrible. You Scotsmen know nothing about bread!"

"What would a Frenchman know about—oh, I do suppose you have a point," Kincaid said. "But my pride won't let me admit it. I do rather like your wines."

"I made them myself, you know."

Kincaid chuckled, "All of them?"

"Yes! All of them!"

It was then that Georgiana interrupted them, thereby announcing her entrance, "William, what are you doing to my poor brother?"

"No worse than what he's done to himself, I assure you," Kincaid said, smiling at his betrothed.

Georgiana smiled and kissed Grégoire on his tonsure. "Do not let Darcy see you, or he will tie you down and *force* you to sleep."

"'Kay."

On the fifth day, he decided to stop sitting down, as it had a tendency to lead to slumping over. He was also quite sure he was hearing things, because every time he asked, no one had heard anything, other than the endless chirping of that bird. Grégoire could no longer read because his eyes could not focus, so he paced back and forth, reciting the psalms he knew from heart.

"God help me," he pleaded, this time a very legitimate plea. "I fear I have made a promise I cannot keep." He was drinking tea with more leaves than water, in it, eating almost nothing, constantly on his feet, and yet at any moment, darkness seemed imminent. "Holy Father, I beg of you, please bring about a speedy conclusion to Nicoleta's term so that I may sleep," he said, blinking. "Precious, precious sleep." He did not know the Latin for that.

"*Somnus* is sleep," said his abbot.

"That I know!" Spinning around a little too fast, so much that he lost what little balance he had, he grabbed the edge of the pews to stay standing. "Father, forgive me I—" Again, he forgot what he was apologizing for. "I am seeing you. I mean, you are not here. Nonetheless, I think one should pay his respects."

"Yes," a new voice said. It was his abbot from Austria, where his monastery was no more. "Do you remember what I said to you?"

"You—the saint—" It was all blurring together. "You said the saint talked to you. He is here with us—you can speak again if you want!" He pointed to the reliquary. "I brought him back to England—was that the right thing to do?"

"That was not what he told me. It doesn't mean it was wrong, but it did not enter into our conversation."

"Holy Father, I hope I have not erred." He knelt on the floor. He could feel the cold of it through his heavy robes. "I have tried to do as you said, Father."

"I did not ask anything of you. I gave you a choice. I said there would be a choice," said the abbot. "But not a moment where it is clear that it is so, at least, not now. What did Saint Sebald say?"

"He said—he said that it is in fire and under hammers that strong things are created," Grégoire said miserably.

"Your path to greatness will be a terrible one," the abbot said. "That is not an easy message for me to convey. But it is through suffering that you have the potential for spiritual perfection. People will lead you astray—within the Church and without. You are not expected to succeed."

"That is… depressing." Grégoire was upset that he could not find a better answer for his abbot. He was sure his earlier one had been more appropriate.

"I believe it anyway," the abbot said. "After all, without belief, we would truly have nothing."

"Is that also what the saint said?"

"Ask him yourself."

Grégoire sat down on the wooden pew. His feet simply hurt too much to keep standing. The bearded man beside him spoke in Latin, or Greek, or something that made sense and yet was foreign, "You requested a favor."

"I—am to pray for the safe delivery of Nicoleta's child," he stammered.

"That has already happened. You know she was due a month ago, or you would have, had the count told you. After all, one cannot expect a letter to arrive so soon, even with a courier."

"I—suppose." He didn't really have an answer to that. "So… why am I doing this?"

"Why are you doing this, Brother Grégoire?"

He didn't know how the answer came to him. "Because people need my help, and I don't know any other way to do it."

Sebaldus met his eyes. "You knew I was Saxon? English?"

"Yes. Yes, I knew that; I must know that because my mind is making you up—"

"That is your wish—for a woman to safely deliver? For a womb to be opened? Like Sarah, who laughed when the angels came to tell her that her wish was granted, having waited a hundred years for that day to come."

"Yes."

There was something calm and peaceful in Sebaldus's eyes, even though his features were foreign, his beard long. The saintly halo did much to lighten his eyes. Grégoire realized he was looking at that image of him painted on the plaster of the church walls at Nuremberg, an old one from centuries past. "This miracle I will perform, and you will bury me. I wish to do my miracles from heaven now, not a box," Sebaldus said, standing up. He put his arms on Grégoire's shoulders. "You will know because her name will be the first you hear after your rest. Good night, Grégoire."

"But I can't rest until—"

"Mr. Darcy?"

Grégoire opened his eyes. He hadn't realized they were closed. The voice he heard was unfamiliar, and piercing in its reality. He rubbed his eyes and looked over his shoulder. "What?"

"Mr. Darcy?" the man said with his heavy Austrian accent, and looked again at the label of the envelope he was holding. "Mr. Grégoire Darcy?"

"Yes—that is me," he said, his legs aching as he rose to greet the man in the overcoat.

"This is for you," said the man in German and passed Grégoire the envelope with the seal of some local nobility.

"Thank you," Grégoire said, his eyes opening in excitement as he realized what it was. "Thank you so much." He grabbed the man's hand and shook it so harshly the man actually shook. "The uh—Mr. Thomas will pay you."

The courier bowed and saw his way out. Grégoire did not wait to tear open the envelope, revealing the letter inside, which was in French.

Dear Brother Grégoire of the Order of Saint Benedict,

As you have surmised, Nicoleta has delivered. It is a beautiful boy. We have named him Sebald, and wish you much luck and joy in your own earthly (and heavenly) endeavors.

Count Olaf Cisnădioara of Sibiu.

He was laughing somewhat hysterically when Thomas entered. "Brother Grégoire, I—"

"It's over. Thank you," he said. He leaned over and kissed the reliquary. "And thank you. And thank God. Thank everyone!"

With that, he left the chapel, returning to his quarters, not far away, where he laid down on the mattress. He was still clutching the letter when he fell asleep.

Grégoire woke ravenously hungry the next morning, after sleeping some twenty hours. Still rubbing his eyes from sleep, he put on his sandals and headed straight for the breakfast room, where Darcy and Elizabeth were having a quiet breakfast.

"Grégoire," Elizabeth said, rising to greet him. "We weren't sure when you would awaken. The apothecary told us to just let you keep sleeping."

"Yes," Darcy said as his brother sat down next to him. "Despite appearances, I was concerned for you. But now, it seems, you are well and, this time around, have done no permanent damage to yourself—except that you might possibly choke."

"I feel fine," Grégoire said between mouthfuls of the muffins he was stuffing into his mouth.

"We were just discussing the Fitzwilliams," Elizabeth said. "Richard and Anne would like very much to visit us. They would like to be here for the wedding."

"Of course," Grégoire said. "Excuse me—did you say Richard and *Anne* Fitzwilliam?" Something struck him, like a person emerging from a haze that was really an idea.

"Yes," Darcy said. "Do you know any other Fitzwilliams beside myself?"

"No," Grégoire said, taking a mouthful of juice and swallowing soundly before answering, "I would love to see them."

Lord Richard and Lady Anne Matlock's intention was to arrive early in February, since such a mild winter made the roads passable. They came later, however, by a few days. Elizabeth was now nearing her last week or two of confinement, or so they estimated, and they were relieved for the distraction from the usual anxiety surrounding a birth.

"I'm so sorry we are late," Fitzwilliam said as he shook Darcy's hand. "You wouldn't possibly have a doctor on hand, would you?"

"Dr. Maddox should be up later this week—do you need one now? I have our local doctor, and he is very good."

"It is probably nothing," Fitzwilliam said, but his voice didn't sound like it was. "The road made Anne a bit ill. I'm sure she would do fine with rest—"

But Darcy would hear nothing of it. "The doctor will be called immediately."

Lady Anne Matlock was helped out of the carriage, but insisted on walking up the steps to Pemberley's doors herself, with her shawl wrapped tightly around her and her husband following very closely by her side. She did look a little pale. "I am fine. It is nothing to fuss over."

But a few minutes later, she was upstairs, ill in her quarters. Elizabeth got out of bed, despite her sister's protests, to greet her own guest. "I need to walk around, anyway."

"I'll get the doctor," Darcy said and excused himself from the company of Fitzwilliam and Grégoire to do so.

Fitzwilliam was about to go join his wife when Grégoire stopped him. "She's been ill for about three weeks now, hasn't she? Lost weight, loss of appetite? And now this?"

"Y-yes," Lord Matlock said, caught off-guard by Grégoire's tone of certainty. "How did you know?"

"The doctor will confirm it," Grégoire said, "but congratulations. Your wife is with child."

Grégoire insisted on digging the grave himself. In an unused corner of Pemberley's cemetery, he broke into the ground that was now just beginning to soften and unfreeze. He was still doing the job when they brought forth the light wooden coffin. Geoffrey squirmed impatiently and everyone else (besides Elizabeth, who had to watch from a window) withheld their laughter at the sight of Darcy, wearing a white frock over his clothing, swinging the golden incense-bearer that represented the host as an altar boy. His expression said perfectly, *Not smiling—it is not funny.* "I'll kill him for this," he mumbled, so softly that only Bingley next to him heard it.

"Pass him to me," Grégoire said from inside the grave pit, as Fitzwilliam and the newly arrived Dr. Maddox, designated as pallbearers, brought forth the coffin, unadorned but for a cross carved on the lid. With Grégoire's help, it was set in the ground, and the four men (aside from Darcy, who was still stuck with host-bearing duty) quickly covered the relatively shallow grave made for the saint. The tombstone, already prepared with a few days' notice, said, "Saint Sebald the Saxon."

The funeral service was short and entirely in Latin. Too many tears had been shed in the past few days—tears of joy, at the confirmation of Anne's state—for any to be spared now, as the old bones of Saint Sebald were laid to rest. In fact, it was almost a joyful service, even though no words to that effect were spoken, but even Grégoire was smiling as he finished the service and blessed the grave. "Amen."

They stood there, momentarily out of wit for what to do, when a servant came running up to them. "Mr. Darcy—Mrs. Darcy has requested the midwife."

For Mrs. Darcy's fourth set of labor pains had begun.

BIRTH, MARRIAGE, AND THE GRAVE

"THIS IS ALWAYS A fascinating experience," Bingley explained to Lord Kincaid.

"I would not dare to call it *fascinating*," Darcy said from the corner of his study.

Bingley, brandy already in hand, continued unabated, "Since Darcy is prohibited from overindulging in spirits for the sake of his health, we all sit around to comfort him by getting drunk ourselves, while he grows increasingly angry and we grow increasingly insensible."

"Yes, 'tis all terrific fun," Darcy sneered, pacing frantically in his little corner, "for the rest of you."

The brandy and whiskey was passed around, and only Dr. Maddox restricted himself to a single glass that he nursed over time, as he might be called on if there was an emergency. As the hours passed, and Elizabeth's cries increased, Lord Matlock looked increasingly pale and took more brandy.

"Buck up," said a very smiley Bingley.

"He can say that because his wife is not currently known to

be with child," Darcy said. "If this were Jane's confinement, he would have his head on the desk by now."

"That is true," Dr. Maddox said.

"Hey!" Bingley said, and turned to Kincaid, who didn't seem at all affected by the vast quantities of whiskey he was drinking. "You know, Miss Darcy was meant to be *my* wife. *You* should thank *me* that I did not care for her… in that way."

"What?"

"Careful, Charles," Dr. Maddox said. "While being strangled by Darcy may be a suitable distraction from his wife's travails, it will also be adverse to your health."

Bingley turned around to face Darcy's cold stare, which was more intense than usual.

"What's all this business?" Kincaid repeated.

"Some past, irrelevant nonsense," Darcy said, and continued pacing. "Where is Mrs. Maddox? Is she with the children?"

"She is one of Elizabeth's nursemaids, I believe," Dr. Maddox said.

"Really? My sister?" Charles said before Darcy could say anything. "My sister?"

"There is only one Mrs. Ma—Well, now I suppose there are two. But yes, I do mean my wife." Dr. Maddox answered.

"I would assume, then, that all previous animosities have been forgotten," Darcy ventured.

"A strange thing indeed, happenstance is," Fitzwilliam said.

Elizabeth's labor was relatively brief. Each one had decreased in length, or so Darcy was wont to notice. It was barely midnight, and only some of the guests had retired—Bingley and

Fitzwilliam mainly, because otherwise they would have slumped into some chair and been sleeping anyway. Darcy was called upstairs, bowing politely to his sisters-in-law and the midwife as he entered the mistress's chambers and sat down (as was now family custom) to receive his new child, so tiny and wrapped so heavily in cloth that he had to inquire as to its gender. He was so happy that he was not marred by drunkenness to experience this, to hold his new child, so small and perfect.

"A daughter," Elizabeth said.

A daughter. Another little girl to lavish his attention and love on, to hold in his arms until she was too big to do so, to give her the best clothes and ribbons for her hair, and then to stress about her coming of age and being out—another addition to his wonderful life. Even though it was night, there was no darkness in his world. "She is perfect." It was as if she was made of light. She squirmed as if she found her new surroundings too strange, her tiny, pink fingers slowly flailing until he offered his pinky finger for her hand to rest on. "So perfect," he laughed. He could not remember such joy. He was sure he had felt it for his other children, but that was all so distant, so marred by time that it was like a new experience, all wonderful all over again. "I am at a loss. What shall we name her?"

Elizabeth replied, "Nothing that starts with a 'G.'"

The Bennets arrived in good time, as there seemed to be an entire month of celebrations. The christening of Cassandra Darcy in Pemberley's chapel was followed a week later by Georgiana Bingley's eighth birthday, and then two weeks later by Geoffrey Darcy's. According to tradition, Georgie spent the two weeks lording it over Geoffrey that she was "a year older than him." The Bennets were housed at Pemberley and all of the Maddoxes (now including Brian and Nadezhda, and Mugin) at Chatton.

On the last day of March, a beautiful spring day, Lord William Kincaid and Georgiana Darcy were united in marriage in the Parsonage church. The Kincaids (and other relatives) who arrived to see William married were not the kilted rabble that the Englishmen generally imagined all Scots to be. In fact they looked very much the same as them, even if they spoke differently, to the point where some of their accents were almost incomprehensible to a southern Englishman like Mr. Bennet. "I'm afraid my hearing's gone out, sir. What did you say?"

It was with no small emotion that Fitzwilliam Darcy gave away his sister. He endured through the ceremony in his usual manner of smoldering emotion hidden behind an expression of calm stiffness, but his eyes betrayed him to Elizabeth as he rejoined her. She slid her hand over his, squeezing it as the vows were said. He returned her gesture with a smile.

Georgiana, the former mistress of Pemberley from her father's death to her brother's wedding, went out in style. The wedding breakfast at Pemberley was unparalleled, mainly because not only had Darcy spared no expense, but he had also invited many tenants and workers who had served Georgiana over the years, or to whom she had paid sick visits. Lord Kincaid was anything but a snob himself and welcomed all of the well-wishers in whatever form they appeared, and Derbyshire had its own party for Lady Kincaid.

There was one last family member to whom the blushing bride wished to say her good-byes before departing for the north.

Lord and Lady Kincaid paid their respects to her parents—to the father she remembered fondly but vaguely and the mother she knew only from her portrait. Darcy and Grégoire caught up with them, and they stood silently in front of the grave, mainly because no one could think of quite what to say of or to George Wickham. Kincaid knew him not at all, Grégoire, barely. To Darcy and Georgiana he had been a maelstrom, but he had been their brother, however unwittingly.

"One of the last things he said was that he loved me," she said, "as a person, as a sister. That he should have acted like a Darcy and been a good brother."

"If he had known, maybe that would have happened," Darcy said, not unkindly. He turned to see his sister leaning on her husband. Darcy was no longer her main support—William Kincaid was. That was what the giving away someone meant, he supposed. The way the earl held her, Darcy thought it might not be such a bad thing.

The wedding preparations had been Elizabeth's first major venture from bed in the few weeks since Cassandra's birth. Two babies in little more than a year, taking over Rosings, a rushed trip to rescue her husband, caring for him, watching him descend into darkness and emerge only with her insistence and Dr. Maddox's help had finally caught up with her. She was not ill so much as exhausted and, after the wedding, slowed back down for the next month, for what sleep was afforded to a mother with a newborn who insisted upon nursing herself. Sarah, fortunately, had been weaned. Elizabeth was still Elizabeth, however, and not content to sit inside. She sat out on the terrace, watching her children play with her nieces and nephews, often with Jane by her side. Grégoire, for the moment resolved to the fact that he was stuck in England for as long as the war continued, worked in the garden, and Darcy plunged himself into estate matters. He still had moments where he seemed lost, or where he needed a cup of that special tea to find sleep, but his heart seemed to warm with the sun.

Jane Bingley and her children were often at Pemberley for meals, as Charles was back and forth to Town, where he had taken Brian Maddox on as a partner in exchange for his stock. No one but the two of them (and maybe Nadezhda) knew the actual numbers, but the Chinese silk Brian returned with was worth no small fortune, and as long as the embargo lasted, retail prices continued to soar. After hiring some slightly more reputable workers, the business was back in high profits, with plans to have a ship sail to Nagasaki within the next two years. Brian and Nadezhda comfortably selected a country house but ten miles from Town, and got a very good price because it was relatively small and one section was in complete disrepair. This they had immediately torn down and begun to rebuild in a fashion to their specifications, and would spend years perfecting the Japanese wing of their home. They also had wide grounds, which they kept empty and wild, and lived in some isolation. The local market did quickly become accustomed to the Oriental in a basket of a hat running in for supplies. Mugin would leave in the fall or late summer—whenever the Dutch ship sailed again for the east.

The Bennets, who so rarely traveled, remained at Pemberley for two months, happily overlapping Elizabeth's convalescence. Even though Mrs. Bennet's nerves could wear on anyone, they were now directed at the children, who laughed at their grandmother and took no offense. Kitty Townsend was now two months with child, and Mr. Townsend was a polite companion who enjoyed fishing and talking business with Bingley, as he had made his own fortune in trade. Mary Bennet conversed with Grégoire (which Mr. Bennet was more than happy about, as it was a load off his ears), and Joseph Bennet was beginning to learn his letters, even if he only knew a few of them. He had black hair and a slightly darker complexion than most of his relatives, but nothing as bizarre as some of their other guests of late. Joseph Bennet was used to the company only of George Wickham, almost four significant years his senior, and enjoyed Charles and Geoffrey. The company was not decidedly divided by gender yet, as Georgie and Eliza Bingley were still in the mix and apparently delighted their mother in their disputes, and Anne followed her brother Geoffrey around as if candy was attached to his back. Only Frederick and Emily were missing, as their father had returned to work, and therefore they remained largely in Town.

When the Bennets departed in May, Brian and Nadezhda came up to Chatton. Their relationship with Darcy was still awkward. Dr. Maddox had always been close to his brother despite their understandably rocky relationship, and was quick to be understanding about the steps Brian had taken to secure the safety of himself and his wife. Darcy, more removed and with less invested in the physical person of Brian Maddox, was still uneasy, no matter how Brian apologized or how much Elizabeth badgered her husband. That bridge remained unmended, though he was not uncivil to his guest when the Maddoxes did dine at Pemberley.

Princess Nadezhda Maddox was universally loved by the children and the adults. She was kind, resourceful, and wise in many ways. That Brian was utterly devoted to her was something that even Darcy saw as a shining quality. She did not plan to make the social rounds during the Season, though she would have been the talk of the town and Mr. Maddox's money now restored him to good standing. While not afraid or shy, she was modest, always covered up in either Eastern European or Japanese styles, and carried herself with a hardened dignity. With the children, she was wonderful and kept them out of a good deal of trouble.

Mugin was another matter. He remained a rogue, unwilling to conform to anything foreign to him (which was just about everything) beyond the basic necessities of life, but still amused by their "barbarian" behavior. Only Brian and Nadezhda seemed to be unruffled by anything he said, and he rarely spoke in English except when absolutely necessary, often using them as translators when it didn't seem necessary. He spent his time mainly outdoors, and despite his weaponry and his obvious tendency towards (or appreciation of) violence, he was a gentle giant to the children, even though without his shoes he was shorter than every other adult, even the women. When they weren't afraid of him, they loved him. If he made anyone uncomfortable, they wisely kept their mouths closed in front of him.

BRIAN'S STORY CONCLUDES

1811

THEY LEFT AS SOON the weather permitted. The landscape changed, slowly, as the road became endless again.

They were forced to take a breather in another nameless, small town, for other reasons. Nadezhda's courses had descended again—this was the first time since the winter—and she was rendered an invalid for those terrible three days. The two of them stayed in their room at the inn, keeping the door shut to everyone but Mugin and Miyoshi, who seemed to be finding enough to do in town.

As usual, by the third day, Nadezhda lost her lucidity from exhaustion, pain, and blood loss. The Japanese seemed to have very little to offer in the way of herbs or medicines, but they had numerous teas and broths. "Here. Try this one," Brian said, holding another bowl up to her mouth. "I don't know what it is, but it smells good."

On the fourth day she regained her sense, but not her strength, and remained in bed. Her hair was uncovered and not in braids, which was a rarity, and he loved to run his hands through it. "How are you feeling?"

"Better." She smiled weakly.

The door slid open behind them without a call, which meant it was Mugin who shambled in. "Any food around?" He had his own room with Miyoshi, but it was connected, and neither of them had been in last night.

"Here," Brian said, not bothering to put up a fight, and offered up a bowl of rice. He had once asked them where they went at night, and the answer was the obvious one, which he had so politely overlooked.

"Well, where would you go at night if you didn't have regularly available access to a woman?" Mugin had answered, and that was the end of the discussion.

Now, he was more polite. "How are you, Nadi-chan?"

"Better," she answered. "I'll be able to travel again in a few days."

"*Sa!* It doesn't matter to me," Mugin said.

"Does anything matter to you, Mugin-san?" Brian asked with a smile.

"Food, women, and money for the other two things," Mugin said, grabbing at the globs of rice in his bowl with the chopsticks. "Maybe Shiro-chan; I like picking on him, and he hasn't killed me yet. He has tried though. So, Nadi-chan—you can't have children, right?"

Brian gave Mugin a cold stare, but Nadezhda merely said, "No. Brian, he's going to do it again."

"What? Oh," Brian said, and turned again to Mugin. "The three-way is still a no and will always be so. You can stop asking."

Mugin huffed. "*Gaijin* are no fun."

"—*Doko doko yukuno*—"

"Mugin."

"*Hito mo nagarete*—"

"Mugin!"

"*Doko doko yukuno*—" Mugin's singing was only stopped by Miyoshi's blade inches from his neck. Mugin stopped walking. "You complain about everything. First I'm not allowed to gamble with our money, and then I'm not allowed to sing—" He turned to Brian and Nadezhda. "What's wrong with my singing?"

"The song was good," Nadezhda said.

"The first hundred times," Brian added.

"So why don't you sing something, Brian-chan?"

Brian put his hands together in a prayer position. "I am merely a pilgrim. I would not know any English sailing songs. And those are all I know."

"He has a point," Miyoshi said, replacing his blade. "We should get moving."

"That's all you ever say!"

"It's true," was Miyoshi's defense.

They continued on, the path sloping down, until they were forced to take a break in the shade of some trees. It was not unbearably hot, but nearly there. There was still an occasional passerby on the road, so Brian kept his hat on, doing his best to cool his brow beneath it with cloth. "Nady, do you want—"

Miyoshi raised his hand. Even Mugin stopped making noise.

"Fuma-no-Shiro," said the voice from behind them. "I thought it was you."

Miyoshi stood up. "I'm sorry; you are mistaken."

They turned to the fat man with only one sword. He held up a scroll while samurai emerged from the woods, flanking him. "Ha! I remember you from court. Do you know how many *ryo* the *shōgun* put on your head? I never thought you would come as far south as this. Did you know this is my prefecture? No, I suppose not."

"I am sorry," Miyoshi said, turning away from them and gesturing with his head for the others to move along, "but again, you are mistaken. I am a samurai to these pilgrims, and we must be on our way."

The man wasn't listening. "When I heard a Fuma samurai was this far north, I knew it had to be you. So you might as well admit it and surrender to me, and I'll let the pilgrims go."

All eyes were on Miyoshi, who stood quietly, his expression hidden beneath his *ronin gasa*. His hands were limp at his sides, not on his swords. Was he planning his battle strategy or contemplating the offer?

"There're too many of them," Brian whispered to Mugin, watching the samurai emerge. There were half a dozen, all similarly attired, and more behind them.

"You think that way, you give up before the battle begins," Mugin said, one hand on the hilt of his sword. "You can run or stay, whatever you think is best. No one will think less of you for it."

"Will he fight them? It's ridiculous."

"As opposed to giving in? It's more honorable to die in battle. This prefect knows that."

Brian felt Nadezhda's hand over his in silent confirmation.

Miyoshi did not speak. Instead he removed his hat and tossed it at the head of the closest samurai. Before the warrior recovered, Miyoshi had drawn his katana and cut his head off.

"Get—" but the prefect got no further before he got a flying *geta* shoe to his head. It distracted him long enough for Mugin to jump in front of him, retrieving his shoe in one hand and stabbing the fat man in the shoulder with the other. He pushed the dead prefect, spurting blood all over him, off his blade with his foot.

"Is that all you have!" Mugin shouted. It was not a question.

"All they had" was quite a lot. Nearly a dozen samurai now surrounded Mugin and Miyoshi. "Kill them!"

"Halt!" Brian shouted, drawing his blade and stepping forward. He and Nadezhda threw off their tengai hats. "You are disrupting this mission, and we cannot allow that."

"Foreigners!" said the nearest samurai, but the revelation had its intended affect. Miyoshi took the time to slay him while he wasn't looking, and Mugin slid beneath another two, cutting off one's leg with his free arm and somersaulting on the other.

"Kill the foreigners, the *ronin*, or the convict? Hard decision, samurai!" Mugin mocked them when he was back on his feet, parrying the swinging blade with his own and punching the samurai in the face hard enough to draw blood.

"Stay back," Brian said.

"I suppose someone will have to rescue you," Nadezhda said. Or at least, that was what he thought she said as Brian raised his sword and charged at the nearest samurai, who was too busy attacking Miyoshi from behind to see him coming.

He would always remember the sound of metal cutting through flesh, muscle, and bone. Everything else about that battle was a bloodied haze. He tried to remember what Miyoshi had taught him, at least long enough for the real warriors to do their work. He saw the coins from behind, tossed by Nadezhda, and a man fell merely from the coin landing in his skull, right between the eyes. The blood sprayed in Brian's face, and he was sure, as he went to wipe it, something hit him from the side, hard enough to make the haze turn to black.

He had not felled them. Even though Brian was sure of it, the samurai stood all around him, in full ceremonial armor, more than they had on before. They stood in a circle around his body, saying nothing, their long spears planted firmly in the ground.

"Is this it?" he said, not fully aware of what language he was speaking. "Is this how I am to die?"

They stood in silence.

"Have I already passed? Did I say good-bye?"

They did not move, but he felt as if they were moving closer.

"Please, tell me I said good-bye. I owe her that. 'Tis nature for a wife to outlive her husband, but I cannot bear it." He sighed, but there was no pain. "I have to wish her well. I suppose she deserves more than a scoundrel like me."

He did not move himself from his position on the ground, which he realized was empty, he felt as if he was floating.

"But—I have not been a scoundrel. I have been a good husband. At—at least, I've tried. Good Lord, I've tried. In every way I knew. Granted, all I knew was how to cut and run, but… I'm quite good at it." He looked up at the masked samurai warriors without moving. "You think I will accept this? You think I will not try to flee one last time?"

They did not answer him.

"You are pulling me down, and I won't go. I have but one love in this life, and not even all the soldiers of Nippon can take her from me."

Their poles became longer, as their bodies melted.

"See? Even you cannot intimidate me, the helpless, lame *gaijin*! Now bring me my Nadezhda, and leave me alone!"

Because he had to see her one last time. The poles were the only thing he could see now and the haze surrounding them, as his eyes slowly focused, and he realized he was looking at the bars of a window. Prison? No, just the Japanese way of things. He was, most definitely, looking at a window. Though he was not alone, the samurai were gone. Beside him he heard labored breathing, but it was a very long time before he could bring himself to turn his head, for his own aches had returned.

On one side, Mugin, without his jacket or shoes, unarmed; so odd to see him that way, not at the ready. He looked like a wild beast, but a wild beast that was uneasily asleep.

On the other, Miyoshi, wearing a different kimono, in a similar position.

"They are asleep." The shadow crossed over him as her figure sat, in front of the light, next to him on the mattress. "We are alone, in a way." She kissed him on the forehead. "You should drink, darling."

He could not, of course, refuse her. With Nadezhda's help, he was able to sit up enough to drink from the bowl. When he was let back down, some of his senses were regained. "Where—are we—in prison?"

"No."

"How—"

"Miyoshi Shiro is dead," she said. "Or so the authorities believe. He took all of the men seeking him with him, but he died in battle. His body can be identified by his clothing, but the fugitives made off with his swords when they saw he was lost."

It took him a very long while to understand, but she was patient. "You switched his clothing with one of the soldiers?"

"Yes."

"We all escaped?"

"We went north. I paid the innkeeper to say so while she harbors us and you recover."

He smiled. "A scheme truly worthy of the Maddox name."

"Have I ever been unworthy of it?"

To this, he could give no proper response but to return her kiss.

In what, they later learned, was the spring of 1812, Brian and Nadezhda Maddox arrived in Nagasaki. They saw it first on the hill overlooking the port town and the ocean beyond it—the ocean that would lead them home. Brian sighed and put his arm around his wife's shoulders.

"Are we going to go already? Lazy *gaijin*," Mugin said. "We didn't come for you to admire the view!"

But they had come, however long the last length had been, riding in a wagon that moved more slowly than a man could travel on his feet, as they recovered from their injuries. When they were well enough, they abandoned it and took on the road on their feet again.

"Foreigners are still not allowed in Japan," Miyoshi explained as they descended the path that would lead them to the massive wooden city before them. "There is some wooden city where the traders live—out on the water."

"Really take things to extremes, don't you?" Brian said. Miyoshi just smiled. A vast improvement.

Not far off was Dejima, the artificial island beyond the massive stone walls of the city's edge. The sun was already setting, and the gates that kept the foreigners from the Japanese and the Japanese from the foreigners were closed. One last inn, before their parting, however it would be. Brian realized then, he'd spent little time contemplating how they would split apart, or if Mugin and Miyoshi could enter the city at all.

They took two rooms at the inn, overlooking the waters. As Nadezhda went to find dinner, Brian sat down at the window and stared at the Japanese-style houses of the floating city, but the people he could see there were not Japanese. They had hair in colors—red, blond, brown. They wore pants and waistcoats. They had sideburns. Brian had just been mindlessly shaving, because it was easier to manage his tengai with. Tomorrow, he wouldn't need his basket helmet anymore. It would all be over.

There was a call at the door. "Come."

It was Miyoshi. "Madokusu-san."

"Miyoshi-san," he said, uneasy at the stance of his old protector, which was tenser than normal. "What is it?"

Miyoshi removed his katana from his belt and held it up before Brian. "I would be honored if you would be my second."

Brian's immediate response was a blank stare.

"You cannot present innocence of *bushido* after all this time, Bry-an," Miyoshi said, his eyes lowered, his voice intense. "My final task is completed. You are safe in Nagasaki and you will be returning to your homeland soon."

"Not that soon."

"I have no wish to delay it." He did not lower the offered sword. "It is the only way."

"After all this time, Miyoshi-san, I still cannot say that I do not find the custom outright nauseating and against my very beliefs."

"Your beliefs are not relevant. It is a matter of honor."

"And Mugin has no honor?"

Miyoshi, for a moment, faltered; his eyes flickering up before he forced them down again. "Mugin refused. Please, I have no one else."

"This goes against my beliefs, my morals, my God—everything," he said, and reached out to also hold the sword. "You understand that?"

"Yes. But you do me a great honor."

Miyoshi relinquished his own grip, and the blade fell to Brian's. He bowed stiffly. "Thank you." And he was gone, closing the door behind him.

Brian placed the katana down respectfully, as if he was afraid to touch it, and then ran outside to the small patch of grass to be sick.

"I can't do it."

"You can," his wife said as she dressed him, like a manservant. It turned out that the pleated hakama pants a swordsman wore were complicated in their tying, and she readily offered to help him.

"It goes against our beliefs. Both our beliefs, I'm assuming, Nady."

"Of course," she said dismissively, "but not Shiro's. This is his country, and he is the master of his own soul. He can do as he pleases. Who knows—he may even be right." She kissed him on the cheek. "You will just be relieving his suffering, darling."

"Mugin wouldn't do it."

"How could Mugin be expected to do it?" she said. "Take the head of his own lover?"

Brian stared at her, dumbstruck. To this, his beloved Nadezhda only laughed. "What? This is news to you?"

"I—I—assumed—"

"Assumed what?"

He colored. "I had no idea."

"Really? Despite the fact they've taken a room together almost every night in an inn? Despite the fact Miyoshi would have never tolerated someone like Mugin from his first appearance unless there was something between them otherwise?"

"B-but they've both been... active. In—you know—houses."

"I didn't say they were—how do you say, monogamous." She turned her head. "Am I the only one of the two of us that realizes we are so far from Christendom and all the beliefs we hold to be commonplace?"

"Apparently so," he said.

Mugin did not attend the ceremony. As they stepped onto the porch, they found him slumped against the wall; he only huffed when they passed by.

They had to walk a good distance away from the city proper. Nadezhda held his hand. Brian allowed himself a moment's respite from his horrible thoughts to realize she looked beautiful in a kimono instead of pilgrim's clothes, with an umbrella over her shoulder to protect her from the sun. He smiled at her before returning to his grief.

Miyoshi was dressed all in white, his instruments laid out on the ground before him.

"I will make one last attempt to talk you out of this," Brian insisted.

Miyoshi ignored the request completely. "I grant my swords to you, Madokusu-san. Both of them." He turned his head down. "I have not completed my death poem."

"We have time."

"No." He smiled. "I have always been terrible at poetry. A gentle art I never mastered."

"No great sin."

Miyoshi nodded. He seemed content; Brian could not deny that, much as he wanted to, as Miyoshi passed Nadezhda the jar of water, which she, as previously instructed, poured over the drawn katana in Brian's shaking hands.

"It has been an honor serving you, Madokusu-san."

Brian's voice wavered as he said, "It has been an honor to have you as our protector. One I can never repay."

"You know how," he said calmly, clasping his hands together. "*Namu Amida butsu.*" His sword, carefully drawn against his stomach, was impossibly quick.

Brian saw his friend suffer. The rest came naturally.

A sudden appearance was made by Mugin in the clearing, after Brian had cleaned both swords and placed them in his obi, to help bury the body and the head. He appeared without a word, and the two of them worked in silence. According to custom, he was not placed deep in the ground, creating a mound, where offerings could be left. Nadezhda placed Miyoshi's prayer beads, which he had given her the night before, on the grave. The three of them bowed their heads and said, silently, their good-byes and prayers for the soul of Fuma-no-Shiro, Miyoshi Shiro, in three different native tongues, but as one.

Descending the steps, only the great courtyard was left to cross before reentering the gates of Dejima. Mugin came with them. Brian did not ask him why. He was too drained, the weight of the two swords on his belt too heavy as they approached the gate.

"*Tomare!*" (Halt!) the samurai guards said as they approached. "Only foreigners, their servants, and officials beyond this point."

Brian and Nadezhda removed their tengai as Brian answered in perfect Japanese, "I would like to speak to the head of Dejima and be granted entrance."

The spears were uncrossed, and a runner sent ahead of them, as the three ascended the bridge. When they came down on the other side, a man in a brown waistcoat and wearing an admiral's black hat was standing there. "*MIJ ben Opperhoofden Hendrik Doeff.*"

Brian bowed. "I'm sorry, I don't speak Dutch," he replied in Japanese. "I am an Englishman," he said in English, which sounded strange as he heard it come from his own mouth. "My wife is from Transylvania."

Nadezhda bowed.

"Then we'd best continue in the local tongue," said Doeff. "I am Commissioner Hendrik Doeff, in charge of Dejima for the Dutch East India Company and under the authority of the *shōgun*."

"Brian Maddox," Brian said. "This is my wife, Princess Nadezhda of Sibiu, Transylvania."

"An honor, sir and Your Highness," Doeff said, removing his hat and bowing deeply to Nadezhda.

"This is Mugin," Brian said, and Mugin bowed.

Doeff paid him little attention. "You are welcome here, of course, but I am a bit surprised to find an Englishman and a member of the Hungarian aristocracy—"

"We came here by way of Russia," Brian explained. "Landed in the north. We made our way down with Mugin-san's help."

"I see," Doeff said. "Well, I assume you mean to return to Europe?"

"Whenever the next ship leaves, we would like to go to England."

"You are aware that Emperor Napoleon's blockade—"

"That is still going on?"

"Yes sir, it is," Doeff said. "In fact, it is more severe than ever. But I can show you to an Englishman who can catch you up—one of the sailors. The next ship leaves for the Continent in a month. Welcome to Dejima, Your Highnesses." They interchanged English and Japanese words when needed as Doeff led them into the bizarre hybrid city that was Dejima—Japanese buildings with European people.

"You never said you were royalty," Mugin said from behind him.

"Nady is," he explained. "I just married her."

Nadezhda swatted him with her fan.

They were shown to the house of a man named Henry

Moss, a first mate currently off duty. "Aren't you a sight for sore eyes?" he said after they were introduced. "You've gone native, I see."

"I suppose," Brian said, one hand instinctively falling near his swords. "We are in need of some shelter for the next month. All of our money is in Japanese currency."

"That's no problem here, obviously. In fact, if you want to do business with the locals, it'll probably help you," Moss said. "And rent is cheap, what with the war going on. But what you look like you really need, sir, is a whiskey."

Brian exhaled with delight. "Oh God, yes."

As much as there was the temptation for idleness, the next month was extremely busy for all of them. Mugin did not leave their side, mainly because they kept sharing their food with him, but also because he helped Brian on various missions back in Nagasaki.

"Now I have an idea and it may either be incredibly stupid or make us a fortune. Or both," he said to Nadezhda, and she just nodded with amusement.

Slowly but surely, a good percentage of the fortune he had carried for so long was spent on Japanese goods. The *tengai* came into use again, as Brian played the *ronin* looking to buy for his master and Mugin played the part of his servant. Selling to their own, the Japanese salesmen had significantly lowered prices, and Brian secured a place on the ship for almost ten trunks of embroidered and raw silk, and various other items he would either want to remember the place by or for sale to the East India Museum in London.

Their last night, they spent in town behind the closed doors of a private room of a Japanese tavern, drinking hot sake with Mugin. "What am I going to do?" he said. "I've been living off you forever."

"You will manage to live off someone else, I'm sure," Brian said.

"So... you're not drunk enough for—"

"No, Mugin!"

Mugin pleaded, "Nadi-sama..."

She shook her head. "Mugin, our affection for you runs as deep as a mighty river of your song poetry. That said, we're not jumping into bed with you."

"*Sa!* No fun, either of you!"

As they emerged into the early morning light, Mugin showed his own affection the same way he did with Miyoshi, which was by leaving in an angry huff.

After they slept a few hours, it took the rest of the day to load the last of the trunks onto the Dutch ship that had agreed to stop in England. It was actually a Danish vessel, neutral enough to cross the complex waters of the channel. Still clothed in their kimonos, Brian and Nadezhda watched the lines being untied and the ship beginning to sail.

"Wait!"

"Mugin?"

The ship had moved away from the edge of the dock, but the clunk-clunk of Mugin's *geta* was unforgettable as he launched himself over the water and grabbed on to the edge of the boat, a large pack on his back. "Help me up, lazy *gaijin!*"

The husband and wife exchanged glances and each grabbed an arm, hauling him over the edge and onto the floor of the deck. They heard shouting in Japanese, and looking back at the disappearing dock, they saw several local policemen waving their swords and juttes. "Get back here and pay your debts!"

"It took you half a day to get in debt?" Brian said, and Mugin just shrugged haplessly.

"Apologies," he said. "Can I go to England with you for a little while? Just until they forget about me?"

"Mugin, they'll probably forget about you in a few hours, and this ship takes months to get there and back!"

"So?" Like everything else, he waved it off as if it was nothing. "Even better for me."

Brian turned to his wife, who just smiled, and he couldn't help but join her.

Present

"Mugin-san! Mugin-san!"

Mugin looked over his shoulder as Georgiana Bingley approached. "*Hai*, Binguri-chan?"

She curtseyed. "What are you doing?"

He looked around, as if it wasn't obvious and something was missing from the picture. He sat on a rock next to the stream behind Chatton. "You not know fishing? Stupid *gaijin*."

"Of course I know fishing," she said. "But why are you doing it?"

"Why not? I catch fish; eat fish. Not complicated." He took a closer look at her. "You good, Binguri-chan?"

"I'm good," she said, her voice still wavering. Without lowering his fishing pole, Mugin reached out with one hand, picked her up, and set her on the rock beside him. They sat in silence for some time before she said, "I think I made my father upset."

"Eh?"

"I was playing with Geoffrey and George, and I got all wet and muddy. I've gotten dirty before, but Mama said it's different now. I'm a little lady, and I shouldn't be messing about like that. She sent me up to my room, and Nurse washed my hair and put in these stupid bows that she knows that I hate," she said, pulling one out and releasing the complicated braid attached to it. Mugin just watched. "And I shouldn't say 'hate.' It's not proper. But I do hate these stupid bows. I don't like lying and saying I *dislike* them." She was tempted to toss it in the river, but realized she would probably have to explain it later, and decided not to. "I don't like being told what to do."

"Disobedient child, make parent upset," Mugin said.

"I'm not disobedient. They didn't say I couldn't play. They just decided one day that it was suddenly wrong because I'm a girl, only they didn't put it that way. And while Mama was talking, Papa just had this expression on his face like I've never seen before. But he didn't say anything."

"Mother yells at you?"

"No, never. But she can be very insistent."

She held up the bow, a little pink ribbon. Mugin took it from her and said, "Is stupid color."

Georgiana laughed. "Why does everybody look at me like I'm strange?"

"Keep secret?"

"What?"

"You. Keep secret of mine. Promise?"

"I promise," she said eagerly.

Mugin was quiet, staring at the ribbon before handing it back to her. "You're not strange. Englishmen think everyone should look the same, act the same, and even dress the same. Like soldiers on a battlefield. In Japan, it is similar, but it's not really true. People are not the same. The only thing that is the same is that everyone dies." He smiled wickedly. "If they fight me, definitely, they die."

Georgie stared at him before managing to mumble, "You speak English!"

"Of course, I've been here seven—eight months, and another three on a ship with Brian-chan. I'm not an idiot." His voice, though perfectly fluent, was heavily accented, and it altered some of the words, but the structure was far more sophisticated than his regular pidgin English. "Our languages are very different, though. It was still very hard."

"Then—why do you act like you don't speak English?"

"Two reasons," he said, picking up his pole properly again but still looking at her. "First, your language is the language of barbarians. I don't lower myself to speak your language if I don't have to. I am Japanese, and you are uncultured *gaijin*."

"Uncultured!"

"Very. You all smell horrible because you don't bathe or use enough perfume. You don't understand warfare, death, or religion. Many of you can't even read. You're so stuffy about sex that I'm surprised you have any children." He sighed. "Hmm. The last comment was not appropriate. Still, you'll figure it out sooner or later."

Georgiana gaped. Here was a simple man in sandals, fishing for his dinner and calling her countrymen barbarians! But the way he said it was like he had really been thinking it all out for some time.

"The second reason is more important," he continued. "It's like… card games your parents play at night. You know of them?"

"Yes. A little."

"They say, 'Play your cards close to your chest.' Brian-chan said that to me. He meant it in cards, but I mean it in life. Everyone has secrets, Binguri-chan. You should always appear weaker in the eyes of your enemies—or people who might be your enemies someday. Let everyone underestimate you." He patted her on her head. "You can be so easily underestimated because you are a girl. There is an advantage. You should take it."

"What are you saying?"

"Everyone wants you to be the same. Sometime you have to act like you are, but it doesn't mean you have to *be* the same. You are a very special girl. But you must be very clever not to appear different… and upset your parents. Understand?"

She swallowed. "I think so."

"You play your cards very close to your chest," he said, putting his hand on her chest.

"Will I always be different?"

"I will be very upset if you are not, very disappointed." He took the bow from her hands. "You should retie this. Here." Copying the other side, he retied the bow as it had been. "Japanese are good with knots."

Come to think of it, all of his clothing was knotted. He didn't have a belt or a buckle on him, and neither did the Maddoxes when they dressed up. "Thank you."

"You should go," he said. "Your parents will worry about you."

"But—you're leaving soon."

"Not so soon. I'll be here tomorrow."

"Promise?"

He smiled. "Promise."

Notes from the Underground

1771

DESPITE ITS BEAUTY, MR. Geoffrey Darcy always had a certain apprehension in his heart when approaching the island. It was a glorious spring day, and the winds were not so strong that he had to hold down his wig to prevent its escape when standing on the bow as the landmass seemed to approach.

"Mr. Darcy, sir," the dockworker bowed to him and offered a hand for him to step off the boat and onto the dock. As usual, he was immediately directed to the head nurse.

"Your brother is out by the rocks, Mr. Darcy. In the usual spot."

He smiled uncomfortably. It was good to know Gregory was still going outside on occasion. He left the house and walked up the ancient stone steps that had once led to an abbey, now in ruins covered by weeds. There his elder brother sat, playing with a ribbon in his hands. He had let his hair grow out, and was no longer wearing a wig, but otherwise was in proper attire. "Hello, Geoff."

"Hello, Gregory," he said, not entirely surprised when his

brother didn't stand. He sat down next to him on the old stone bench. "I have been remiss in visiting you—"

"—since our father died, yes." While his expression was emotionless, he nervously fiddled with the ribbon in his hand like it was a toy. "Well, I can understand you have been intolerably busy. You need not say it."

"Yes. Yes, I have." He sighed, relaxing. Now he could come to the news, which was not nearly as awkward or depressing as their previous topic. "I am engaged to be married."

His brother's face lit up as he chuckled. "You work quickly, do you not? Is she to be solely for the production for an heir, or are you in love? Oh, but I can see that you are." He smiled. "Or at least, infatuated. But you have never been one to fail in female company."

Geoffrey Darcy blushed, as his brother's insinuation brought to mind any number of situations, each brought along with them a sense of embarrassment. "I am in love. I would not marry into that family under other circumstances."

"Oh ho, ho, this will be a good one. Yes, tell me of her awful relations."

"No, I will not do that injustice, though you do tempt me. Her name is Lady Anne Fitzwilliam and she is the most beautiful woman I have ever met." He added, "And before you say it—yes, that is including my own experience, which you would deem vast."

"Any man would be tempted to deem it vast," Gregory said, because Gregory could get away with it. After all, the elder brother had helped the younger brother out of any number of embarrassing and possibly scandalous situations, without their parents the wiser, in his time in society. "Does she have any other exemplary qualities?"

"She has all of them." Geoffrey had to give his brother a most intense stare to prove he wasn't joking.

"And her terrible family?"

"Her brother has inherited the earldom. He is tolerable, but obviously would not begin to consider anyone less than a peer if not for our fortune."

His brother interrupted, "*Your* fortune. Remember, I no longer exist."

"Yes." Geoffrey swallowed uncomfortably. "Anyway, she has one elder sister, Lady Catherine, who makes even less of a pretense of only tolerating me for Pemberley and Derbyshire and *all that*. In fact, upon our first meeting, she began a long series of suggestions as to how I may improve it."

"And your blushing bride just sat there?"

"She rolled her eyes on several occasions during the speech."

"Ah, sisterhood. Is this Lady Catherine married?"

"To a knight. Sir Lewis de Bourgh."

"Bah! I was never one to abide by those horribly pretentious French names, especially d'Arcy. You know they side with those colonists?"

"Us or the French?"

"Your wit never fails you, Geoffrey." His brother smiled again, but it was sadly. "You were always a better speaker than I was, and shall always be."

Geoffrey Darcy paused, and then said in a much quieter voice, "How are you?"

"Why don't you ask my doctor?"

"He said you refused his newest treatments."

"Did he tell you what they were?" his brother answered. "It seems lancing is now all the rage, as if there was a boil in my brain." His voice was severe. "He is not to take any more blood from me, unless you order it, of course. But I will not go down without a fight. Do you know what they will do? They will tie me down to the bed and gag me. Maybe they'll leave me that way for weeks, all because of this fever in my blood. I hide my episodes from them. I won't let them hurt me if I can avoid it. You may think I have given up on life, but there is fight left in me!"

"What about the pills?"

Gregory looked exhausted from his outburst. "They made me ill. I was up late, vomiting. I was so weak I could barely get out of bed. How will that improve my mind?" He looked at his brother with haunted eyes. "How will any of this improve me? Father already legally killed me—why don't you just *leave me alone?*"

Geoffrey said nothing. He had nothing to say, nothing that would comfort either his brother or himself as he watched his elder brother break down into weeping. Gregory was right—all of the proposed cures were painful in one way or another, and none of them worked. In fact, each seemed to weaken his spirit further. Fortunately, Geoffrey held the reins of his brother's treatment, and for as long as he lived he would protect him.

"No more doctoring," Geoffrey announced, "unless *you* want it."

His brother took his face out of his hands, still wet with tears.

"You're my brother," Geoffrey said. He wanted to put his arm over his shoulder, like he used to when they were children, but Gregory made it clear long ago that he did not want to be touched. "I'll always take care of you."

About eight years later

"The nurses will watch him?" Lady Anne said nervously as she watched her five-year-old son frolic on the beach, kicking up the water with his bare feet and splashing the woman put in charge of him.

"They *are* nurses," Geoffrey said to his wife. "It is what they do, or are supposed to be doing, anyway. We will watch him from the window."

Mrs. Darcy was increasingly nervous as they wound their way through the one-story home, sort of a sprawling affair where previous owners had just attached more and more rooms as they saw fit. The sitting rooms—and there were many of them, all unused—were filled with books. Books were in piles, in cases, stacked against the wall—all gifts that had obviously been handled, at least, and probably read. Gregory was a voracious reader, thankfully. He had little else to do with his time. He used to whittle small objects—chess pieces, animals, and boats for his bath—until they took away his knives. Somewhere in the tight, frightened mind of Gregory Darcy, former heir to Pemberley and Derbyshire, was a wealth of knowledge of literature, science, and history. Geoffrey sent him whatever he saw in shops that he was sure he had not already read.

Gregory did emerge from his chambers to greet them in the sitting room immediately outside it, closing the door behind him. "Lady Anne," he said with a stiff bow. He had never seen her before, but there could only be one person Geoffrey would bring. "I see you are wearing Mother's jewels."

"Mr. Darcy," she said, curtseying while unconsciously grabbing her husband's hand.

"They suit you," Gregory continued. "Hello, Geoffrey."

"I was to present my wife," Geoffrey said, "but I see little point now. Darling, this is my brother Gregory. Fitzwilliam is outside."

"I saw." He pointed to the window, and indeed, he did have an adequate view of the coastline. "I would so like to meet him."

"He was very excited to learn he has an uncle," Geoffrey said. "Though he had a few questions we could not answer."

Gregory just nodded. He looked older—older than he should have been. His eyes betrayed him even when his expression was stiff. He was obviously uncomfortable in Anne's presence, and she in his. On cue, she excused herself to collect Fitzwilliam, and as soon as she was gone, Gregory sat down and leaned his head against his hand. "She is—quite beautiful."

"Thank you. And stop ogling my wife."

Gregory smiled. His hands were shaking. "I am sorry my presence upsets her."

"Your presence? This is your home, and we came here. Anne came of her own free will."

"But she has never been in the room with an insane person before."

"Then you have forgotten what a Town ball can be like," Geoffrey said. However, it didn't make Gregory's statement any less true. "Do you want to go outside?"

"No! No, no going outside," his brother shouted, then slowly recovered, steadying his breathing. "If you would let me see him, bring him here." He continued, "We have established how I am doing. How have you been?"

"Good. Very good."

"You have a son. An heir. All is well in the house of Pemberley."

"Yes."

"You are lying."

Geoffrey looked away. "How do you know me so well?"

"You are so easy for me to read. What did you do this time?"

"I'm not a child."

"You have been known to act like one. What did you do?"

He shook his head. Gregory was still his older brother, however infirm he might be, and could still say these things. "I have another son."

"The other's name?"

"George. After the man he thinks is his father. And his father thinks is his father. And Anne thinks is his father."

"George?" He frowned. "Wickham? Your steward?"

Geoffrey put his head in his hands. "Please don't make it worse."

"You have to tell her."

"How am I supposed to do that? How would that help? It was years ago! George is four. It was a mistake." He added, "I'm his godfather."

"How appropriate."

"Don't scold me!"

Gregory stood up. "Geoffrey Darcy, you may be the master of Pemberley, you may be married to the daughter of an earl, and you may be the master of all those beneath you—but I am *still* your older brother. I held you in my arms the day you were born. If *anyone* is to say *anything* to you about your conduct with our parents gone, it is me!"

For the first time in a long while, Gregory was not helpless, mad, wild, or sick. He was the older one, the bigger one, the stronger one, who towered over his cowering baby brother.

"I can't do it," Geoffrey pleaded. "I can't tell her. She loves me, and I need her to love me, for Fitzwilliam, at the very least. He should know two parents who love each other."

Gregory frowned, rubbing his chin. "What is right for your wife or your child? What a terrible position you've put yourself in." He shrugged, letting his shoulders sink as he voluntarily put a hand on his brother's shoulder. "At least you didn't run away from everything."

If either of them had further comment, it was interrupted by the return of Lady Anne and the young Fitzwilliam Darcy.

Gregory put on a smile. "Well, well. Who do we have here?"

1790

"Fitzwilliam, you wait outside," Geoffrey said as he entered the sitting room and knocked on his brother's door. Books were piled up outside, having been stacked up by someone standing within the doorframe. When the door was opened from the inside, he discovered why. There was no room left in Gregory's bedchambers for any more books. Every wall was lined with cases. There were stacks of them on the floor. Besides that, the desk, and the bed, there was barely room to walk. "Gregory."

"Geoffrey. Sit, sit!" Gregory got up from the desk, freeing the only chair for Geoffrey, who uneasily sat in it as his brother sat across from him on his bed. Geoffrey sighed. They said his brother wouldn't leave the room, but he hadn't expected... this. Gregory's whole life was now confined to that little room. He looked well—for someone who never ventured out of his only door—but there was a tiredness around his eyes that Geoffrey had never seen before. He had a beard, small but already wild, and seemed to be snipping his own hair (after many good years, he was allowed sharp objects again), the results of which did not provide for a good appearance. "It has been a while."

"It has."

"Much has changed."

Geoffrey said nothing, but nodded.

"I am truly sorry for your loss," Gregory said. "I did not know her—I did not take the time. I should have—I should have let her in. I should have been open."

"We were only here a few hours."

"I scared her off. It was all my fault. She was perfect—perfect!"

Geoffrey shook his head again. "That is not my purpose for coming here."

"So now you need a purpose?" Those eyes—they said so much about him. Geoffrey watched his brother retreat from him, like he did with everyone else, or had done when he'd known other people.

"No. I didn't mean to imply such a thing," Geoffrey said. "I've been terribly remiss in visiting you—before *and* after Anne's death. I should have been a better brother." He looked back at the door. "I should have been a better father." He sighed; his chest was so tight, his stomach full of nerves. Was this how his brother felt all the time? He had no way of knowing. He would never know. "I need your help with Fitzwilliam."

"With his homework? Does he want my advice about running an estate? You've come to the wrong person, brother. You should—" But then, it was as if the idea was a light in his head, like a match had been struck. "Oh."

"He is my only son, Gregory." He swallowed. "My only son in wedlock. The only one who can inherit. I cannot—" Words failed him. He stood up and paced, even though there was very little room to do it in. "He must inherit Pemberley. You understand? This *must happen*."

"Good Lord, it is just a building—"

"It is *not* just a building!" Senselessly he grabbed his brother. He knew he wasn't supposed to do that at all, especially to Gregory, but strangely, Gregory was too surprised and weakened to oppose him. "If you had been its master like you should have been, you would remember that! Don't you understand? You cannot do this to him!" He was shaking him—or shaking the edges of his coat. "*Fitzwilliam cannot get sick!*"

The horror of it—even just spoken—was enough to knock him out of his state. He released his brother, who fell back on the bed without complaint and stepped away. "I cannot appear weak in front of him. I must be the shining example." He leaned against the bookcase. "All of my deeds, all of my failures, all of my mistakes—they can be forgiven if they don't fall on him. But even *I* am lost here."

"You are mistaken," Gregory said slowly, "if you think I know what to say to him."

"Don't say—what we're both thinking," Geoffrey said. "Tell him—I don't care. Just talk to him. Advise him. You've always been wiser than me."

"And look where I have ended up."

"You would have made an excellent master of Pemberley," Geoffrey said. "The best. If not—if you could deal with people. It could have gone so differently." He shook his head. "Just talk to him. Or listen to him. *Anything*."

After a pause, Gregory quietly said, "Very well. Send him in."

Geoffrey opened the door and went out to retrieve his son, who was pacing in the long hallway. Fitzwilliam Darcy had had his growth spurt, and was now almost as tall as his father, but he did not stand proud. He looked uncomfortable in his own skin, though most boys did at that age, when so much was happening to their bodies and minds. The transition to adulthood could make or break someone. George Wickham had already made his choices, by getting caught with one of the chambermaids. Thankfully, neither Georgiana nor Fitzwilliam were in that part of the house, and the servants had been suitably warned to say nothing while the girl was quietly dismissed. Fitzwilliam rarely spoke to anyone, much less while horizontal. In school, it was even worse. It would have given a normal father who loved his son a moment to pause. Geoffrey Darcy had sleepless nights.

As Fitzwilliam entered his uncle's room and shut the door behind him, Geoffrey Darcy slid down onto the floor of the empty hallway and cried.

Chapter 37

THE LAST MONK OF SAINT SEBALD

CASSANDRA DARCY WAS JUDGED by both parents to be the loudest Darcy, a title formerly held by the infant Geoffrey. Nonetheless, even when Elizabeth was exhausted, Darcy never tired of the sound of her coos, murmurs, or wails. "Very well then, you feed her," said a sleepy Elizabeth as he got up to tend to his hungry child in the early morning light.

"Sadly, some things remain out of my own extensive capabilities," he said, handing her to her mother. Elizabeth could not help but be relieved, not just that everything was finally in order, but that new life had awoken new life in Darcy's eyes. He loved all of his children, but the timing of Cassandra's arrival brought something out of him that had been asleep. The only thing missing was his sister, but her letters indicated nothing but the best. She was happy in her new home and quite occupied giving the old castle a much-needed woman's touch. As Georgiana was still by birth a Darcy, not a single word in her letter could be doubted.

Even though Geoffrey was eight and growing quickly, the Darcys were spared the burden of hiring a governess for a time.

Grégoire was a natural teacher, and his knowledge was not just restricted to the Good Book, though that would do for the moment, with the children so young. Charles and Eliza were old enough to understand, and Anne and Edmund just liked to listen.

"Enough for today," he said, closing the book and shooing the children away as he saw his brother approaching. Grégoire leaned against the tree, removing his spectacles as Darcy sat down next to him.

"You work very well with children," Darcy said. "You should consider having some of your own."

"You may have this conversation with me as many times as you wish, and I will sit patiently through it, but my answer will always be the same," Grégoire said with a smile. "I have no desire to leave the Church."

"I couldn't imagine you as anything but a clergyman," Darcy said, "but in case it passed your notice, we have a system in England where clergymen can have families."

"And I believe that system is full of clergymen who became so because they were a younger son and desired a living."

"But they do get to enjoy themselves," Darcy said. "I heard about Munich."

"About the abbey? What about—*oh*." Grégoire reddened under Darcy's amused stare. "Please—it was a mistake."

Darcy slapped him on the back. "Manhood is not a mistake, little brother. It is a very wonderful thing."

"Please be silent."

"Why, you might even imagine it happening multiple times—"

"Please, *please*, brother—"

"Quite possibly on a regular basis—"

"Darcy, please," Grégoire said, covering his face with his hands. "There is more to life than the physical experience."

"But it is *part* of life."

Grégoire frowned. "I made a promise—to my abbot, myself, and to God. I have always believed I was meant for the contemplative life." He added, "And I still believe it."

"The world doesn't agree with you," Darcy said. "Where can you go? Spain? Rome? Egypt? Why can you not consider Pemberley your home?"

"Because I am not a priest. I am a monk, Darcy. I am part of a brotherhood. What brotherhood, I do not for the moment know." He shook his head. "I cannot explain it, but I know it. It is what I stand on, as you stand with your wife and your children."

Darcy sighed. Somehow the question he had unknowingly been asking had been answered. "As long as you're running to something, not away."

His brother smiled. "That, I assure you, is true."

The summer passed peacefully for the family at large, even though the world around them was in chaos. Derbyshire was quiet, and Bingley's business was thriving under new leadership. He was back and forth between Chatton and Town, often staying at the Maddox house outside London. Georgie begged him to come along, and he could hardly deny her anything. She became especially close to her Aunt Nady. Everyone privately knew that Nadezhda would never have children, as Brian had taken her to nearly every doctor in England to confirm it. If her nieces and nephews adored her, so much the better. Brian and Bingley would sit in the office and work out the details of unloading their stock, and Georgie and Nadezhda would play in the grove.

"Look! Look! I can do it!"

Georgie did finally manage the handstand—for about five seconds before she went toppling over. Mugin caught her from landing flat on her back by grabbing her legs and holding her up. Fortunately she was wearing boy's breeches underneath for this exact purpose. "Very good. Nadi-sama?"

"I can't do that. Very good, Miss Bingley."

"Heh." Mugin released Georgie, who managed to flip back to being upright again. "Now, with one hand!"

"Awww! Mugin-san!" Georgie groaned.

"You must practice," he said. "At your age I was—how old are you, Jorji-chan?"

"Eight!"

He looked to Nadezhda, who held up eight fingers. "Ah. Well, I don't know what I was doing at that time, but I am sure it was hard!" He tried to stare Georgie down, who switched tactics and immediately looked up at him with her sweetest, most heart-melting expression. "You're too clever, you know that?" he said, patting her on the head.

"You're a softie is what you are," Nadezhda said. Between their accents, their English was barely understandable to the average Englishman, but Georgiana was accustomed to both of them.

"You tell anyone, and I'll kill you," Mugin said. "It goes for you too, little *ookami*."

"Mugin, do you really have to leave?"

"There is only one ship."

"But you can stay here! Forever! Aunt Nady's staying!"

"Nadi-sama is a *gaijin*. She belongs with her husband, in a *gaijin* country."

"Besides, I believe Uncle Brian needs my help doing… anything," Nadezhda said. "That man needs a good woman."

"I need a good woman," Mugin said. "For a night, maybe two, depending on how good she is."

"*Mugin!*"

"What? She didn't get it. Did you, Jorji-chan?"

"Get what?" Georgie asked as she put her hair braids back together.

"See?" Mugin said with a broad smile. Nadezhda just folded her arms and shook her head.

"Daniel? Daniel!"

Dr. Daniel Maddox groaned, moving only enough to reposition his head. "What time is it?"

"Two in the afternoon," Caroline said, entering his chambers. "The servants are not aware of your return time last night. They were all asleep."

"It was—very late," he said. "Early. Light in the streets."

"The Regent had a late night, I take it?"

"His Highness always has late nights. You'd only need to read the gossip columns to know that. Which you do, as I see them crumpled up on our nightstand."

Caroline sat down on the bed, pushing up against him so he would make room as she scratched his head. Ever since his hair had come back in, he adored that. He was like a cat, she'd say. "He had a late night with some emergency, I mean."

"Perhaps," he said, his voice still slurred from sleep. "Or perhaps he was so drunk he rather abruptly fell asleep standing and tipped onto the Prime Minister's lap."

"What happened to patient confidentiality?"

"As the man in charge of the *Courier* was right there, I doubt it's *confidential*," he said, turning onto his back so he could see her properly. "Is there a reason you woke me? Am I late for something?"

"Do you know what today is?"

He blinked. "The twenty-seventh? No, it must be the twenty-eighth—why?"

"The twenty-eighth. Four months."

It took him a moment. "Really?"

"Yes. Really."

He smiled, pulling her in for a kiss. This close, he could see her perfectly. He didn't need to; he knew Caroline. He could see her from far away, when his eyes were closed, when she was in another room—she was his wife, and he *knew*. "You know," he said between kisses, "technically, this could be four—and—a half—"

"I know," she said. She didn't resist being pulled down, or his hand stroking her belly. They hadn't made it to four months since Emily, when the morning illness lessened and her body truly began to change. Once her body had made it three-and-a-half, but never four. "I want to announce it."

"Right now? At least let me get dressed—"

"No, silly man—next week, when we go up for Edmund's birthday."

"Oh right. Of course," he said. "What was I thinking? I was distracted by something."

476

Anne had a few months left to her increasing, which so far had been successful. She suffered only the normal aches, pains, and illnesses of a woman with child, but she had the experienced Mrs. Collins to aid her through the worst of it, and the best doctors lined up in case anything went wrong. As she approached confinement, even the normally subdued servants hummed with excitement at the idea that Rosings and the Fitzwilliam family might see an heir. Though nervous, Lord Matlock was otherwise in the best of spirits, at least in front of his wife. Mr. Collins offered to sit in vigil, but when Grégoire mentioned fasting alongside prayer, Mr. Collins lost interest in the idea and decided to put his faith in the Lord to do what was right.

The Darcys paid a call on Rosings as soon as Elizabeth was well enough to do so. They listened patiently to Lady Catherine's declarations that if Anne's child was a girl, she of course must be married to their Geoffrey, and if it was a boy, all the better, because he would have his pick of their three daughters (though she thought the eldest was a bit shifty-eyed and no good would come of her). They nodded politely, saying almost nothing, and left the room with some amusement and no intention of taking a word of her advice.

"Son, if Anne has a girl, would you like to marry her?" Darcy proposed to Geoffrey, who was sitting on the stairs.

"What?" Geoffrey said. "I thought I was marrying Georgie."

"I hope not," Darcy said. "Or I owe Bingley five pounds."

"*Darcy!*" Elizabeth said, and swatted him.

Edmund Bingley turned two largely without his knowledge, though he certainly enjoyed the attention that was lavished on him by those around him. It was, in the end, as much a celebration for them as it was for him. No one needed to say it, but everyone knew it was a marker date, when the idea of Darcy and Dr. Maddox's ill-fated departure became real. Their family was whole again (and seemed to have gained a few members), their prayers answered, and life as they knew it was returning to normal, even better than normal. It was the summer of 1813, and Wellington first successfully routed Napoleon's troops.

"I hope nothing happens to that poor man," Grégoire said at the news.

"Who? Wellington?"

"He means Bonaparte," Caroline said to her husband.

"Don't let the rest of the country hear you say that," Charles suggested, lifting his glass to Grégoire.

"He was very polite," Grégoire said, "and he quite possibly saved my life. I will say nothing against him."

"You are too good for this world," Darcy said. "Dangerously so. One of these days you will get in trouble for it, and this time... Elizabeth and Mrs. Maddox will not be there to save you." He glared at Bingley, who was chuckling beside him. "Be quiet. You stayed at home and got a thrashing from your own employees. You are lucky you have an insane brother-in-law."

"Why does everyone keep saying that in front of me?" Brian Maddox said. "I won't begin to deny it, but normally it is not wise to insult a man thoroughly more armed than you are." Brian relinquished his Japanese costume and swords only when it was absolutely necessary, and often had at least the small one hidden inside his waistcoat when he did.

"Because you are wearing a skirt," Caroline said.

"Pleated trousers. A *hakama* is a set of pleated trousers." He turned to his wife. "Nady, you tell them how manly I am. What? Why are you laughing? Don't do this to me!" But he could not truly raise his voice at his wife, who hid her laughter with her hand, but not very successfully. "At least you could support me."

"Mr. Maddox, if you expect your wife to always be your sternest supporter when your honor is insulted in any family event, you are not well educated in the English customs of marriage," Darcy said. "I need not turn my head, and I already know Elizabeth is staring at me and deciding whether to laugh or to look enraged." She was doing precisely that. "See?"

"You are a quite accomplished husband," Elizabeth said. "Already you know that I am thoroughly plotting my revenge with a story you wouldn't want told."

"What about this noodles incident I keep hearing mentioned?" Dr. Maddox said.

Bingley looked down at his drink. "No, no, that was me. Well, involved me. And everyone present was sworn to secrecy. Right, my darling?" He looked so very sweetly at Jane, whom he had not insulted.

"You are an accomplished husband for not upsetting me during the course of this conversation."

"I'll help him along," Brian said. "He told me last week he wants to go to India."

"India!"

"Oh God." Bingley slumped in his seat. "Joking! I was partially—*mainly* joking when I said that I might be interested in thinking about possibly *considering*—"

"INDIA!"

Elizabeth turned to her husband, whose well-practiced mask of indifference was set on his face. "Mrs. Darcy, I can soundly promise you I will never venture to India, Africa, or quite possibly beyond the British shore, and if by chance someone is foolish enough to visit a country filled with snakes, vermin, pagans, and disease, I will leave him to stew in his own mistakes."

"Darcy!"

"Bingley," Darcy said, moving away from the fireplace and towards Bingley. "We have been friends since the moment we met. I have stood by your side when you made a fool of yourself and you have forced me into the social sphere in which I met my wife. However, when one must choose between a friend and a wife, one must strategically choose the wife."

Bingley sighed but gave his friend a smile in agreement.

That was when Elizabeth piped up. "Good sir, what do you mean by *strategically?*"

While the adults enjoyed themselves and the younger children slept, the older children played on Chatton's lawn. Eliza stood on the stump and was the captive princess, and Geoffrey was her jailor, as her brother was the knight to rescue her, which involved a lot more chasing than actual fighting.

"I give you this," Mugin said, off to the side with Georgie Bingley. In his hands was a book, little more than sheets of paper bound with two hard pieces and loops of string poked through to tie it together. She opened it to find crude drawings of a human figure—distinct only in the position of the limbs, which changed on every page with instructions in Japanese and Nadezhda's best

English handwriting under it. She recognized all of the moves in the form he had taught her. "When you understand it, come find me."

"But you are going to Japan!" she cried, holding the book close to her chest.

"So? If you asked me five, six years ago if I would be in England, do you know what I would have said?"

"No. What?"

"'What is England?'"

The joke brought a smile to her face as she hugged him, but she did not relinquish her tight grip on the book.

The fall, as had the previous one, required two good-byes, but these were longer and more definitive. Mugin left with the only ship that would for certain take him to Shanghai, and from there, he could easily get to Japan. Brian gave him money for the trip. "Try not to gamble it all in one place. Spread it out over several places."

Brian, Nadezhda, Bingley, and Georgie were there to see him go. Wearing his upside-down basket hat, he climbed up the ramp, his shoes making their "clack-clack" noise the whole way up. They waved good-bye until the ship was out of sight, and long after he could possibly still see them.

To everyone's relief, Anne delivered safely in October. Though severely weakened, she would recover, and was strong enough to hold her minute-old son in her arms and hear his first wail.

Mr. Collins had the honor of christening Viscount Henry Lewis Fitzwilliam. After the meal, Anne was requested in her mother's room, and she had the nurse bring along Lady Catherine's grandson.

"I always wanted a son," Lady Catherine said as she held the squirming infant in her arms. "I prayed so fervently. I had two, but both died within days. And then you came along, and I was so happy that at least I could produce something in this world of worth." She looked up at her daughter. "I may have smothered you with doctors, but I did it for you."

Lord Matlock entered the room, and Lady Catherine acknowledged him with a nod but continued on to her daughter. "I wanted a family for myself. But you were sick, and Lewis died, and I saw that it would not be possible. So I wanted a family for you. I did everything in my power to arrange for this family, and it only brought misery to everyone."

"Mama—"

"It is in the past. It is all in the past." Lady Catherine smiled as she looked down at her grandson.

The hectic years of the end of Napoleon's reign on the Continent were not mirrored in Derbyshire, where life passed as normal. There was less tenant and worker rebellion in that particular county than most others, at least in Darcy's half because of his masterful overseeing of his lands. Bingley purchased some land, but had no real interest beyond his family's needs, not with his business thriving.

To everyone's great relief, Caroline Maddox carried to term, and Daniel Maddox Jr. was born. He had his mother's red hair, with the curling tendency of his father's, so they concluded that he was a hopeless case in that respect.

As abruptly as the horde of children had come into the world, the spell seemed to end. Kitty Townsend (née Bennet) had three children in four years, but otherwise, there were some failures and periods where there was no conception. Jane and Elizabeth did not complain; they were tired, both having had four children (which they now had also to *raise*). They were content. Charlotte Collins had another child—another girl, though Mr. Collins expressed no consternation (at least not openly or to his wife, whom he was always very kind to). There were whispers about the Bennet curse resurfacing, which Mr. Bennet laughed at much as he laughed at everything else, and remained living, and therefore master of Longbourn, with his wife, daughter, and grandson at his side.

Brian and Nadezhda lived in peace. Count Olaf sent them their crowns and chains, having wrangled them from Count Vladimir, so Brian could finally wear his princely regalia in front of his brother, which amused the doctor to no end. Besides working on his business, Brian sat down to turn his letters to his brother into a travelogue, which sold fabulously well, and he became the talk of the town as a famous author, but he stayed largely out of the limelight because Nadezhda did not want to be ogled, and her needs came first.

When the war ended, Grégoire left for Spain, now safely sovereign again. There was an old monastery in the northwest that seemed perfect for him. It was Benedictine and near the coast, so he could travel to England in a few weeks by ship, a trip he relished only for its brevity. He returned the following summer, content in his community there but happy to visit his family and the saint, now buried in an obscure grave in the corner of a private cemetery in England. At the end of his allotted time for the visit, Grégoire kissed his nephew and all of his nieces, hugged Elizabeth, shook Darcy's hand, and began down the path that would lead him south to London.

Later that day, as he always did when he missed his brother, Darcy slipped away from the others and went into the cemetery, to that small tombstone, and sat down beside it.

"So," he asked the saint, "what now?"

The End

HISTORICAL INACCURACIES

Princess Nadezhda Maddox (who could not have had that title for real, as there was no princess of Transylvania, and she was the daughter of a count who did not marry a prince) speaks Romanian in the book. Though Romanian is a language, Romania as the country we know today did not come to exist until after World War I, though there were several independence movements in the mid-to-late 1800s. As Transylvania was part of the Austria-Hungarian empire, and Nadezhda and Count Vladimir are descendents of *boyars* (nobility), they would probably consider themselves Hungarian based on their geography, which is why she is referred to as Hungarian, even though today she would be Romanian. The nobility of Transylvania probably didn't speak Romanian, the language of the peasants, and spoke whatever language was most popular in court. Covering one's head with a scarf is a Romanian custom, though she carries it to an extreme in the book.

It would have been safer for Brian and Nadezhda to simply take a boat (which they tried) instead of walking through Tokugawa, Japan—although it would have been a less interesting story.

There were no wolves in England in the 1800s. They were driven to extinction centuries before, which is why I had to introduce the plotline about the crazy nobleman who reintroduced wolves to Derbyshire by accident to get the wolves to remain in the story in revision, as I didn't discover the extinction business until well after the story was written.

Napoleon was heavily involved in the Russian campaign around the time that Grégoire meets him in Austria. It is unlikely he would have been in that precise part of Austria at that time. He had mixed feelings about the church, alternately respecting it and degrading it during his career.

Rabbi Shneur Zalman of Liadi (zt"l) (1745–1812), otherwise known as the Alter Rebbe and the founder of Chabad-Lubavitch Hasidism, moved to Liadi after being released from a Russian prison in 1798. He left Liadi before his death in 1812, though the dates are not precise. He probably was in Liadi around 1810, when Brian and Nadezhda meet him. He probably never wrote a letter about the birth of Nacham Flanzblau (born 1810), but I threw Nacham in because he was my great-great-great-great-grandfather.

Sebaldus of Nuremberg, the patron saint of Bavaria, has conflicting stories of his ancestry, and was possibly a German, a Frank, or a Saxon from England, and either lived in the eighth or the twelfth century, depending on your sources. What is known is that his body was not stolen away for safekeeping in 1812 and still remains in Nuremburg, in his tomb at the St. Sebaldus Church.

You cannot fight wearing wooden *geta* shoes. They will break. I've tried.

ACKNOWLEDGMENTS

All praise belongs to the Holy One, blessed be He, who in His infinite mercy will now understand when I contradict myself and go on to praise other people.

Brandy Scott, who has continued to edit all of my work long after it stopped being a sensible use of her time as a human being, really went beyond the call with this book, the longest and perhaps most convoluted of the books. Also the editing period fell during the Christmas season, so, she gets extra praise for this one.

Deb Werksman purchased this book for Sourcebooks without knowing how crazy it was, and for that I thank her and hope she will continue this lovely trend. Susie Benton worked out the kinks in the editing process, which is difficult for all twenty people who seem to be involved in putting a book together. At the time of my writing these acknowledgments, I am sure that Danielle Jackson will continue to do an incredible job at publicity. Sarah Ryan did, as always, an excellent job on copyediting.

Katie Menick, my agent, continues to represent me for some reason. I can only thank her by hoping she actually sees some profit from her hours and hours of hard work.

To all of my readers at Fanfiction.net and other fan fiction websites, thank you for continuing to read the series and for giving advice, catching mistakes, and providing translations. You guys are the reason this series happened.

The following people are responsible for translating dialogue:

Elena Luiña—Japanese

Lory L—Romanian

Lise, colinette—French

Franziska Herberger, fanficaddict, bette, Angelika—German

I would like to thank Amazon.com for its industry-crippling used book market, as I could never afford all of the history books I need to work on this series if I actually had to pay anywhere near full price for them.

My boss, Diana Finch, provided contract and promotion advice when I needed it. And this was while I was on the clock.

To my grandmother, for supporting me all these years, and no doubt making her friends buy and make some attempt to read my books.

To my brother Jason, thanks for talking me up to your friends, which I heard you actually did.

To my roommate, Shir Lerman, thanks for being my room-mate. (Roommates get a freebie acknowledgment.)

Alison Hale, my old college roommate, tried to teach me how to accurately pronounce the name "Nadezhda." She really did put her back into it, but my tongue is too many generations away from my Eastern European ancestry to pull it off.

To all the members of Congregation Agudath Israel, thank

you for buying my first book, even though there was no Jewish content in it except the word "Jew." *This* is the one with the Jewish content in it. A whole few pages' worth. Enjoy.

Rabbi Mendel and Chani Laufer have put me up in their home in Providence on almost no notice, and all I've ever given them is a copy of the first book and some baby toys. As the Laufers are Lubavitch Hasidim, a branch of Hasidim founded by the Alter Rebbe, he appears in this book partially as a tribute to them and the many Lubavitchers who have supported and counseled me over the years. Others include Rabbi Zalman and Toba Grossbaum, and Rabbi Baruch and Devorah Klar. Also, the Alter Rebbe was alive in 1810, so that really helped.

Thank you to Jamie and Ruth Nachinson, my long-lost relatives in Israel, who found me on the Internet and contacted me in time to learn the identity of my great-great-great-great-grandfather Nacham Franzblau, who now has a mention in the book. Thank you, Uncle Arthur and Aunt Donna, for helping out with the family tree.

And to everyone I forgot to thank, as usual, I apologize.

ABOUT THE AUTHOR

Marsha Altman is an author and historian specializing in Rabbinic literature in late antiquity. She has a bachelor's degree in history from Brown University and an M.F.A. in creative writing from the City College of New York. She works in the publishing industry and is writing a series continuing the story of the Darcys and the Bingleys. She lives in New York.